COLLATERAL

BY BRIAN ANDREWS AND JEFFREY WILSON

Tier One Series
Tier One
War Shadows
Crusader One
American Operator
Red Specter
Collateral

Tier One Origins Novellas
Scars: John Dempsey

Writing as Alex Ryan
Nick Foley Thriller Series
Beijing Red
Hong Kong Black

Other Titles by Brian Andrews
The Calypso Directive
The Infiltration Game
Reset

Other Titles by Jeffrey Wilson
The Traiteur's Ring
The Donors
Fade to Black
War Torn

COLLATERAL

A TIER ONE THRILLER

ANDREWS & WILSON

This novel is dedicated to you, dear reader.

Without you this series would not exist. So please accept this dedication with our heartfelt gratitude. We consider our Tier One fans to be family, Thank you for your love, generosity, and kind online reviews.

Be well, stay safe, and always remember we've got your six.

NOTE TO THE READER

We've provided a glossary in the back of this book to define the acronyms, military lingo, and abbreviations used herein.

PART I

Breaking a country is no different than breaking a man;

all you have to do is take away hope.

—*Matias Zinovenko*

CHAPTER 1

The Ferry House English Pub
London, England
September 14
2147 Local Time

John Dempsey ducked just before the bottle flying at him could slam into his temple. It sailed over his head instead and smashed into a life-sized ceramic English bulldog positioned just inside the pub's entrance. The bottle, and the bulldog, shattered into a million comingled pieces. The barmaid behind the counter released an eardrum-piercing shriek—full of outrage and anguish at the loss of what must have been the pub's mascot.

"Get ooooout!" she screamed. "All of you brigands!"

Nobody listened . . . except for the man Dempsey was there to kill. The Russian operative darted out the pub's double doors, running like a man on fire.

"The target has just left the building," said a professorial voice through the wireless microtransmitter stuffed deep in Dempsey's right ear canal. The voice belonged to Task Force Ember's Signals Chief and Acting Director, Ian Baldwin, located in a Tactical Operations Center five time zones away.

"I know," Dempsey—a former Navy SEAL turned American assassin—said as he blocked a punch from a burly middle-aged local with his forearm. He was about to drive a hook into the guy's jaw but decided the poor bloke didn't deserve to spend the next six weeks drinking all his meals through a straw. So instead, he sent the tough-guy wannabe flying backward and onto his ass with a two-handed shove. He whirled toward the exit to pursue his quarry, only to find another angry brawler blocking his path.

"Dude, where are you?" said another voice, this one belonging to former SEAL and combat surgeon Dan Munn, who was also sitting in the TOC in Florida. "He's getting away."

"I know!" Dempsey growled, ducking a jab flying at his face.

"Well, what the hell are you doing?"

"Somehow Alpha has managed to get himself into a bar fight," came a third voice, this one belonging to Elizabeth Grimes, Ember's sniper in residence and overwatch for tonight's assassination mission.

"Of course he has," Munn said, and Dempsey could practically hear him shaking his head. "Screw this. I say we have Lizzie shoot the target."

"No," came Baldwin's clipped reply. "The DNI was very specific about the approved lethal methods for this operation. No sniper action unless we can disappear the body without incident. Bravo, you are relegated to spotter and exfil activities only."

"Check," Grimes said, acknowledging the directive.

The chatter in Dempsey's ear was beginning to piss him off,

and so was the asshole in front of him trying to channel Rocky Balboa. The dude threw a gut punch, which Dempsey caught in a scissor block. The block made the brawler wince, but he was committed and drew back his other fist to try again. Dempsey didn't give him that opportunity; he drove a knee into the man's groin, buckling the wannabe boxer at the waist.

"Behind you," Grimes said in his ear.

Dempsey dropped into a crouch and spun on the balls of his feet. A third dude, the bottle thrower, was charging with a fresh bottle raised overhead and primed to split open Dempsey's skull. Dempsey grabbed him by the shirt, pivoted, and used the attacker's momentum to send him flying into tough guy number two, who was still bent over, clutching his nuts. Both men crashed to the ground in a tangled heap of arms and legs amid a pile of overturned wooden chairs.

Dempsey did a quick scan for the next threat, but there was nobody left standing in the tiny pub. For an instant, he locked eyes with the woman behind the bar. Thank God this was London and not Houston, or else he would be staring down the barrel of a Remington 870. As it was, the only targeting lasers fixed on him at the moment were the invisible ones streaming from her angry eyes.

"Sorry about your bulldog," he said with an Irish brogue as he turned to leave.

"Get the fuck out," she screamed as he barreled out the pub's doors and onto the street. "And never come back!"

"Which way did he go?" Dempsey asked to the ether, scanning right, then left, for his target.

"North on East Ferry Road," Grimes answered.

"Check," he said and took off after the Russian spy. After one block, the ancient and uneven brick pavers underfoot transitioned to asphalt, improving Dempsey's footing and letting him push to a full tilt. "How are your eyes, Omega?" he asked, noting the misty, overcast night sky.

"We have the target on satellite thermal," Baldwin said. "He has a two-block lead on you and is headed toward Mudchute Park."

"Is that the giant fucking goat farm?"

"Yes, John," Baldwin said, breaking OPSEC as usual. "Mudchute Park and Farm is the largest working farm in London. It's heavily wooded and spans twelve hectares, so I suggest you hurry before you lose him."

"I know, I know. I'm running. I know you can see that," Dempsey puffed.

"Oh, we see you. Is that all you got, old man?" Munn chimed in.

Dempsey didn't answer, preferring to conserve precious oxygen. He hated this shit. Lately, it seemed like every op ended in a footrace—either with him chasing down some fleet-footed asshole, or with him running for his life while being shot at by Russians. Ember didn't need operators; what it needed was Olympic middle-distance runners.

I'm too old for this shit, he thought as his quads began to burn.

"Alpha, this is Bravo," Grimes said in his ear. "I'm coming down. Gonna bring the car around to the east side and reposition on Stebondale Street. If our tango crosses Millwall Park playing fields, I'll plink him with the long gun."

"I said *no* sniper action." Baldwin's voice had an uncharacteristic hard edge. "Accidental death or poison—that was the OPORD."

"We tried poison and that didn't work out so well," Munn said. "So now it's time to try accidental death."

"Enlighten me, Dan, if you will. How does a sniper round to the head qualify as *accidental* death?" Baldwin said.

"It qualifies when the target *accidentally* walks into Lizzie's bullet while it happens to be flying in the vicinity of his head," the former SEAL doc said, oozing with sarcasm.

"OPSEC, people, OPSEC!" snapped an acerbic fourth voice on the line. "I'm good, but so is British Intelligence. GCHQ is listening." The rebuke from Richard Wang, Ember's cyber and IT expert, was as out of character as truth was from a politician.

To Dempsey's surprise, everybody shut up and locked it down. *Thank God . . .*

He pulled up a mental image of the nearby greenspace complex, consisting of Millwall Park and Mudchute Farm. He didn't have an eidetic memory, but he'd always had a knack for remembering topography and details from satellite imagery. As a SEAL with the Tier One back in the day, it had been his responsibility to plan the ops and know the terrain cold. Yes, they'd had GPS, Suunto watches, slick tablet computers, and eyes in the sky to monitor their position, but Dempsey knew better than to put all his faith in technology. Because unlike his teammates, technology seemed to have an annoying habit of letting him down when he needed it most.

Mudchute Farm was a genuine anomaly; nothing of the sort existed in American cities. At thirty-two acres, it was huge and situated on the Isle of Dogs, a peninsula inside a buttonhook bow of the Thames in central London, where real estate was going at a premium. More than just a greenspace, the farm had a wooded perimeter, an equestrian center, and grazing pastures for cows, pigs, goats, sheep, and llama. The farm had caught Dempsey's attention not only because of its size, but also because it was the perfect place to disappear or wait in ambush.

"Target is approaching the Chapel House Street intersection," Baldwin reported. "And he just vectored east toward the park."

"Check," Dempsey said.

"And he appears to be opening the gap, Alpha. Can you possibly run any faster?"

"If I . . . could run . . . any faster," he said, his words punctuated by heavy exhales, "then I would . . . be."

"Target is crossing the northwest quadrant . . . heading for the woods and Mudchute Farm," Munn said. "Bravo, where are you?"

"Driving, but not in position yet," Grimes said. "Ninety seconds."

"Shit, you're gonna be too late," Munn said, as if sniper action were still on the table.

Arms pumping and legs churning, Dempsey crossed the Manchester Grove intersection. In another two hundred meters, he'd reach the park entrance. Two-story brown-brick row houses zipped past him as he sprinted up the middle of Ferry Road between twin columns of parked cars. As he ran, he noted how he could barely feel the formfitting body armor protecting his torso. This was his first time wearing the brand-new tech Baldwin had procured for all the SAD team members.

Unlike traditional antiballistic Kevlar vests with heavy, rigid SAPI plates, this new vest was light and flexible. The puncture-resistant woven shell concealed a honeycomb interior filled with "liquid" body armor. Originally conceived at MIT and then refined by DARPA, liquid body armor—or shear-thickening fluid—was flexible and viscous in normal conditions but instantly hardened when struck by a projectile, deflecting and dispersing the impact force. He'd rolled his eyes and chuckled when Baldwin had presented him with the vest, but after unloading a thirty-round magazine of 5.56 at the range and finding it intact, his skepticism had melted away. Wearing it now, however, he couldn't help but wonder what critical little piece of information Baldwin had "forgotten" to mention.

He could almost hear the Signal Chief's voice in his head.

Antiballistic STF performs flawlessly against all calibers of ammunition . . . so long as it doesn't get wet. Or maybe, *Liquid body armor is positively impenetrable . . . provided the gel temperature stays below ninety-one degrees Fahrenheit.*

He suddenly found himself wishing for his old rigid, heavy, uncomfortable-as-fuck body armor. He'd been shot plenty of times in that rig and had walked away every time.

Well . . . almost every time.

"Target is in the woods," Munn reported, just as Dempsey reached the park entrance.

He hurdled the entry gate and ran a dogleg path left, slowing and looking for cover as he scanned the tree line. His spidey sense was tingling as the risk profile shifted. The Russian was in cover now, and Dempsey was exposed—especially while crossing the field.

"Do you have eyes on my tango?" Dempsey said, panting and dropping into a crouch.

"Hold," came Baldwin's reply. "The target is loitering just inside the tree line four hundred feet from your position."

Dempsey took a knee and pulled a compact Sig Sauer from his underarm holster. Wishing he had night vision goggles, he scanned the tree line over the new, low-profile SAS fiber-tritium sights. "Bearing?"

"Zero four five, true."

"Check," Dempsey said, verifying his watch compass heading and adjusting his aim right.

"The target is moving," Baldwin said, his voice ripe with tension. "Moving north and east, through the trees."

Dempsey popped up from his crouch and sprinted along the line he'd just been sighting. He crossed a walking path and wove his way into the trees and underbrush.

"Target is out of the woods, crossing what looks like a very large vegetable patch. He's heading for one of the paddocks," Baldwin said.

"I'm on it," Dempsey said, pressing forward through the surprisingly dense undergrowth with a cringeworthy lack of stealth.

"Oh dear . . ."

"'Oh dear' what?" Dempsey said, his voice low and hushed.

"We lost him."

"How is that even possible?"

"He must suspect we have him on satellite thermal, because he moved in among the animals—sheep, I suspect—and entered a barn-like structure. He must be on all fours, because we cannot identify which heat signature is his."

"Are you telling me you can't tell the difference between a man and a bunch of sheep?" Dempsey said through clenched teeth.

"Dude, he's telling you straight," Munn interjected. "It just looks like a bunch of yellow-orange blobs huddled together."

"Ridiculous," Dempsey murmured and couldn't help but think how he'd gone from being a kitted-up Tier One SEAL, fast-roping with his unit out of Stealth Hawks behind enemy lines, to *this* . . . a dude stalking sheep in a petting zoo.

In the distance, sirens began to wail.

"There's a police cruiser en route to the Ferry House Pub," Wang reported, his voice all business.

"Time to wrap this up, Alpha," Baldwin said. "You have five minutes to eliminate the target, or I'm terminating the op."

Yeah, yeah, easy for you to say over your tea and biscuits, Dempsey thought as he grudgingly acknowledged Baldwin's order with a double-click of his tongue.

He advanced silently and methodically toward the animal pen where the Russian operative was hiding. The perimeter was kept by a sturdy four-foot-tall slat-and-wire fence with two swing gates. Inside, the turf had been grazed down to bare dirt. A simple, twenty-foot-long windowless shelter with a flat metal roof occupied the south end of the pen. With his pistol trained on the building, he eased along the fence until the opening of the shelter—wide enough to permit free and easy movement in and out by the animals—came into view. The inside of the shelter was pitch black, but he could make out greyish blobs moving just inside the opening.

A second later, the smell hit him and one of the animals let out a throaty, prolonged bleat.

Yep, definitely sheep.

If this were Afghanistan, the tactical solution would be simple—toss a grenade in the barn and hose down everything that came out. But this wasn't the 'Stan. In central London, lobbing grenades and shooting anything, even a bunch of sheep, was off the table. Which meant he had no choice but to go in after his target. And he could predict how that would play out. The minute he entered the barn, commotion would ensue. The animals would bleat and shit and scuttle, and while he milled about trying to find a crouching human in the chaos, his adversary would plink him with an easy headshot.

Dempsey cursed to himself, trying to decide what to do.

"What is the problem, Alpha?" Baldwin said, his tone more annoyed than concerned.

"He's trying to figure out how to get the sheep out of the barn without discharging his weapon," Munn answered for Dempsey.

"Ah yes, do be careful not to kill any sheep, John," Baldwin said. "This needs to look like a mugging gone bad, not a shootout."

Dempsey clenched his jaw in irritation and stood there motionless, sighting over his Sig at the entrance. For the first time in his long and decorated career, he was experiencing tactical paralysis . . .

Tactical paralysis in a petting zoo, he thought. *God, what have I become?*

He crept back to a position with a perpendicular firing angle on the enclosure. The side walls didn't have any windows, just a series of drilled ventilation holes that would be virtually impossible to sight and fire through.

I need a distraction, he decided.

He scanned the ground until he found a rock the size of his fist. He knelt and picked it up.

"Fuck it," he murmured, looking at the rock, and then lobbed it in a high arc at the shelter.

The rock hit the metal roof dead center with a loud, metallic clang that echoed through the park. Terrified sheep poured out of the enclosure in a wooly, stinky stampede—bleating, stomping, and defecating en masse. At the same time, Dempsey jumped the perimeter fence and charged forward in a low crouch. A sheep screamed to his left. The animal's cry was so uncannily human that he reflexively swiveled and sighted before dismissing the threat.

He pivoted back toward the enclosure and felt the shift he'd been waiting for—into the combat slipstream where all anxiety, uncertainty, and doubt evaporated. His mind and body unified into a state of hyperawareness and fluidity. With his weapon up in a two-handed grip and index finger tension on the trigger, he closed on the doorway. Then something happened he did not expect . . .

The sheep recoalesced into a compact herd and charged back toward the enclosure—apparently collectively deciding it was safer back inside than out here with him. On instinct, he went with them. Ducking as low as possible, he grabbed a fistful of wool on the back of a fat ewe and went in behind her like she was his blocking fullback. As he broke the plane of the doorway, he pulled the sheep tight to his chest, dug in his heels, and revectored her momentum radially. As they rotated in place, he scanned over her back for anything human-shaped in the shadows.

A crack of gunfire exploded inside the metal structure, three deafening bangs along with three brilliant muzzle flashes from the back right corner. His sheep-shield bleated and shuddered—a fat wooly bullet cushion—as it took all three of the rounds. Dempsey returned fire, two rounds of his own into the corner, but the Russian was already rolling right and the slugs punched two holes harmlessly in the wall. Dempsey's ovine bodyguard suddenly became dead weight as the sheep's legs buckled. Its decision to die in that instant was unfortunate for Dempsey, because the Russian squeezed off another round. This one hit Dempsey center mass, square between his pecs. Instead of the familiar impact jab he was accustomed to when taking a round in Kevlar, he felt a sharp rippling tension across the breadth of his chest and then nothing.

The bullet had gone through his vest like a knife through butter.

Motherfucker, he thought as he returned fire at the Russian shadow. *I knew this shit was too good to be true.*

He scrambled right in the chaos—the gunfire having sent the sheep into blind pandemonium. Any second now, his breath would grow wet and raspy as his chest filled with blood. His blood pressure would drop, his arms would grow impossibly heavy, and his legs would turn to jelly. But none of those things happened. Was it possible that Baldwin's vest full of magic slime had actually friggin' worked?

Still strong and in the fight, Dempsey grabbed a fleeing ewe—smaller than the last—and ducked down behind her. Instead of firing over her back, he sighted around her ass. Muzzle flashes lit up the inside of the shelter as the Russian emptied his magazine. Multiple rounds slammed into Dempsey's sheep, and it sprayed the side of his face with shit pellets. He returned fire, aiming just below the muzzle flashes.

Crack, crack, crack . . .

A human-shaped shadow dropped, hitting the dirt with a thud.

Dempsey released his grip on his second sheep, and the ewe collapsed beside him. He shifted from a crouch to a tactical knee, his Sig trained on his target, with whom he was finally alone in the barn. The Russian groaned and wheezed as he made a futile belly crawl toward the pistol he'd dropped, now a meter away.

"Stop," Dempsey said in Russian, surprised how the word came to him automatically. He'd been taking lessons from Buz—who claimed Dempsey had the worst language skills of anyone he'd ever taught. This was the first time the language had come to him without trying.

The Russian stopped and strained a backward look at him.

Dempsey pressed to his feet and walked over to the man, keeping a proper standoff in case the Russian operator wasn't quite as wounded as he was letting on. The two men locked eyes, victor and vanquished.

The spy said something to him, but the only word he caught was "Zhukov." It didn't matter, though, because he knew his enemy well enough to infer the question. Dempsey was hunting Zetas—the Russian Federation's most secret and lethal black ops task force—taking them out one by one until he'd worked his way to the top.

"No, Zhukov didn't send me," Dempsey said, answering in English this time. "Shane Smith did."

Confusion washed over the other man's face, the murdered Ember Director's name clearly unknown to him. Dempsey wasn't

12

surprised; only one Zeta had survived the horrific attack ordered by Russian spymaster Arkady Zhukov on Ember's secret compound in Virginia three months ago. Apparently, this dude wasn't that guy.

"*De oppresso liber*, comrade," he said and squeezed the trigger, completing the mission and ending the life of yet another Zeta.

"Well, *that* certainly didn't go as planned," Baldwin said in his ear as the last wisp of smoke from Dempsey's muzzle faded into the ether.

Where there had been only one siren wailing before, now a chorus screamed in the night.

"What do you want me to do with the body?" Dempsey asked.

"Leave it," Baldwin said through a defeated sigh. "And you can explain to the DNI why you violated the OPORD."

"Roger that," he said, holstering his weapon as he ducked out of the barn.

"Exfil north," Grimes said in his ear. "I'll pick you up in the Asda superstore parking lot."

"Check."

"Hurry, they're coming," she said.

"I *know*," he said, a surge of fresh adrenaline helping get his sluggish legs moving. As he ran, thoughts of the next mission began to take shape. "Hey, Omega?"

"What is it, Alpha?" Baldwin answered, still irritated.

A malign smile curled Dempsey's lips.

"I'm ready for the next target."

CHAPTER 2

Unregistered Domestic Detention Center

Tampa, Florida

September 15

1715 Local Time

The buzzer sounded, the lock clicked, and the man Amanda Allen knew simply as Doug opened the door for her.

"Thanks, Doug," Amanda said. "How are the kids?"

"Doing great," he said, his serious expression mismatched with the amiability in his voice. "Mark just started band, and the triplets joined the swim team. Coach said too bad we didn't pop out one more girl, 'cause then we could have our own relay team."

This answer surprised her and she chuckled.

The exchange was a little running joke between them that had developed organically over the past month. She doubted he had kids. Hell, she wouldn't be surprised if he wasn't married. Each time, he gave her a different answer with different kids' names, sexes, ages, and activities. Doug was a glorified jail keeper, guarding one of Russia's most highly trained covert operatives—a Russian Zeta named Sylvie Bessonov. Under no circumstances did Doug want his charge to learn anything personal or of consequence that could be used to manipulate him. But Amanda suspected he was also bored out of his mind and this was the only novelty in his daily routine.

"I thought Jasper was taking skydiving lessons?" she said, pausing at the threshold.

"Who's Jasper?" he asked, his expression deadpan.

She flashed him a conspiratorial smile and headed inside. He shut the door behind her with a thud and she heard the lock mechanism engage.

Amanda worked for Task Force Ember.

In strange turnabout, she'd been recruited by the same people who'd rescued her from terrorists less than a year ago. Her abduction had been a false flag operation, devised by Arkady Zhukov and executed by a Zeta operative, Valerian Kobak, who had functioned under the legend Anzor Malik. The same Russians were responsible for the murder of Ember Director Shane Smith, Operations Officer Simon Adamo, and SAD operator June Latif during the attack on Ember's previous headquarters in Newport News, Virginia. Dempsey had made sure Malik paid the ultimate price.

But Zhukov, the mastermind behind the attack, was still at large.

Since that fateful day, life at Ember had been a roller coaster ride.

No, not a roller coaster, she thought. *More like post-hurricane disaster recovery*.

Sure, they'd all rolled up their sleeves and put on brave faces, but if she was being honest with herself, all was not well with America's premier covert black ops task force. The stability, purposeful leadership, and tactical clarity that Smith and Adamo had brought to the organization were missing. The vacuum left in their absence was tangible. Signals Chief Baldwin was functioning as Acting Director and Munn had stepped into Adamo's old role as Ops O. The thing was, neither man wanted his respective "promotion," and it showed.

Baldwin, while knowledgeable and undeniably the most intellectually gifted member of the organization, lacked the operational experience and leadership skills to effectively lead and manage an organization as complex and dynamic as Ember. Munn, on the other hand, had the operational experience and a doctor's sensibility for reading and relating to people, but did not have the calculated, methodical disposition that had made Adamo so successful as Ops O. From the stories she'd heard about Munn, she knew he had the capacity to be cool and analytical under pressure, but that was not his default state. The man wore his heart on his sleeve, tended to be reactive rather than proactive, and wanted nothing more than to be back out in the field as Dempsey's wingman. The "lumberjack" wanted his old job back and wasn't shy about letting everyone know it.

We all just need a little more time, Amanda told herself. *Just a little more time and everything will sort itself out.*

She stepped into what was essentially an efficiency apartment where Sylvie Bessonov was incarcerated. Instead of being dumped into a dark hole at some black site overseas, the DNI had agreed to keep Bessonov close and accessible. The whack-a-mole operation they were presently running—finding and assassinating embedded Zeta field operators around the globe—was only possible because of the intelligence Bessonov had given up. The operation to break the Russian woman had been a psychological mind fuck of epic proportions, one in which Amanda had played a critical and unwitting role. In the days and weeks since, Amanda had taken over as Bessonov's interrogator and, dare she say, handler. During that time, she had successfully extracted the names of five Zetas and their assigned cities of operation, an accomplishment she was feeling pretty proud of, especially since she had achieved it without resorting to any enhanced interrogation techniques.

"Hello, Sylvie," Amanda said to the back of the Russian girl's head. Bessonov was sitting on a sofa watching television with the sound turned off. She had not turned around to look when Amanda entered, nor did she say anything now.

Amanda walked around the sofa, giving the Russian a wide berth. The Zeta had never shown any aggression. Still, Amanda's ordeal at the hands of Malik had permanently rewired her psyche. She knew what human beings were capable of—the scheming, the hate, the violence. Bessonov could snap at any time, and the Russian's past interactions and behavior could not be relied upon as a predictor for this or any future engagement between them.

It was imperative to be careful.

She sat in the lone chair beside the sofa and looked at her charge. Bessonov was slumped in her seat, feet up on the coffee table, legs apart, fingers knitted together and resting on her stomach. Her unblinking eyes were fixed on the TV, which was playing what looked like an episode of *Survivor*.

"Why do you watch with the sound turned off?" Amanda asked.

"Because it doesn't matter what they say," Bessonov said in Russian-accented English. "I can discern the hierarchy and lies from their body language and expressions alone. The words are a distraction from the truth."

"Interesting," Amanda said and flashed the Russian her *it's all good* smile—an expression that lived halfway between a flight attendant's *I'm paid to smile at you* and a coworker's *let's grab a beer and catch up* grin. In her experience, smiles were the transactional currency that powered business, politics, friendship, romance, and even interrogations. How she smiled, when she smiled, if she smiled . . . these were the variables that Sylvie cued off of. How, when, and if Sylvie smiled was equally insightful.

Amanda shifted her gaze from Bessonov to the television and watched in silence for thirty seconds or so before asking, "Do you have reality shows like this in Russia?"

"I like to watch these idiots," Bessonov said, ignoring the question. "Walking around in their underwear, arguing all the time. It's quite funny . . . Take away our jobs, our technology, and our houses, and this is what humanity becomes—a troupe of monkeys, fighting for table scraps and sexual hierarchy."

Amanda looked from the TV back to Bessonov. She tried to think of something to say, but her mind was stuck on the monkey metaphor. She remembered what it had felt like when Malik had reduced her to her primal state—stripping her naked, withholding food and water, and controlling her most basic and fundamental biological liberties. She'd been caged and dehumanized, and so in one respect that made her and her charge kindred spirits. She empathized with the Russian girl and wondered if that was why Baldwin had tapped her to manage Ember's MVP detainee.

"You seem quite melancholy today," Amanda settled on. "Is everything all right?"

"What a ridiculous thing to ask me," Bessonov fired back, making eye contact for the first time. "You've taken everything from me. My profession, my colleagues, my country, my dignity—"

"Not your dignity," Amanda snapped. "We've never taken that.

And trust me, I'm someone who can speak with authority on such matters. The decision to abandon your dignity is yours and yours alone."

"How can there be dignity without purpose? You've made me a traitor. You come here asking for names and I give them to you so you can murder my countrymen. There is no dignity in that. No dignity in betrayal and weakness. No dignity in self-preservation when you sacrifice all your principles in the process . . . I should have kept quiet. I should have let you torture me until I was dead."

Amanda laughed. She didn't mean to. It wasn't scripted or deliberate—it just came out.

"So you're laughing at me now," Bessonov said, her voice a serpent's hiss. "I'm a joke to you?"

"No," Amanda said, shaking her head. "I'm not laughing at you. I'm laughing at the stupid irony of it all. We're both here because of *him*—our lives forever maligned and spinning, like two billiard balls sent careening off course."

Bessonov just shook her head at this.

"Your old life may be over, but your future is unwritten. I made you a promise, that when this was over, you would be given a new identity and the resources to start a new life. Yes, Sylvie Bessonov may be dead, but you are young and have a second act in you. There is nothing stopping you from pursuing a new career, finding love, becoming a mother . . . the possibilities are limitless. There's more to life than espionage and cold wars."

"Fuck you," the Russian girl murmured under her breath.

"Excuse me?" Amanda bristled.

Bessonov exhaled loudly through her nose. "Dimitri Godunov. Last I knew, he was working as a professor in Berlin, under the alias Erich Habicht." Her gaze was fixed back on the television, her voice flat and lifeless.

"What is his mission?"

"The same as every Zeta—to do his job so well no one suspects he's a Russian spy."

"That's not what I meant."

"I know, but it was a stupid question, so you got a stupid answer."

"Am I to take that to mean you haven't run any ops with him?"

"That's correct. He's been embedded for a long time. Not one of the more active Zetas. He's not been running any significant operations."

"Then what is he doing in Berlin? He must be there for some reason?"

"I don't know all the details. I've told you, the structure in Zeta is very compartmentalized."

Amanda pursed her lips in irritation at the other woman. "Then speculate."

"Fine," Bessonov said through a sigh. "Supposedly, his father was a brilliant theoretical physicist who worked for decades at the Lebedev Institute. The hope was that Dimitri was as gifted as his father, but he wanted nothing to do with academics and pursued a career in soldiering. But Arkady misses nothing and snatched him up—enchanting Dimitri with 007 dreams of spy craft and glorious covert operations. But the reality was, Arkady needed someone smart enough to understand and steal cutting-edge research and intellectual property in the fields of theoretical and applied physics. So, the old man put Dimitri in Berlin because the Germans are very good at this sort of thing."

"Is Dimitri married?" Amanda asked.

"I don't know."

"Dimitri's German NOC is Erich Habicht?" she said, confirming the name. The room was under twenty-four-hour surveillance and all their conversations were recorded, but maintaining pretenses and authentic conversational rhythms was important. "Habicht spelled H-A-B-I-C-H-T?"

"That's right," Bessonov said. "Now run along, little sister. Come back when he's dead and I'll give you another name."

Amanda stared at her for a long moment, then pressed to her feet. "Is there anything I can get you?"

"A Makarov would be nice, but any gun will do . . . I just need one bullet."

"Good night, Sylvie," she said with a sad smile, and walked to the door. Doug let her out.

After the door was shut and locked behind her, he said, "How's she doing?"

Amanda paused, surprised by the question, as the big man had never once inquired about his charge. "It's a PF Chang's night," she said, running her fingers through her dirty blond hair. "Mongolian beef."

Once, in a moment of sororal weakness, Sylvie had confessed that Mongolian beef from the popular Asian fusion chain was her favorite. Ordering it for her on the days she gave up a name had become something of a tradition between them.

"Roger that," he said. "See ya next time."

"Back at ya," she echoed with a nod and headed to her car. Once she was seated inside with the engine running and doors locked, she called Ember.

"Munn," a familiar gruff voice said, picking up the secure line.

"I got a name. Erich Habicht," she said, with a bittersweet undertone that she didn't try to hide. "He's in Berlin."

"Nice work, Amanda," Munn said. "Head on home, and we'll get to work putting together a package."

CHAPTER 3

Hotel Intercontinental Berlin
Berlin, Germany
September 18
1430 Local Time

"I hear you, Buz, but that makes absolutely no sense," Dempsey said, shaking his head at the Russian grammar worksheet in his hand. "This sentence says *cat caught mouse*, correct?"

"Koshka poymala mysh," Buz said, with a patient nod. "Yes."

"And this sentence translates to *mouse caught cat?*" he said, pointing to the next line.

"That's right. *Mysh poymala koshka.*"

"And this one, *poymala koshka mysh*," Dempsey said, struggling to pronounce the Russian himself this time, "translates to *caught cat mouse?*"

"Correct," answered the old spook.

Dempsey exhaled with aggravation. "How the hell can *mouse caught cat* and *caught cat mouse* mean the same thing as *cat caught mouse?*"

"This is what I've been trying to explain to you," Buz said with an empathetic smile. "The Russian language is very flexible. Word order by itself is irrelevant. You can write the same sentence with these three words six different ways and the default translation will always be *cat caught mouse*. And remember, the Russian language doesn't use articles like we do. You don't have to put a *the* in front of *cat* or an *a* in front of *mouse*."

"So all I have to do is memorize the verbs and nouns and then I can say them in any order I want and people will understand me—is that what you're saying?"

Buz chuckled. "No, that's not at all what I'm saying. Context, intonation, and the application of the six cases are what differentiate and provide the meaning to the sentence."

"But word order doesn't matter? I can at least bank on that."

"Well, no, sentence structure does matter sometimes, but we'll get to that later."

"Oh for Christ's sake, this is hopeless," Dempsey said, setting the paper down on the desk. "I'll never learn Russian."

"Never say never," Buz said. "You learned to speak Arabic, right?"

"Yeah, a little, but that's only because I was around people speaking Arabic for fifteen years," he grumbled. "And I'm not even close to fluent."

"Sounds like you're an auditory learner; most people are when it comes to languages," Buz said, giving his shoulder a pat. "I'm just going to have to start talking to you only in Russian during these lessons. We'll see if that causes things to gel."

"I hope you're a patient man," Dempsey said with a self-deprecating shake of his head. Then he glanced at his watch. "I should probably get back to the room and prep for the op."

"You up for this?" Buz said, with an undercurrent that made Dempsey wonder if the killing was beginning to weigh on Ember's most seasoned spy.

"Easy day," Dempsey said, flashing a crooked grin. "See ya in a few."

He let himself out of Buz's hotel room, walked down the hall to the suite he was sharing with Grimes, and let himself in with the key card. The bathroom door was closed and he could hear the water still running in the shower.

How long does it take for this woman to wash her damn hair?

He walked over to the mini-fridge and grabbed himself a bottled water, spun off the cap, and chugged half its contents. A second later, he heard the shower finally turn off.

"About friggin' time," he murmured. For this evening's op, he needed time in the bathroom to prep. But instead of getting cleaned up, he was about to get dirty.

And smelly.

Very dirty and very smelly.

This particular disguise had been Munn's idea, and at the time had seemed reasonable to Dempsey. But now as he contemplated the specifics of what was required to achieve *authenticity*, he was having second thoughts. He sat down on the corner of the bed and began to unlace his boots.

The bathroom door swung open.

When he heard footsteps approaching, he looked up to find a very wet—and very naked—Elizabeth Grimes standing in front of him, her head wrapped in that post-shower towel-turban thing that women do.

"Christ, John!" she exclaimed, her hand pressed in between her bare breasts. "I thought you were in Buz's room practicing Russian."

"I was," he said, mouth agape, watching her heavily freckled chest flush to match her cheeks. "But I . . . I came back."

"Instead of just sitting there gawking, do you mind handing me one of those towels, please?" She thrust an index finger at the stack of white towels that housekeeping had left on the corner of the bed beside him.

"Uh, sure," he said, *mostly* averting his eyes and handing her the top towel off the stack.

"What's that grin for?"

"I never really noticed your freckles before, but I guess that's because I've never seen you . . . um . . . naked."

"You know, *roommate*," she said, as she wrapped the towel around her torso, "you could have looked away sooner."

"Yeah, well, you could have turned around and run back into the bathroom, *roommate*," he said.

"Are you implying I have something to be ashamed of?"

"Nooooo," he said. "Quite the opposite. Your body is definitely, shall we say, beach ready."

"Damn right—and don't you forget it," she said, then turned on a heel and disappeared back into the bathroom.

This was the fourth hotel room they'd shared in as many weeks as they posed as husband and wife during this string of city-hopping Zeta assassination ops. Unlike the intimate experience he'd had pretending to be newlyweds with the Israeli operative Elinor Jordan, he and Grimes had kept things strictly professional—no kissing, no hugging, no bed sharing. With Elinor, he'd instantly felt the tug of attraction. With Grimes, it was the opposite. She was like his cousin or a stepsister . . .

He heard a hair dryer turn on.

Chuckling, he finished taking off his boots. While doing so, his right ankle cracked, triggering the sudden sensation that everything was out of whack. He'd put his forty-year-old body through the wringer over the years, and the last three years had arguably been the hardest. Waking up was the worst. Most days he ached pretty much everywhere he had a joint, and that was a lot of places because the body has a lot of joints. He rolled his neck, then each wrist, and cracked his knuckles—sounding very much like a popcorn machine popping a fresh batch. Next, he arched his back and twisted his spine—cracking the vertebrae to relieve the pent-up tension and get himself back in alignment. He got satisfying pops from all the usual offenders except one, the vertebra right between his shoulder blades. He twisted right and then left, trying to get it to shift, but it stubbornly refused to pop. He took a knee, then lay down prone on the carpeted floor. He pressed up, his hips against the floor, while lifting his head skyward and arching his back.

Nothing.

He rolled onto his back and tried crossing his left arm across his chest and pulling on it. No crack. Right arm pull . . . *nope.* The more he focused on it, the more the damn thing bothered him. He knew it wasn't possible, but the bone felt completely crooked in its slot, like it was cocked forty-five degrees out of whack. He rolled back onto his stomach and tried reaching behind to see if he could press the spot with his thumb . . .

"What the hell are you doing?" Grimes said.

He looked up and saw her standing directly in front of him—fresh-faced and now fully clothed—looking down at him.

"I'm trying to get this one stupid vertebra to pop," he said in an irritated grumble. "It's driving me fucking crazy."

"I told you not to do that. The more you crack your joints, the more they want to be cracked. It's like an addiction, JD. You're a crack addict."

"I'm not a crack addict," he said, chuckling. "I'm a *cracking* addict."

"God, you look pathetic down there," she said, shaking her head. "I don't think you're going to get it that way."

"Ya think?" he said, straining with futility.

She sighed, and then with resignation said, "What do you want me to do?"

With an anticipatory smile, he moved his arms to his side, turned his chin to the left, and lay completely straight and flat on his stomach. "I need you to stand on my back."

"What? No," she said. "I'm not doing that."

"Trust me, it's fine. Kate used to do it all the time."

"Seriously?"

"Yes, seriously. It works. Trust me. Just step up onto the middle of my back between my shoulder blades. You can hold onto the wall to steady yourself."

"Fine," she said and walked to his right side. She put a reluctant bare foot onto his back and began to step up, but after applying marginal pressure quickly stepped off. "I'm going to hurt you. I can't do this."

"You're not going to hurt me," he said with a laugh. "I promise . . . unless you step on T8. That would be bad. Don't step on T8, that's the one I shattered that's held together with pins. The one that's bugging me is T4. Or maybe T3. I can't really tell. Between my shoulder blades."

"No, no, no, I can't do this. I have no idea what the hell you're talking about, and I refuse to be the person responsible for putting John Dempsey in a wheelchair for the rest of his life."

"Lizzie, please," he said, craning his neck to look up at her.

"Trust me, you're not going to put me in a wheelchair. Just don't step on my lower middle back and I'll be fine."

"This is stupid," she said, grudgingly placing her foot between his shoulder blades. "I'm heavy."

"I'll be fine . . . and no, you're not."

With a pained expression on her face, she stepped up with her other foot until all her weight was on him.

He let out a groan.

"Did I hurt you?"

"No," he said. "But I was wrong, you *are* heavy."

"You're such a dick."

"Kidding, kidding, I'm only kidding," he said, trying not to laugh. "You're absolutely perfect, Freckles."

"Freckles?" she snapped indignantly. "All right, that's it. I'm getting off—"

"No, no, not yet," he protested. "You didn't get it."

She shifted her weight and the offending vertebra popped loudly underfoot. "Oh my God, I felt that. Did I get the right one?"

"Yeah," he said with a satisfied groan, closed his eyes, and smiled. "Thank you."

In that moment, the door's lock beeped. The handle turned, the door opened, and Buz Wilson stepped in. The old spook looked at Grimes, then down at Dempsey, and a crooked grin curled his lips.

"It's not what you think," Grimes said, stepping off his back and folding her arms across her chest.

"I'm not judging," Buz said, then, twisting his shoulders, added, "Come to think of it, I could use some good back-walking myself."

"What? You do this, too?" she said, her tone incredulous.

"Oh yeah, back in the day Bonnie used to walk on my back all the time," Buz said.

"But not anymore?"

"No," he said, his tone almost wistful. "It feels damn good, but the thing is if you don't stop cracking your joints, then they get all loose and you have to crack them every day . . ."

"See, I told you," Grimes said, wagging her finger at Dempsey as he did a push-up and got to his feet. Then, turning to Buz: "That's exactly what I told him."

Dempsey smiled defiantly at them both. Punctuating each word with a crack of his knuckles, he said, "Not gonna happen."

They chuckled collectively at this, and Buz checked his watch.

"You guys about ready?" he said, his dubious gaze traveling between them but settling on Dempsey.

"Almost," Dempsey said, grabbing a wadded-up pile of ratty clothes off the nearby desk. Tucking them under his arm, he headed for the bathroom. On his way past Grimes, he looked at her and said, "I'm sorry, about . . . you know, earlier."

"It's fine," she said with an easy smile. "We're roommates. Bound to happen sooner or later."

He nodded, any guilt assuaged.

"To stay on the timeline, we need to get moving. We don't want to miss the professor," Buz called after him.

"I know," Dempsey said with a dismissive wave over his shoulder. "I just need a couple of minutes to shit my pants, and I'll be ready to roll."

CHAPTER 4

Bistro at the Hotel Grenzfall
Berlin, Germany
1745 Local Time

Professor Erich Habicht glanced at the woman sitting alone at one of the outdoor dining tables. She was looking away from him, which had happened each time he'd glanced at her table and also when he'd first spied her following him on campus yesterday. Her clothes were different from the last time he'd seen her, as was her hair, but this was definitely the same woman.

And that was a problem.

He had spent most the last four years, seven months, and eleven days teaching theoretical physics at Technische Universität Berlin, or TU Berlin, as it was known. Entropy and quantum mechanics was his specialty. But how could one express in equations the truly cold and nefarious nature of entropy? It was the great disintegrator of order. The universe's original serial killer—a relentless hunter that always and eventually ended every living thing. Cells age and fail. The organs they are part of lose their fight, until the entire organism—the ultimate conductor of the orchestrated battle against entropy—falls into randomness in the form of death and decay. All systems, be they natural or man-made, eventually succumb to disorder. He had come to accept this, and to accept that life was nothing more than a concerted effort to fight entropy. To persist and survive requires that energy be put into the system . . .

In his other life—in what he slowly found harder and harder to remember was his *real* life—the phenomenon had a different name. Entropy was a term for philosophers, chemists, and *real* physicists; in the world of spies and spycraft, complacency was the killer. Today, the Zeta known in Berlin as Professor Erich Habicht would let neither complacency nor entropy take his life. He would bring order to chaos, which would require the expenditure of a hefty energy toll. But he didn't care, because for the first time in years he felt alive again.

He tipped back the last of his beer and nodded to the hostess as he exited the bar through the street-side door, stepping down onto Ackerstraße and turning right. It was only a few paces to the corner of Bernauer Straße, and he chose the corner that would cross north—because the crossing light had just turned red. There was no traffic, but he waited patiently—as most native Berliners would because Berliners loved order above all things. Across Bernauer Straße sat an open corner lot with a lone, antiquated guard tower, part of the Berlin Wall Memorial that stretched on in both directions—an enduring Cold War reminder of what Berlin had once been.

Regrettably, there was no car at the corner whose window reflection he could use to check behind him as the pedestrian light turned green and he began to cross.

No matter. She won't be there. Not yet.

It struck him that he'd had this thought in German—something that was beginning to happen regularly as the legend slowly consumed him from the inside—like the aliens in the old American film. Eventually, he feared, he would *become* Professor Erich Habicht and lose all sight of the way back.

The once and future spy walked slowly north, taking his time, enjoying the cool of the evening, and occasionally checking his six in the side mirrors of cars parked along the road. Three blocks north, he came to the corner of Brunnenstraße, stepped from the curb, then stopped as if distracted by a phone vibrating in his pocket. He turned to step back onto the curb as he pulled the phone from his overcoat and placed it to his ear.

"Hallo . . .? Ja, das ist Herr Habicht. Wer is das, bitte?" he said to his imaginary caller.

Sweeping his gaze across the street, he spotted her—standing just beyond the newsstand at the corner, laughing. Phone pressed to her ear, she stepped up to the newsstand and bought a magazine.

"Wir solten morgen sprechen, okay?" he said, keeping up the charade. *"Ja, ja. Danke Sehr, Fraulein Schimmler."*

He sighed as if put upon—an anticipated rendezvous now cancelled—and returned the phone to his pocket. Then he looked in both directions, searching for the rest of her team while feigning checking the road for traffic. He tapped his hand on his thigh, as if uncertain what to do now that he didn't need to meet whoever Fraulein Schimmler might be, then shrugged and turned north, toward Humboldthain Park with its thick trees and narrow trails.

I will lure her there and take her. If she is an agent I will kill her . . .oh, how good it will be to operate again. And with my cover blown, I will finally have an excuse to return to Russia for reassignment.

His heart soared at the thought. He had not endured the years of training to become a Zeta only to waste the best operational years of his career teaching theoretical physics. He was tired of waiting for a message to activate him to the life he had chosen—a life of action and danger. But now he had a target, and that made him stifle a smile.

He continued north, his pace relaxed. He didn't greet or nod at anyone he passed—that was not the Berliner way. He took his time, his leather satchel over his shoulder, as he worked out his plan. Humboldthain Park was small, but he knew it well. He could think of several areas where he could take the woman, so long as she didn't have other team members supporting her. He was unarmed, after all, living the genteel life of a professor. Even the occasional woman he took to bed—mostly graduate students at TU—would describe him as a tender, even sensitive, man. The irony was that inside he carried so much rage, rage he had no outlet for. Unable to spar and train properly without jeopardizing his cover, he'd lost twenty pounds of muscle during this assignment. He barely felt a Zeta anymore, and he hated the weak shell of a man he'd become.

Entropy, it seemed, had done its work well.

He entered the park, shuffling slowly, his hands behind his back, taking in the cool evening air as he wandered along the paths. His plan was to give himself a chance to look for spotters and agents who might be part of the woman's team. He could not be sure how long they'd been surveilling him, but he'd not come to this park once in the past month, which meant it was extraordinarily unlikely assets were pre-positioned here. They would not think of this place—why would they? It was a perfect site for killing, but one would have to be a killer to know so.

He passed a woman sitting on a bench, reading a magazine, but she paid him no mind. As he walked north, he passed an old man with a cane, but the man was heading south, away from the trap. The spy resisted a smile, content with his plan.

Unless this is a test—a test I might fail. What would Arkady expect of me? Would he want me to remain in my legend and try to salvage it?

Surely not.

If I'm being followed, then my legend is compromised already. Unless she's following me for other reasons? Something related to the university?

But he could think of nothing—of no reason that anyone would take any interest at all in the soft man who was Professor Erich Habicht or the boring work he did. There was no obvious military application to his esoteric research or teachings. And this woman was highly trained—a government agent for certain.

Either I've been made by the BND or it is the Americans. Regardless, the legend must be sacrificed.

He veered east to enter the rose garden. He didn't see her, but he could feel her trailing him.

I will re-establish myself in a nonofficial cover of my choosing—outside of Germany but inside Europe. That will please and impress Director Zhukov. Then I will make contact, hopefully through Bessonov—she was my operational handler before infiltration, and I trust her.

He entered the garden and began his counterclockwise circle, stopping at the first bend to check a text message he pretended to receive, and in his peripheral vision he spotted her. Her appearance had changed again—an oversized green fleece pulled over her jeans, a grey ball cap—but he recognized her by her gait and her build. He suppressed a grin. God, how he had missed this—the thrill of the hunt. At the moment, he was the hunted, but when the time was right he would flip the script. The satisfaction of turning his hunter into his prey would be doubly rewarding. He could feel his edge returning, even felt his muscle tone improving, and he no longer walked with the lazy shuffle of Professor Erich-fucking-Habicht.

The smell of liquor mixed with body odor and urine filled his nostrils as a hunched figure rose with great difficulty from a supine position on a bench along the path. The bum was dressed in little more than layers of rags and reeked of a smell impossible to acquire in less than months of living on the streets. Habicht tensed nonetheless, preparing himself for an assault. But the man stumbled, then fell face-first onto the gravel path, cursing in German. Habicht gave the derelict a wide berth, circling him while he puked on the gravel path.

Disgusting . . .

As he distanced himself from his legend, the Russian spy struggled against the urge to kick the pathetic creature in the head. The bum looked up at him, puke dribbling through his shaggy beard, and raised a filthy hand.

"Kannst du mir bitte helfen? Kannst du etwas geld für essen sparen?" the vagabond said, begging for money for food, a drunken smile splitting his tangled, wet beard.

"Nein, Sie warden es nur für alkohol verwenden."

The homeless man's face clouded and his smile disappeared. *"Fick dich dann,"* he choked out before doubling over, wracked by a coughing fit.

Habicht shook his head, leaving the bum coughing on all fours as he continued north. He walked to a fork in the footpath and turned west to make a counterclockwise circle around the garden. In his peripheral vision, he saw neither the woman nor the disgusting drunk. He forced himself to slow his pace, while dropping his shoulders and shoving his hands into his pockets. For just a few more minutes, he needed to be Professor Habicht, and the professor didn't walk with such strength and confidence.

The path continued in a circle at the periphery of the rose garden, and as he turned south, he stopped near a bench to ostensibly check his phone. A quick glance in all directions showed that, for now, he was alone. A cluster of trees obscured the sightline from the observation tower to the west, where his enemy might have positioned a spotter or a sniper. Satisfied he was still in control, he pocketed his phone and stepped over the knee-high black metal chain to exit the walking path. Behind him, he heard the faint crunch of footsteps on gravel.

She's coming . . .

He slipped into the trees, disappearing among the long, dark shadows as the sun fell. He removed his coat, dropping it to the ground, and repositioned behind a large tree just a few yards from the edge of the path. There, he waited—his muscles tight and ready to strike, his breath long and controlled, his pulse rate paradoxically slowing.

My God, it is good to be me again, he thought as the footfalls of his prey grew louder.

A heartbeat later, she rounded the corner. He watched her approach the bench where he had stopped only moments ago and throw her hands up in frustration. Then she pulled her phone out of her back pocket.

"It's me," she said softly in English.

Ah, I was right. It's the Americans . . . so arrogant. So overly aggressive.

He wished he could take her captive so that he could learn how they'd penetrated his legend. The risks in doing so, however, would greatly outweigh the potential gain. He needed to kill her and disappear as quickly as possible.

"I lost him, but I know he's in the park . . . No, I'm by myself . . . Because how the fuck was I to know he would break routine today of all days and take a stroll?" She waited while someone spoke to her. "Look, I don't need you in the park. I'll reacquire and shadow. Position the team at both south corners and the van at the southeast corner. That's where he'll likely exit. If the opportunity presents, we grab him; otherwise, we take him at his apartment later."

He watched her slip her phone back into her pocket and resume her search for him. When her back was turned to him, he moved swiftly, his feet silent on the pine needle carpet. He closed on the walking path, keeping just inside the chain to avoid the gravel until he was upon her. He lowered his shoulder—intending to wrap an arm around her throat, choking off any scream—when a putrid smell overwhelmed him.

Gravel crunched, and a slurred voice said, *"Gib mir etwas verdammtes geld!"*

Damn it! Where did he come from?

The drunk bum was back, stumbling toward them.

The American woman whirled, wide-eyed, and her hand slipped under her fleece.

Habicht leapt onto the path and used his forward momentum to shove her violently to the ground before he turned to grab the bum's filthy outstretched arm. He clutched the man's wrist, intent on pulling him off balance so he could deliver a blow to the temple, then immobilize the woman before she pulled her gun. But the drunk twisted out of his grip, and with lightning speed seized his forearm and pulled *him* off balance. Before he realized what was happening, he felt searing pain as his forearm shattered against the vagabond's knee. Next, he felt his shoulder dislocate as the man in rags executed a second crippling strike.

I'm such a fool, he thought as he tried to get back in the fight.

Ignoring the pain in his arm and shoulder, he tucked and spun, dodging the bum's third strike. He tried to drive a kick into the other man's groin, but his assailant was like a wolverine—savage and relentless. He felt his strike blocked and then took a blow to the temple. Stars exploded in his eyes and he lost his sense of balance and spatial awareness. An iron claw clutched his throat. As his vision cleared, he found himself staring up into the derelict's eyes—eyes burning with fire above a dirt-and-vomit-speckled beard. The fist closed on his throat and he felt a sickening crunch.

The woman—his prey—stepped into view, her expression cold apathy as she peered down at him over the monster's shoulder.

Deprived of oxygen, his lungs burned and his vision began to dim.

He felt cool metal under his chin—the wide barrel of a suppressor.

The wolverine man's eyes bore into him. "De oppresso liber," the American assassin growled.

Then he heard the pistol discharge, felt the burn under his chin.

And the world went red.

CHAPTER 5

Ember Van

Westbound on Königin-Luise-Straße

Berlin, Germany

1850 Local Time

No matter how many layers of filthy clothing he removed, Dempsey still smelled like shit. Not the manly stench of protracted combat—sweat, dirt, and testosterone. No, he was an homage to excrement—urine, vomit, and shit. He'd made sure all the orifices were represented, electing to piss and puke himself in the field to complete the look of a homeless drunk.

And it had worked.

When it came to role-playing, authenticity was key.

"Coming up on the embassy in just a moment," Buz said from the driver's seat.

Beside him, as he stripped naked, Grimes stared absently out the window at the passing grey buildings.

He held his breath as he pulled the final layer of stench-laden clothes off his body, shoved them into a garbage bag, and sealed it. The smell in the truck improved immediately, but it would probably take antiseptic soap and a fire hose shower to make him palatable. Grimes bent over the backpack at her feet, retrieved a sweat suit top and bottoms, and handed it to him.

"Thanks," he said. "Sorry about the smell."

"No problem," was all she said as she looked back out the window.

See, this is why I need Munn, he thought as he pulled on the sweatpants. *I'm sitting here buck naked and filthy, and she doesn't even take the once-in-a-lifetime opportunity to bust my balls and get back at me for earlier today.*

Munn was an operator, a former SEAL like Dempsey, and as a SEAL, Munn knew how to be a proper wingman. Dempsey didn't want a "no problem" from Grimes. He needed someone to give him shit about the smell. He needed someone to comment on his appearance and call him a fucking stinky hobo when he was decked out like a stinky hobo, then compliment him for "smelling better than usual" after an op. But Grimes was locked up soooo tight. The only actual banter they'd shared for months was this morning when he'd caught her naked . . . and he certainly couldn't rely on *that* to happen every time he wanted to talk smack with her.

"You okay?" he asked, looking at her.

She shrugged, but then seemed to think better of it and turned on him. "Do you have to say that *every* time?" she asked through clenched teeth.

"What?" he asked, feeling heat in his face. "I'm not allowed to ask if you're okay, now?"

"No, not that, John," she said with exasperation. "I mean, dear God, do you have to call out *de oppresso liber* every time you kill one of them? Why not just wear a T-shirt with an American flag and sing the national anthem while you pull the trigger?"

"It's for Shane," he said softly, barely biting back anger that didn't really make any sense. "Shane was a Green Beret, damn it. And in the moment before I end each and every one of those Russian bastards, I want them to understand. I want them to understand who is killing them and why. And so to answer your question, yes, I'm going to call out *de oppresso liber* every time. Because I want it to be the last fucking thing every Zeta hears before they die."

"Yeah, well, it's a gut punch for me every time you do it. And second, it compromises the mission. Who knows who might be listening? Wang's not perfect."

"Yes, I am," Wang said on the still-active comms channel. But instead of his usual swagger, his voice was flat and monotone.

"No, you're not," she said, "which means every time JD satisfies his neurotic compulsion, he risks blowing our NOCs. What do you think our allies will do when they all start comparing notes and figure out there's an American assassin on a killing spree across Europe who recites the US Army Special Forces motto before he murders his victims?"

Dempsey shrugged but said nothing. She was right, of course, but he simply couldn't make himself care.

"I hold you a half block from the Clayallee gate," Wang said, also choosing not to continue the debate.

Since the attack just months ago on Ember's TOC, and the deaths of Smith, Adamo, and Latif—not to mention the crippling spine injury to Chris Noble, aka Dale—Wang had been morose and depressed. No jokes, no bravado, none of the tech genius pointing out how flawless his ISR—intelligence, surveillance, reconnaissance—was on a daily basis. Dempsey was worried about Wang. Maybe the most of anyone on the team. Even Ember's relocation to Tampa, a town with plenty of attractive girls and a hopping nightlife, had done little to buoy Wang's spirits. On the flipside, the kid's operational performance had gone to the next level. He was faster and more precise, and without all the self-aggrandizing commentary, he'd begun to make tactical observations and strategic contributions during ops. Yet despite all that, Dempsey missed the kid's irritating babble.

Just like he missed having Munn as his smack-talking wingman.

And I miss Smith playing mother hen, and Latif picking on Martin, and Adamo talking about "cold facts"—whatever the hell those are—while incessantly pushing his stupid glasses up on his nose. When Zeta hit us at home, we lost more than just a building and our brothers—we lost our soul.

Dempsey shook off thoughts of lost souls. He was an operator, a weapon, an instrument of policy. At the moment, that policy was to exact retribution on Spetsgruppa Zeta and every one of its operators they could find. And when that was done, they would find and eliminate Russia's legendary spymaster, Arkady Zhukov, too.

Buz braked.

"Why are we stopping?" Dempsey asked, looking up.

"So the Marines can open the gate," Buz said.

"Why are the gates closed?' Grimes asked.

"They close them whenever there's an op underway in the city," Buzz said, and quickly held up a hand before Grimes could speak. "And yes, I am aware that they might as well run a flag up the embassy flagpole saying *American covert operation in progress*, but we're guests here. I assure you, CIA has bitched about it for years. Marine Corps security dictates policy for the embassy, and 'gates closed during operations in Berlin' is that policy."

"Someone should tell them keeping operations covert is way better security than an eight-foot-high iron gate," Grimes mumbled.

Buz looked like he might say something but simply nodded instead.

With a wave from the Marine guard, the former CIA man and Russian operations expert piloted them through the gate and across the wide courtyard nestled behind the main building. The square stone building they headed to was officially the United States Trade and Investment Bureau Mission, but anyone who knew anything about the history of Berlin knew this was the nerve center for CIA operations in the city—a city once surrounded by a stone wall and ground zero for covert operations during the Cold War. Buz had been here then, Dempsey knew, and he watched the spook purse his lips under his Magnum P.I. mustache as he parked tight to the building and shut off the engine.

Something was clearly eating at Buz, but the old-timer always kept his thoughts to himself.

Dempsey climbed out of the vehicle, tossed the trash bag full of soiled clothes into a dumpster beside the access ramp at the back of the building, and fell in behind Grimes. Buz pressed the door buzzer, waved his hand in front of the camera, and a second later the door clicked open. The trio walked to a borrowed conference room they were using for an ops center, and Dempsey collapsed into a leather task chair. Grimes selected a chair across the table from him—the smell, he assumed—and Buz took a seat at the head where a closed laptop waited. He opened the screen, logged in, and brought up a video feed on the wall-mounted monitor. Baldwin's face filled the screen just as Wang walked in. The cyber whiz gave a somber nod to Dempsey, who returned a thumbs-up.

"Everyone all right?" Baldwin asked. Dempsey sensed his concern was genuine, but his demeanor lacked the academic enthusiasm that had always been his hallmark. The Zeta attack on Ember had affected Baldwin, too. Dale, now a paraplegic, had been one of his protégés. Baldwin had hardened in the aftermath.

Maybe embittered *was a better word*, Dempsey thought, staring at the screen.

"Jesus, JD, you look like shit," Munn's familiar voice said as the doc entered the frame. "Or I should say, you look like you *smell* like shit. Is it even worse than in Thailand that one time?"

Dempsey smiled and felt himself relax. *Thank God for Munn.*

"Not quite that bad, bro," he chuckled, trying to capture the camaraderie from a memory that felt like a lifetime ago.

"What's this make?" Munn said. "Three in a row you managed to complete without me? I guess miracles do happen."

Grimes crossed her arms against her chest. "Getting back to business, we're all fine and the operational objective was achieved. No reaction from local law enforcement and we believe our NOCs are intact," she said while giving Dempsey the stink eye.

That's okay, sis. You're allowed.

"Any collateral, problems, things you would have done differently?" Munn asked.

"No sheep were harmed on this op," Dempsey said, suppressing a grin. "If that's what you're asking."

"Yes, good, as you know, livestock welfare is always my primary concern," Munn said.

"The park was mostly empty. Wang disabled area security cameras, but in any case, we could not ID any surveillance in the vicinity of the hit—something I suspect Habicht knew. He lured me there, just like we predicted," Grimes said.

"Yes, which is why we should always take advantage of ISR conducted by a target in advance," Baldwin said. "We must strive to work smarter, not harder."

"Right," Dempsey grumbled, and then, looking at Baldwin in his suit coat and tie, wondered why the hell Jarvis had put a man who, despite his brilliance, had no special operations experience or qualifications in charge of Task Force Ember. But then again, if not Baldwin, who? Baldwin had been with Jarvis and Smith from the beginning, and other than Dempsey, nobody else had the clearance and organizational experience to assume the role on short notice.

"Okay, well if there's no additional constructive input," Baldwin said, "let's move on to preparations for the next mission."

"Hold on," Dempsey said, raising a hand. "As much as it gives me great pleasure to end these fuckers, I'd like to open the door to revisiting the operational strategy. We've now capped a half-dozen Zetas and we're still no closer to cutting the head off the snake than when we started. I appreciate the work that Allen is doing harvesting names from Bessonov, and every Zeta we take out weakens the organization—but when are we going to start focusing on Zhukov? Kill Arkady Zhukov and all these other assholes wither on the vine."

"We tried that with the first target, remember?" Grimes said before Baldwin or Munn could respond. She was looking across the table at him. "And it was a colossal waste of time. The Zeta field operators are completely compartmentalized. They're read into their NOCs and the details of their specific operations. We could interrogate them for months or years and never harvest any actionable intelligence beyond the training pipeline in Vyborg, and that's provided we could break them at all. Bessonov is different. She was support. She ran C4 and accumulated personnel and operational knowledge during her tenure. If you want Zhukov, then she's key. Break her, and you find him."

"Allen is convinced Bessonov is already broken," Baldwin said.

"Okay." Grimes shrugged. "I'm not, but you've made your position crystal clear on enhanced interrogation, Ian, so here we are."

Dempsey felt a surge of anger, but he wasn't sure why. He wasn't even sure he disagreed with her. Maybe it was a programmed reaction because Grimes was behaving like the know-it-all firebrand she'd been during the early days when they both joined Ember. He pushed back from the table, got up from his chair, and began to pace. "Look, I guess the point I'm making is that I'm sick of playing whack-a-mole. I want to find Arkady Zhukov and I want this to be over."

"As do we all, John," Baldwin said, in a tone Dempsey usually found so patronizing that it chapped his ass. For some reason today, however, he found it strangely endearing. "But the hope has always been that if we hit enough Zeta assets, then Zhukov will be forced to adjust his strategy. How many losses can he tolerate without action? How many assets must he lose before he changes tack, breaks protocol, or calls them in from the cold? Rest assured, with each prosecution, we're collecting signals intelligence. We are aggregating, analyzing, and trying to correlate thousands of data points about his network of operatives. At some point, we will have a breakthrough—intel that leads us to him or predicts his next move. Eventually, Zhukov will make a mistake, and then we will get him."

"And until that happens, the world is a better place without each and every one of these assholes we eliminate," Munn added. "We don't know what Petrov and Zhukov are going to cook up as their next big false flag operation. What is the next ship they plan to sink and call it an industrial accident? What is the next strategic facility they plan to attack and call it terrorism? Every Zeta we kill is like taking out a midlevel officer in charge of a squadron of assets. I don't know what the dude you just whacked in the park was planning, but I do know that eliminating him made Berlin a safer place. The same is true for London, Helsinki, Bangkok, and Bucharest.

God only knows what Russian operations we thwarted in those cities."

"Don't get me wrong," Dempsey said. He stopped pacing and leaned against the high-back leather chair he'd been sitting in. "I thoroughly enjoy ending these bastards. More than you know, maybe. And you're right, every field operative we take out is sand in the gears for Zhukov's mayhem machine. But once they're gone, I'm worried that the trail will go cold. The thought of Zhukov disappearing into the night . . ." He sighed.

"I get it, JD," Munn said, "but I think we all need to trust the process."

Look at you, playing peacemaker, Dempsey thought. *I gotta get you back in the field with me before it's too late.*

"Do we have the next target?" Grimes said, in her *let's get on with it* voice.

Baldwin and Munn nodded in unison and disappeared from the screen. In their place, a headshot appeared of a woman who looked thirty-five, but Dempsey decided could be older depending on her level of fitness. She was smiling in the photo—a genuine and happy smile, the smile of someone living their best life. She looked like a business executive, or perhaps an attorney, but certainly not a killer.

And therein lay the con . . . because that was exactly what she was.

"This is Selina Pichler," Baldwin began. "According to her CV, she's a thirty-five-year-old French pharmaceutical executive . . . and she is our next Zeta target."

CHAPTER 6

Bocharov Creek 2
Sochi, Russia
September 19
1340 Local Time

Arkady Zhukov shrugged off his suit coat and folded it over his left forearm while he stood and watched Russian President Vladimir Petrov exercise. Petrov had converted what had probably been a very nice dining lanai into a self-indulgent, open-air fitness center. Very expensive-looking exercise contraptions of every shape and size were arranged in a U shape around a section of padded, open floor space. When the opportunity presented itself, Petrov liked to make a spectacle of his workouts, often inviting guests, VIPs, and even visiting heads of state to join him for a "training" session. Most refused to participate, but Petrov didn't care. Exercising, per se, was a charade. The point was to create an asymmetry. Make his guests uncomfortable. Knock the other party off kilter so they became distracted, insecure, or both.

No one was immune to the treatment.

Once, Petrov had insisted Arkady conduct a post-op debrief in a dry sauna—heated to an unbearable eighty degrees Celsius—while Petrov sat naked, trimming his toenails. Another time, the President had demanded Arkady accompany him to a hydration therapy session, and he would not let Arkady speak until they were both hooked up to IVs with vitamin-infused saline flowing. It was growing harder and harder to get the Russian President's attention, and the man was taking ever greater pleasure in pushing the boundaries of subservience and sycophancy. The unspoken message was clear: *You may be standing beside me, but there is a canyon between us.*

"I'm sweating and I'm not even working out," Arkady said with a chuckle, his second attempt to get Petrov to engage.

The Russian President grunted, not in acknowledgment but from strain. The machine he was presently using, a seated chest press, faced away from Arkady so its user could look out onto the lush and manicured grounds of Bocharov Creek 2. Petrov loved Sochi and took every opportunity to govern from his half-billion-dollar summer "dacha" nestled on the coast of the Black Sea. Arkady recognized the allure. With its mild climate and Russian Riviera aspirations, Sochi glowed with an aura of self-importance, attracting money and power brokers like moths to a flame. But not Arkady—at his core he was a Muscovite. Strategic briefs somehow didn't feel, well, *Russian* when conducted on a terrace with the sea breeze blowing in his face.

"If you prefer, I can come back another time," Arkady said, making a quarter turn to leave.

Petrov finished his last rep, arched his back, and shook out his arms at his sides. Then, with a sigh, he climbed off the seat to face

Arkady. "You should change into a tracksuit and join me," he said with a humorless smile. "You could probably use the exercise, old man."

"I'm retired," Arkady said. "Old retired Russians don't exercise."

"You're not retired. You're just lazy, Arkady."

A dozen clever, biting retorts populated Arkady's mind, but he held his tongue. Petrov was in one of his moods and verbal sparring would only antagonize the Russian President. Petrov had lost his sense of humor years ago, and after all . . . tsars don't self-deprecate. "Anyway, I don't think I'll—"

"What do you want, Arkady?" Petrov said, cutting him off as he walked to a new machine.

Arkady swallowed and forced his cheek muscles to relax.

One thing at a time, he reminded himself. With Petrov it was best to limit each interaction to one topic and one topic only. As of yet, he'd neglected to inform the Russian President that he'd lost six Zeta field operatives to American-led assassinations over the past two months. Now was *not* the time to break that news. And if he was honest with himself, the window for disclosure of the truth had probably closed. Best-case scenario, Petrov would see the repression of the information as a failure of professional judgment; worst case, he'd view it as treason. In Petrov's mind, all Russian assets—even human ones—belonged to him. All intelligence was his to know. All decisions were his to make. In his mind, he was the nexus of all things within and touching the Russian Federation. For Arkady to interfere with or disrupt the flow of information was an unpardonable sin. And so, this morning, they would not be discussing Zeta's recent losses in the shadow war raging with Ember. Instead, Arkady would chum the water with much more enticing bait for the great white shark eyeing him from two meters away.

"There's been an interesting development in Ukraine I wanted to brief you on," the spymaster said.

"Tell me," Petrov said, adjusting a pin in the weight stack in preparation for his next set.

"I have a man embedded inside Ultra in Kiev . . . sowing dissention and stirring up trouble. Typical stuff."

"A Zeta?"

"Yes."

Petrov nodded his approval. "Remind me, what is this other group? Ultra, you say?"

"They're Ukrainian ultra-right-wing nationalists, like National Corps and C-14, only more extreme."

"In other words, a nuisance," Petrov said, starting a set of seated rows. "Why are you wasting my time with this?"

"Because something interesting and unexpected has happened with this group . . . they're planning to assassinate Ukrainian President Zinovenko."

Petrov released the handlebars mid-pull and let the stack of weights slam home with a resounding metallic clang. "What! Are you serious?"

"Da," Arkady said with a nod. "Dead serious."

"Why would they do this?"

"Because, they are furious about the Donbas treaty. They think by ending the war and giving the separatists in the Donetsk People's Republic autonomy, Zinovenko has betrayed them and betrayed Ukraine. My man has convinced Ultra leadership that Zinovenko is weak and that he's a puppet—catering to western liberalism while at the same time taking Russian bribes. He's promulgating the narrative that the Donbas agreement is only the first step and that Zinovenko plans to cede control of more Ukrainian territory in the coming months."

A giddy smile spread across the Russian President's face, the likes of which Arkady had rarely seen. Petrov clapped his hands together and then suddenly did a little celebratory dance to some imaginary party track before saying, "Glorious. I couldn't make this shit up in my wildest dreams!"

"I know, but wait, there's more . . ."

"More?" Petrov said, eyes wide with delight.

"Yes, they are planning the attack when the American Vice President arrives to sign the treaty. They want to kill Zinovenko and Tenet at the same time."

The smile faded from Petrov's face as the wheels in his head processed this new detail. Vice President Tenet's assassination changed the calculus completely—the stakes, the opportunities, the risk of retribution, the geopolitical aftermath . . .

"Hmmm," Petrov said and started to pace.

"What to do, what to do, what to do?" Arkady said, vocalizing what they both were thinking. "It's a quandary, isn't it?"

"Da," Petrov said, walking to the railing and looking out into the garden. "My first inclination is to shut it down, but on the other hand . . ."

"I know. Your head's in the same place as mine when I got the report."

"How do they plan to do it? The security is going to be insane. I know these ultranationalists are fighters, but short of lending them a squad of Spetsnaz, I don't see how they can pull it off."

"They stole a Javelin missile from the Eastern front and plan to shoot it from a half-kilometer offset, outside the patrol perimeter. This weapon is not like a sniper round or a rocket-propelled grenade. It uses a seeker guidance system. It doesn't have to fly a straight trajectory to hit the target."

Petrov spun around, the giddy enthusiasm returned to his face.

"Unbelievable! I love these Ultra guys. They've got balls . . . very big balls." His gaze went to the middle distance while he considered, and then he nodded. "Okay. I like it, but what is our contribution?"

"Very limited. My man helps them plan the hit and makes sure they don't chicken out at the last minute."

"Good."

"Most importantly, Ultra takes all the blame. It was their plan, they stole the missile, they take credit for the attack."

Petrov nodded, the decision made. "Very well, I will send Prime Minister Vavilov to the treaty signing. That way we lose somebody important, too."

"What?" Arkady said, a lump suddenly forming in his throat.

"It's a fair trade, one Russian Prime Minister for one serving Ukrainian President and one future American President. Besides, Russia doesn't need a Prime Minister. I was going to ask Vavilov for his resignation in the coming months anyway. This just accelerates the timeline and gives us ironclad plausible deniability on the world stage. In fact . . ." Petrov stopped midsentence.

Arkady felt a shift—one that caused gooseflesh to stand up on the back of his neck. "Go on," he coaxed.

"I'm getting ahead of myself," Petrov said with a dismissive wave of his hand. "We wait and see if the operation is a success before we talk next steps. You have the green light, Arkady. Make it happen."

"Mr. President," Arkady said, a cautious timbre to his voice. "Are you sure about Prime Minister Vavilov? I'm certain we could identify another, less *significant*, cabinet official to attend."

"No," Petrov said, his voice a hard line. "It has to be Yuri. It should be Yuri. The timing is perfect."

"Respectfully, I disagree. Vavilov is—"

"Is what?" Petrov snapped. "An important figurehead who in reality contributes nothing? A politician's politician, patiently loitering in my shadow so he can drive a knife in my back when the winds change? Say it, old man—Vavilov is what?"

"I was going to say that Vavilov is a loyal and competent ally. That he has done everything you've asked of him and more, while playing his role perfectly without drawing undue attention to himself. He will be a hard man to replace."

"Were you not listening?" Petrov shouted, spittle flying from his lips. "I don't need a Prime Minister. Russia doesn't need a Prime Minister. Russia needs *me*. Only me. Forever."

Arkady inclined his head. "My apologies, Mr. President. You're right, of course. I'll set the operation in motion and keep you updated as things develop."

"Very well," Petrov said and walked back to the seated row machine. "On your way out, if you see Tatia, send her in with a lemon water. I'm thirsty."

"Yes, sir, Mr. President," Arkady said, turning to leave. "I'll see if I can find her."

He walked out of the gym and didn't stop until he reached the Mercedes G wagon parked in the drive at the front of the property. The driver, one of Petrov's staff, looked up from his mobile phone when Arkady approached.

"Airport," Arkady said and let himself into the back seat.

The driver nodded, walked around the vehicle, and climbed into the driver's seat. "Are you in a hurry, sir?" he asked, starting the ignition.

"Nyet," Arkady said, propping an elbow on the armrest. "There's no need to rush."

"Was everything okay with your visit?" the driver said, glancing at him in the rearview mirror.

"Everything was perfect," the old spymaster said, looking out the window as they pulled away.

But this, of course, was a fiction. Everything was not perfect.

Far from it.

He pulled out his mobile phone and sent a simple text message to his man in Kiev confirming the assassination operation was greenlit: мечта. The reply from Gavriil Osinov, the most capable Zeta in his rapidly thinning ranks, came less than a minute later: пробудиться.

He exhaled audibly and returned his phone to his pocket. With that out of the way, his mind turned to Petrov and the conversation they'd had only moments ago. He'd not anticipated the Vavilov move, and he silently cursed himself for not seeing it. Prime Minister Vavilov was an important part of Arkady's endgame. The man was feckless, but the Russian people liked him. Losing Vavilov now would make things much more difficult for Arkady later.

Petrov's getting worse. Maybe it's time? Arkady thought, scratching an itch on the side of his neck. *No, not yet.*

Not yet . . .

CHAPTER 7

Warehouse Along the Dnieper River
Kiev, Ukraine
September 21
2045 Local Time

"I'll do it," Gavriil said, speaking up for the first time during the heated debate. The comment immediately silenced the chatter in the room and all eyes went to him.

Viktor Skorapporsky, the outspoken rising star of Ultra, fixed him with a hard glare. "This is not a democracy. Who said you could talk?"

Gavriil smiled, though he didn't let the men see it. He had them right where he wanted them—where he needed them. They didn't know he was Zeta Prime of Russian Spetsgruppa Zeta. They didn't know he was a master manipulator and killer of men—a weapon of anarchy honed by Russia's greatest spymaster over many years. To these men, he was simply Artem, his backstory part of a carefully crafted NOC designed to make him into one of them—an angry, testosterone-fueled fascist. He found slipping into legends like this one as easy as shrugging on a coat. He liked wearing masks and had trouble imagining a life where he was constrained by having to occupy a single identity in perpetuity.

As Artem, he would fulfill a role none of these men had the skill or courage to execute, and he would do it without turning the hierarchy on its head . . . or at least not completely. Some of these Ukrainian militiamen had seen combat, but none of them had operated at his level, not even close. His combat skills were something that would earn him envy and respect, but how and when he made this reveal was critical.

Gavriil got to his feet, puffed out his chest, and met the other young man's gaze with unflinching eyes. "First of all, I don't need your fucking permission to talk. And second, if you're all going to be a bunch of pussies about it, then let me do it."

"You better watch your mouth, Artem," the big Ukrainian hothead said, calling Gavriil by his legend's name, "or you're going to find my fist in it."

"I'd like to see you try," Gavriil taunted.

True to form, Skorapporsky took the bait, balling his right fist and letting it fly. Gavriil leisurely sidestepped the jab, deflecting it downward with a modest flip of his forearm. He drove his fist into the big Ukrainian's right kidney. Skorapporsky grunted, arched his back, and dropped to a knee. Face contorted with rage, he tried to get up but hesitated, clutching his side.

"Hurts, doesn't it?" Gavriil said, extending his right hand to the other man.

"Shit, yes," said the bested Ukrainian, coughing and laughing at the same time. He clasped Gavriil's hand and let himself be pulled to his feet.

"At least we both get to keep our teeth," Gavriil said with a make-nice smile, "but if you start pissing blood, I recommend going to the hospital."

"To move and hit like that, you must be a boxer," Skorapporsky said, collecting himself in front of the group of soldier-activists.

"I confess, I've spent many hours in the ring," Gavriil said, and it was not a lie . . . but it was not the whole truth either.

Flashbulb memories from his indoctrination and training at Zeta's Bright Falcon compound in Vyborg played in his mind: bare-knuckle boxing after being waterboarded, Krav Maga matches after days of sleep deprivation, knife fighting after hypothermia conditioning in Vyborg Bay . . . and so on and so on. This had been the method and madness of Zeta's sadistic taskmaster-in-chief Arkady Zhukov: stress the body and mind of his recruits to the breaking point, then make them fight. To become a Zeta, Gavriil had faced down death and brutality on more occasions than he cared to remember and had emerged victorious. Today's test was nothing for him, but it was a test he had to pass nonetheless to achieve his strategic objective.

Everywhere, no matter the country, culture, or company, *hierarchy* reigned supreme. Even in so-called "flat" organizations, the proverbial pecking order was the secret sauce that drove all decision-making. Tasking flows downhill—everyone understood that and jockeyed for position accordingly. From the day he'd joined Ultra, Gavriil had worked diligently to understand the power hierarchy of Ukraine's most vocal, violent, and fastest-growing ultrarightist group. Like in most fractious organizations, political thuggery was the modus operandi. The biggest dog in the room called the shots, and in this gathering of a dozen angry young men, Skorapporsky was that big dog. But one defiant kidney punch later,

58

Gavriil had suddenly called Skorapporsky's alpha status into question.

"Listen, Artem, you recently joined our movement. I appreciate your enthusiasm, but all of us here have been fighting on the front in Donbas for years . . . all of us except for you," Skorapporsky said, putting a *thoughtful* hand on Gavriil's shoulder. "The decision who fires the missile is not a matter of who has the most courage or enthusiasm. It is a question of tactical competency. We have one chance at this—one chance, that's all."

It took all Gavriil's willpower to suppress a smile. Skorapporsky believed himself the architect of this afternoon's operation, but the idea had not been his. Gavriil had mentioned the idea to Sacha, who had told his brother, Josef, who then predictably suggested it to Skorapporsky. Josef followed Skorapporsky around like a pup, and Gavriil had correctly anticipated how the events would play out.

Now it was time for the masterstroke.

Gavriil put his hand on Skorapporsky's shoulder, mirroring the Ukrainian's patronizing posture, and said, "The FGM-148 Javelin is a fire-and-forget, ultraportable antiarmor missile system. Unlike other weapons in its class, the Javelin uses an automated infrared guidance system that locks the target's image into memory, allowing the missile to track and follow the target during flight. The missile's guidance unit performs calculations in real time to determine what trajectory is best—either direct horizontal action or a top-down attack. The Javelin has a ninety-four percent target-engagement reliability rate and a novel 'soft launch' rocket propulsion design to minimize backblast and visible launch signature. The carry weight is twenty-two kilos and the F variant we smuggled from the front has a fragmentation warhead that makes it ideal for attacking soft targets."

"Well, it appears you've done your homework, Artem," the Ukrainian said with an irritated smile. He released his grip from Gavriil's shoulder and stepped away to pontificate. "But these are just words you memorized from the internet. The real question is, have you fired a Javelin?"

"No . . . have you? Has anyone in this room fired a Javelin?" When no one spoke, Gavriil said, "None of us have fired this weapon because the Americans only sent them to Ukraine two months ago. But I have fired a Russian Kornet-E as well as a FIM-92 Stinger. I imagine this makes me the most qualified person here to fire the Javelin."

"Where did you do these things?" Skorapporsky demanded. "What army did you serve with?"

"I don't talk about such details," Gavriil said. "All that matters is that I am the most qualified man for the job."

"You're a Russian, aren't you?" Skorapporsky's voice oozed with accusation and suspicion.

Gavriil ran the calculus in his head and shifted into empathy-inducing confession mode. "My father is Russian, yes, but my mother is Ukrainian. I was born in Kiev but taken by my father to be schooled and trained in Russia. I was Spetsnaz. They sent me to Crimea . . ." He let the words hang in the air for effect. "I did not want to be there. I was so angry to be there, helping Russia steal a piece of my homeland. After that, I decided I could no longer serve in the Russian army. But once you're Spetsnaz, they don't let you go."

"What did you do?" sensitive Josef asked, taking the bait just like Gavriil knew he would.

"I had to do some bad things . . . things I will not talk about here. But it's okay, because now I'm finally home. Now, I'm finally able to use my Russian military training for a purpose—to help build a strong Ukraine that can stand up to Russia and America. We don't need anybody telling us what to do. We don't need anybody trying to control our land. When Zinovenko was elected, I thought he would stand up to Petrov. I thought he would fight for Ukraine, but he has ceded control of the Donbas to the separatists. This cannot be allowed to stand. In six months' time, Petrov will annex the region and call it Russia. Then he will push east and pursue his Novorossiya fantasy. He'll claim all of Donetsk, swallowing Mariupol, then push east into Kherson and Nikolayev, and he won't stop until he's claimed Odessa and annexed all of southern Ukraine. It is time for a second Maidan Revolution. The first one did not go far enough, and I'm ready to lead the fight."

His fiery speech earned him a moment of stunned silence followed by shouts and whoops from half a dozen of the members. With a single punch and an improvised speech, he'd ascended the hierarchy and wrested control of the operation from Skorapporsky.

"All right, Artem, you can fire the missile," the big Ukrainian said, recognizing that granting this concession was the only way for him to retain the illusion of control.

Gavriil nodded, accepting the other man's authority rather than pushing to dethrone him entirely.

"I appreciate the honor, but know my only motivation is victory—well, that and getting to kill the bastards who would sell off our country piece by piece and divide our people. Your plan is brilliant, Viktor, and I wish only to do my part to see it succeed."

Leading Ultra was not his mission objective. Making sure the Javelin missile was fired on time, on target—that was all that mattered.

Skorapporsky extended his hand to Gavriil, who shook it while meeting the Ukrainian's gaze. In that moment, the two men made a wordless pact.

I'm still in charge here . . . you better not fuck this up.

Don't worry, I know what I'm doing.

"We have our rocketman," Skorapporsky said, turning back to address the room. "Now I need volunteers to round out the assassination team."

Every hand in the room shot up.

Gavriil smiled.

His mission—for Mother Russia—was certain to be a success.

CHAPTER 8

Mariyinski Palace
Kiev, Ukraine
September 24
1549 Local Time

It's imperative that the Ukrainians and the world see the Donbas treaty as a victory for the West, Thom. We must control the narrative here. Your job is to sell it to the world.

Those words—President Warner's parting instructions before departing Joint Base Andrews—echoed in Vice President Thomas Tenet's mind as he smiled and nodded at the room full of strangers. He took a sip of his wine, forcing himself not to gulp it down too quickly, as he tried to avoid eye contact with Russian Prime Minister Vavilov, who was seated kitty-corner across the table from him. Tenet imagined Vavilov's marching orders from Petrov were nearly identical to his own: *Russia must control the narrative. Your job is to con-*

vince the world that the Donbas treaty is a victory for Russia and Russian-speaking people everywhere.

Games and games . . .

Thank God Petrov had done as Warner had and sent his second instead of coming in person, because the blue-eyed bastard gave Tenet the creeps. The Russian Prime Minister, on the other hand, seemed to be a decent-enough fellow; he'd even made an effort to speak exclusively in English during this morning's meetings and this very late-running lunch. Maybe the world would get lucky and Petrov would decide to retire and not run in the next election. Just the thought buoyed Tenet's already hopeful plans for the future.

"Mr. Vice President," Ukrainian President Matias Zinovenko said, his voice loud and confident so that all the room was certain to hear. "Will you please tell President Warner how grateful I am for his support since I've taken office. This treaty, and the wave of anticorruption, pro-Western legislation we've passed over the past six months, would not have been possible without America's expression of confidence in my leadership and policies."

Zinovenko raised his glass toward Tenet, as did all the Ukrainians at the table. The Russian contingent, however, looked at Vavilov to check his reaction to this not-so-subtle slight.

But the Russian PM didn't miss a beat; he smiled without malice and raised his own glass.

"Thank you, President Zinovenko. I'll be certain to tell him," Tenet said, returning the toast. "And rest assured, this White House's policies and practices are ones I intend to continue when I'm President."

The comment earned him a polite round of laughter and applause, along with some sycophantic fawning from those seated nearby. He accepted it all with a genuine smile, a practice he'd honed to perfection during a lifetime in politics. He'd been Warner's toady for seven years, and now, finally, that chapter in his life was paying off. As incumbent VP, he was the party's presumptive choice for the ticket, and Warner had already publicly given his endorsement. As long as he made it scandal free to the convention in San Antonio, the nomination was his, virtually guaranteeing he would be the next President of the United States.

After lunch—and a painful series of pictures shaking hands with the newly elected heads of the provisional separatist governments in Donetsk and Luhansk; the Russian contingent; and Zinovenko—Tenet's stint in Mariyinski Palace came to an end. Opulent, ornate, and oozing with baroque one-upmanship, Mariyinski was the type of building that existed only in Old Europe. The White House was impressive, but nothing like this. Like its sister palaces—the Louvre, the Hermitage, and Buckingham Palace—Mariyinski was a product of unchecked monarchial hubris. People didn't build shit like this anymore, Tenet lamented to himself as Secret Service led him out. It was just too damn expensive.

A shame, really . . . I could get used to this.

Tenet grunted as he ducked into the Ukrainian President's up-armored stretch Cadillac limousine. This had been a sticking point for his Secret Service detail, but President Zinovenko had refused to budge on them riding together and the vehicle being one from *his* fleet. Tenet understood. The optics were just too delicious for Zinovenko to pass up, and so, after much negotiation, they had settled the matter—with two of Tenet's heavily armed Secret Service agents riding along, flanking a much smaller and clearly unhappy security man from the Ukrainian detail. Another American agent was up front with the driver, and their limo was in convoy with an American-flag-streaming Secret Service SUV in front and behind—a symbol of unity the Ukrainian President had been delighted to agree to. Best of all, the Russian Prime Minister was relegated to traveling behind in his own motorcade.

How's that for optics, Tenet thought with a smile.

"You must be happy," he said, now that he and Zinovenko were finally alone together. "After six years of war in Donbas, a peace has finally been brokered with Russia and the separatists."

"Yes, I am happy, but many have died. Fourteen thousand Ukrainians," Zinovenko said, pausing with somber reverence. "Now we take steps to move forward and put this terrible chapter behind us."

A silence lingered between them for a long moment, as an invisible third hand coaxed them both to dispense with the small talk and say what was truly on their minds—for this was how real politics was conducted. No reporters. No lawyers. No intermediaries. Just two men, talking face-to-face behind closed doors—with their security agents sworn to secrecy beside them, of course.

Tenet broke the silence first, deciding it was the presidential thing to do. It was important that he got used to taking the initiative, because as Commander in Chief it was what would be expected of him. Filling President Warner's shoes was a tall order—Tenet had no illusions about that—but he was up to the task. People had underestimated him his entire life, and always to their public chagrin or political peril. He deserved to be President, because damn it, he'd put in the work, soldiered through the years, and kissed all the requisite asses. In fourteen short months, the American people would go to the ballot boxes and elect him leader of the free world, and he could hardly wait. It was his turn, damn it.

"Let's talk about messaging," he said, keen on executing his tasking and keeping Warner happy. "*We* want to control the narrative on this armistice with the separatists, not Moscow. Undoubtedly, Petrov considers this a victory for Russia, with the Donetsk

People's Republic and Luhansk People's Republic earning recognition as independent states. In his mind, he's orchestrated the secession of two Ukrainian oblasts. It's only a matter of time before DPR and LPR go the way of Crimea and get absorbed into Russia. Petrov is not going to say that publicly, of course, which is why he sent Prime Minister Vavilov to the signing. Vavilov will talk about how the Russian-speaking citizens of Donetsk and Luhansk finally have their freedom and autonomy, and how Russia plans to support their fledgling governments to ensure their success and survival."

"I agree we want to control the narrative, but make no mistake, this was not the endgame Petrov was hoping for," Zinovenko said, crossing ankle over knee.

"What are you talking about?" Tenet said, genuinely surprised. "We all know what happened in Crimea: a secession vote administered at gunpoint by Russian soldiers and the results tabulated by Moscow. Donetsk and Luhansk are just one illegitimate vote away from joining Russia. Petrov is literally carving away pieces of your country and laughing about it behind closed doors."

"Respectfully, I disagree. Did you see Petrov smiling at the press conference last week? No. He was unable to hide his displeasure at the outcome. He did not expect my government to concede to the separatists' demands. If annexation were the goal, it will be much harder to achieve now that DPR and LPR have autonomy. The people will not want to join Russia now that they are independent. It's the main reason why I signed the treaty, to avoid another Crimea."

Tenet shook his head, unconvinced.

"Besides, I'm not so sure Petrov's goal for the Donbas was annexation. Maybe in the beginning, yes, but not after he saw the destructive power of a never-ending civil war in Ukraine. The past five years have driven a wedge between Kiev and the EU. Everyone is afraid to do business here, which undermines economic stability in my country. And you see, without Mariupol, the secession states do not have the same geographic, economic, and military value as Crimea. The cost of annexing and supporting their new governments might even exceed the economic benefit they bring." He shook his head. "The civil war in Donbas was a cancer of Petrov's design, and my goal in signing this treaty was to cut it out. Yes, we lost some land, but in the process, I excised a dangerous, painful tumor and prevented the disease from spreading to the rest of Ukraine."

Tenet nodded and realized he may have vastly underestimated this man. He was about to respond, but the Ukrainian President wasn't finished.

"You see, Mr. Vice President, breaking a country is no different than breaking a man: all you have to do is take away hope. Petrov prefers Ukraine in shambles, because he doesn't want his own countrymen looking across the border with jealous eyes. If Europe embraces Ukraine and my presidency is a success, the Russian people will begin to question Petrov's authoritarian regime. Russians weather austerity better than any other people. It's in their DNA. But if Ukraine can flourish outside of Petrov's control, if democracy and the rule of law can elevate the standard of living and the pride of the Ukrainian people, then Russians might see the light. Petrov cannot permit this to happen."

Tenet nodded. "I see what you're saying, but I also think Petrov has not given up his dream of Novorossiya. He talks about it all the time—restoring the Russian Empire to its former might. He wants to turn the clock back to 1915 and reclaim those House of Romanov territories he believes were lost. I would not be surprised if he has plans to annex all of southern Ukraine, dividing your country in half and cutting off the remainder from the Black Sea completely."

"No, no, that would be insanity. Ukraine would not stand for that. The *world* would not stand for that. Such brazen aggression would cause World War Three. Petrov is greedy and arrogant, but he's not an idiot. To understand Petrov's desired endgame, one must understand the mind of the Russian oligarch. They rise from the chaos they create in others. They ascend on the backs of those they tear down, rather than lifting themselves up. It is a Western misconception to see them as you do, but then that is why we must partner so closely, isn't it?"

Tenet felt his stomach tighten. In the limo, at least, he was most certainly *not* controlling this narrative.

"Rest assured, we understand Petrov much better than you think," he said. "Our relationship with Ukraine is honest and true. Together we will weather any storm, whether it comes from your far-right nationalists or from Russia."

Instead of the awe and reverence he expected his words to inspire in the Ukrainian President, Zinovenko looked almost bemused.

"We will see, I suppose," the man said with a smile. "Let us hope we can get a lasting peace in place before you take office so that we can build on what we accomplished today."

Unsure what to say, Tenet nodded and looked out the window as the limo pulled into Independence Square. He had underestimated Zinovenko's geopolitical savvy. Was he a victim of his own American elitism? He would need to purge this weakness moving forward. As President of the United States, underestimating his contemporaries would be disastrous.

The motorcade came to a stop, and Tenet sat a moment in familiar silence as his Secret Service team, in tandem with Zinovenko's security detail, cleared the area outside the vehicle. Then he exited his own side of the limo, knowing better than to emerge *behind* the Ukrainian President.

My God, how would that look?

He and Zinovenko walked together up the wide steps behind the stage set up for them to address the crowd. Russian Prime Minister Vavilov and his retinue joined them on the platform. Diplomats, aides, and bodyguards all shuffled for position, and eventually everyone who was supposed to be there had found a place to sit or stand. From behind the clear ballistic acrylic barrier, he scanned the smiling faces of the thousands of Ukrainians gathered in Kiev's most famous square, and as he did, Zinovenko's words echoed in his mind.

Breaking a country is no different from breaking a man: all you have to do is take away hope . . .

There was so much hope everywhere he looked, and yet like an earworm, the words played over and over and over again. It wasn't so much the phrase itself, but rather the *way* the Ukrainian President had said it—with such earnest resignation and certitude. Zinovenko was a native-born Ukrainian, which certainly qualified him to speak with authority about purloined hope . . .

And nation breaking.

As the crowd cheered, Tenet was unable to shake the feeling that something important had happened that he'd failed to register. He saw Zinovenko turn and smile at him from the podium, but he hadn't been paying attention to the speech, nor to the whispered blow-by-blow from the American ambassador who was tediously translating what was being said in his ear.

He was still processing the conversation he'd had with Zinovenko during the ride over. As he waited for his turn at the podium to address the crowd, he remembered his mission. Yes, he was speaking to the Ukrainian people in Independence Square, but he was also addressing a global audience. His job was to remind the world that America, not Russia, was Ukraine's true and reliable partner. America, not Russia, was the world's one and only superpower.

He felt a tap on the back of his right hand, pulling him back to the present. He turned to look at the American Ambassador to Ukraine.

"President Zinovenko is finishing up his remarks, Mr. Vice President," she said with a tight smile.

"I'm speaking before the Russian Prime Minister?" he said, suddenly questioning whether the optics were better if he followed Zinovenko or spoke last.

"It appears so. Are you ready?"

"I was born ready," he heard himself say, and cringed inside at the cliché. Warner would never say something so lame, and going forward, neither would he.

The Ambassador chuckled politely, but her attention was fixed on Zinovenko. "Okay . . . he's introducing you, sir. You can head to the podium," she said.

Tenet stood, and his trademark vice presidential smile spread across his face. *Hey there, people of Ukraine, I know I'm not the guy you wanted to hear from, but I'm the guy you get.*

Zinovenko turned to face him, his own smile broad, eager, and genuine. His speech had clearly gone well, because the roar of the crowd was deafening. The war of secession was over. The war with Russia was over. Now, Ukraine could finally move on to the business of being and becoming the Ukraine of tomorrow. They were happy and hopeful . . . at least, most of them were.

A commotion in the crowd to his right caught his eye. A group of angry protestors were pushing and shoving their way through the throng toward the dais. They held signs and shook their fists. Some of the signs were written in English: ZINOVENKO IS A TRAITOR; PETROV'S PUPPET; and DON'T GIVE UP DONBAS.

Tenet turned and smiled at the Ukrainian President, while using his eyes to pose the burning question on his mind: *What the hell is this all about?*

"Ultra-right-wing nationalists," Zinovenko said through a smile as he shook Tenet's hand for all the world to see. "They're upset about the treaty. They see this as capitulation. Don't worry. It's fine."

Tenet nodded and saw a squad of Ukrainian police dressed in riot gear moving to intercept the protestors. He glanced over his shoulder at the lead agent in his Secret Service security detail, a man he'd known for seven years and trusted implicitly. The square-jawed agent had two fingers pressed to his ear, holding his earpiece in tight. He nodded at Tenet and mouthed, "We're good."

Sufficiently reassured, Tenet took the podium behind a transparent bulletproof screen. The crowd noise ebbed in anticipation of his opening remarks. He scanned the eager faces and refreshed his smile.

"Thank you, President Zinovenko, for your wonderful introduction. And thank you, people of Kiev—" He stopped midsentence. "What the hell is that?" he murmured, squinting at the thing streaking toward him just above the heads in the crowd.

"Incoming!" an American voice yelled.

He tried to move. Tried to run, but his legs were lead.

He felt someone tackle him.

Then there was only heat and pain and the agonizing sensation of his body being ripped apart. And in a bizarre moment of final clarity, as the world was consumed by fire, he thought: *Damn, I guess I don't get to be President after all . . .*

PART II

You may be standing beside me,

but there is a canyon between us.

—*Vladimir Petrov*

CHAPTER 9

Kelso Jarvis, the Director of National Intelligence, resisted the urge to condescend.

But he wanted to . . . God, he wanted to.

"Ian, I'm going to say this as plainly as I can," he said, keeping his voice measured and steady. "My concern is not about Amanda Allen's interrogative acumen or professional competency. I simply do not trust Sylvie Bessonov. She is a Zeta. She was trained by Zhukov. We cannot and should not take her word at face value."

He was alone in the SCIF for this call with Ember. Since the discovery and confirmation that his Deputy Director of Intelligence Integration, Catherine Morgan, was a Russian spy, Jarvis had ultra-compartmentalized the flow of information inside his ranks. The Morgan infiltration, followed by the Zeta hit on Ember, had been a one-two punch that knocked him to the deck. Now he was operating with an overabundance of caution, something he'd eschewed his entire career. Micromanagement, control of information, second-guessing the motives and intentions of direct reports—these were the hallmarks of an insecure and ineffective leader.

And yet here he was, doing what he despised.

On the video monitor, he could see Ember's Signals Chief and Interim Acting Director sweating—not from nerves but from the heat. An overtaxed air conditioner hummed loudly in the background. Ember's present accommodations at MacDill Air Force Base were nothing to brag about. Truth be told, they'd moved from the penthouse to the outhouse. Where the previous Ember HQ had been a high-tech underground bunker worthy of James Bond, America's premier counterterrorism black ops task force was now working out of a double-wide construction trailer on the Tier One compound. Completing the motif, a brownish-green mottled gecko casually climbed the wall behind Baldwin.

"With all due respect, sir, the intelligence Bessonov has provided has been one hundred percent accurate. She's given us six names and six loci of operation, resulting in the successful neutralization of six Zeta operators. Now we're in position to move on number seven," Baldwin said, mopping his brow with a handkerchief. "Statistically speaking, that makes Bessonov a golden outlier."

Jarvis shifted his gaze to Munn, who was sitting beside the bespectacled genius. Where Baldwin was dressed in his signature tie and sport coat, Munn was wearing a truly obnoxious Hawaiian shirt. "Dan, what do you think?"

"I agree with Baldwin," Munn said. "I've watched the recordings, sir, studied the way she interacts with Allen, and the girl is clearly broken. I know the Russians are tricky bastards, but there's not the slightest indication she's deceiving us. We are batting a thousand off Bessonov's intel so far."

Jarvis knitted his fingers together and squeezed just enough to subdue the resting tremor in his hands. He was taking medication now, which helped keep his symptoms under control, but some days it wasn't enough. Today was one of those days. If he squeezed, he could shut the tremors down. It was exhausting, but he did it anyway because it made him feel like a SEAL.

Always fighting and always in the fight.

Since his Parkinson's diagnosis, he'd made exercise a mandatory part of his daily routine—weights, core, and cardio—and the parts of him that had started to go soft since becoming DNI were resolidifying. Tremors and vertigo be damned, he was going to get back in fighting form if it killed him.

Jarvis was about to speak when Baldwin scooted to the left, making room for Amanda Allen at the table.

"Director Jarvis," she greeted him as she stepped into the frame.

"Ms. Allen, we were just talking about the work you're doing with Bessonov," Jarvis said. "You're harvesting some solid intelligence from her."

"Thank you, sir," Allen said. "She's been incredibly forthcoming."

"That's what I understand," he said, before pivoting. "Is she still dribbling out the names one at a time?"

"Uh, yes, sir."

"Have you pushed for more than one name?"

"I have . . . on multiple occasions."

"And what happened?"

"She says the same thing each time." Channeling Bessonov's

Russian accent, she added, "'One cut at a time, please, Amanda, lest I bleed to death during the night.'"

Jarvis screwed up his face at this. "Has she threatened or hinted suicide?"

"Not overtly," Allen said, "but she's not in a good place—emotionally, that is."

"Has she been subjected to enhanced interrogation?"

"No, sir. One hundred percent mind games. It was the CGI session with Malik that broke her," Munn said, referring to an Ember ploy that had convinced Bessonov that she was watching one of her Zeta colleagues being brutally tortured and executed. Bessonov had believed it real and cracked under the pressure.

"Does she know the truth now?" Jarvis asked.

"No, sir," Allen said, "we've maintained the ruse. And as you know, the real Malik is dead, so we see no reason to dissuade her of the fiction."

"All right, well, let's try to get more out of her during the next session. Step it up, Ms. Allen. I want operational details, communication protocols, and Zeta tradecraft methodologies. I want to know how Zhukov trains them to operate. I want to know how he trains them to think. And I want two names next time. Do you understand me?"

"Yes, sir."

A pounding on the door behind him usurped Jarvis's attention. At the same time, text message alerts chimed on the video feed, prompting Baldwin and Munn to glance at their phones.

"Excuse me," Jarvis said and scooted his chair back from the table. He opened the SCIF door and was greeted by his Deputy Chief of Staff, Commander Mike Casey. "You look like you just saw a ghost, Mike. Is there a problem?"

"There's been an attack in Kiev. The treaty delegation was targeted. Vice President Tenet, Ukrainian President Zinovenko, and Russian Prime Minister Vavilov were targeted. Preliminary reporting indicates they're all dead," a grey-faced Casey said.

"Fuck," Jarvis said, and the adrenaline dump that followed sent lightning into his veins. He jogged back to the conference table.

"We just heard," Munn said on the livestream. "I'm terminating SAD's current tasking and pulling them back to the airport. We'll be ready to go wherever you need us in ninety minutes."

"Check," Jarvis said and dragged his index finger across his throat. The feed went black, and he turned to his deputy. "Is POTUS secure?"

"Yes," Casey said. "He's in the Situation Room along with SecDef, Secretary of State Baker, General McMillan, and the National Security Advisor."

"And Petra?"

"She's in the NCTC ops center with Buckingham," he said.

"Good," Jarvis said. *She'll be safe there.*

"The President is requesting you at the Situation Room," Casey said, quickstepping to catch up with Jarvis, who was already moving down the corridor with speed. "Your motorcade is ready."

Jarvis stopped abruptly in his tracks. A mental street map of the route from ODNI to the White House formed in his mind. Potential ambush locations appeared as bright red dots. Born of paranoia or prudence, he could not be sure, but it didn't matter. Arkady Zhukov was in his head now.

"What?" Casey said, stopping beside him.

Jarvis executed an about-face and marched back to the SCIF. "We're not going anywhere."

"Sir?" his deputy said, trotting at his side.

"I've been in a motorcade that got ambushed. It didn't go so well," Jarvis said, stopping at the SCIF door. He pressed his thumb on the biometric security reader. When it flashed green, he entered his six-digit code. "Until we have a better handle on what the hell is going on, we're not going anywhere."

Casey nodded, but hesitated at the threshold.

"From now on, where I go, you go," Jarvis said and waved the former submarine skipper into the room. The only person on his staff *fully* read into his health status, Task Force Ember operations, and the weeds of the Russian threat was his Chief of Staff, Petra Felsk. Time would tell if Zeta was behind this attack on the Vice President, but Jarvis didn't have the luxury of time. Petra was stuck at the National Counterterrorism Center and he needed a second set of eyes and ears to back him up. The stakes were too high to fly solo. "Consider yourself officially read in," he said, making the unilateral decision.

"Yes, sir." Casey stepped into the SCIF, and shut the door behind him. "You want me to drive?" he asked, gesturing to the computer workstation.

Jarvis nodded and Casey slid into the seat. With deft and swift competency, Casey established a secure conference channel with the Situation Room and sent the video feed to a large monitor on the opposite wall. A young man in a Marine uniform appeared on the screen. He looked back and forth between Casey and Jarvis, then said, "Stand by for the President."

The screen flickered and the image refreshed to a camera feed looking down the length of the massive table in the large conference room, which was packed with the most important and powerful people in the United States government and military. Jarvis knew all of them.

"Director Jarvis," President Warner said from where he stood at the head of the table. "Where the hell have you been?"

"In a SCIF, sir," Jarvis replied.

"Are you up to speed, DNI?" Warner fired back.

"Getting there, sir."

"It's been confirmed, the Vice President is dead," the President said. "I've just ordered SecDef to go to DEFCON Three."

Jarvis glanced at Casey and watched the color drain from the other man's face. The defense readiness condition was an alert system developed in the late 1950s by the Joint Chiefs of Staff and the North American Aerospace Defense Command, with the perceived nuclear threat from Russia playing a driving role. In the current incarnation, the system prescribed five levels of military readiness that corresponded to the severity and imminent nature of a threat to the nation. DEFCON 5 was normal military peacetime readiness; DEFCON 1 implied maximum readiness in preparation for nuclear war. DEFCON 3, which Warner had just set, was the highest Jarvis had seen in his thirty years of service, and he'd only seen it once before, on 9/11 after the towers fell.

"I'm not prepared to make a statement yet, but it is being drafted as we speak. I will address the nation at sixteen hundred hours . . ."

While the President talked, Casey powered on a second monitor and established a secure conference channel with the NCTC ops center. Next, he pulled up CNN and BBC on mute on a third monitor. Jarvis glanced at the second monitor as a grim-faced Reggie Buckingham appeared with Petra standing beside him.

". . . Preliminary reports indicate that the attack was carried out by right-wing Ukrainian ultranationalists protesting the Donbas treaty, but that has not been confirmed and no specific group has claimed responsibility. I need ironclad confirmation of who is responsible for this, DNI, and I'm putting that responsibility on you."

"Yes, sir, Mr. President," Jarvis said, meeting Warner's gaze over the live feed.

"Is the team that investigated the sabotage and sinking of that LNG ship in Klaipeda anywhere near Kiev?"

Jarvis resisted the urge to cringe at the President's mention of Ember. Most of the people in the Situation Room were not read into Ember's file, let alone its existence. It was the one asset in Jarvis's arsenal that never appeared in his daily intelligence brief. "Yes, sir. That group is in the neighborhood."

"Mobilize them," Warner said, wagging his index finger at the screen. "Find out whose fingerprints are on this, and then God have mercy on my soul for what happens after."

CHAPTER 10

Every time Dempsey had an opportunity to observe Wang in action, he was mystified. The kid was working on three laptops simultaneously—which he had arranged in an arc on the table—establishing his own mini tactical operations center. It was like watching a master pianist in concert, except instead of making beautiful music, the cadence of Wang's keystrokes was wreaking havoc in the digital dimension, a dimension that Dempsey accepted the existence of but had no access to or understanding of. Kind of like astrophysics, politics, and women's fashion. He couldn't help but wonder: If Baldwin were standing here instead of him, would he see beauty or artistic genius in Wang's performance?

"Target acquired," Wang said robotically. "I have Pichler on the security feed in the lobby. She's crossing to the elevators, heading up to her room, I assume."

Dempsey nodded and slipped the subcompact Sig Sauer P365 into a shoulder holster beneath his black hotel staff waistcoat. He looked down at Wang, but the kid didn't even bother looking up. Before the attack on Newport News, Wang would have jumped on the opportunity to make some smart-ass James Bond—or better yet, Austin Powers—dig at Dempsey in his penguin suit, but not today.

Today, he was all business.

"She's in elevator three . . ."

Dempsey straightened the Westin name tag on his lapel and confirmed in the mirror that the Sig was not producing a detectable bulge beneath his left armpit, even with the seven-inch SRD9 suppressor in place.

"Ready," Grimes said via the microtransmitter in Dempsey's ear. "Call the ball."

Grimes was in a room on the third floor, just beside the service elevator, also dressed as hotel staff. When their target, Selina Pichler, ordered room service—dinner and a glass of Rioja—as she had the last three nights at this time, Grimes and Dempsey would arrive early and surprise her. The plan was to take her in her room, clean up the mess, and disappear the body . . . a straight-up Cold War hit job that would make Robert Ludlum proud.

Dempsey paced back and forth, glancing at Wang occasionally, but the kid was laser focused on his work. He watched Wang's hands fly over the three keyboards, pulling up images from multiple cameras, clicking icons to listen in on phone lines, and streaming a live audio feed from the advanced bug adhered to the wall of the room adjacent to Pichler's.

"She's in her room and already placing the order," Wang said. "Two glasses of wine and, oh, look at her go, she's ordering a piece of cake as well. Soooo decadent tonight."

Dempsey said nothing, aware that Wang was not talking to him. This was the running patter Wang always had going when he worked, but only now did Dempsey notice that Wang was toggling his mike back and forth between mute and vox.

Interesting, he thought and now understood why the cyber jibber-jabber that SAD had historically been forced to endure while on target seemed greatly reduced of late. Oh, Wang still babbled all right, only now he was keeping it to himself. A wan smile spread across Dempsey's face as he thought of simpler times, before Wang had fallen down this dark hole. A kid with his skills should be pulling down seven figures in the private sector, coding trading algorithms for a hedge fund or designing video games in California. But here he was, morose, haunted, and spiraling down into the fiery hell of a life ruled by vengeance and regret—a hell that Dempsey knew all too well. He looked at Wang's profile and said a silent prayer that the kid would find his way out of the pit and become the fun-loving man-boy he had once been.

Me . . . I'm content to stay in the pit. It's where I do my best work.

Minutes clicked by in awkward silence.

"Pichler's order is filled and headed to the service elevator," Wang said.

"Moving into position," Grimes said in Dempsey's earpiece, and he picked up the tray containing an elegant fruit platter and a pony bottle of expensive red wine. He was heading to the door when Wang stopped him.

"Wait," Wang said sharply.

Dempsey swiveled to look at him. "What's the target doing?"

"It's not her," Wang said, his attention fixed on the leftmost computer monitor. "We just got a flash message from Home Plate. Mission abort."

"Two, One—mission abort," Dempsey repeated, making sure to reach Grimes before it was too late.

"Check," came her reply. "Where do you want me?"

"In the dugout," Dempsey said, indicating the hotel room.

He set the tray down on a table and glanced at Buz, who was sitting on a sofa, computer on his lap. The old spook exhaled, set his computer aside, and joined Dempsey looking over Wang's shoulder at a video chat window Wang had opened with Ember HQ.

There better be a good fucking reason they turned this off, Dempsey thought, irritation blooming in his chest.

Baldwin appeared on the screen, looking as haggard and depleted as Dempsey had ever seen him.

"Jesus, Baldwin, are you all right?" he said. "You look like hell."

"There's been an incident," Baldwin said.

An incident? What the hell does that mean? Our whole world is one big-ass incident, he thought, but restrained himself from vocalizing.

The hotel room door lock clicked and Grimes walked in. Dempsey waved her over. When he looked back at the monitor, Munn was on-screen, leaning over Baldwin's shoulder.

"Guys, the Vice President has just been killed. There's been an attack in Kiev. He was in Independence Square with the Ukrainian President, addressing the crowd, when there was an explosion. Reporting on the ground is that Tenet and Zinovenko are both dead, along with the US Ambassador to Ukraine and most of Tenet's security detail."

Dempsey felt the blood drain from his face. "Anybody claiming responsibility?" he asked.

"No. We don't know much, but a BBC reporter in Kiev has made an unconfirmed report that the attack was carried out by Ukrainian ultranationalists. It's looking like this could be an act of domestic terrorism fueled by anger over Zinovenko granting autonomy to the separatists in the Donbas."

Dempsey had once overheard Jarvis joking with a Pentagon official about the Navy SEAL mentality, saying: *You have to understand that to a hammer, everything looks like a nail.* At the time, Dempsey had been mildly offended. Now, as his mind automatically assigned blame for the attack to Zeta, the analogy hit home.

"It's just like Istanbul all over again," he muttered, then being the hammer that he was, added, "I think we have to consider Zeta as the primary suspect."

"Unlikely, John," Munn said with a hard grimace. "Russian Prime Minister Vavilov is listed among the dead."

"What?" Dempsey screwed up his face. "What the hell was the Russian PM doing there?"

"Russia is a signatory to the Donbas treaty," Baldwin answered. "I imagine Petrov sent Vavilov for the same reason the White House sent Vice President Tenet—to take credit for brokering the armistice."

Dempsey turned to Buz, looking for an ally. "What do you think?"

The old spook smiled. "I wouldn't put anything past Petrov and Zhukov. Vavilov is very popular in Russia, and word on the street is he's become increasingly out of step with Petrov. Maybe Petrov saw this as an opportunity to kill two birds with one stone—get rid of a potential domestic rival and use Vavilov's death as ironclad plausible deniability so nobody could suggest Russian involvement."

Dempsey nodded and enthusiastically jerked a thumb at Buz. "Yeah, what he said."

"Look, I'm not ruling out the possibility that this was a Zeta false flag," Munn said, uncharacteristically landing on the other side of an issue from Dempsey, "but we can't let our own personal biases color our judgment. Maybe Zhukov was the mastermind behind this, maybe not, but that doesn't change the fact that the DNI wants hard evidence and he's tasking us to get it."

A tense silence hung in the room until Baldwin said, "Elizabeth, you look like you have something on your mind."

"Absolutely I do," she said with her jaw set. "A thousand dollars says Bessonov has delayed confessing critical intelligence that might have prevented this attack. I think she's been slow-walking us from the beginning—giving us the lowest priority Zeta NOCs first to give Zhukov time to move his other chess pieces on the board."

"The DNI has expressed similar frustration and concern with our handling of Bessonov," Baldwin said, his shoulders visibly slumping, "And I take full responsibility for that. If this attack in Kiev was a Zeta operation, then my methodical approach of systematically eliminating Zeta field operatives will prove to be a mistake. But hindsight is twenty-twenty, and everyone on this call knows my position on torture. We must address the situation at hand before events spiral out of control. So, while we figure out how to step up the pressure on Bessonov and extract everything she knows about Zeta operations in Ukraine, SAD is going to Kiev. The DNI wants a loaded gun ready to point and shoot the minute we have a target."

"I hear you, Ian, but here's the deal," Dempsey said, "*this*"—he drew an imaginary hoop in the air to signify the four people in the hotel room—"ain't Ember SAD."

"I understand that we have been operating shorthanded for too long," Baldwin said, "and while it's not an excuse, please keep in mind that recruiting for Ember is a much greater challenge than for other organizations. Nonetheless, I hear you, which is why Munn and Martin will be augmenting you for the foreseeable future, and Buz will be returning to Florida to round out the Head Shed."

"Is Martin ready to go?" Dempsey said, shifting his gaze to Munn on-screen.

"As luck would have it, the doc cleared him to return to unrestricted duty earlier today," Munn said with a shit-eating grin.

A wide, toothy smile stretched across Dempsey's face. *Well, it's about damn time . . . Hooyah!*

"Copy that," he said, straightening. "If you guys can call ahead and have the Boeing ready to go, we'll pack up here and be at Portela Airport within the hour."

"Will do," Munn said. "See you jackasses soon."

The feed went black.

Dempsey shook his head, then locked eyes with Grimes. Her face was a mask he couldn't read. Next to her, Wang was staring at his hands, while Buz stowed his computer.

Three heads of state assassinated at once, including the Vice President of the United States!

He felt the ground tilt a little as the news hit home. All the pundits believed that Tenet was likely to be the next President. By taking him out, it opened the door to all kinds of political chaos . . . chaos that Russia could exploit. When Dempsey was just a door kicker, he didn't care about politics. So long as he had ammunition and a target, it didn't matter which administration was calling the shots. But now, because of his time in Ember, the geopolitical ramifications started percolating in his mind. All indications were that a Tenet administration would continue President Warner's hawkish and hardline policies toward Petrov's Russia. If what Buz had said were true, and Russian Prime Minister Vavilov had been a potential rival to Petrov, was it really that big of a stretch to think this attack was yet another brilliant and ballsy Arkady Zhukov operation? The Russians were the ultimate chess players, which meant they weren't above sacrificing their own pieces to win the game.

He blew air through his teeth. All this time he'd felt like they had Zhukov on his toes, when in reality, the Russian chess master was still playing two moves ahead.

"You okay?" Grimes asked, but the question was hollow.

"No," he said, turning to pack his things. "We're losing."

CHAPTER 11

The Kremlin
Moscow, Russia
September 25
0922 Local Time

Arkady had never seen the Kremlin buzzing like this.

Never.

The hallways were packed with men in uniform—their expressions granite serious, their heel strikes echoing as they moved with purpose up and down the hallways. Armed security personnel had seemingly been posted at every doorway, and administrative staff were zipping about like frantic drones in a rattled hive. And for a moment, Arkady just stood in the middle, taking it all in with the wide-eyed fascination of a child visiting Disney World for the first time.

If these idiots only knew the truth . . .

"Director Zhukov," a voice said, and he felt a light touch on his left shoulder.

He turned to find Petrov's assistant, Tatia, standing behind him.

"Hello, Tatia," he said, smiling at the young woman. "They wouldn't let me past this new checkpoint."

"I know," she said with an insider's smile. "That's because you're not on their list . . . Thankfully, you're on mine."

He shrugged. "One can never be so sure. Opinion in the Kremlin changes like the seasons. I was wondering if I'd been excommunicated."

"Quite the opposite," she said, showing the uniformed soldier her gold Presidential badge. "From what I understand, you're the man of the hour."

The guard nodded at her, handed Arkady a temporary gold badge on a lanyard, and waved them past.

"Man of the hour, huh?" he said, resuming their conversation.

"Indeed. Your circle of admirers is small, but noteworthy."

Interesting, Arkady thought. *She's been read in on the false flag Ultra operation in Kiev. Apparently, Petrov is not immune to pillow talk. I'll have to keep that in mind . . .*

"And what about you, Tatia? What circle do *you* find yourself occupying these days?"

"An interesting question," she said, glancing at him sideways as they walked. "Is it possible for my heart to be in one place, while my body is trapped in another?"

"Oh, I think so," he said, nodding. "A conundrum only a true Russian could appreciate."

"Like deciding between tea or coffee?" she said, her voice dropping to just above a whisper.

"Yes, very much like that." He slowed their pace, lest they arrive too soon. This conversation was just starting to get interesting. "As you know, I prefer coffee. While our President prefers tea. Which do you prefer, Tatia?"

"Well, this morning I had tea, and it was so hot it scalded my mouth," she said, her heels clicking hard with each step. "As the day wanes and the sun begins to set, I could see myself yearning for a nice iced coffee to soothe the burn."

"I completely understand," he said, admiring her brazen and skillful attempt at tradecraft. They'd had so few interactions over the past year, and all of them had been in Petrov's presence. He'd once thought he'd sensed her reaching out, but he'd written it off as coy posturing. That was not what was happening now. "Maybe sometime our paths will cross on the street and I can introduce you to my favorite café in Moscow. It's quite a remarkable place. So many options, depending on your mood and palate."

"What is it called, this place?" she pressed.

"Café Tchaikovsky, on Triumfalnaya Square."

"I think I know it. It would be fun to try . . . *someday.*"

"I travel a lot, as you might imagine, but when I'm in Moscow, I often stop there after work on Thursdays."

"And if I miss you?"

"Oh, not to worry. The barista who works on Thursday afternoons, Svetlana, is very knowledgeable, and she can walk you through the menu of choices and help you find something to your liking."

"I'll keep that in mind," Tatia said and flashed him an inscrutable smile.

She escorted him to the closed doors outside the Security Council Meeting Room, where they waited, both silently contemplating if the other's overture had been made with malign intent. It was entirely possible a paranoid Petrov had tasked Tatia to open a backchannel dialogue with Arkady to probe for indications of treachery and betrayal, but her style seemed to lack Presidential coaching. Petrov was too vain to permit an underling, especially a bedfellow, to even hint at personal dissatisfaction in a relationship with him. And he was too controlling to let Tatia come up with this script on her own. And yet, if Petrov *was* capable of getting out of his own head, if only for a moment, he would recognize this would be the only approach capable of fooling Arkady.

He looked at her—standing perfectly still and tall, her lithe body at rest and yet her posture so brazenly confident.

"Were you a dancer?" he asked.

"Everyone asks me this question," she said through a sigh, "and I'm always tempted to say yes. Men love their romantic visions of Russian ballerinas, but no, I was never a dancer."

"Too bad," he murmured.

"You're disappointed?"

"Not with you, but with myself. It seems I've proven myself as shallow and predictable as the rest of my kind. Now you will forever think of me as no less boorish than the rest."

She looked up to heaven and pursed her lips in the Parisian fashion, as if to say: *C'est la vie.*

Ah yes, there it is, he thought, resisting the urge to smile. *She was a model . . . an Aphroditic beauty Petrov probably saw in a photograph, stalked relentlessly, and then wooed into conscripted service.*

"You're not like the rest," she said at last, fixing him with her glacier-blue eyes.

"Oh?" he said. "How so?"

"You're much more dangerous."

And on that cue, the doors to the Security Council Meeting Room opened and a legion of flag officers in the finest dress uniforms filed out in twos and threes. The tension and energy in their ranks was palpable; he could practically taste adrenaline on the air. Most of them glanced at Tatia as they walked past—a programmed reaction in the presence of such beauty—but a small handful looked past her to Arkady. Those who did, men who knew him by name or reputation, offered silent, deferential nods. Tatia's words from before echoed in his mind: *Your circle of admirers is small, but noteworthy.*

Arkady accepted the acknowledgments from Russia's top military brass with stoic mutual respect, all the while wondering what the hell was going on. He'd not been told about this meeting, let alone been invited to it, nor had he heard whispers in his network about the agenda. His stomach immediately went to acid as thoughts of Russian jets bombing Kiev and Russian armor rolling into Ukraine popped into his head. He shifted his gaze into the room, where only one man remained. Seated at the head of a vacant conference table— a table as long as a city bus—sat Vladimir Vladimirovich Petrov, President of the Russian Federation. And he was smiling.

Oh dear God, what has he done? Arkady thought as Tatia closed the doors behind him.

"What is that look, old friend?" Petrov said, gesturing to the empty seat at his right hand. "You look like you ate a bad oyster."

Arkady didn't even try to put on a mask. This was no time for games. "What the hell is going on?"

Petrov laughed, incredulity ripe on his face. "What a ridiculous question, especially coming from you." When Arkady didn't respond, the Russian President's expression turned serious. Like a stage actor performing his lines, he said, "The Prime Minister was murdered by terrorists in Ukraine, Comrade Zhukov. This brazen act will not go unpunished."

"And who, Mr. President, do you intend to punish?" Arkady asked, taking a seat.

"That's the trouble," Petrov said, his eyes still smiling. "It's very difficult to know who was behind this egregious plot. Some people are saying that a right-wing Ukrainian ultranationalist group was responsible for the attack, but I'm not so sure. I told our military commanders that an in-depth investigation would be required to discover the truth. But I also told them that something like this would never happen in a stable, uncorrupted Ukraine. I am deeply concerned for the safety and welfare of our Russian-speaking brethren living across the border, not only in the Donbas, but across all of southern Ukraine. There are reports of Russians being attacked in the streets of Mariupol and rumors of civil unrest brewing in Odessa."

"I've heard no such reports," Arkady said, meeting the other man's gaze.

"That's because the Western media is suppressing the truth. But rest assured, anti-Russian forces are coalescing as we speak. I told Admiral Kresinoff that I'm growing increasingly worried about the safety and security of our naval base in Sevastopol. Crimea could be overrun by these Ukrainian nationalists at any minute."

"I see . . . and you have decided to do what about it?"

"Two things," Petrov replied. "First, I've instructed our military commanders to send peacekeeping troops into Mariupol and our Navy to take control of the Black Sea north of the forty-fifth parallel. We simply cannot risk things spiraling out of control."

"And second?" Arkady said, dreading what could possibly be coming next.

"I want your Zetas to conduct an operation to make it look like the Ukrainian military has fired missiles at our forces in Mariupol. I need justification to escalate and you're going to give it to me."

"You can't be serious."

"I'm dead serious."

Arkady tasted bile. He swallowed it down and said, "Vladimir, please, don't do this."

His use of the familiar visibly irked Petrov, confirming that the strength of their bond was strained to the point of fraying. Twenty-five years of friendship, mentorship, and cooperation mattered little to a mind thoroughly and completely corrupted by power.

"I'm going to pretend you didn't say that," Petrov said with a frosty smile.

"If you do this, then you're starting World War Three," Arkady said, undeterred. "You caught the world by surprise with Crimea, and that time it worked. The Donbas treaty is another victory. But this obsession with reclaiming Novorossiya must end. We've pushed President Warner into a corner, and there is nowhere left for him to retreat. If you do this, mark my words, he will send American ground troops to Ukraine. Any moves we make, he will counter. And when shots are fired—which is inevitable—and American soldiers are killed, Warner will escalate. Under no circumstance will the United States and NATO permit us to annex southern Ukraine."

"I've already spoken to President Erodan of Turkey and received his commitment. All it takes is one dissenting vote and NATO is powerless to act. Unanimous consent is required, and they will not have it."

"Then Warner will act unilaterally. America doesn't need NATO to challenge us." Arkady shook his head. "Please, I beg you, let it go."

"Get out of my sight," Petrov said. When Arkady didn't react, the President thrust an outstretched index finger at the double doors. "I said get out!"

The spymaster stood, nodded to Petrov, and began walking toward the exit.

"Do your job," Petrov called after him, "or else you can spend the rest of your days thinking about this conversation from the basement of Lubyanka."

"Understood," Arkady said, without a backward glance. When he stepped out into the hall, instead of finding Tatia waiting for him as he'd hoped, a pair of uniformed MPs flanked the doors. He looked at them each in turn, his eyes asking the question: *Are you here for me?* But instead of taking him into custody, they nodded deferentially and closed the doors behind him.

He exhaled silently with relief and walked away with solid, confident strides. But in his mind, the ground was crumbling beneath his feet.

CHAPTER 12

The Situation Room
The White House
Washington, DC
0624 Local Time

Jarvis, along with the rest of the National Security Council members, stood the moment President Warner entered the room. The President said nothing, just waved them all to be seated as he took his place at the head of the table.

"This situation is the most treacherous and perilous any of us will face in our careers. A foreign power has assassinated the Vice President of the United States, and I hold all of you personally responsible for this intelligence failure." Warner dragged his laser beam eyes across everyone at the large conference table, his gaze eventually settling on Jarvis. "Not the Secret Service . . . but you, each and every one of you in this room. You are my National Security Council, and in case you've forgotten, that means you're responsible for *national security*."

"Yes, sir," Jarvis said, having no choice but to answer for the collective. "And we accept full responsibility for this tragedy."

Warner shook his head and looked down at his hands, which were balled into fists on the table. "Satellite imagery shows Russian armor and troop carriers repositioning along Ukraine's southeastern border, correct?"

"Yes, Mr. President," General McMillan, the Chairman of the Joint Chiefs of Staff, said.

"And the Russian Navy has parked a small armada of ships off the coast of Mariupol in the Sea of Azov?"

"That's correct, sir. And the guided-missile frigate *Admiral Grigorovich* appears to be steaming toward Odessa in the Black Sea. Three Kilo-class submarines moored at Sevastopol have also gotten underway and submerged."

Warner nodded. "The question I want everyone in this room to ask themselves is, why would the Russian military reposition both land and naval assets in such a manner? The pro-Russian separatists in the eastern oblasts already won their autonomy. Why would Petrov take such actions unless he's planning to capitalize on the chaos and use this as an opportunity to invade Ukraine?"

"Mr. President, if I may?" Secretary of State Baker interjected.

"You may not," Warner said with an admonishing glare, then looked from Baker to the Secretary of Defense. "Bob, I don't know how else to say this other than *make preparations for war*. I will not, under any circumstance, allow Russia to invade Ukraine. Petrov's dream of Novorossiya dies today."

At first, the SecDef, Robert Frank, didn't react. But then, very slowly, he began to nod. "Yes, Mr. President. Is it premature to brief the Gang of Eight?"

Warner thought for a moment. "No, and I'm going to need Congress on my side for this. Go ahead and start a dialogue with Senator Rutledge. He's a hawk. We'll let him take point." The President turned to his Chief of Staff and said, "David, who's that reporter at the *Post* who's always a pain in my ass?"

"Well, sir, there are several: Greg Olsen, Christina Morales, Ben Bradshaw—"

"Bradshaw, that's the one. Why don't you send him a Black Sea maritime-activity status report and include a note about a previously unannounced Russian military exercise that appears to be unfolding along Ukraine's southeastern border. When he connects the dots, tell him my administration is gravely concerned about these developments. If he presses you, tell him, off the record, that we believe a Kremlin-directed clandestine operation is underway to further destabilize Ukraine following the tragic death of President Zinovenko. I want to get ahead of this in the press and I want to control the narrative."

"And what do we want in return?" Warner's Chief of Staff asked.

"Nothing, other than his verbal assurance that he will report on the situation with the same tenacity he's used to scrutinize my presidency."

This comment momentarily broke the tension in the room, giving the assembled powerbrokers something to chuckle about in a situation that otherwise warranted no levity.

The President turned his attention back to the Secretary of Defense. "Bob, get to work with the Joint Chiefs. I want containment scenarios and options on my desk by eighteen hundred hours. It's going to be a late night, people. The first of many. Clear your calendars and hug your kids, because you're living here for the foreseeable future. Meeting adjourned."

After a moment of hesitant silence, the room buzzed to life with commotion as a half-dozen side conversations fired up between various principals, and a legion of staff personnel—aides, deputies, and directors—scrambled from the "cheap seats" along the perimeter to find and support their bosses. And so it was with Jarvis; when he slid his chair back from the table and turned, he was met by Petra and Mike Casey.

"Let's go grab one of the small rooms before somebody else does," Jarvis said, chopping a hand toward the exit like he was on an op back in the day. "We need to talk."

Petra spun on a heel and led the way, parting the sea of bodies like a fast boat cutting through the surf. Casey followed her, with Jarvis bringing up the rear, as she strode at a brisk pace to one of the nearby breakout rooms. She snagged it a split second before Secretary Baker's aide could, tossing her notebook on the table like she was planting a flag on virgin ground and claiming sovereign territory. Baker's aide shot Petra an irritated look, turned on a heel, and went for another room. Casey shut the door behind Jarvis and they both grabbed seats at the table.

"This is an open session," Jarvis said. "I want to hear everything on your minds, unfiltered. There are no stupid ideas, no stupid theories. Petra, you first."

"I talked to the CIA station chief in Kiev this morning and picked his brain in preparation for this meeting," she said, resting her hands on the table. "He confirmed there's no love between Ultra and Russia. Ultra is an organization whose stated mission is to fight for a strong and independent Ukraine, free from Russian influence. They are *ultra*nationalists, many of them veterans of the war in Donbas, where their brothers died fighting the Russian army. Any narrative proclaiming that Ultra is somehow a puppet of the Kremlin is not based in fact."

"What else did he have to say?" Jarvis asked.

"As of five hours ago, Ultra is still denying responsibility for the attack."

"That means nothing," Jarvis said. "Does CIA have embedded assets in any of the far-right nationalist groups in Ukraine?"

"No," Petra said. "I asked him that specifically."

"What are his snitches in Kiev saying?"

"The consensus on the street is still that Ultra was behind the strike, but he's got nothing concrete."

Jarvis blew air through his teeth. "Look, the President wants ironclad confirmation of who was behind this attack, and we need to find a way to give it to him. Petra, I want you to contact CIA Director Hartigan's office and give them a heads-up we're going to be coordinating with his Chief of Station to run ISR on Ultra in Kiev. Ember has to start somewhere, and I think Ultra is the logical choice."

"Roger that," she said, jotting a note with his pen.

He turned to Casey, who was now fully read in on Ember. "Mike, give Baldwin the green light to raid Ultra's base of operations, pick up some guys, and see what we can learn."

"Timeline?" Casey said.

"ASAFP," Jarvis replied, then returned his attention to Petra.

"I know that look," she said. "You think Russia was behind this, don't you?"

He shrugged. "It does have the hallmarks of a Zeta false flag operation—well orchestrated, plausible deniability, and massive geopolitical stakes for Russia. Vice President Tenet's stance on Russia was the same as Warner's. Had he been elected, he would have continued the Warner doctrine of targeted sanctions against Russia and a hard stance on rebuffing Russian expansionism. And when you factor in Zinovenko's recent statements indicating

Ukraine's intention to seek membership in the EU following the Donbas treaty signing . . . well, let's just say the future wasn't looking so bright from Petrov's perspective."

"I hear you, but Russian Prime Minister Vavilov was also killed in this attack. Would Petrov really task Arkady with an operation to murder Russia's parliamentary head of state just for the sake of plausible deniability? That seems highly unlikely to me, even for a man as vicious and power hungry as Petrov."

"Maybe you're right," he said, flexing his fingers below the table. "Ever since we lost Shane, I see Arkady's fingerprints everywhere I look. Maybe I've lost my objectivity on the matter."

"I'm not so sure," Casey said. "Since when has sacrificing their brethren in the name of country ever bothered the Russians? The Red Army suffered eight-point-six million casualties in World War Two. Some historians estimate an additional twelve million Russian civilians died in the war against the Nazis. After the war, Stalin branded millions of his countrymen dissidents and had them executed. Millions more were sent to die in labor camps to cement his grip on power. Let's not forget, Petrov had his main political rival gunned down on the streets of Moscow in plain sight. Why is it so inconceivable to imagine he'd dispatch his Prime Minister to Kiev knowing the man would die? Remember, in two thousand seventeen there was speculation that Vavilov was going to run for President against Petrov. Vavilov denied it, but early polling showed he had a higher approval rating than Petrov. From what I understand, Petrov got spooked and offered Vavilov the Prime Minister job to preempt a Presidential bid."

"I think the one thing we can all agree on is that Petrov will do *anything* to cement his power and promote Russian hegemony in the region," Jarvis said, his mind going back to Buz Wilson saying something similar about the Russian mindset on the day he'd recruited the old spook for Ember. "Politics and power for Petrov is a zero-sum game. For him to rise, others must fall. Tenet, Zinovenko, and Vavilov all threatened his reputation, agenda, and grip on power in different ways . . . How he would outmaneuver all of them in the coming years certainly had to be on Petrov's mind."

"Agreed," Petra said.

"Mike, give me your thoughts on the Black Sea and these naval movements General McMillan mentioned," Jarvis said, turning to his Deputy Chief of Staff.

The former submarine captain retrieved a notebook computer from his bag and flipped open the screen. He clicked on a mapping application and pulled up satellite imagery of arguably the world's most strategically important captive body of water.

"As you know, access to the Black Sea from the Mediterranean is controlled via the Turkish straits—the Dardanelles on the Aegean side and the Bosporus on the Black Sea side. The straits and the body of water between them, the Sea of Marmara, are sovereign territorial waters of Turkey. Since the nineteen thirty-six Montreux Convention, Turkey has exercised full control over the straits. The agreement guarantees free passage of civilian vessels in peacetime, but grants Turkey exclusive power to restrict and control the transit of warships not flagged under one of the Black Sea countries—Bulgaria, Romania, Ukraine, Russia, Georgia, and Turkey. There's no governing treaty between those countries that limits how many naval ships they can maintain and deploy from Black Sea home ports."

"Do we have any ships in the Black Sea now?" Petra asked.

"Yes, two ships, in fact. Historically, Ankara has limited US Naval presence to one combatant vessel at a time, but right now 6th Fleet is conducting a training exercise with the Romanian Navy, and so the USS *Oak Hill* and the USS *Donald Cook* are there. The *Oak Hill* is carrying a detachment of Special Operations–capable

Marines, as well as supporting air assets—namely AH-64 attack helicopters and their UH1s. The *Donald Cook* is an *Arleigh Burke*-class guided-missile destroyer, homeported out of Rota, Spain."

"Is that for the annual Sea Breeze exercises?" Jarvis asked.

"Exactly," Casey said. "The *Oak Hill* is docked in Odessa for liberty and the *Donald Cook* is running around with a couple of Ukrainian fast boats and their flagship, the late Soviet-era frigate *Hetman Sahaydachniy*."

"Ukraine's flagship is a frigate?" Petra asked.

"Yeah, and it's their only frigate at that," Casey said with a pitying expression. "What most people don't understand is that when Ukraine forfeited Crimea to Russia in two thousand fourteen, it lost more than just a chunk of land—it lost its status as the dominant naval power on the Black Sea."

"Go on," Jarvis said.

"Petrov didn't want Crimea, he wanted Sevastopol. Eighty percent of Ukraine's naval personnel and sixty percent of its maritime assets—ships, amphibious craft, aircraft, and helicopters—were stationed on the Crimean peninsula, with the lion's share operating out of Sevastopol. When Petrov annexed Crimea, he took everything. In one fell swoop, Russia neutered the Ukrainian Navy and ripped up the two thousand ten Kharkov Agreement, which was preventing Russia from growing and modernizing its Black Sea fleet. Petrov gained an ice-free deep-water harbor and shipyard and took control of the land mass on both sides of the Kerch Strait—the only passage connecting the Sea of Azov to the Black Sea."

"Didn't Petrov recently blockade the Kerch Strait?" Petra asked.

"Yeah, but not just once—five times in the last twelve months. Which is a major problem for Ukraine because its two largest seaports—Odessa and Mariupol—are on opposite sides of the strait. Eighty percent of Ukraine's maritime traffic is between these two cities. Petrov knows this and he's using his Black Sea fleet to create chaos. The US Naval Institute estimates Mariupol maritime-related revenues were down fifty percent last year entirely due to Russian maritime interference."

"I don't think Congress, the American people, or the media ever understood the strategic implications of annexing Crimea," Petra said. "The news reports focused on the bogus election and Moscow's sob story about native Russians in Crimea wanting to be part of the motherland again. Never once, did I hear anyone explain that this coup was all about the Black Sea."

"That's exactly right, and since two thousand fourteen, the size and capabilities of the Russian Black Sea fleet have increased dramatically." Casey pulled up a list of ships, with the dramatic post-Crimea additions highlighted in yellow. "And I haven't even touched on the aviation assets relocated and the missile batteries they've installed all across the Crimean peninsula. They've got supersonic antiship missiles, ballistic missiles, antiaircraft missiles, submarine-launched cruise missiles—basically, every type of missile imaginable—and their Air Force recently stood up a squadron of Sukhoi Su-30s in Sevastopol. In other words, all of the Black Sea and every country that borders it are well inside their strike radius. From a military standpoint, Russia dominates the Black Sea, and there's absolutely nothing anybody, including the United States, can do about it."

"Mike, let's pretend for a minute that I'm President Petrov and you're my chief strategist," Jarvis said, rubbing his chin. "We took Crimea and that worked out great. With Ukraine in chaos, I'm ready for my next land grab. Walk me through the sequence of events."

"Novorossiya?" Casey clarified.

Jarvis nodded.

"Okay, Mr. President," Casey said with a wry grin. "Kinda has a nice ring to it, doesn't it?"

"Not hardly," Jarvis grumbled and glanced at Petra. She smiled and shook her head, knowing better than anyone how much he loathed politics. "Never gonna happen."

"All right, Novorossiya," Casey said, turning his attention back to the computer. He centered the map over southern Ukraine and the upper half of the Black Sea. "First, we deploy a couple hundred professional dissidents to Mariupol and start stirring up unrest. We launch a propaganda campaign, the same one we used for Crimea, only this time we're much better at it because we know how to exploit social media. Then, the Kremlin issues a statement of concern about instability in the local government and Ukraine's failure to ensure the safety of native Russian speakers, not only in Mariupol, but in all of southern Ukraine. We organize riots and protests and make sure plenty of shots are fired, killing some civilians. At the same time, we harass Ukrainian merchant traffic, prompting the Ukrainian Navy to deploy patrol ships. When they show up, we manufacture an incident in the Sea of Azov and blockade the Kerch Strait. We have lots of practice doing that now, so we go one step further and claim the Sea of Azov as Russian territorial waters. The next day, we declare a state of emergency in Mariupol and send Russian 'peacekeeping' troops into the city. At the same time, we declare an Economic Exclusivity Zone everywhere north of the forty-fifth parallel and blockade all maritime traffic in and out of Odessa. We then move our dissidents from Mariupol to Odessa and stir up trouble over there. Some Russian peacekeepers unfortunately are going to have to die in Mariupol, but when they do, we roll armor across the border and move west. We take control of the M14 roadway from Nova Kakhovka, just north of Crimea, all the way to Mariupol—cutting off all east-west ground traffic—and we blockade the Dnieper River there as well, halting all north-south river traffic . . . Then, we pause and assess, before making the decision to move peacekeeping troops into Odessa and start holding secession votes for the occupied oblasts to leave Ukraine and join Russian—supervised at gunpoint, of course—like we did in Crimea."

Jarvis shot Petra an impressed look, then said to Casey, "A reasonable plan, comrade. I will take it under consideration."

Casey chuckled. "Or not . . . Feel free to do as you wish, Mr. President."

Jarvis steepled his fingers. "In all seriousness, is that something you just threw together off the cuff, or have you been thinking about this?"

"I have some experience war-gaming from my time at the War College," Casey said. "And as a submarine CO, I suppose I know a little something about what-if scenarios."

"Sure, sure," Jarvis said, no stranger to war-gaming in his own right. "And if I asked you to game this scenario out, what do you predict the most likely outcome to be, assuming US intervention?"

"With Warner at the helm—hot, bothered, and acting unilaterally?"

"Yes."

"World War Three," the submariner said, all the humor gone from his voice now.

"That's what I thought," Jarvis said. "Hey, Mike, do you mind giving us the room for a moment?"

"Sure," Casey said, closing his computer screen and stuffing the laptop into his bag. As he slid his chair back from the table, he said, "Did I say something wrong?"

"No," Jarvis said, with an easy smile. "I just need a couple of minutes alone with Petra."

"Yes, sir." And with a dutiful nod, Casey excused himself.

"What do you think of Mike?" Jarvis asked once the door to the breakout room was closed.

"With each and every engagement, he continues to impress me," she said. "He's sharp, well-informed, and best of all, doesn't beat everyone to death with a big ego. What about you? What do you think?"

"I think he's outstanding. Which is why, I'm afraid, I have no choice but to fire him."

"What?" Petra screwed up her face.

"Yeah, as much as I'd like to keep him for myself, I think his talents could be put to better use elsewhere."

"By elsewhere, you wouldn't happen to mean in a trailer in Tampa?"

He nodded.

"When you told me to find you candidates for Deputy Chief of Staff with command experience, I wondered if the real reason was so you could vet for Shane Smith's replacement."

"Great minds think alike," he said, grabbing her hand and giving it a squeeze. "At first, when you brought me a sub driver, I balked."

"I remember," she said.

"That's because while submarine operations have both tactical and strategic components, sub driving and leading direct-action missions in the field are completely different animals."

"But at Ember, he's not going to be leading the missions. That's Dempsey's job."

"Exactly," Jarvis said. "Listening to Casey war-game out that Novorossiya invasion scenario, I realized that he checked all the boxes . . . plus one or two I hadn't considered."

"Hold on, someone else thought of something before you did?" she said, her voice ripe with sarcasm. "Has the human supercomputer met his match?"

"I probably deserve that," he said with a chuckle, downplaying what was actually a new and troubling personal development he'd yet to discuss with her. Ever since he'd started taking antitremor meds for Parkinson's, his synesthesia and the perceptual insights he gleaned from the rich sensory cross-pollination in his mind had been dramatically suppressed. The analytical part of his brain seemed unhampered by the drugs, but his ability to perceive novel and creative connections across disparate datasets was disturbingly diminished. In his youth, he'd viewed his synesthesia as a curse. As an adult, he'd embraced it for what it really was . . . a gift, and now that gift had been taken from him.

"Kelso, did you hear what I said?" Petra asked, with a characteristic tilt of her head.

"Sorry, zoned out there for a moment. How do you think Baldwin is going to take Casey coming in as Ember's Director? I hope it doesn't cause him to shut down on us."

"Are you kidding me?" she said with a laugh. "He's going to be elated."

"You think so?"

"Oh my God, Kelso. I can see it in his face and hear it in his voice every time I talk to him. Ian doesn't want to be Director of Ember. He accepted the promotion out of devotion and respect for you and love of country. This has been very difficult for him."

"I know . . . and probably more than I should have asked of him. But he was the least worst alternative."

"Agreed," she said, giving his hand one final squeeze before letting go. "But not anymore. Mike is exactly what Ember needs at the time it needs him most."

"All right, then it's settled," he said, loosening his necktie, then taking it off completely. "If you don't mind, why don't you call him back in here so I can give him the bad news."

CHAPTER 13

Zeta Safe House

Kiev, Ukraine

1340 Local Time

Gavriil's encrypted mobile phone rang.

He glanced at it, sighed, and put down his Nintendo Switch. This was the first time he'd been able to play *Fortnite* in weeks. He'd pulled off the mission—a fucking impossible mission at that—and all he wanted was to be left alone for just one day.

One day . . . is that really too much to ask?

"Prime," he said, answering the call.

"Are you alone?" Arkady asked; Gavriil recognized his voice instantly.

"Yes, lying low and following standard post-operational protocols."

"Very good," the old bear said, then, with what Gavriil imagined was a fatherly smile on his face, added, "Congratulations on the operation. Excellent work."

"Thank you," he said. "Are you calling with new tasking?"

"What? I can't call to congratulate my top asset on a job well done?"

"So, I *don't* have new tasking?" Gavriil asked, glancing with hopeful eyes at the video game console.

"I didn't say that," Arkady said with a wry little chuckle.

"In that case, I'm ready," he said.

"Before we get to that, what is the status of Ultra?"

"A fractured response to the pressure. Some have gone to ground, others are running scared, and the rest are pretending nothing happened."

"Have you severed ties with them?"

"*Nyet*, not officially, but I haven't checked in since the day of the attack either. Do you want me to check in?"

"No, no," Arkady said, and in the pause that followed, Gavriil knew his mentor was weighing the pros and cons of sharing whatever piece of information he was contemplating. Finally, the spymaster said, "I'm going to let you in on a secret."

"Okay . . ."

"For the past several months, the Americans have been systematically eliminating your brothers and sisters in the field."

"How many?"

"Six and counting."

"And you have elected not to warn any of us, I presume?" Gavriil said, working to keep his voice detached despite the hot geyser of anger in his chest.

"That is correct."

"Do you know where they are getting their intelligence?" he asked, although he suspected he already knew the answer.

"Bessonov, of course."

Gavriil got to his feet and began to pace. "She's a traitor."

"Perhaps," Arkady said. "Perhaps not. We don't know her circumstances. We don't know what intelligence she's been able to gather during her internment. I see a methodology in her actions. From my outside perspective, she appears to be cooperating in a manner to provide the least value over the longest possible time period. I believe she's still in the game."

Gavriil pursed his lips and considered the underlying complexities and ramifications of this last statement. "And so, you decided to let the game play out in the hope she will win the Americans' trust and she'll become a mole in their ranks? Or better yet, maybe we'll get her back in a prisoner exchange, and Petrov can call her a hero and parade her around like fucking Anna Chapman? Is that it? All sins are forgiven?"

Arkady laughed. "In our business, what is sin? What is absolution? Both are nonsensical constructs for a spy. There is only risk and value—my job is to extract the latter while managing the former."

"That's not an answer."

"Then ask me the question that is upsetting you so much. As Prime, you are not only permitted to ask questions, it is your duty."

"Fine," he said, hating this cat-and-mouse game they were playing. "Why? Why didn't you warn us we were being hunted?"

"There are three reasons," Arkady said. "I'll tell you one and leave the other two for you to ponder."

"Fair enough."

"I did not warn you because to do so would be a violation of this program's charter. Any Zeta worth their salt must be able to execute their mission in the cold. That is the job—disavowed, deep-cover work, alone. Now your turn, Prime. What are the risk-value propositions for taking action versus not taking action?"

Gavriil exhaled and found his center. He swallowed down his petty anger and tried to think like Arkady. "Because to warn the others would have required opening lines of contact with deep-cover assets, creating new electronic trails for the Americans to follow. Trails that could have led them to other network assets and operatives outside of Bessonov's knowledge base. I'm sorry. How foolish of me to speak without thinking it through first."

"That's correct. And the other?"

Gavriil rubbed his temples, which were beginning to throb. "Maybe Bessonov found a way to signal you?"

"Very good," the spymaster said. "In this case, she has been unsuccessful on that front, but I was hoping to see a pattern and predict the next name she would give up."

"And that way you could set a trap," Gavriil said, puzzle pieces suddenly fitting together, another reminder that it was impossible to *over*estimate the depth of his mentor's intellect and cunning.

"Da," Arkady said. "And my instincts tell me the time is now. If I were Kelso Jarvis, I would immediately suspect Zeta had a hand in the assassination attack in Kiev. He knows how I think. He understands now that Russians are willing to sacrifice pieces on the board, and he's learned this lesson the hard way. He's going to be angry. He's going to order his people to squeeze Bessonov until she gives him a name in Kiev. He'll assume that operative was working with Ultra and he'll send the Ember task force to prosecute."

"But I didn't work closely with Bessonov. Also, I wasn't occupying the Artem NOC at the time she was taken," he said.

"That's right," Arkady said. "Nor does she know that you've ascended to Prime. But she did work with Bondar. She knew about him."

"Bondar?" Gavriil said with a laugh. "He's more cuckold than killer. Bondar could never have infiltrated Ultra."

"*Da*, but the Americans don't know that."

Gavriil nodded. "That's true. Maybe they will think he procured the Javelin missile and devised the attack."

"Precisely," the old spy said.

"What do you want me to do?"

"When Ember comes for Bondar, I want you to be ready. Set the trap, my son. And maybe Bessonov's suffering and the sacrifice borne by your Zeta comrades who died to protect our brotherhood will not have been in vain."

CHAPTER 14

Ember Executive Boeing 787

Boryspil Airport

Kiev Oblast, Ukraine

September 29

1345 Local Time

"Damn, it feels good to have the band back together," Dempsey said with a smile, scanning the faces of the freshly reconstituted Ember SAD team around the conference table.

"Getting Martin out of the spa took some effort, but his vacation is over," Munn said, raising his coffee mug at the former MARSOC Marine whose discharge paperwork Munn had ramrodded through every administrative barrier possible at Portsmouth Naval Hospital. "Isn't that right, Luka?"

"Took ya'll long enough," Martin said, toasting with his water bottle. "If I'd stayed much longer, I think the PTs would have taken a baseball bat to my knee or something. They said I was demoralizing all the other patients in rehab because I was healing so fast. Guess they'd never treated a Marine before."

"Is that so?" Baldwin said on the monitor, shaking his head in disapproval. Clearly, the Acting Director was still chafed by the decision to cut Martin's convalescence short by a full month.

Dempsey ignored the look. If the operator said he was good to go, then that was enough. They played by big-boy rules at Ember, and Martin knew the stakes. In any case, who the hell else was there? Even with Martin and Munn back, they were pretty damn lean. Dempsey had toyed with the idea of requesting Lieutenant Commander Redman and a small, handpicked squad of SEALs from Team Four to augment this mission, but the fuse had proven too short. They'd have to do it with their four shooters plus Wang.

We've done more with less, Dempsey thought, *but not with everybody in this fucked-up headspace.*

He glanced at Wang, expecting to see the kid staring at his hands, but instead their cyber lead was sitting up straight with fire in his eyes.

"Are we going to brief this fucking thing or what?" Wang said, looking from Baldwin to Dempsey and back again.

"Elizabeth," Baldwin said. "As you've taken point interfacing with the Ukrainians and local CIA since your arrival, why don't you kick things off."

"Sure," she said, clicking a few keys on her laptop. A photograph of a powerfully built, square-jawed Ukrainian appeared on the large wall monitor. "Meet Viktor Skorapporsky, the twenty-nine-year-old cofounder and leader of the right-wing ultranationalist Ukrainian terrorist group known as Ultra, which we are now highly confident was involved in the Independence Square missile attack."

"So this guy, Viktor, is a Russian mole?" Martin asked.

"No," she said, shaking her head. "He's definitely Ukrainian.

We have his birth records: he served in the Ukrainian Army, and his family all lives in Kiev. The Ukrainian Security Service, or SBU, has been keeping tabs on Viktor since he discharged from the army and formed Ultra. Of all the ultranationalist groups in Ukraine, Ultra has the most formidable paramilitary capabilities. Most of their members have seen combat in the Donbas War, and they pride themselves on being the most outspoken, aggressive, and ultraright voice in Ukraine."

"Does the SBU think this guy is the mastermind behind the attack?" Munn asked.

"Yes, in fact, it's been a bitch to get them to back off. If not for DNI Jarvis's pull, the SBU would have already raided Ultra safe houses and apartments and hauled in as many members as possible. They've lost their President and the Ukrainian people are calling for blood. The station chief had to intervene to shut down an SBU operation *in progress* meant to grab Skorapporsky the day we landed."

"Viktor must be shitting his pants right now," Dempsey said.

Grimes flashed him a sly smile. "In the beginning, yes, but not anymore. Since not a single member of Ultra has been arrested, we've observed a gradual shift in his movements and communications."

"He's starting to think he got away with it," Dempsey said.

She nodded. "Precisely."

"Where do things stand now?" Munn pressed.

"I've been sitting in on a joint CIA-SBU task force conducting ISR on active Ultra members. About half of them have dissociated—severing all communications and appearing to be going about their daily lives. Probably until they think the risk of getting arrested has blown over. A few members have fled Kiev. The rest, the diehard members and leadership, are continuing to meet. A small core group, including Skorapporsky, are hunkered down in a commercial building owned by Skorapporsky's father."

"Talk about amateur hour," Martin said, leaning back. Dempsey thought he saw a grimace ripple across his teammate's face, but it disappeared quickly. "Do they really think they're not being watched? What a bunch of rubes."

Wang laughed at the comment, which Dempsey took as a good sign. He hadn't heard the kid laugh in weeks.

"Indeed," Baldwin agreed. "Ultra is a grassroots organization . . . a politically motivated street gang, if you will. Or better yet, a paramilitary activist—"

"They're terrorists, Ian," Dempsey said, cutting him off. "We're not writing a thesis paper. Let's move on. Can you give us an update on the warehouse where they're lying low?"

The screen refreshed momentarily with a close-up of Baldwin's left nostril, and then his distorted face was replaced by a static satellite image of an industrial park along a bend in the Dnieper River, the main waterway running through the heart of Kiev. A bridge crossed the river, but instead of handling residential traffic, it appeared to be intended for shuttling material back and forth between the warehouses on the southwest bank and the manufacturing facilities on the north. A red arrow appeared on-screen, pointing to a building just north of the bridge.

"A half-dozen individuals appear to be living in this warehouse building and up to a dozen others come and go." As Baldwin talked, the satellite image switched from a daytime color to a perfectly matched static thermal image. "As you can see, they are using a rotating security schedule, with two perimeter sentries roving and a pair stationed inside at all times."

"What about Skorapporsky?" Munn asked.

"We're tracking his phone," Baldwin said. "He's sleeping at the facility and rarely leaves."

"So, we're sure Viktor isn't a Zeta?" Dempsey said.

"Ninety-eight percent confidence interval."

"Then which one of these guys is? Because there's no way Ultra pulled a hit like that off by themselves."

"We don't know, but we've been working overtime to answer that question," Baldwin said. "And we believe it is this man."

The screen split and a new photograph appeared—an insanely grainy black-and-white security cam capture of a clean-shaven, dark-haired Caucasian. In the image, the man's head was turned in profile. Without even asking, Dempsey knew the image quality was too poor for an effective facial recognition database search.

"*Greaaaaat* picture," Wang grumbled.

"Yes, I know, Richard," Baldwin said. "It is not ideal, but it is the only face shot we have. However, the Ukrainian Security Service has been very helpful and given us access to all relevant archive data. Using our body-form algorithm, the system flagged this man dozens of times in the vicinity of Ultra's previous meetinghouse. With a ninety percent confidence interval, I can say he attended the last all-hands Ultra meeting the day before the attack."

"But you didn't get any other face shots?" Munn asked, incredulous.

"No, he seemingly knows the exact location and angle of every camera in the vicinity of the Ultra safe houses."

"Then that's Arkady's guy," Dempsey said. "Only a pro could pull that off. What about at the industrial park? Have we picked him up on any cameras there since the attack?"

"Unfortunately, no."

"That makes sense," Dempsey said, a fire growing in his chest. "More confirming evidence. After mission accomplished, there wouldn't be any reason for this guy to continue associating with Ultra. The best plan would be to cut ties and not leave any direct link between Ultra and Zeta."

"That's why grabbing Viktor Skorapporsky is our best play," Munn said. "He's just one link removed from this dude."

"All right, Skora . . . pporsky, or however the fuck you say his name, is the mission. Whatever you do, people, do not kill this guy," Dempsey said. "Everyone clear?"

"Clear," the team replied in unison.

"All right, let's brief it," he said. "Is Ground Branch good to go as our quick reaction force?"

"Yes," Baldwin said, and a new red dot appeared on the satellite map. "The CIA safe house they'll be staging from is located here. You'll have a four-man team as backup."

"Are they read in on the op?" Dempsey asked, his tone implying he hoped to hell not.

"Negative," Baldwin replied. "I will parlay your instructions after we conclude here, but DNI feels, and obviously I agree, that the less the world knows about Viktor Skorapporsky's fate, the better. We want to keep the circle tight and control the narrative."

"Good," Dempsey said and got to his feet. He paced toward the big screen and Munn handed him a laser pointer. Dempsey lit up the cargo bridge leading over the river.

"I think a waterside infil here is best," he said, the SEAL inside taking over. "We'll insert upriver here . . ." He lit up a point a quarter mile north of the bend in the river, trying to keep the swim short for Martin, who had still not fully recovered. "Munn and Martin will exit the water here, while I continue south another hundred yards to move from the other corner."

"What about me?" Grimes asked.

"You'll set up as overwatch here," Dempsey said, pointing at a six-story apartment building across Naberezhno-Khreshchatytska Street, a good two hundred and fifty yards east.

Grimes shook her head. "I'm of no use to you there, John. Maybe

I get a line on the roadside sentry, but after that I just sit and wait, with no line on anything inside, nor on the best exfil, which is waterside."

"Here, then," Dempsey said, pointing at a taller building southeast of the X and past the bridge. "No obstruction, line on the waterside, and still some angles streetside."

"But nothing gives me a line inside, where all the shitheads will be." Grimes held his eyes.

Dempsey knew what she was going to say. He also knew she was right, but he made her ask anyway. Sure, it was immature, but since when had that ever stopped him? He folded his arms across his chest and raised an eyebrow.

"You need me inside, John," she pressed. "You know that. Hitting a building with only two outside sentries and a half-dozen or more shooters inside calls for another assaulter rather than an overwatch."

"Yeah, well, have you ever done a maritime infil?" he asked, knowing the answer.

"No," she said. "But I've trained for it. I'm good on scuba." She mimicked him by crossing her arms and raising an eyebrow. "And you've seen me swim a three-K in the pool. Besides, this body is beach ready, remember?"

With that comment, he broke. "Okay, so Grimes is with me," he said through a laugh. "That means Baldwin's overwatch. Any chance you can have an *armed* drone in orbit, just in case?"

"For tonight?" Baldwin said, making a show of checking his watch. "Unlikely, but miracles have been known to happen."

"Tell me we're good on the exfil; if not, we'll have to push it back," Dempsey said.

"As luck would have it, Ground Branch has an experienced boat driver in theater. Both he and his boat are standing by. You just need to finalize details with him."

"Excellent," he said, then doing his best George Peppard, added, "I love it when a plan comes together."

Only Munn chuckled.

"C'mon, really? Hannibal from *The A-Team* ... Nobody?" Dempsey said, then waved a hand, dismissing all of them. "Ahhh, you guys suck."

"Med ops?" Grimes asked, looking past him to Munn, keeping them on task.

"We're tiny, so it's just me for now. CASEVAC is back here to the Boeing unless it's urgent surgical. If that's needed, we fall in on a civilian hospital—the Cardiac Hospital on Melnikova Street, which I've already loaded as a waypoint on everyone's GPS app. DNI will deconflict this for us if needed, but it'll raise a big-ass flag nonetheless, so best to avoid it if we can. Don't get shot," Munn said and looked at Martin. "That means you, dude."

"Roger that," Martin said with a chuckle. "Don't get shot."

"But if you feel you must," Dempsey said, "then get shot somewhere relatively unimportant."

This finally got a laugh from the group, and Dempsey felt more like himself than he had in a while. Now this was an operation worthy of a frogman—not some assassination in a park dressed like a hobo who'd shit his pants. Finally, they were back to doing the Team-level operations he did best.

He looked at his watch. "All right everybody, we've got seven hours to prep and get set. Let's go, let's go, let's go ..."

As the world's most elite operators cleared the room, Munn clapped Dempsey on the back and smiled. They locked eyes but no words were needed between them. Ember SAD was back, and God have mercy on anyone who tried to get in their way.

CHAPTER 15

Home of Dr. and Mrs. Oleksiy Honchar
Kiev, Ukraine
2130 Local Time

Gavriil dragged the Queen Anne–style upholstered chair in front of
the French doors and took a seat. Then, he pulled back the ornate
silk curtains, revealing a set of arched glass balcony doors. Pity he'd
had to kill the couple who lived here . . . it was a very nice house, and
from the pictures on their dresser they seemed like a happy couple.

It wasn't personal . . . just bad luck.

From this vantage point, he had an unobstructed view of Denys Bondar's mansion. Bondar was the opposite of what one would
expect from a Russian covert operative—brash, colorful, public,
and always in the tabloids with a new woman. He'd splashed onto
the Kiev scene a few years ago as a millionaire playboy architect,
and he ran in circles with Kiev's most important and influential

elite—politicians, lawyers, bankers, and business tycoons—and was rumored to have had affairs with many of their wives. The rumors, he dismissed with a perfunctory wave of his hand, but also sometimes with a wink. He'd made many allies in the capital city, and twice as many enemies. His antics and scheming brought him constant attention from the paparazzi as well as scrutiny from the Ukrainian government's watchful eyes.

Bondar was a covert operations nightmare.

And yet another demonstration of Arkady's brilliance. Bondar had been the source of some of the most important intelligence coming out of Ukraine and Eastern Europe.

Gavriil rolled his neck and got a satisfying crack on the left side, where he carried all of his stress. He raised the boxy binoculars to his eyes, scanning in thermal mode across the yard and street and seeing nothing of concern. Next, he scanned the back of the house, a curious blend of Russian and Italian contemporary architecture, and saw no movement in night vision or with thermal imaging. Next he scanned the downstairs rooms, before moving up to the second floor. He switched from thermal to night vision with the flip of his thumb and peered through the open French doors of the balcony off the master bedroom. Inside, Bondar was sitting on the edge of a king-sized bed while a young and completely naked woman knelt in front of him, her head bobbing up and down.

Lucky bastard.

Gavriil tried to remember the last time he'd been with a woman . . . a year? Longer? He exhaled. The women he was drawn to were confident, successful, and attractive—the alpha females. Wooing women of that caliber took effort, commitment, and time, none of which he could spare in his profession. And so, for the foreseeable future, he'd chosen abstinence.

No attachments. No liabilities. It was the best way.

It was the only way.

Gavriil watched the woman stand up and push Bondar down onto the bed. Then she straddled him. Gavriil looked away and, with a chuckle, resumed sweeping the exterior for any sign of the American operators, whom he felt in his gut were coming for Bondar tonight.

He just knew it.

"Specter Two—One," he said, his wireless earbud transceiver transmitting to his colleague on the stakeout. "Any movement on the front approach?"

"Negative, One. All quiet."

He pictured the Zeta sniper, Ruben, in his roost two houses south of the intersection and across Redutna Street. The operator had the advantage of setting up in a house that was unoccupied; the family normally in residence was away on holiday in Greece.

"Odin?" he queried, calling his field operations coordinator, who was managing cyber, comms, and surveillance for the mission.

"No movement on satellite. No suspicious vehicle traffic. Nothing unusual in the comms from the American embassy. We don't have ears inside the known CIA safe house, but no unusual traffic or activity there," Odin said in clipped, precise tones.

The young, bearded Muscovite was undoubtedly seated in front of myriad open computers, streaming data from multiple sources, including city camera feeds, satellites, pirated feeds from local law enforcement, and even streaming audio from the American embassy, where a trusted source had recently placed a new listening device. Odin was one of Gavriil's favorite coordinators. Never any emotion—just streams of useful information devoid of passion or editorial comment. He sometimes wondered if the man might be half machine . . . the first of Arkady's next generation of Zeta cyborgs.

"Check," he said and frowned.

Perhaps the arrival of the American 787 a few days ago in Kiev had been a ruse or a red herring. He was certain it heralded the arrival of the American Ember team—as predicted by Arkady. And yet, still nothing. They had detected no activity around Bondar to suggest new ISR. The Americans were crafty—nearly the equal to Zetas, perhaps—so not detecting any new ISR did not mean it wasn't happening. By putting himself in the Americans' place, he had assumed that the hit would be tonight. He'd arrived at this conclusion by estimating the time *he* would need to conduct reconnaissance and counterintelligence operations before making the hit.

Unfortunately, he had made many other assumptions to get to this point. The *assumption* that the Ember team would come to Kiev, the *assumption* that Sylvie Bessonov had given up the Denys Bondar NOC to the Americans, and the *assumption* that the Americans would choose to disappear Bondar to a black site to interrogate him about the Javelin missile attack rather than executing him like the other Zetas. For a target like Bondar, someone always being watched by the paparazzi and the public, taking him at home was the logical choice.

It has to be here, Gavriil reassured himself. *Just be patient and trust your instincts.*

He raised the binoculars again, and unable to resist, zoomed in on Bondar's bedroom. The bed was empty.

"Where'd you go?" he murmured, and with a flick of his thumb, switched to thermal imagery. "Oh there you are," he said with a grin, seeing, in glorious heat map color, Bondar working the girl bent over the love seat in the corner.

He watched until he became bored, which wasn't long, and lowered his binoculars.

Although Gavriil had never met the man, he imagined the Zeta agent was as lazy, callous, and overconfident as an operative could be and still be in play. Such irony . . . at the pinnacle of his professional success, Bondar was tactically comatose. His hubris had made him vulnerable. Gavriil saw the man's future with perfect clarity. Soon, Bondar's ego would make him unmanageable. He would forget why he was here and no longer appreciate the man who'd made him. He would forget that his money was Petrov's money, that he was standing on the shoulders of giants—only giants hidden in shadow. Soon, he would ascend above his legend and demand fealty and obedience from his master, and when that day came Arkady would send someone like Gavriil to remind Bondar of his mortality. But that day was not today, and before it could happen, they all needed to survive the Americans.

Gavriil exhaled and swept the exterior of the house. Seeing nothing, he scanned the downstairs first and then the upstairs again. The lovebirds had now decoupled, with the woman sitting on the toilet in the en suite bathroom and Bondar standing fully naked just inside the open balcony doors, lighting a cigarette.

How can you not know you are being surveilled? How can you not sense death creeping nearby, my Bright Falcon brother?

Gavriil would never, ever allow the pursuit of carnal pleasure to dull his tactical edge. Bondar was an easy sniper headshot where he was standing. An amateur could take him.

Fucking pathetic. Maybe I should order Ruben to take the shot and save us all a lot of trouble.

For a moment he actually contemplated the idea, before shooing it away.

"That's my own hubris talking," he said to himself. "And besides, Arkady would kill me."

Gavriil set his binoculars down and decided to finally relieve the pressure that had been building in his bladder for hours. After slinging a black backpack onto his left shoulder, he crossed the bedroom toward the bathroom. En route, he carefully stepped over the two corpses on the floor beside the bed. When the couple was found in a few days, the double homicide would look like a robbery gone bad. He had already ransacked the house for jewelry, collectibles, and taken the man's wallet. As a finishing touch, he'd break a window downstairs on his way out once the operation here was complete.

Standing over the toilet, he retrieved a wide-mouthed plastic bottle from his backpack and relieved himself into it. The dark yellow stream—a negative side effect of keeping his hydration to a minimum to avoid the distraction of frequent urination—filled it only halfway. Without spilling a drop, he replaced the cap with a glove-covered hand and slipped the bottle back into his backpack. He glanced at himself briefly in the darkened mirror, amused by the bouffant hairnet cap on his head, designed to decrease the likelihood of leaving hair for the forensic detectives to find. It wouldn't really matter—he had used a blood sample from a known heroin addict to leave DNA evidence spattered on the floor beside the bodies. He'd executed the older couple with a cheap pistol, which would be found in the addict's flophouse apartment along with blood from the victims.

Feeling better, he returned to the chair by the window and looked out into the night.

Ember had conducted six assassinations in a row and encountered zero resistance. That sort of winning streak has consequences, even for professionals. Overconfidence creeps in. An expectation of victory dulls the reflexes, even if ever so slightly. Like Bondar, Task Force Ember was undoubtedly inebriated by its own success.

Tonight, Gavriil would use that to his advantage.

He put the binoculars back to his eyes.

They were coming . . .

And this time, Zeta was ready.

CHAPTER 16

Dnieper River
One Hundred Yards South of Havanskyi Bridge
2145 Local Time

Dempsey looked at Grimes in profile—decked out in full scuba and kitted up like a SEAL—as she stared unblinking into the night. Tough as nails she was, this woman who never ceased to amaze him. No matter the challenge, no matter the risk, she wanted in the fight. Tonight, was no exception.

Feeling his eyes on her, she turned to look at him. "What?" she said with a half-accusatory smile.

For a second, he was about to quip that all the gear she was sporting had to weigh more than she did, which made her a drowning risk, but instead he said, "You're a badass, you know that?"

"That's not what you were going to say." She narrowed her eyes at him. "Spill it."

"You're right," he said with a frat-boy grin. "With all that gear on, make sure you use your buoyancy compensator. This river's so dirty, if you sink to the bottom we'll never find your body."

"Now that's the kind of advice a girl expects to hear from you." Under her breath she added, "And everything was right in the world."

"At the drop," the boat driver said over the comms channel.

Dempsey looked up, caught the pilot's eye, and nodded as they slowed into a right turn, north and upriver of the industrial park. Dempsey gave the hand signal to his teammates to get wet, popped his regulator into his mouth, and slipped over the side and into the cold, oil-slicked water. He allowed himself to sink to a depth of perhaps fifteen feet, then stopped his descent by adjusting his buoyancy with the button on the side of the integrated buoyancy compensator. They were on regular scuba rigs tonight, as this mission didn't call for bubble suppression in the dirty, turbulent waters of the Dnieper. He waited in a static hover, peering through his night-vision-capable hybrid dive mask, as Grimes swam up beside him. A moment later, Munn and Martin joined them. They all exchanged the obligatory underwater okay signs, then Dempsey rolled onto his side, extended his right arm, and began swimming. The navigation device he wore on his left forearm displayed a magenta track line—grey in his enhanced night-vision world—for him to follow. Submerge any deeper, and he would lose the satellite signal, but the navigation device had a memory function that made an intermittent signal less taxing, and for now the little triangle representing his team tracked on course as they finned toward the target.

The infil distance was much shorter than any SEAL mission, but nevertheless, Grimes stayed true to her word and never fell behind, finning with triathlete efficiency at his side, her long gun tight against her right flank. Eventually, Dempsey stopped checking on her, confident she'd let him know if she had a problem. After fifteen minutes of exertion, a yellow X flashed on the left side of his nav device. In his peripheral vision, he saw two shadows—Munn and Martin—peeling off. The pair would vector toward a preprogrammed point just north of the cargo bridge, designated "Rays," while he and Grimes would continue on to "Dodgers." It had been Martin's idea to use baseball teams as the checkpoints for the op as a tribute to Smith. It was also the reason their mission call sign was Astros—Smith's favorite team.

God, how Shane loved baseball, Dempsey thought, remembering the man who'd been both a brother and a mentor when he'd needed it most. He pushed the image of Shane's smiling face out of his mind and finned a bit harder toward the checkpoint. As they neared shore, he gradually ascended until he was holding at five feet below the surface.

"Two and Four are Rays," came the report from Munn in his ear.

Dempsey double-clicked the transmit button on his left upper chest, acknowledging the report.

Moments later, he reached a concrete pier and finned against the current to station-keep. He turned to Grimes and pointed up, and she nodded acknowledgment. With a gloved right hand, he grasped a rusted barnacle-covered ladder rung, loosened the sling securing his assault rifle to his chest, and pulled up. The barrel of his rifle broke the water just before his head. His vision cleared a heartbeat later as his mask breached the waterline.

He scanned the cement pier above him for targets, while letting his fin-covered boots find the crunchy ladder rungs below. Beside him, Grimes surfaced and began scanning over her rifle.

"Clear," she whispered.

He signaled for her to shed her gear and covered her as she shrugged out of her scuba rig—submerging it and securing her tank and vest to the ladder underwater and out of sight. In all likelihood, they'd need to exfil quickly and would be forced to leave their gear behind. All of Ember SAD's gear was stripped of serial numbers or potentially compromising markings, to facilitate this protocol. She swapped her dive mask, with its alien-looking built-in night vision, for a helmet and NVGs, then secured the mask and her fins to the ladder, too. Then they swapped roles, with her covering him as he did the same, finally getting his footing much easier with his amphibious boots unencumbered by the oddly curved fins.

He switched his radio to hot mike. "One and Three are Dodgers," he said, while clicking his NVGs into place.

"Standby, One," Munn came back in a whisper, his voice amplified in Dempsey's earpiece. "We'll clear north and cover your infil."

"Check," Dempsey said and quietly ascended the ladder until his head was just below the edge of the pier. He exhaled, popped his head up to eye level, and scanned the grounds for shooters and cover positions before quickly ducking back down.

"One, Two—I have the backside sentry at my corner, smoking a cigarette," Munn said in his ear. "You should be clear, but we have a shot if he makes you."

"Check," he said and motioned to Grimes to climb up and crowd in beside him on the relatively wide ladder.

"Go now, One," Munn said.

Dempsey climbed off the ladder and cleared right, knowing Grimes would perform in mirror image left, their movements as fluid and in sync as a ballet. He advanced in a low tactical crouch, clearing around the corner of the rear of the first of two parked trucks. A moment later, Grimes tapped his left shoulder and he surged forward again, this time clearing between the two trucks and taking a knee behind the corner of a metal shipping container.

"Clear," she whispered, after clearing north from her covered position.

"Two, we're set."

"Roger that, One. We'll drop the sentry on your call and move around the building."

Dempsey double-clicked acknowledgment. Then, to Wang, who was in the TOC back in the Boeing, he said, "Home Plate, Astro One—ISR update." He knew that calling targets and movement made Wang feel closer to the action, and the kid was becoming pretty damn good at it.

"Astros are clear except for Astro Two's tango," Wang said. "There's a second tango at the front of the building, streetside beside the door. No additional players up moving or en route that I can see. We have a hot drone in place," he said, confirming that the armed drone was not only circling overhead, but they were cleared to employ ordnance if needed, with administrative control via Mother coordinated through CIA.

"Mother, confirm interior battle space?" Dempsey said.

"Confirmed, Home Plate," Baldwin reported from the Ember trailer in Tampa. "If you call for air, I will patch direct comms between you and the drone operator, but otherwise Mother will retain control. Total targets inside is nine, including the HVT, whose phone we are tracking. With your two sentries outside, the total threat is eleven."

"Roger, Mother, and nice work, Home Plate," Dempsey said, throwing Wang an over-the-air pat on the back. "Two, take the waterside sentry on my mark and sweep to the front. Take the other sentry and then call 'Braves' and set to breach. We'll go on your call."

"Hold, Astros," Wang interjected. "The waterside sentry is moving north, hugging the rear wall of the building. Probably going to the other corner."

"We've lost the angle for a clean kill," Munn confirmed.

Dempsey flipped up his NVGs and peered around the corner of the shipping container. He spied the sentry, who was now strolling along the back of the building. More concerned about smoking his cigarette than keeping watch, the roving guard had his compact submachine gun tucked harmlessly under his arm rather than in a combat carry.

"We'll take him, Two," Dempsey said. "Standby."

He motioned to Grimes, who joined him at his corner, and sidestepped behind her, giving her plenty of room to work.

"Not until he clears the corner, so we don't risk a through bullet hitting the building and giving us away," he said.

Grimes flashed him her best *duh* look, before shifting into a kneeling firing stance. Steadying herself against the side of the container, she raised her rifle—an MK12 Special Purpose Rifle, which, while very much similar to Dempsey's assault rifle in appearance, had a longer barrel, a much larger Leupold illuminated scope, and side-mounted AN/PEQ-2A Target Pointer/Illuminator/Aiming Light. Grimes's weapon was designed for snipers doing close-in work, whereas his variant was optimized for close-quarters combat. Grimes leaned in on the scope and made a two-click adjustment. He watched her breathing slow as her finger moved inside the trigger guard. She let out a last, long breath just as the shooter reached the corner.

Her weapon burped and the AEM5 suppressor hid the muzzle flash as she sent her round flying. Blood and gore spit out the far side of the sentry's head and the man crumpled to the ground.

"Sentry one is KIA. Go, Two," Dempsey said and automatically began a count in his head.

They would wait until Munn took the second sentry before moving toward the door. Wang had done a full electronic survey of the warehouse an hour before they launched and had identified only a single security camera at the rear, which he had hacked and put on a loop. The other concern was high-flying Russian ISR aircraft, drones, and satellites. Zeta was orders of magnitude more sophisticated an enemy than the terrorists living in caves and compounds he used to hunt.

"If they had high-flight or satellite ISR, I assume we'd be in a gun battle by now . . . you agree?" Grimes asked, cheek still pressed to her rifle and scanning through her sight.

Dempsey smiled. The team—what was left of it—sometimes seemed to think with one shared brain. Especially him, Grimes, and Munn.

"Agreed," he said. "Unless they have a standoff QRF en route we don't know about."

She looked back over her shoulder, a scolding look on her face, and shook her head.

"Just sayin'," he whispered, shrugging and smiling. "Either way we're gone with our bad guy in the next five minutes."

"Two and Four are Braves," Munn announced in his ear. "Sentry two is KIA."

"See," he said with a grin, then tapped her shoulder. "Let's go."

They moved into the open, traveling a straight line to the rear door as they sprinted in combat crouches from cover to the warehouse. Dempsey scanned left as Grimes scanned right, but they encountered no resistance. The only sound was the pounding of their feet on the pavement and the raspy sound of their breathing, both greatly amplified by their comms gear.

"Our breach is your go," Dempsey reminded Munn as they made the door.

"Check," Munn answered.

"Astros is Braves," Dempsey announced, informing all listening that both breacher teams were in position.

"Roger, Astros," Wang said softly. "Godspeed, guys."

Dempsey tipped his NVGs up and worked quickly, pressing a small wad of preformed explosive into the groove between the door and metal frame. Grimes covered him while he worked, scanning over her rifle. He pushed the detonating charge into the lump and moved right, forcing Grimes ahead of him. Holding the detonator box in his right hand, he fished a flash-bang grenade out of his kit with his left. Then, pressing his back against the wall, he turned his head toward Grimes and pushed the red button on the small black box.

The breacher charge detonated with a loud *whump* and a flash of orange that penetrated his closed eyelids. A split second later, he was moving back toward the door, breathing through the smoke and dust. He took a knee at the threshold, tossed the flash-bang through the gap, and brought his rifle up. Sporadic gunfire echoed inside the warehouse, but no rounds were striking near him. The flash-bang popped and the shooting inside stopped. He felt Grimes cross behind him, and in his peripheral vision she appeared on the other side of the door in a crouch, aiming her rifle into the smoke.

"Going dark," Wang said and, almost in synchrony with a second explosion from Munn's entry, the entire warehouse complex plunged into darkness.

Nice work, kid.

Dempsey popped up, clicked his NVGs back into place, and moved through the door, turning immediately right along the wall.

Normally, he would move left, clear the left rear corner, and surge forward with Grimes mirroring him to the right, but not this time, because Munn and Martin had entered from that side. With the other team clearing their six, Dempsey and Grimes's only charge was to sweep right toward where Skorapporsky's cot was located, as determined by Baldwin, who'd triangulated his mobile phone's static position during sleeping hours.

Only, the Ultra leader wasn't there.

With the shock of the breach and flash-bang wearing off, a half-dozen Ultra fighters were regaining their wits. Most were on the floor, scattered among upended cots and folding chairs, but a few were already on their feet pulling weapons. In the grey-green night vision, Dempsey saw the men's panicked expressions as clear as day. While he could see perfectly, the young revolutionaries couldn't make out anything in the pitch black, and they were unsure where to point their weapons. It was this moment of confusion that he and his teammates depended and capitalized on for victory in engagements like this.

Dempsey put his green dot on the closest threat, squeezed twice, and watched two black holes appear in the man's chest as he pitched backward. He shifted the dot to the next shooter and dropped him with a headshot just as he heard double taps of suppressed 5.56 fire coming from Munn and Martin to his left. Grimes added her own volley of fire as she moved right.

Three tangoes plus the HVT remaining.

It was a blacked-out turkey shoot.

"Orioles," Grimes called out behind him, indicating she had eyes on their HVT. Dempsey shuffled to join her as Munn and Martin finished off the Ukrainian paramilitary extremists who had helped assassinate the Vice President of the United States. He followed her IR targeting laser to where the toe of a large boot was sticking out past the corner of a metal cabinet. Also sticking out was the barrel of a large handgun held at chest height. Dempsey angled left, creating separation as Grimes moved in.

"Viktor Skorapporsky," Dempsey boomed. "Drop your weapon and step out with your hands over your head. Resist and you will be shot."

When the man didn't move, Grimes fired a three-round burst into the wall beside the cabinet, letting their prey know they did, indeed, see him.

"Place your weapon on the ground and come out with your hands over your head," Dempsey barked. "We know you speak English, Viktor. This is your last warning."

He watched a hand lower the pistol to the ground and then slide it across the cement floor toward them. A heartbeat later, two hands appeared and Skorapporsky stepped out from behind the cabinet, eyes wide in the dark, mouth turned up in an angry snarl.

Dempsey closed the gap quickly, forcing the big Ukrainian face-first onto the cement floor. He jammed his right knee into the back of Skorapporsky's neck and pressed the muzzle of his rifle into the man's temple. Grimes was beside him in a flash, flex-cuffing the ul-tranationalist leader's wrists behind his back. With the cuffs secure, she expertly searched the man for other weapons—tossing a large pocketknife and then a compact pistol onto the floor beside them.

"He's clean," she said, and together they pulled him roughly to his feet.

"Walk," Dempsey said, tugging the Ukrainian by his restrained right arm.

Grimes held her sights on the back of the man's head as Dempsey guided their crow toward the exit. Skorapporsky shuffled his feet, unable to see in the pitch black, and was panting from the fear and residual adrenaline dump.

"Two, One—secure anything of value and meet us at the primary in two mikes," Dempsey said. "Home Plate, Astros is Orioles. Headed to primary exfil."

"Roger, Astro One. Exfil at primary in three mikes. Still all clear, and no response detected or indicated," Wang said.

"Astros, Stingray," came a less familiar voice—the boat driver who had dropped them. "Pickup in two. Wagon Train is in position."

"Roger," Dempsey said and pulled up short of the warehouse's rear door, which hung half off its heavy metal hinge. He scanned the open pier and observed no movement, no threats. He did, however, see the wake of the approaching Boston Whaler 420. "Thirty seconds, Two," he said.

In lieu of responding, Munn joined him at the doorway with Martin in tow. The former Marine had crammed a bunch of mobile phones and two laptops into a plastic bag and was shoving it all into his backpack.

Dempsey chopped a hand forward and they exited, with Grimes taking point, Munn moving and scanning left, while Martin covered right. Dempsey herded Skorapporsky in the center of the triangular formation. When they reached the edge of the pier, Dempsey retrieved a black hood from his cargo pocket and pulled it over the Ukrainian's head. Grimes took a knee and covered their six as Munn and Martin fell in, just as the Whaler expertly docked pierside.

Dempsey leapt the five feet down to the deck of the boat and slung his rifle on his back. Standing on the gunwale, Munn passed their captive roughly down into the boat. The landing didn't go so well; Skorapporsky wailed in pain after his shin smacked the top rail of the gunwale.

"Shut up," Dempsey barked and pushed the terrorist down into the cuddy cabin with the sole of his boot. When he turned around, Grimes was standing on deck, scanning for converging threats up and down the river through her scope. Munn and Martin jumped aboard, and the pilot buried the throttle. The boat sped away, having been pierside less than ten seconds.

"Astros is Blue Jays," Dempsey reported, indicating their exfil to the boat was complete.

"Wagon Train is Yankees," their exfil SUV driver reported from where he waited at the next rally point.

"Four mikes out," the former Special Warfare Combat Crewman replied, handling the boat, comms, and mechanics of the op like only an ex-SWCC could.

"Going below to keep an eye on Viktor," Grimes said, squeezing past him.

"Roger that," he said and gave her shoulder an *attaboy* squeeze.

The satisfaction of victory spread over him like a warm embrace. It was rare for a real-world op to go off without a hitch. Even training ops usually hit some sort of snag or wrinkle, but this one had been flawless. He looked at his teammates—Grimes covering Skorapporsky, and Munn and Martin sighting over their rifles fore and aft respectively.

Oh hell yeah, he thought and ran his fingers through his hair, raking it out of his face in the wind. *Zeta may have knocked us down, but Ember will never be out of the fight . . . So long as I have this crew, I can do anything.*

CHAPTER 17

Gavriil was completing a perimeter scan of the Bondar estate with his binoculars when his earbud crackled to life.

"Specter One, Odin," said his field operations coordinator.

"One—Go."

"Burst traffic from Delta suggests an attack is underway at Boxcar."

It took a moment for the report to sink in, but when it did Gavriil's heart rate spiked and his mouth twisted into a *fuck me* grin. Delta was the radio tag for the safe house, code-named Boxcar, that Skorapporsky and Ultra had relocated to in an industrial park by the river. Odin maintained surveillance devices at the location that operated by short bursts of large data dumps; the devices defeated routine electronic sweeps by remaining dormant the vast majority of the time.

Damn . . . I should have anticipated this contingency and ordered round-the-clock surveillance of Skorapporsky.

"How old is the data dump, Odin?" Gavriil asked.

"Real time. The device was programmed to transmit only under certain sound parameters that would indicate an attack. I'm sending video uplink now."

Gavriil rose from the chair, slung his Beretta 501, and pulled a tablet from his backpack. On-screen, an alert icon flashed, indicating incoming data. He entered his six-digit code and the screen came alive with a series of static images: what looked like a four-man squad of special operators massacring the Ultra members. He paused on an image of Skorapporsky being cuffed.

"Specter Two, One—the Americans just hit the Ultra safe house and grabbed Skorapporsky. Mission abort, meet me at the vehicle."

"Check," came the reply from the Zeta sniper.

Gavriil slung the backpack onto both shoulders and moved deliberately to the door, stepping over the dead woman's legs.

"Two is clear and headed to the vehicle," said Ruben.

"Three minutes," Gavriil said.

He circled around the back of the house and stepped on the towel he had positioned beside a kitchen window. He tipped on his toes and smashed the glass inward with an elbow, grateful he had placed the blood for the police already, planning for the need for a rapid exfil.

He backed off the towel, careful not to leave any footprints, picked it up and stuffed it into his pack as he ran. He leapt a short wrought iron fence in a single, fluid movement and entered the garage through a cracked-open side door. Inside, he found Ruben already sitting in the driver's seat of the BMW 750i.

Gavriil slipped into the passenger's seat and pressed the button to raise the garage door and open the gate at the end of the driveway simultaneously.

"Take Lavrska south to E95 and we can jump onto Naberezhne Road north," he said as Ruben accelerated out of the garage and down the brick driveway. He pulled his Fort-224 assault rifle and a Fort-17 pistol from his bag, extending the folded stock on the rifle and checking the magazine and the rounds chambered in both.

"Check," his fellow agent said, a hint of annoyance in his voice at what he doubtless considered an unnecessary direction. They were both Zetas, after all.

But there is only one Prime, Gavriil thought, then couldn't help but laugh at the situation.

"What's so funny?" Ruben said with a humorless glance.

"This job is like a video game. You complete all these impossible levels, and just when you think you're going to defeat the boss monster, he does something you don't expect and fucks you."

"Are you talking about the Americans?"

"Of course. I thought they would go for Bondar, but they went after Skorapporsky instead. Good job, Ember. You got me. But the game is not finished, my friends."

"What are you talking about? They'll be gone by the time we get there," Ruben said, shaking his head.

"Maybe, maybe not. They don't know we're coming. And also, they have to get away. As soon as they exfil, they'll let their guard down. And that's when we hit them."

Ruben nodded. "Punch and counterpunch."

"That's right. Let's hit them hard," Gavriil said and pulled an encrypted satellite phone from the backpack and pressed the second number in his Favorites. The phone chirped only twice.

"Da?" the male voice answered.

"I need your help, comrade," he said in Russian.

"Where?" the mercenary answered.

"How quickly can you get half your team to the warehouse location I briefed you on and the other half to the Metro Bridge?"

"Five minutes," the man said. "What are your instructions?"

Gavriil quickly explained what he believed was happening. "Kill everyone, including Skorapporsky. If you miss the Americans, I need the other team at Metro Bridge to intercept."

"How do you know they go that way?"

"Educated guess."

"*Da*. It will be done."

Gavriil slipped the phone into his coat pocket as Ruben maneuvered smoothly onto Naberezhne Road. He pulled extra magazines from his bag and shoved them into the pockets built into the tactical cargo pants he wore. Then he pulled a quadcopter drone the size of a paperback book from his pack and powered it on.

"Odin, One," he said to his coordinator. "I want to put up a microdrone when we're on station. It's powered on, you should be able to sync."

"Understood . . . linking now."

The drone's four ducted propellers whirred individually, then pulsed collectively, causing the little drone to bobble in his hands. "Synchronization complete. Standing by for launch."

The roads were deserted, so they easily managed eighty-five kilometers en route. As they crossed the Dnieper, a boat sped past underneath the bridge. Something about it screamed for his attention, and he glanced over his shoulder but saw nothing of interest beyond that the boat was traveling faster than the posted no-wake speed limit. He refocused his attention on the potential gun battle ahead. Ruben slowed as they neared the warehouse, and Gavriil rolled down his window. He grabbed the lightweight drone with his right hand and held it out the window.

"Ready to launch drone," he said.

A heartbeat later, the quadcopter's rotors buzzed to life and it shot out of his grip skyward.

"I have good eyes," Odin reported.

Gavriil's phone chirped with a text message as Ruben navigated into the warehouse lot and parked behind a black Cadillac Escalade that Gavriil recognized as belonging to his contracted killers.

The message read: *Shooters gone, but you need to see this.*

"They're already gone," he informed Ruben, "but I want to take a look."

Ruben nodded and they both hopped out of the big Bimmer. His contracted Vory shooters had switched on the warehouse's overhead halogen lights. Even as he approached the open front door, Gavriil could see that the carnage inside was breathtaking. The four hired killers were standing in a lake of blood, a half-dozen bodies sprawled about.

"Here," the lead mercenary, Novitsky, called, waving them over.

One of Novitsky's men squatted beside a gurgling Ukrainian. "He says it was soldiers. They killed everyone but took someone named Skorapporsky."

Gavriil raised his Fort-224 and fired, blowing apart the head of the wounded Ultra fighter and spattering blood onto the gangster's shirt and pants. The tattooed thug leapt to his feet and pulled his pistol.

"What the fuck, asshole?" the man seethed in Russian, but stopped raising his weapon when his eyes focused on the muzzle of Gavriil's Fort pointing at his chest.

"Novitsky, is your second team in position south of the Metro Bridge?"

"Yes, they called in position a few seconds ago. All clear."

The Americans were on that boat, he suddenly realized, and a fresh adrenaline dump energized him. *We still have time!*

"Odin, One—do you have eyes on the complex?" Gavriil said into his mike.

"Da," came the reply.

"If you zoom out, do you see a boat heading upriver, north of the bridge?"

"Hold . . . *da*, I have it," Odin reported. "It's docking. I count five—no, make that six—persons on the boat. And there are two black Chevrolet SUVs waiting."

"Check," Gavriil said and turned to Novitsky. "We can still catch them. Send your men north. Look for a convoy of two black Chevrolet SUVs. Kill them all—whatever it takes. Use heavy firepower, and I will clean up any political mess."

Novitsky didn't move. "How much?"

"Five million Euros in your account by morning."

"Ten," the gangster-for-hire said.

"Fine, but tell them to hurry. You guys follow us."

"It will be done," Novitsky said and made the call.

And with that, Gavriil sprinted out of the warehouse, Ruben beside him and the squad of hired guns in tow.

CHAPTER 18

Dempsey felt his tension begin to melt away as they sped past the city ferry pier and he spotted their exfil SUVs parked along the river. But years of operating as a Tier One SEAL had taught him to never, ever fully relax until he was back home in CONUS drinking a beer and turning steaks on the grill. Hell, based on those criteria, since he'd joined Ember that opportunity had come along . . . well, never.

"Pierside in twenty seconds," he called to his three teammates, who'd all moved below for a quick change out of their tactical gear and into civilian clothes. After the proof-of-concept testing he'd done with the new gel-pack body armor in Mudchute Park, they were all wearing the high-tech vests pretty much twenty-four seven.

Dempsey checked the Sig P320 in his small-of-the-back holster and tucked his MCX Rattler under his long brown coat. He rolled up onto the balls of his feet against the slowing of the boat in the midnight water and did a quick scan up- and downriver. Satisfied, he pulled a ball cap onto his head as the boat driver parked the Whaler expertly just inches beside the floating dock.

Dempsey jumped over the gunwale and onto the dock and watched as Munn and Martin dragged the prisoner out of the cuddy cabin, hands under his armpits, then hoisted him up onto the dock. Dempsey led them at a double-time pace up the aluminum walkway from the dock to the cement pier, while Grimes took up the rear.

"Home Plate, Wagon Train—we have Astros," came a new voice in his ear as the two SUVs roared to life.

Dempsey heard the Boston Whaler pulling away behind him as he hopped into the rear of the first SUV, sliding all the way across to make room for Grimes. He turned and looked over his shoulder in time to see Munn shove Skorapporsky roughly into the rear of the second SUV as Martin got in the other side. Three seconds later, their caravan of two was on the move.

"Well done, guys. Thanks for the lift," Dempsey said to the driver.

The man behind the wheel, a neatly bearded twenty-something—dressed in a flannel shirt that to Dempsey screamed former operator rather than organic CIA—grinned at him in the rearview mirror. "Pleasure, bro. Looks like a successful hunting trip. You bag what you were looking for?"

"We'll see," Dempsey said, unable to contain his own smile.

The truth was, this was the first operation in months that might yield intelligence about Zeta operatives *not* provided by Bessonov. Hopefully, Skorapporsky was worth it.

He glanced over at Grimes, who pulled off her cap and shook out her auburn locks, still damp and wavy from their swim. She smiled back at him.

"Feel it?" he asked.

"Feel what?" she said.

His smile broadened. "The momentum."

She chuckled but nodded. "Yeah. So long as our crow"—she

glanced at the two CIA men in the front seat, not wanting to breach security—"really was working with you-know-who."

"I know it was him," Dempsey said with conviction. "This attack had his fingerprints all over it."

The driver made eye contact in the rearview but was too seasoned to ask the obvious question. The "attack" could only mean one thing less than a week after the assassination of the Vice President of the United States. Dempsey gave a slight nod to his fellow operator, then turned back to Grimes.

"If we can get this guy to talk, we're one step closer to our real objective."

"Hope so," she said. "But either way, that asshole in the truck behind us and his dead friends pulled the trigger, so the way I see it, the mission is a success."

"Truth," he said, but did he really feel that way?

As a SEAL, he could have convinced himself that the mastermind behind the Independence Square assassination wasn't his concern. Ember was the President's direct-action weapon of choice. They were America's lethal protector. Ultra was a clear and present danger that needed to be dealt with, so the President had sent them. Yet . . .

Even without proof, I know the Russians were behind this.

Which meant as far as Dempsey was concerned, the priorities needed to shift and shift immediately. Even if it meant traveling undercover into the heart of Moscow to do it, Arkady Zhukov needed to die. And while he was there, he'd take out President Petrov, too.

A little American quid pro quo . . .

But as he tried to puzzle out what the pieces of *that* operation would look like, Dempsey felt himself slip a few more feet down the blood-slicked slope he was forever trying to climb up—falling away from gleaming patriotic warrior toward the kind of black ops killer that slunk and paced in the shadows at the bottom. For two decades he had maintained a professional code of conduct as a Tier One SEAL—to fight his nation's enemies with extreme prejudice but without personal malice. *That* was the difference between a soldier and a killer. He'd always understood that, but then he'd felt the world tilt when terrorists ambushed and murdered his Tier One unit in Yemen. He'd taken his first short slide down the slope when he joined Ember for the sole purpose of exacting vengeance. And he'd done it; he'd killed them all . . . and afterward, he'd clawed his way back up the mountain. He'd embraced a new family and a new charter at Ember, and in doing so had regained his sense of purpose as a warrior. But then Arkady's Zetas had attacked Ember's headquarters and murdered half of his *new* family . . . and suddenly he found himself slipping again.

He grabbed the armrest to steady himself.

Feeling eyes on him, he looked over at Grimes.

Like they so often did, her baby blues bore into him—piercing his armor and reading his thoughts. But that was okay because she understood. Her SEAL brother had died in Yemen with the rest of Dempsey's team. And Smith, Adamo, and Latif had been her replacement family as well.

Are you sliding too? he asked her with his eyes.

"Don't worry," she said, her expression so hard and beautiful. "We'll get him, John . . . and we'll make him pay."

He opened his mouth to say something, but bouncing lights in his peripheral vision drew his attention out the windshield. Two black SUVs jumping the raised median between the north and southbound lanes on an intercept course.

"Oh, shit," the driver said and cut the wheel to the left. Their SUV swerved hard and momentarily tipped up on two wheels before the driver expertly corrected and dropped the vehicle back on the pavement. "Brace for impact!"

A heartbeat later, one of the converging SUVs slammed into their rear quarter panel and sent them spinning in a clockwise rotation. The impact slammed Dempsey into the passenger door and his head bounced off the bulletproof side window. His vision filled with stars, but he shook them clear and reached for his MCX assault rifle. He quickly unsnapped it from the sling and pulled it free of his coat.

Two trucks jumping the median? This is no traffic accident, it's an assault.

The universe nodded its agreement when a hail of gunfire from the two attacking Cadillac Escalades lit a shower of sparks across the hood and raised dozens of stars in the ballistic glass windshield. Thank God the doors were also up-armored, capable of keeping Dempsey and the others safe from up to fifty-caliber rounds. The same could not be said for the engine block and tires, however, and the barrage of fire they were taking could easily render them immobile.

And if those assholes have something more powerful, like RPGs, then we're really screwed.

"Out your side," Dempsey hollered at Grimes, but she had already lowered a shoulder and slammed it into the door on her side.

"Mother, Home Plate—Astros is in enemy contact. We need that QRF!" Dempsey heard Wang say over the comms channel.

"Roger that," Baldwin replied. "I've already made the call."

That's nice and all, but this thing's gonna be over long before those bros show up, Dempsey thought as he crabbed in a tactical crouch over the pavement and toward the rear of the SUV. While he set up at the rear bumper, Grimes joined the driver in cover behind the open driver's side door. Dempsey sighted around the rear of their smashed-up SUV and found a target—a knee sticking out past the front bumper of the stalled Cadillac that had just hit them. He aimed and fired, turning the enemy shooter's knee into pulp. The gunman screamed and fell to the ground, dropping his weapon and clutching his ruined leg. Dempsey put a second bullet in the shooter's head, silencing him permanently.

"Two, One—you good?" Dempsey said, talking to Munn on a hot mike.

"Setting up," Munn grunted.

Dempsey couldn't see Munn or Martin because their vehicle had spun out into the median and Dempsey's line of sight was blocked by his own SUV. When he heard the sound of 5.56 bursts from that direction, however, he knew Munn and Martin were in the fight.

He glanced over his shoulder at Grimes and saw her calmly setting up the MK12 SPR she had somehow already managed to pull from her duffle. She and their driver had moved forward, and while he provided covering fire over the hood, she snapped out her tripod. Meanwhile, the CIA shooter who'd been riding in the front passenger position had climbed across the seats and was in the fight, too. Standing on the driver's side doorsill to give him height to fire over the roof, the operator let out two bursts from his short Sig MPX submachine gun, while releasing an expletive-laden barrage to match.

Dempsey was just about to call for air, when Baldwin's voice crackled in his ear. "Astro One, Home Plate—I am linking the drone pilot into comms. You have JTAC control of the asset, in orbit overhead now."

A big grin spread over Dempsey's face as he dropped another heavily tattooed shooter.

"Predator, this is Astro One—be advised, we are all driving

154

lookalike black SUVs. Astros are the two vehicles on the north side of the firefight, including the one in the median. Shitheads are to the south. I repeat, shitheads are to the south."

"Astro One, Predator—copy all. I have a good visual," the drone pilot said with a hint of bemusement.

"RPG!" Munn yelled in his earbud.

Dempsey glanced around the bumper and saw the unmistakable cylindrical RPG launcher propped up on an enemy combatant's shoulder. The shooter was sighting over the hood of the second Escalade. A split second before he pulled the trigger, his head exploded from one of Grimes's precision sniper rounds, causing him to pull upward as he fired. The rocket-propelled grenade screamed over Munn's SUV and out over the river, where it detonated on the opposite bank.

"Predator, One—let's drop some ordnance on these assholes."

"Astro, be advised you are—"

"Yes, yes we know. Danger close," Dempsey said, cutting him off. "You're cleared hot. Shoot now!"

"Moving . . . need covering fire . . ."

Martin's call brought all of them up and together they poured fire onto the two vehicles, but Dempsey had no clear targets.

"Missile away, Astros," came the calm and very young-sounding voice in his ear. "Get small, you guys."

"Take cover," Dempsey hollered and dropped to the ground just as he saw an orange streak of light coming from the heavens above.

The missile impacted the closer of the two enemy SUVs and the vehicle disappeared in a ball of fire. A wave of intense heat washed over him, and he felt the hairs on the back of his neck curling from the heat as he covered his head with his arms. A split second later, he heard chunks of debris raining down—peppering the pavement and the roof of their Suburban.

"Astros, Predator—I hold two vehicles inbound from the north closing on your position at high speed. I can't take that shot, so don't ask 'cause I don't know who they are. But be advised they will be on you in less than a minute."

"Copy," Dempsey said. "Put a Hellfire in the other SUV. We'll reposition; you're cleared hot."

"Roger—cleared hot," the drone pilot said. "I'm coming about."

"Our vehicle is fucked," Munn said, sounding more annoyed than stressed. "One, what's your status?"

Dempsey looked at the driver, who glanced under the chassis to make sure the opposite side tires were intact, then gave him a hesitant thumbs-up.

"Two, bring the crow to us after the next hit and we'll load up and get the hell out of here. Come from the south side—it sounds like we have more guests on their way to the party."

A bullet tore a chunk of pavement away beside his knee—one of the remaining enemy shooters apparently firing from under their own remaining vehicle.

"Oh, you asshole," Dempsey said, and popped up and repositioned to peer around the corner just as a second orange streak ripped through the night sky. He pulled back and made himself small behind the rear wheel as the missile obliterated the enemy Caddy.

Oh shit, that kid is good, wherever the hell he is.

Another wave of heat poured over him, but he kept his eyes open, searching for the inbound threat on Naberezhne Road. He saw the lights of two vehicles screaming toward them. He assumed this was an enemy QRF, but he couldn't light them up without first confirming hostile intent. Could be police, could be civilians.

"So much for our zero-footprint operation, bro," Munn growled in his ear, echoing Dempsey's thoughts.

"Move now, Two," he called. "South side of the vehicle. We may have incoming."

Dempsey repositioned, clearing for Munn and Martin any potential tangoes who might have survived the Hellfire strikes. As expected, he saw nothing but bodies—and body parts—strewn around the burning hulks of the two Cadillac Escalades.

"That's it for my load, Astros," the drone pilot said. "Loitering for ISR, but I'm unarmed now."

Damn, Dempsey thought, wishing they'd had a tricked-out Reaper instead of the Predator with its load-limited two Hellfire missiles.

He stood at the rear of the SUV, sighting north at the approaching headlights, as the CIA driver slid into the driver seat. Grimes took up a position on the south side of the hood, again setting up her sniper rifle and pressing her cheek into the stock as she took aim.

"Coming to you," Munn said, starting their sprint toward Dempsey's SUV.

Dempsey watched north, and as he did the rear vehicle turned and stopped in the middle of the southbound lanes, about a hundred and fifty yards away. He could see it was a long black sedan now that its headlights weren't in his eyes.

Definitely not police.

A moment later he saw a subtle suppressed muzzle flash from the sedan at the same time as Grimes shouted, "Sniper!"

"Fuck. Need covering fire now!" Munn yelled. He and Martin were crossing no-man's-land between the two Suburbans, dragging the still-hooded Skorapporsky with them.

Dempsey fired a series of three-round bursts at the distant sedan, while ordering Grimes to stop the incoming SUV, which was still rapidly closing range.

A half second later, he heard two burps from her rifle. The inbound vehicle jerked hard left, jumped the median, and crashed into the seawall on the other side of the road.

Long-Gun Lizzie is on tonight, he thought as he saw another muzzle flash from the sedan.

An inbound enemy sniper round slammed into the Suburban's front passenger-side window at head level, leaving a starburst pattern but failing to punch through.

"Damn, he's good," their driver said. "Let's get the fuck out of here."

Munn and Martin arrived in lockstep, dragging Skorapporsky into cover behind the Suburban. The man's arms were still cuffed behind his back, but his legs were jelly and his hooded head bounced lifelessly against his chest.

Martin yanked the hood off. Skorapporsky was missing half his head.

"Damn," Dempsey said. "Leave him."

Munn dropped the corpse onto the pavement, and everyone piled into the vehicle and slammed the doors shut.

"Where to?" the driver asked, looking over his shoulder at Dempsey.

Dempsey looked out the window and saw the target sedan was already bugging out—a pair of red taillights pulling away. "Think you can catch those motherfuckers?" he asked.

"I can try," the driver said with a grin and put the transmission into gear.

"Negative, Astros," came Baldwin's voice on the line, shutting that idea down. "You have law enforcement inbound. Mission terminated, return to Home Plate immediately."

"Copy," Dempsey acknowledged through gritted teeth, then said, "Predator, Astros One—please tell me you have eyes on our runaway tangoes."

"Affirmative, Astros, tracking now. But be advised your tangoes appear to be heading toward city center."

Dempsey looked at Munn, the question plain on his face: *Should we do it anyway?*

Munn gave a heavy exhale, then shook his head. "It ain't worth it, dude. We can't afford to sit in jail, even if it's only overnight. Remember what happened in Riga? And we didn't kill anybody on that op."

Dempsey responded with a grudging nod, then said, "Airport."

"Roger that," the driver said, and punched the accelerator.

"I might have something for you, Astro One," Wang said in his ear.

"Yeah, what's that, Home Plate?" A sliver of hope crept into Dempsey's voice.

"Image capture from the Predator video feed—I've got a pretty clear image of the passenger in that sedan. I'm going to run it through facial rec . . . Boo-yah," Wang said, using one of his signature lines for the first time in months. "Oh, and for what it's worth: the dude looks Russian."

"Send it to me," Dempsey said, pulling his small, waterproof tablet computer from his cargo pants pocket.

"Already done," Wang replied.

Dempsey opened the file and stared at the image of a clean-shaven Caucasian male in the passenger seat—looking through the windshield, hands expertly clutching what looked to Dempsey like a Fort assault rifle. The man in the image looked unperturbed, his face a mask of concentration and confidence. But the eyes—the eyes burned with the fire of a killer.

Dempsey stared at the image, searing it into memory.

He knew the look well.

This man was a Zeta.

And he'd bet his left thumb that the driver who'd been sniping them was a Zeta, too. All the other shitheads they'd killed had just been cannon fodder—hired collateral to slow them down until the pros arrived.

Damn, he thought with a sigh. *We were so close . . . so fucking close.*

CHAPTER 19

Wane Pub

Kiev, Ukraine

September 30

0132 Local Time

After two hours, three changes of clothing, four vehicle switches, and a long painful crawl back and forth across Kiev, Gavriil finally arrived at his destination on a bicycle. Only once he'd stashed the bike in the alley behind a coffee bar just a stone's throw from the Chinese embassy and entered the rear entrance of the basement pub did he allow bone-weary exhaustion to settle in on him.

He pounded on the heavy door of one of several GRU drop sites run by locals friendly to the Russian presence—this one belonged to a man who, more importantly, was a conduit to a safe room for the night.

"Go around to the front, you drunk," an irritated voice commanded.

"I'm Danilo's cousin," he answered.

He heard two loud clicks as deadbolts were undone, and the door opened a crack. Gavriil pushed it open the rest of the way, entered a small mud room, and stomped his feet on the mat.

"How can I help you?" The old man glanced behind Gavriil, and seeing no one else at the door, brought his right hand from behind his back where it clutched an antiquated short-barrel shotgun. Then the man gave him a shrug and a stained-tooth smile, shut the door, and returned the weapon to a hook beside it. "Can't be too careful these days. It is good to see you—it's been far too long," he said. "What do you need?"

Gavriil smiled and shook the old man's worn hand. "You are most generous. Just some food to go, please," he said, "as I'm afraid I still have some work to do."

"Understood," the man said. "I will prepare you some varenyky to take along. It's delicious tonight—mushrooms and venison."

"Sounds perfect, thank you. If it's okay, though, I will wait here. It sounds as if you still have a crowd."

"Of course," the old man gave a bow of sorts, the ties of his apron disappearing beneath his grease-stained shirt and generous pannus for a moment. "I'll be quick."

Gavriil thanked him and clasped his hands behind his back. A moment later, the old man returned with a half-full bottle of vodka.

"We've poured from it, but it's not old."

"Thank you, comrade," Gavriil said, then took a short pull from the bottle, swallowing very little so as not to dull his edge. "Ah . . . a wonderful end to a long day."

The man seemed pleased, held up a finger, then dashed back into the kitchen, returning quickly with what looked to be a Styrofoam box in a brown plastic bag, the handles tied together.

"I put some sausage and cheese in, as well as some fresh bread. Enjoy."

Gavriil nodded, placed the bag and bottle into the weathered leather satchel over his shoulder, then slipped outside and down a short, brick-walled hallway. A few paces later he passed through another heavy door that he heard lock behind him. The passage was dimly lit by exposed bulbs about every ten feet, but it ended at another door three bulbs later. He pressed down on the handle, opened it slowly, and entered a large storage closet behind the three conference rooms on the first floor of the Natsionalny Hotel. Inside, he shoved his long jacket and black cap deep into a trash bin, pulled out and donned a grey knee-length overcoat and business-man's thin Karakul-style cap, then rolled his neck and closed his eyes a moment—becoming this new legend for his short stroll through the lobby. He dropped his brown leather satchel into a larger black leather shoulder case and slipped from the closet into the empty hallway between the conference rooms.

He passed through the gaudy lobby, nodding to the concierge, who looked disinterested but gave a courteous smile, and entered the center elevator. Two minutes later he used the key card in the shoulder case to enter the apartment style suite on the fifth floor.

Gavriil set his bag on the table, shrugged out of the overcoat, then arched his back, feeling the relief of the double pop between his shoulder blades. The smell of fresh-baked dough stuffed with savory meat filled the room as he opened his bag, and only then did he realize the gnawing hunger that filled his belly. He opened the Styrofoam container and popped one of the still hot pierogies into his mouth and was rewarded with a burst of juicy meat and spice. He rolled his neck again, this time received the satisfaction of another pop, then crossed to the closet. Opening the closet safe with the memorized four-digit code, he pulled an envelope out, which he tucked under his arm before reaching for the lockbox inside. He took both to the table and sat down, then shook the satellite phone from the envelope. As he swallowed another pierogi in one bite, he pressed "*1" on the speed dial and held the phone between his shoulder and cheek while placing his thumb on the biometric sensor of his steel lockbox.

"It seems you are well," Arkady answered the call, his mood impossible to read.

"I am intact, but the operation did not go as planned."

"I am aware."

Somehow you are always aware. Somehow you always know everything.

When Gavriil said nothing, Arkady added, "There will be other chances. Are you compromised?"

"I don't believe so, but we live in a world with cameras in outer space, so who ever knows?" He set aside the stack of envelopes thick with cash in a variety of currencies, and focused instead on the passports and other identification cards in the box. When he knew what his boss wished his next step to be, he would know which of his various legends to become.

"Indeed," was all that Arkady said.

"My sniper and coordinator—have they checked in?"

"Yes."

"Then all should be well. We eliminated Skorapporsky, so there will be no intelligence harvested from him. And since the Americans killed almost everyone else from Ultra, it seems they've erased our trail quite efficiently all by themselves."

"That's convenient."

"We are tracking them, I hope?" Gavriil said as he chewed. He was so hungry, he couldn't help himself. "Do you want me to plan a counterstrike?"

"I'm afraid that will have to wait. We have other problems," Arkady said. "Turn on your television."

Gavriil set the phone on the table and crossed to the kitchen bar to pick up the remote control. He turned on the TV and scrolled through the channels, shocked to see scenes of Mariupol in flames. He flipped to another channel, this one a local station reporting that Russian troops and armor were being deployed to southeastern Ukraine. He flipped to the BBC and the headline read, "US Prepares to Counter Russian Aggression in Ukraine."

"What the hell is going on?" Gavriil said with both disgust and disbelief.

Arkady chuckled, apparently pleased by his angst. "While you were working, our brilliant leader decided now is the time to invade Ukraine."

"For what reason?"

"To reclaim Novorossiya, of course, and he's using the death of Prime Minister Vavilov as the excuse."

"Oh shit," Gavriil said through a breath. Then a terrible thought occurred to him. "Did you know Vavilov would be in Independence Square when you gave me the tasking?"

"The tasking, no," Arkady said without hesitation. "The green light, yes."

"Did Petrov?"

"Of course. It was his idea to send Vavilov in the first place."

"I thought it was an oversight. A communication failure." Feeling suddenly nauseated, Gavriil set down a half-eaten pierogi in the food container. "That's what I told myself."

"I know, that's what we do. Pull the trigger, don't ask why, and move on."

"Then why are we discussing this now?"

"Because I need to be sure you're both willing and capable of executing your next mission. I've sent you a file. Read it . . . I'll wait."

Gavriil opened his computer, logged into his anonymous email account, and saw a draft message, unsent and waiting in a folder. He clicked on it and read the mission objective and details. When he was finished, he stared at the screen with disbelief. Since becoming a Zeta, he had done many terrible, terrible things, but this . . . this was something else entirely.

"These orders appear to contradict themselves," he said carefully.

"*Da,*" Arkady said.

Perhaps this was a test? The old fox did such things from time to time to assess loyalty . . . to measure resolve and test an operator's willingness to follow orders.

"You seem uncertain, my son," the spymaster said when Gavriil didn't answer. "You are Zeta Prime now—more than just a foot soldier. I have shown you my willingness to embrace your thoughts and advice, so if you have something to say or a concern you wish to voice . . ."

Was this yet another test? The only thing more legendary than Arkady's cunning was his disdain for incompetence. Gavriil again chose his words carefully. "Executing these orders will kill dozens, if not hundreds, of my own countrymen."

"Mmm-hmm."

"And it will give Petrov justification to escalate and retaliate, perhaps even launch a full-scale invasion of Ukraine."

"That is correct."

Gavriil nodded. "So that is the intent . . . but if that's his plan, then why leave evidence incriminating Russia? I have never done this before on a false flag—" He stopped midsentence, everything suddenly clear. The missile launch was Petrov's operation; the rest of the design came from Arkady. "Ahhh . . . I understand."

"Do you? Do you really?" Arkady said, his voice taking on an unusual timbre.

"I am to take the fall?"

"You and me both. Spetsgruppa Zeta will not survive the betrayal. Petrov is too clever and will understand that such incompetence could only be born of malign intent."

"So, you would see him fall?"

"I will see the devil I have created undone . . . if it's the last thing I do."

Gavriil desperately wished that he could see Arkady's face, though he knew it would provide little clue to whether he was being played by the chess master. He'd never learned to read the man— not really. Was he to be Arkady's pawn, or his knight? He considered what he knew of Petrov, and then considered that information which he was not privy to. For certain, Petrov had a god complex, but he had also—almost singlehandedly—lifted Russia from the ashes. Surely he was . . .

Suddenly, the script flipped in his mind.

"It is naïve to think that if we do this, the Americans and their allies will simply allow Russia to conquer Ukraine and establish sovereignty," Gavriil said.

"You are correct. The Americans are already repositioning assets as we speak. I predict they will deploy Marines to Odessa. Warner will draw the line at Mariupol. The juggernaut of war will be unstoppable. Once the Americans suffer losses, NATO will engage and war will spread across Eastern Europe. Tens of thousands will die, maybe hundreds of thousands, including civilians."

"Then what in God's name is the goal? To start World War Three?"

"The goal, my son, is that cool heads will prevail. That the commanders on the ground, and those giving counsel in Moscow and Washington, DC, do not let it come to that. And in the aftermath of a world war that *almost* was, regime change will finally be possible."

"Do you really want Russia to fall?"

"No," Arkady said with an incredulous laugh. "What I want—what I have always wanted—is for Russia to regain her former glory. That is why I chose Petrov, molded him, and pulled all the levers at my disposal to ensure his rise to power. But now, it has become painfully apparent that he is no longer the right man for the job. He is willing to risk everything he has accomplished—for what? For this dream of reclaiming a Novorossiya that never truly was in the first place . . . It's nothing short of madness."

"What we are talking about is treason."

"No. What we are talking about is patriotism, Gavriil. Sometimes patriots must do the difficult things, must make impossible decisions, for the good of the nation. Russia deserves better than Vladimir Petrov. If we don't intervene, this war will leave Russia in economic ruin and destroy our standing on the world stage. Two decades of progress and growth will be undone. We must turn the ship before it runs aground."

"How can you be so certain it will work?"

"I'm not," Arkady said and laughed again. "The only thing I am ever certain of is uncertainty. But that has never stopped me from trying, and it will not stop me now . . . So, are you with me? Is this a mission you can execute, my son?"

Gavriil hesitated, but only a moment. Was saying no really even an option? He supposed not. The smartest man he'd ever met had made a decision and made it in the interest of Mother Russia. "You can count on me."

"I know I can," Arkady said, but then added, "Ember will undoubtedly try to stop us. We cannot let that happen."

"I understand," he said, powering down his computer.

You outplayed me last time, my American friends, but not this time.

Not this time.

CHAPTER 20

Mariupol Maritime Logistics (MML)
Covert CIA Ukrainian Operations Station
Mariupol, Ukraine
0212 Local Time

Jonah Knight cursed as he tried and failed to correctly enter the combination using the dial on the safe in his office for the fourth time. His fingers were shaking from the adrenaline. And the fear. Probably more fear than adrenaline, although the former stimulated the latter. Or was it the other way around? Regardless, his sympathetic nervous system was to blame for the hormonal cascade causing him to—

Shut up, he chastised himself. Why his brain did shit like this during times of stress, he would never understand. *Mom was right . . . I should have been a doctor.*

"Jonah, what do you want me to do with this stuff?" a nervous female voice asked from the doorway.

He glanced over his shoulder to find Marci Miller holding a cardboard box against her chest.

"I'm not a mind reader, Marci," he said. "Tell me what *this stuff* is."

"All the Kuznetsov transcripts," she said, referring to the rising political activist and regional troublemaker Maksim Kuznetsov. Marci had painstakingly transcribed and translated hundreds of hours of recorded conversations between Kuznetsov and numerous Russians during the months leading up to the recently signed treaty, conversations confirming what Jonah had long suspected . . . Kuznetsov worked for the GRU.

"That's just the print copies you have there?" he asked.

"Yeah."

"Are you positive everything is on the UMBRA dumpster?"

The "UMBRA dumpster" was what he and everyone in the office had taken to calling the CIA's confidential cloud server. Jonah had mixed feelings on the matter. On the one hand, putting shit on the cloud made things *soooo* much easier than having to worry about managing the integrity of local data servers and computers. On the other hand, was it really the best idea to put Amazon Web Services in charge of safeguarding the nation's most sensitive and confidential intelligence?

"I haven't checked today," she said. "But last time I looked it was all there."

"Then burn it."

"Okay," she said, then, "Do you want me to . . . ?"

"Yes, please," he said, waving her over. "You know how bad I suck at these stupid fucking things."

"It's fine," she said, setting the cardboard box down on his desk and kneeling beside the safe. "What's the combo again?"

This was the little game they played every time, with her pretending she couldn't remember the combination and him reciting it slowly like he believed her. "Thirty-seven, two, twenty-nine . . . Why I have to use this old piece of shit instead of a biometric safe—"

An explosion somewhere outside shook the windows, cutting him off and making them both flinch.

"What the hell was that?" she said, glancing up at him.

"It's starting," he said, as a car alarm outside began to wail, undoubtedly triggered by the shockwave from the blast. He'd always known this day would probably come, but now that it was here, he wasn't ready for it. Photos of Russia's little green men—so called for the lack of insignia on their green uniforms—on the streets of Mariupol had started appearing on social media this morning. The riots, led by Russian GRU agents pretending to be Ukrainian civilians—undoubtedly spearheaded by Maksim Kuznetsov—had started by late afternoon. By nightfall, Mariupol was burning.

Marci turned her attention back to the safe, and with steady fingers, finished dialing the combination and jerked the lever to open the door.

"There you go," she said and got to her feet.

"Thanks."

"No problem." She flashed him a brave smile, but her eyes told a different story.

"It's going to be okay, Marci," he said. "We're going to close up shop and get out of here without a hitch . . . I promise."

She met his gaze, nodded once, and jogged off.

God, I'm going to miss tapping that, he thought as he watched her disappear around the corner. Assuming they both survived this, one thing was certain: Mariupol Maritime Logistics would soon cease to exist and he and Marci would both be reassigned.

Setting up this outpost operation had been Jonah's idea—an

idea born of frustration because of the amount of surveillance and scrutiny all the players in Kiev were under. The CIA liked to piggyback its operations on the State Department's diplomatic missions. As such, the vast majority of CIA stations were located either in or in close proximity to a US embassy. This made sense for many reasons. First, modern embassies were hardened structures, built with physical and cyber security in mind. They had a stout security presence, staffed by the Marine Corps Embassy Security Group and duly equipped to rebuff a wide range of potential threats. The other advantage to working out of the embassy was the close proximity and access to the actual diplomatic staff, including the US Ambassador—a billet with significant clout and political sway.

But in Jonah's opinion, the embassy in Kiev was too far away from the eastern front to be of any value. To truly understand what was going on in Crimea and Donetsk, the CIA needed to have officers closer to the action. Mariupol, he'd argued, was at the epicenter when it came to Petrov's aspirations in Ukraine. As the largest Ukrainian seaport on the Sea of Azov—and only thirty miles west of the Russian border—Mariupol was strategically significant in any annexation scenario. Popular wisdom held that if Mariupol absconded to Russia, then all of southeastern Ukraine would follow, forcing Kiev to concede its eastern coastline, and thus the entire Sea of Azov, to Moscow.

After convincing the station chief in Kiev to let him set up his own shop, Jonah and his team had been busy recruiting local assets. His focus had been threefold: one, assess and report Ukrainian separatist activities; two, identify Russian GRU agents and assets operating in southern Ukraine; and three, monitor potentially compromised public officials in Mariupol and Odessa based on their interactions, or lack thereof, with GRU-connected persons.

The results had been worse than he'd expected. The GRU had deeply penetrated the local government ranks.

Jonah knelt in front of the safe and started emptying its contents. Everything went into his backpack except for the Glock 23, which he slipped into the waistband of his trousers. He zipped the main compartment closed, then turned his attention to the open notebook computer on his desk. He checked his secure email account for any updates or instructions from Kiev. Finding nothing new since the last time he'd checked, he opened the self-destruct protocol application from his desktop. After logging in, he authenticated with his sixteen-digit passcode and pressed "Enter." A pop-up window appeared:

ARE YOU SURE YOU WANT TO ERASE ALL DATA?
THIS ACTION CANNOT BE REVERSED.

He clicked the "Yes" button. The computer's processors fired up and the cooling fan whirred as the machine went about the business of rendering itself into a brick. With that done, he looked around his office. For all intents and purposes, it looked like it was supposed to—the unassuming office of a small local logistics company. With a heavy sigh, he slung the backpack over his right shoulder and headed out to address his team. He had five organic CIA—three officers from clandestine services and two analysts—as well as two Ground Branch shooters who provided security. Seven souls whose lives he was responsible for, and the weight of that realization hit him for the first time.

I will not let this be my Benghazi, he told himself as he made his way to the back room where his team was shredding and incinerating documents. Despite having jury-rigged the incinerator exhaust duct into the cold air return, the atmosphere in the room was heavy with smoke. A large-screen television, sound muted, streamed live news from the streets of Mariupol. As soon as he entered the room, the frenetic activity stopped and everyone looked at him with expectant eyes.

"Where are we?" Jonah asked, his gaze going to Nathan, his unofficial second-in-command.

"All the computers are wiped, or in process, except for the one handling the external security camera feeds. We swept and sterilized the offices, and document incineration is well underway, as you can see."

"How long until it's done?"

"Twenty minutes."

"All right, good," he said, then let out a heavy exhale. "Look, everybody, here's the deal. When we signed on for this gig, we all knew this could happen and, well, it's happening. Troop carriers were spotted on the M14 rolling into town this morning, and there's chatter on Twitter and VKontakte documenting the progress of Russian armor rolling south on the H-20. Last tweet I saw had a nine-MBT convoy at Volnovakha, which means that it could be here within the hour. This is the exact Russian pincer move we've feared. Mariupol will fall; it's only a matter of time."

"Then we need to get the hell outta Dodge, Jonah," Nathan said.

"We're going to exfil, but we're not going to try to do it alone. The station chief is working on a plan to get us out. In the meantime, we shelter here in place."

"By the time the bureaucrats come up with a *plan*, it'll be too late. Russian tanks are en route. We need to go right fucking now, man."

"Go where, Nathan?" Jonah said, his voice as hard as granite. "We can't go east, because that's Russia. We can't go north, because that's where the tanks are rolling. We can't go south, because the Russians have just declared the entire Sea of Azov Russian territorial waters. So, where do you want to go?"

"Fucking west, of course!"

"And you don't think the Russian Army stationed in Crimea is going to drive the hundred kilometers north to block the bridges in Kherson?" he fired back. "Of course they are. They will set up multiple roadblocks on the M14 and we'd have to talk our way through all of them."

"As opposed to what, shooting our way out later? No thank you, I'll take my chances with diplomacy and tradecraft any day. Our NOC is solid. We've never had any indication that Russian intelligence is onto us," Nathan argued.

"We think that's true, we hope it's true, but it's not something I'm willing to gamble all of your lives on. I've been assured help is on the way. We just need to hang tight until then. So, let's finish up with the incinerator, get it cooled down and hidden, and then we can open the windows and get back to work looking like a logistics company." When nobody said anything, he scanned their faces and said, "Okay?"

"Okay," came several replies in unison, and everyone returned to their tasks at hand.

"Hey boss, a word?" the lead GRS guy said with a lift of his chin.

"Yeah, Brock," Jonah said, walking over to him.

"Probably a good time to read me in on the plan?"

"Like I said, our orders are to execute Omega protocol and shelter here until the cavalry arrives."

"Yeah, I heard that, but uh, what if the cavalry don't show up?" the shooter said, running his tongue over his front teeth. "What then? You got a contingency plan?"

Jonah met the other man's steely, grey-eyed stare. "Look, Brock, I get it, I do . . . you're looking at me, thinking, 'This dumbass is going to get us all killed because some lying bureaucrat told him to shelter in place.' But I can assure you, I am not going to let this turn into another Benghazi. I take your expertise and your counsel seriously. If you tell me we need to relocate, then I'll consider it."

"And if not, then it's up to me and Steve to hold down the fort?"

Jonah nodded.

"Awesome," Brock said with that fatalistic sarcasm that only SOF guys could pull off. "Do we have *any* shooters in this crew, or is everyone baggage?"

"Nathan, Marci, and Sergei all graduated from the Farm, but Sergei is the only one you guys would consider tactically proficient. Nina and Bess are analysts."

"What about you?"

"I can plink targets, but me on my best day couldn't handle you on your worst," Jonah said, telling it straight.

"I appreciate the candor, boss," Brock said as automatic weapons fire echoed outside. "And now I'm going to return the favor. If the shit hits the fan and nobody comes for us, then we're fucked. As a base of operations, this building and location is fine, but as far as security goes, it sucks. So, here's what needs to happen. One, I'm going to get the van and park it at the back door. When it's time to go, we all pile into one vehicle. Two, you're going to fire up that sat phone of yours and inform the station chief that Russian armor is rolling into town right fucking now and see if that changes the calculus on us sheltering in place. And finally, you're going to give your guy an alternate pickup location." He slapped a scrap of paper in Jonah's hand with hand-scribed lat-lon coordinates.

"What's this place?" Jonah said, looking down at the paper, committing the digits to memory, then looking back at his head of security.

"That is a house in Nikolske that I've been renting for a scenario just like this," Brock said with a tight grin. "Always be prepared. That's my motto."

Jonah arched an eyebrow at the operator. "Funny, I never took you for a Boy Scout, Brock," he said.

"There's probably a lot about me that would surprise you," the shooter said, giving Jonah's shoulder a squeeze. "And if we're lucky enough to get outta here alive, maybe I'll read you in on some of it."

CHAPTER 21

The Situation Room
The White House
Washington, DC
0823 Local Time

Jarvis watched President Warner take control of the chaos in the room and slay it with a single word.

"Enough," the President barked, his voice silencing the din of chatter and the half-dozen side conversations going on across and around the table.

More so than with anyone else he'd ever met, Jarvis's opinion of Warner had radically evolved over time. In the beginning, he'd dismissed the man as a bumbling bureaucrat. But during his tenure as DNI, that disdain had transformed into grudging respect. And now, Jarvis found he admired the President . . . maybe even thought of him as a mentor.

"It's time to stop calling what's unfolding in Mariupol something other than what it is. Russia has just invaded the Ukraine, and the time for debate is over. Give me options, people."

All eyes immediately turned to the Chairman of the Joint Chiefs, former Air Force fighter pilot General McMillan.

"Mr. President, we are all in agreement that the current threat cannot go unanswered and we are prepared to execute military operations consistent with your stance that Russia cannot be permitted to annex any more territory from the Ukraine . . ."

Jarvis listened intently as the General outlined a scenario almost identical to what Mike Casey had war-gamed for him and Petra days ago. He glanced at his Deputy Chief of Staff—and soon to be Director of Ember—who was standing beside Petra. The former submariner must have felt the look, because he gave Jarvis a tight smile and a humble shrug.

On the main screen, a mouse cursor moved over a map of southern Ukraine and the Black Sea.

"The USS *Oak Hill* is in port here," McMillan continued, pointing at Odessa, "with its contingent of Special Operations–capable Marines from the 13th Marines Expeditionary Unit. Due to rising tensions, ship's company and the Marines have all been called back in preparation for departure. However, with your authorization, we could deploy the Marines in Odessa. Have them set up defensive positions and checkpoints to discourage troop incursion and, perhaps more importantly, to quell Russian-sponsored destabilizing activity in the city. We could try to preempt what's happening in Mariupol from repeating itself in Odessa. But for the Marines to be effective, we would need to control access to the city, which means establishing checkpoints on the highways—here and here—and we will need to control the skies. Regrettably, it's too late for a defensive posture in Mariupol, especially considering the proximity to the

Russian border and the tremendous buildup of troops and armor we're already seeing—"

"Hold on," Warner snapped. "You're not suggesting we just hand Mariupol over to Petrov without a fight, I hope?"

"No, Mr. President," the General said, keeping his cool. "Of course not. However, rushing ground troops into Mariupol is dangerous and logistically impossible. Russia has taken control of the Sea of Azov, and the Economic Exclusion Zone Moscow just declared in the Black Sea is mere window dressing for what's really going on. The truth is, they've blockaded the entire northern half of the Black Sea. Moreover, not only is Turkey not permitting any additional US warships to enter, they're demanding that *both* the *Oak Hill* and our other vessel in theater, the USS *Donald Cook*, exit the Black Sea to deescalate tensions."

"So Erodan is backing Petrov," the President said, shaking his head. "The day has finally come that proves Turkey is a NATO member in name only."

"Yes, sir," Admiral Kellam, Chief of Naval Operations, chimed in. "Our situation in the Black Sea is desperate. The *Oak Hill* and *Donald Cook* are completely cut off and surrounded by the Russian Black Sea fleet."

"Well, I'm not pulling the only two warships I have in theater," Warner said, glancing from Kellam to Jarvis.

Jarvis nodded his agreement, not sure if the President was looking for an ally on that point or not. "We don't have to pull them out, we could simply pull them back—dock in Constanta, Romania. The Russians wouldn't dare hit us there, because then the conflict moves from a US-Russia-Ukraine conflict to all-out war with NATO."

"Agreed," Admiral Kellam said.

"But we have another problem, sir. Unlike in Afghanistan and

Iraq, where we own the air, in the Black Sea theater we're facing a fierce air superiority presence and antiair capability from the Russians."

"Are you saying *they* control the skies?"

"Not on my watch, sir," General McMillan said. "I will commit to controlling the airspace and establishing a no-fly zone over the Black Sea and southern Ukraine, including the Crimean peninsula. Russia might own the water, but *we* will own the skies."

There was a loud snicker and Admiral Kellam grumbled, "A no-fly zone over Russian airspace? Yeah, Petrov will like that."

"Fuck Petrov," President Warner said. "I love it."

"Control of this no-fly zone is imperative, sir, because it limits Russia's ability to support ground operations with close air support and prevents an offensive air campaign against Ukrainian military targets. But make no mistake, Moscow has been preparing for this. Last summer the Russian military conducted an exercise simulating air strikes on targets in Odessa and on the Ukrainian Navy. If this becomes a hot war, we're going to have to win it from the air."

"And how exactly do we plan to do that?" Warner said, leaning in and resting his elbows on the table.

"We have a detachment of F-22 Raptors from the 94th Fighter Squadron out of Langley kicking sand in Kuwait at the tail end of a three-month deployment. This unit is the absolute best to control the air over the battle space, including incursions into Russian airspace to enforce the no-fly zone. For one thing, they have the stealth to control a no-fly zone west of the border, but they are also armed with antimissile capabilities, as you know. Stealth and antiballistic missile ordnance is the best defense we have against the Russian Kalibr cruise missiles, P-800 antiship missiles, and those damn S-400 batteries they've stood up on the Crimean peninsula. I have the F-22s and their support teams heading to Mihail Kogălni-ceanu Air Base in Romania as we speak. We've been operating Rap-tors out of MK for years. We have a maintenance squadron there, and ammunition depot and fuel. The 94th will be our primary Air Superiority asset, but once we establish superiority, we will augment with F/A-18s from the carrier strike group in the Med," McMillan explained.

"Very well," Warner said.

"May I, General McMillan?" said a gruff voice to Jarvis's left.

Jarvis turned and saw Marine Corps General Jericho Zimmer-man tap his left breast pocket, where he always kept a fresh cigar, then make a *tsk* sound when he remembered smoking was forbid-den in the Situation Room.

"Of course, Zim," McMillan said. "What have you got?"

Jarvis watched as the man most likely to be the *next* Chairman of the Joint Chiefs cast his vision onto the map on the screen.

"I agree with the Chairman that the Air Force and her stealthy Raptors are best for the air superiority mission over the Black Sea and defense of the *Oak Hill* and *Donald Cook*. But the F-35s from VMFA-122 aboard the *Essex* are the best platform for supporting our Marines in Odessa and the Army's 1st Battalion, 16th Infantry Regiment Armored Brigade Combat Team—which as luck would have it is still deployed to eastern Europe in support of the Joint exercise Atlantic Resolve. The *Essex* is in the Med as part of the carrier strike group, and in addition to F-35s from VMFA-122, she has Marines from I MEF and additional support personnel which can be rapidly deployed into theater when we need them."

"*If* we need them, right?" Admiral Kellam raised a cynical eye-brow.

"Yeah . . . right. If . . ." Zimmerman said. "And speaking of *ifs* . . . we should probably consider mobilizing the 101st Airborne to augment our Marine presence and the 1st Infantry Division in MK."

McMillan stared at the map a moment, his lips pursed. "Using F-35s from all the way down in the Med is a helluva reach. They'll have zero loiter time without refueling and it'll be much riskier providing refueling over the Black Sea when things hit the fan."

"Won't keep them on the *Essex*, Mac," the Marine said, unconsciously tapping his cigar again, his steel-blue eyes on fire now as he stared at the map. He tapped his own station computer and added an orange arrow to the map on the large screen over what looked to Jarvis to be the middle of nowhere. "Our Marines aboard the *Essex* are expeditionary, and that includes our aviation assets, and I say expeditionary they will be. I think it's time we deploy the F-35s and F-22s together. They can both operate out of MK *and* execute the missions they were designed for. While the Raptors maintain air superiority over the Black Sea, the Lightnings will provide air support for our troops on the ground in Ukraine. I would also deploy the Navy expeditionary FRSS team surgical unit to MK for casualty support. We would then coordinate with the battle group surgical assets on a master MEDEVAC plan to move stabilized casualties to the carriers before sending them for tertiary care back in Italy."

"Okay, Zim, you sold me," McMillan said.

"But how do we get the *Oak Hill* safely out of Odessa to Constanta?" the CNO asked. "She's going to be an easy target as she steams south through the Russian blockade."

Jarvis nodded toward Mike Casey, reading in his eyes that he had something to say.

"Excuse me, sir," Casey said, holding Zimmerman's hard gaze. "I might have an idea."

"Anything is appreciated, Commander Casey," McMillan said.

"What if we have the President announce that, in an effort to de-escalate tensions in the Black Sea, the Navy will be exfiltrating the *Oak Hill* and the *Donald Cook* from the region. We make a statement that the *Cook* is steaming north to link up with the *Oak Hill* and to escort her from port. It would be difficult for the Russians to justify an attack on them under those circumstances."

"Won't fool anyone," Kellam grumbled. "The Russians aren't a bunch of sheepherders in Afghanistan, Commander. The Kremlin will know we've disembarked our Marines from the *Oak Hill* and they'll be watching our buildup of forces in MK."

"I can take care of that," President Warner beamed. "Commander Casey has the right idea. Strategy is not just about the tactics and logistics, but also messaging and optics. Wars are waged in the media and the court of international opinion as much as on the battlefield these days. Proper messaging could give us time to move both ships to Romanian territorial waters, and if we hurry we can get it done ahead of the arrival of the Marines and Army Airborne troops."

"I agree with all of that, Mr. President," General McMillan said with an overt nod of support to his fellow Joint Chiefs. "Obviously, the support and logistics footprint to backstop this is significant, but we now have a starting point."

"Do it," the President said. "Get me a full plan including all movements of troops and materials for signature in the next two hours, gentlemen. We need to move now."

"Yes, sir, Mr. President," McMillan said.

Warner turned to Jarvis, apparently reading his thoughts. "DNI, you look like you have something on your mind. Spit it out."

Jarvis nodded. "As if things weren't complicated enough, we have a CIA annex in Mariupol that's been operating under a nonofficial cover for several years. Everything happened so fast, they weren't able to evacuate before the Russians took control of the city."

Warner's cheeks went crimson. "No, no, no—we are not going to let history repeat itself. One Benghazi is enough. We need to get them out of there. What are you doing about it, DNI?"

"Well, sir, this is one call that only you alone can make. We can go big and overt with the Marines and hope that Moscow backs down, or we can go small and try to extract them under the Russians' noses. There are potential risks and benefits associated with both options."

"What do you recommend?"

Jarvis resisted the urge to smile at the question. "I recommend the latter, sir."

Warner nodded and turned back to Chairman McMillan. "General, finalize your plans as briefed and leave the sale of our counteroffensive to Congress and the American people to me. I'll provide the political cover. We are not letting Russia annex southern Ukraine."

"Yes, sir, Mr. President," the Air Force four-star general said.

Warner pushed back from the table and turned to Jarvis. "DNI, join me in a breakout room."

"Yes, sir, Mr. President. I'd like Mike and Petra to join, with your permission."

"Sure," Warner said, and they moved as a group to the nearest soundproof breakout room. Once inside, the President shut the door, but no one took a seat. Jarvis jumped in, anticipating the agenda.

"Sir, I have Ember in Kiev as we speak and an element from SEAL Team Four in the Med. My recommendation is Ember plans the rescue op and augments Team Four on the extraction."

"Make it happen," Warner said. He collapsed into the large seat at the head of the table. On cue, Petra and Casey took their own seats. Kelso decided to remain standing. "What else has Ember been able to turn up in Kiev?"

"While we were prosecuting the Ukrainian right-wing paramilitary group Ultra, the mission was interrupted by a hit squad. They killed our HVT while we were exfiltrating him. He was our best chance at giving you hard evidence that Russia was behind the Vice President's assassination. I'm sorry, sir, but we don't have anything you can use in the public arena."

Warner waved his hand, unconcerned. "To be honest, Kelso, I never thought you would. These bastards cover their tracks too well. Besides, the time for gathering proof has passed. Petrov has already moved the goal posts. Russia has invaded Ukraine, and all the evidence I need to prove that is on TV. It's time for Ember's priorities to shift."

"Yes, sir."

"Priority one is getting our CIA folks out of Mariupol alive. Priority two is heading off whatever covert operations nightmare Petrov has planned next."

Jarvis nodded. "Agreed."

"And Ember is up to the challenge despite the leadership gap?"

"Yes, sir, and I have a plan to bring them back up to their full operational level. I've asked Mike"—he indicated the submarine commander—"to take over the role of Director at Ember. This will free Baldwin to focus on what he does best: cyber and signals."

"You ready for this, Commander Casey?" the President asked, eyeing the submariner.

"Yes, sir, Mr. President," Casey said.

Warner nodded. "I don't second-guess my people, Commander," he said. "If Director Jarvis says you're the man for the job, then I trust his judgment and will extend you the same confidence. But understand there is zero margin for error in Ember operations. Get up to speed quickly, because Ember is my go-to denied asset. And I have a feeling we're going to need them for more than disappearing terrorists in the coming days."

"Yes, sir. I will, sir," Casey said, his eyes suggesting the full weight of the job he had accepted was now settling squarely on his shoulders.

"Get to it, then, son," Warner said, dismissing the Naval Officer. "There's a plane to Tampa somewhere that has an empty seat waiting for you."

Casey rose and made eye contact with Jarvis. "Thank you for the opportunity, Director." Jarvis saw the man's reflexive need to salute, which he suppressed. "We'll get it done."

"I know you will, Mike."

Petra gave Jarvis a tight smile, then followed Casey out of the room. The President gestured and Jarvis finally took a seat.

"How are you holding up, Kelso?" Warner asked, the timbre of his voice changing now that they were alone.

Jarvis raised both eyebrows. He'd never been asked that by the President—or, hell, by anyone except Petra, and then only in their rare private moments.

"I'm fine, sir. Getting Ember back on its feet has been a top priority, but they're on track. I think—"

Warner held up his hand. "I'm not talking about Ember. I'm asking how *you* are doing."

"I'm afraid I don't understand sir," Jarvis said, crossing his legs and folding his hands in his lap. "Is there something specific you want to ask me?"

Warner leaned back in his chair and knitted his fingers together behind his head.

"Kelso, I'm sure it will come as no surprise to you that if

187

someone crucial to my administration were to, let's say, seek medical care at Walter Reed for a crisis they're having, I would catch wind of it. Right?"

Warner held his gaze but gave away little else.

"Sir, again, if you have a specific question for me, I'll address it frankly and honestly."

"I asked it, Kelso," Warner said and leaned forward. "How are you holding up?"

Jarvis let out a deep sigh.

"Sir, I am perfectly well. If you have solicited information on my health, you know that I have an issue I'm dealing with, but that it is under control. I am on medicine that has no side effects that would affect my performance of my duties, and in any case, the possible sequelae of my condition are more long- than short-term, and for the duration of your administration will have no bearing on my ability to function."

"Jesus, Kelso," Warner said, smiling, and his eyes suggested it was genuine—not the political smile that had landed him the most powerful job in the world. "If I had concerns about your abilities, you'd be gone already. I trust your judgment—and the counsel of the neurologist at Walter Reed you're seeing—to determine that. Hell, I can't do this right now without you, so if I had concerns they wouldn't matter, not for the task we have before us. I'm asking as a friend. How are you doing, and is there anything I can do to help?"

Jarvis felt himself relax.

"Mr. President, I am quite well, and I greatly appreciate your support and friendship. I'm good. I'm getting back into fighting shape, the medication has erased all but the subtlest of symptoms, and I'm prepared to serve my country for the foreseeable future. And I promise"—flashing Warner a genuine smile of his own—"if I need anything I will not let my pride get in the way of asking."

"Great." Warner stood and extended his hand. "Because I will need much more from you moving forward, Director Jarvis. I have a few things to work out in the coming hours, and then I will have new tasking for you."

Jarvis shook the President's hand, relieved that he felt not even the slightest tremor as he did.

"Something I should prepare for, sir?" he asked, curiosity getting the better of him.

"Not something you can prepare for, Kelso. We'll talk soon. In the meantime, get back to work and bring me Zhukov's head on a pike."

"Yes, sir," he said and left the breakout room.

Petra was waiting for him and fell into step with him as they headed through the chaos of the Situation Room toward the hardened exit with two Marines guarding it. The Marines opened the door for them, and as they started alone down the long hallway, Jarvis turned to his most trusted confidant.

"You hearing any rumblings about something *else* brewing we should be preparing for?" he asked as he swiped his CAC card across a panel to activate the elevator.

"No," she said, her curiosity impossible to mask. "Why?"

"Not sure," Jarvis said. The elevator doors opened, and they stepped in. "The boss was rather cryptic about some new tasking." The doors closed and he looked at Petra—who had become far more than just a confidant. Truth be told, and as hard as it was to admit to himself, without her it was unlikely he could have gotten through what he referred to as "the diagnosis," especially when compounded by the devastating Zeta attack on Ember and the loss of Smith, Adamo, and the others. He held her eyes and shook off the urge to kiss her. Instead he said, "Guess we'll find out when he's ready. Plenty to do in the meantime. And by the way . . . thank you."

She looked up at him, truly puzzled. "For what?"

He allowed himself a brief squeeze of her forearm, a physical gesture equivalent to a passionate embrace, coming from him and under the circumstances.

"Everything," he said simply.

Then the doors opened and they double-timed it toward the White House exit together.

CHAPTER 22

USS Donald Cook (DDG-75)
135 Nautical Miles South of Odessa
The Black Sea
1702 Local Time

Commander Dustin Townsend loved his ship.

He loved her design. He loved her capabilities. He loved her hull number, her crest and shield, and her motto: *Faith without Fear.* But most of all, he loved her crew—and he bragged on them every chance he got.

"The *Donald Cook* has the finest crew in the United States Navy," he'd said, addressing the ship before this underway to the Black Sea. "And do you want to know why? Because you have pride. Not the overconfident, dangerous kind of pride. Not the conceited, *we're better than you* kind of pride. No, I'm talking about the pride that comes from knowing you can count on each other—

for support, for encouragement, for help, and most importantly, to do the right thing when the right thing is not the easy thing. Every day that we're forward deployed, each and every one of us is putting our lives in our shipmates' hands. That takes an incredible amount of trust. As your commanding officer, I want you to know that I do not, and will not, ever take that trust for granted."

After the speech, the ship's Command Master Chief had come to see him in his stateroom and asked him if he'd meant what he'd said. Did he really think the *Cook* had the finest crew in the Navy, or had that just been a pep talk? Dusty had simply smiled at the CMC and said, "I meant every word of it." Now, three weeks later, the Navy was asking him to lead the ship he loved, and the crew he loved even more, on a mission that some—and quite possibly all— of the crew might not survive. His words about trust echoed in his head. The two hundred and eighty-one souls aboard the *Cook* trusted him to keep them safe. They also trusted him to do the right thing. But what was a captain to do when keeping his crew safe and doing the right thing were mutually exclusive?

This, he thought, *is what they mean by the "burden of command."*

He exhaled as he pushed open the door to the wardroom. He'd assembled his senior staff—both officers and chiefs—for a strategic brief and tactical planning session. Despite the propaganda campaign the Kremlin was running claiming otherwise, Russia *was* invading Ukraine, and it was up to the United States to stop them. Admiral Greer, the Strike Group Commander presently on the aircraft carrier USS *Gerald R. Ford,* had called their tasking "escort duty," and *technically* that was true. And yet, it was also the understatement of the year. The *Donald Cook*'s tasking was to steam north, rendezvous with the USS *Oak Hill* off the coast of Odessa, then escort the *Oak Hill* south and out of the hornet's nest. The rub, however, was that in order to do so, *Donald Cook* would need

to cross the forty-fifth parallel and enter the bogus Economic Exclusion Zone that Russia had declared. Yes, Russia's EEZ violated
international maritime law, but when had international law ever
stopped Russia? According to satellite imagery, the Russian Navy
had blockaded a thirty-thousand-square-mile chunk of water boxed
in by Crimea on the east, Ukraine on the north, and Romania on
the west—stopping all traffic in and out of Ukraine's largest and
most important seaport. The *Oak Hill*, along with four hundred
Marines, had been docked in Odessa at the time the Russian blockade was established.

"Captain, I don't get it," said the ship's Operations Officer.
"Why not just leave the *Oak Hill* in port? If she stays at the pier,
then she's not going to provoke a response from the Russians.
Leaving port violates the blockade and provokes a response. Us
steaming to Odessa to escort her out also violates the blockade and
provokes a response. Why poke the bear?"

"Because the blockade is fucking illegal," the ship's Combat
Systems Officer, Lieutenant Commander Brewster, quipped. "Since
when do we let the Russians decide where we can go and when
we're allowed to go there? C'mon, dude, did you forget your balls in
your stateroom? The Russians don't own the Black Sea. I say fuck
them and their blockade."

When Dusty didn't say anything, both department heads
looked at him to adjudicate. "As usual, the two of you are on opposite sides of the issue, and as usual, you both make good points," he
said, wishing he could somehow magically merge the two officers
into a single person who would have all the characteristics of a
great future CO. As it was, neither man was ready for that next
step. But that was okay; they still had time. He glanced at his XO,
and she nodded at him to keep going. "Ops makes a good point,
one I made to the Admiral when he gave us this tasking. It would

be irresponsible not to consider leaving the *Oak Hill* in port, because make no mistake, ladies and gentlemen, tensions are at an all-time high in the Black Sea. One miscommunication, one misconstrued intention, one itchy trigger finger and this mission could spiral out of control, drawing both nations into a war that makes Iraq look like child's play."

"Which is why I think that antagonizing the Russians out of the gate isn't the smartest idea," Ops pressed. "They have eight Kilo-class submarines homeported in Sevastopol. Last satellite imagery had seven of them at sea. We'd be lucky to track one of them operating on battery, let alone seven! They have a squadron of Su-30s and two squadrons of Su-24s, all of which are undoubtedly on standby and all of which carry antiship missiles. And on top of that, their *Admiral Grigorovich* frigates each carry eight Oniks-M *supersonic* antiship cruise missiles."

"Dude, we're on an *Arleigh* fucking *Burke*," Brewster replied. "The most badass, capable warship in the world. We have enough firepower on this ship alone to sink every surface ship in Russia's Black Sea fleet and enough Tomahawks to obliterate Sevastopol."

"Even if every missile hits its mark, they will retaliate. All it takes is one torpedo or one supersonic Russian cruise missile, and we're on the bottom of the Black Sea. The *Oak Hill* is safer in Odessa than it is out here with us. If we get in a shooting match, the Russians will sink both ships! I don't understand why we have to risk our lives—"

"Enough," Dusty said, summoning his command voice. "The reason why is simple. The *Oak Hill* and her crew are trapped behind enemy lines. And you're right, the chances of the Russians sinking her at the pier are small. But the chances of the Russians seizing her and taking her crew hostage are not. As your captain, I am responsible for your safety and the safety of this ship, and I am not going to lie to you—the risks we are about to take are grave. I do not make this decision lightly. I was up all night thinking about it, and the conclusion I ultimately came to is this—*we don't leave our shipmates behind*. Period. If I confine my sphere of concern to only the hull of this ship, then the decision is easy. We should definitely play it safe and not cross the forty-fifth parallel. But, if I extend that sphere to include the sailors and marines on the *Oak Hill*, if I accept responsibility for their safety and welfare, then suddenly, playing it safe is not an option. I'm not leaving them behind, just like I would never leave any of you behind. And if that means we have to swim into a school of sharks to get them out, then by God that's what we're going to do."

"No man left behind," the CMC said, with perfect timing.

"No man left behind," the XO repeated.

"No man left behind," a chorus of voices echoed around the table.

Dusty nodded with approval at his team while a swell of pride blossomed in his chest. "Now that we're all on the same page, I'd just like to point out that the irony of this situation is not lost on me—that of all the *Arleigh Burkes* in the fleet, it is the *Donald Cook* at the tip of the spear, going toe-to-toe, or bow-to-bow, rather, with the Russians. In two thousand fourteen, when Russia seized Crimea, it was this ship standing watch in the Black Sea . . . this ship that fended off two Su-24s. And in two thousand sixteen, while in the Baltic projecting power off the coast of Kaliningrad, the *Cook* once again faced down a pair of Russian fighters. I expect this time around will be no different. And I know it might sound a little hokey, but I don't believe in coincidences. This ship's namesake, Captain Donald Cook, was a Marine awarded the Medal of Honor for putting the welfare of his men before his own. This ship's motto, *Faith without Fear*, could not be more fitting . . . more prophetic . . .

more ironic. We are going to go rescue our brothers, with the faith that it is the right thing to do, and navigate whatever threats the Russian Navy throws at us without fear."

For a long moment, no one spoke, the power and poignancy of his words hanging in the air like the ghost of Donald Cook himself. Finally, the XO said, "We're with you, Captain. Whatever the challenge, whatever the risk, you can count on us."

CHAPTER 23

Ember Executive Boeing 787

Boryspil Airport

Kiev Oblast, Ukraine

1845 Local Time

Dempsey leaned forward, his hands and forehead against the cool wall of the shower, and let the cold water assault his neck and back until he was shivering. It was a popular myth that BUD/S and a career of swim training and ocean operations made Navy SEALs immune to the cold. For Dempsey, it was the complete opposite—he hated being cold. But the cold brought the comfortable familiarity of being on mission, and it helped focus his weary mind and renewed his aching muscles when he needed it most.

When the shivering was no longer bearable, he toweled off and pulled on a black long-sleeve pull over and BDU-style cargo pants.

Then he padded on bare feet to the bunkroom, where he grabbed fresh socks from his locker. A printed screen capture image taped on the inside of the locker door drew his eye. In the image, his son Jake—dressed in his high school graduation robes—was standing next to his ex-wife, Kate. They had their arms around each other and they were smiling. Not those fake *smile for the camera* expressions people had perfected for their curated social media selves, but real, genuine, and loving smiles. Instinctively, Dempsey smiled back.

Then his smile faded and another emotion took its place . . . *regret*. The picture was six months old.

He shut the locker door, put on his socks and boots, and headed to the conference room, where the after-action debrief on last night's Ultra snatch-and-grab was already in progress.

Baldwin was talking on the center screen of a bank of monitors, livestreaming from Florida, while Munn stood at the head of the table, tapping away with one finger at a time on a laptop.

"Oh, for God's sake," Wang said, reaching under Munn's beefy arms with his own spindly appendages to jam out a flurry of keystrokes in less than a second. "Just let me do it."

The screen split and a static image of the wrecked SUVs on Naberezhne Road filled the left side of the screen, map coordinates and the date in green at the bottom suggesting the image originated from the drone supporting their mission last night. The right side of the screen showed the face of the man in the sedan—the one they believed to be a Zeta operator. Baldwin's video stream shifted to the adjacent monitor.

"I wanna send a bottle of hooch to that dead-eye drone operator who saved our asses," Dempsey said, slipping into the high-backed chair beside Grimes, who had changed into jeans and a 5.11 Tactical half-zip fleece.

"Done, JD," said Chip, who was serving as Baldwin's sole

mentee while Dale was learning how to breathe without his trach back in Virginia.

Dempsey gave the kid a thumbs-up, which Chip mirrored back over Baldwin's right shoulder.

"It's regrettable that we were not able to reacquire what we assume to be our primary target, the man on the right side of the screen—whom we are now designating by the call sign Ipabog—"

"I'm not calling him Ipabog, bro," Martin said with a chuckle.

"It was my idea," Chip chimed in enthusiastically. "Ipabog was the Slavic god of the hunt, so I thought it would be—"

"I don't care if it's the name on his fucking birth certificate, dude," Munn interrupted. "We ain't calling him Ipabog. Call him Oscar, since he's our primary objective."

"See? I told you," Baldwin said, turning to Chip.

Dempsey chuckled and shook his head. Now *this . . .* this is what normal felt like. They all needed less moping and more of this.

"So," Baldwin continued, adjusting his glasses. "Oscar remains at large with no discernable trail. Our programs have been scanning real-time imagery and historical data from cameras throughout Kiev for facial matches, but suffice it to say, we have not received any notifications. That suggests he moved through Kiev with practiced and determined countersurveillance efficiency."

"Hardly surprising," Munn added. "He's a Zeta."

"Are you implying they're better than we are?" Martin quipped from his corner.

And we were doing so well there for a minute, Dempsey thought, shaking his head. He shot the Marine a *let's not go there* look.

"Sorry," Martin said. "My bad."

"So . . . as I was saying, Oscar remains at large," Baldwin continued, as Buz and Allen appeared in frame next to him. "But before all of you start pushing for follow-on resources and tasking to prosecute him, DNI Jarvis asked that once the team was assembled, we set aside a moment for him to share some staffing and tasking changes. Chip, if you could loop Director Jarvis in for us, please?"

The screen flickered and the drone images disappeared, replaced with a shockingly grim-faced Jarvis. Heavy, dark bags hung under the DNI's eyes, and he looked like he was carrying the weight of the world on his shoulders.

"Thanks, Ian, and thanks, team, for your commitment and all the sacrifices you have made and continue to make to serve your country in the capacity you do. I know your ranks are thin and I know you are reeling from your recent battle damage, but the work you're doing is critical to this administration and to moving the nation forward. We *will* find and prosecute Spetsgruppa Zeta and Arkady Zhukov, but right now I have more pressing matters to discuss with you. First and foremost, I want to thank Signals Chief Baldwin for rising to the occasion and filling the billet of Acting Ember Director for the past months while we all tried to regain our footing. I know I asked a lot of you, Ian, and you worked tirelessly and without complaint to hold the team together during a very dark and difficult time. We are grateful and we are proud."

Dempsey glanced away from Jarvis and saw that Baldwin's eyes had gone wet with emotion. He looked like he was about to say something, but instead he just swallowed hard to keep his composure and nodded. Chip reached up and gave Baldwin a squeeze on the shoulder. The poignant moment took Dempsey by surprise and tugged on his own heartstrings. Until hearing Jarvis say it, he'd not fully appreciated the burden their Signals Chief had been expected to carry. The man was not an operator, not a SEAL. He was an academic who had shown the mettle and commitment of a SEAL under pressure.

"And I'd like to thank Munn for stepping in as Operations Officer," Jarvis continued. "Bravo Zulu, Dan, for all your hard work and for wearing two hats when we needed you most."

Wang gave Munn a fist bump, and then everyone—on both sides of the Atlantic—raised their fists in solidarity and gratitude to Baldwin and Munn.

"And with that, effective immediately, Buz Wilson will be taking over duties permanently as Ember Operations Officer."

On-screen, Buz nodded. "Thank you, Director Jarvis for this opportunity. I won't let you or my Ember teammates down."

"I know you won't," Jarvis said with a knowing smile. "Next up, I'd like to introduce everyone to the new permanent Director of Ember, Commander Mike Casey. Mike . . ."

Dempsey looked around the room at his colleagues' faces that appeared just as stunned as he felt.

Who in the holy fuck is Commander Mike Casey?

Jarvis shifted to the left side of the frame to make room for a man dressed in a navy blue suit. "Thank you, sir," said the man, who appeared to be in his early forties. "I'm honored you and the President have entrusted me with the opportunity to lead and serve with the brave men and women of Ember."

Dempsey leaned forward and strained his eyes to see the miniature gold warfare insignia on the man's suit lapel.

Are those dolphins? Is this guy a fucking submariner? He screwed up his face and looked at Munn. *Is this some sort of joke or have we died and gone to hell?*

Munn just shrugged.

"As some of you may or may not know," Casey said, "for the past two months I've been serving as Director Jarvis's Deputy Chief of Staff—where I worked closely with Petra Felsk. Prior to that, I was the liaison between General McMillan's staff and the Pentagon's Strategic Capabilities Office. Before my Pentagon tour,

I did a stint at the War College and before that served as CO of the USS *Tucson* (SSN-770), a fast boat nuclear submarine out of Pearl . . ." He paused and took the time to look at all of them. "I wish we had time for a proper indoc so we could get to know each other, but as you are no doubt aware, the crisis in the Ukraine is reaching critical velocity. I'll be flying to Tampa tomorrow morning to relieve Director Baldwin. In the meantime, I'm going to brief you on what is going on in Mariupol, then discuss new tasking that the President and DNI Jarvis have for us. Any questions before I dive in?"

It was as if he were daring Dempsey to ask how in the holy hell a submariner was qualified to lead the most lethal, covert direct-action team in the world. But Dempsey was too smart to take a bite at that apple.

"Very well," Casey said and briefed the team on the chaos unfolding in the Black Sea and Mariupol.

Dempsey listened intently as Ember's new Director spoke with a quiet confidence that made it hard for him not to feel his knee-jerk cynicism at having a submarine brainiac at the helm of Ember begin to dissolve. After several minutes, the Hollywood-handsome Naval Officer's face disappeared and was replaced by a video clearly captured on a mobile phone. The footage showed several armed paramilitary thugs with no discernable insignia, standing around a kneeling man pleading desperately in Ukrainian. As the kneeling man spoke, a different man in a dark-blue Nike zip-up sweat jacket walked up from behind and executed him with a headshot. The crowd around him raised rifles in celebration as the shooter turned casually on a heel, slipped the pistol into the waistband of his jeans, and brought a cigarette to his lips. The frame froze.

"What you just saw was the execution of Mariupol Mayor Bohdan Volovshyn." The frozen video was replaced by a black-

and-white photo of a man with close-cropped hair, wearing the uniform of Russian Infantry. "This is Maksim Kuznetsov, former Spetsnaz who was later recruited by GRU. He disappeared from known GRU activities about four years ago. Facial recognition confirms this is our shooter in the tracksuit. Apparently, he's been living in Mariupol, existing and operating under a pro-Russian, anti-Zinovenko NOC for the past several years."

"So Russia has covert agitators stirring shit up in Ukraine just like they did in Crimea and Donetsk?" Munn said.

"And executing Ukrainian government officials?" Grimes added, her expression incredulous.

"Yes on both counts," Casey said. "Over the past twenty-four hours, the situation in Mariupol has deteriorated into a war zone. Petrov announced that Russia is sending 'peacekeeping' troops into Mariupol to protect native Russians and quell the violence. Russian troop carriers are moving in from the east and Russian armor is rolling south toward the city as we speak. Which brings us to our short-fuse mission."

The screen image refreshed to show a building with a sign that read: MARIUPOL MARITIME LOGISTICS.

"Mariupol Maritime Logistics is a CIA front company. The staff includes four CIA clandestine service officers, two analysts, and two GSR contractors for security."

"Did you say only *two*?" Munn said.

Commander Casey's face was on the screen again and his slow blink suggested he found the constant interruptions irritating.

Welcome to Ember, bro. You ain't briefing bubbleheads anymore. This is how we operate. We question other people's stupid-ass decisions, which is why we're so damn good . . .

"Correct. It caught me off guard as well, but keep in mind that up until forty-eight hours ago, this operation was not considered a high-risk outpost. Hindsight is twenty-twenty." His lips pressed into a thin line. "Regardless, we don't have time to worry about why, and instead need to focus on how to get these guys out of there before the Russians pierce their NOCs and hold them hostage, or worse."

"Sorry to interrupt, sir," Dempsey said, with a tone that, he was fully aware, suggested he wasn't the least bit sorry and might even be enjoying it. "But we're a little light here in SAD, as you may know. It's really just four of us at present—"

"Five," Wang interrupted. "Five of us."

"Yeah, sorry, Dick," Dempsey said with a smirk, before turning back to Casey. "As I was saying, it's just the five of us in SAD, so I'm not sure how we got tasked for a rescue operation that pits us against the entire Russian army."

Another tic of the man's mouth suggested that, while he had no doubt been briefed on the very different style of management required at Ember, he wasn't enjoying this first engagement so much.

Didn't learn how to run a band of covert killers when you were at the War College, eh, Commander?

"From the after-actions I've been made privy to—most notably your superhero antics in Tehran—I would have thought that you in particular, Mr. Dempsey, would be chomping at the bit for a chance like this," Casey said.

"Sick burn," Munn whispered, half covering his mouth with his hand.

Dempsey shot his *best friend* a look.

"In all seriousness," Casey continued, "you're absolutely right. The DNI does not expect Ember SAD to go it alone. We're going to augment for the operation." A map of southern Ukraine filled the screen, and a red arrow appeared, pointing at a dot labeled *Dnipro*.

"This is the city of Dnipro, located approximately one hundred fifty miles northwest of Mariupol. Ember's SAD will head there immediately, under a war correspondent journalist team NOC, where you will join up with a platoon from SEAL Team Four."

Munn looked over at Dempsey and smiled broadly.

Please, god of covert warriors, let it be Chunk and his boys.

"From what I understand, you have a history of working closely with these particular gentlemen . . ."

"Chunk, Chunk, Chunk," Martin chanted and offered a high five to Grimes, but she crinkled her nose at the Marine and left him hanging.

"Oh c'mon, Lizzie, you know you love Chunk and his guys," Munn said.

"Sure, just like I love how they can't stop undressing me with their eyes every five minutes. You'd think those guys had never seen someone with tits before," she said, shaking her head.

Sharing a brain, Munn, Wang, and Dempsey collectively turned and stared at her chest.

"You guys are such assholes," she said, but the corners of her lips lifted, nonetheless.

"As I was saying, Lieutenant Commander Select Keith Redman is the OIC," Casey said, appearing unfazed by their antics.

As a fast boat captain, maybe Casey has been around Team guys before, Dempsey thought. *And I bet he hated it.*

"Redman and his team will meet up with you at Dnipro, where you will together plan an operation to exfil the CIA contingent from Mariupol and, if possible, snatch Kuznetsov. If the opportunity to take him isn't there, then kill him."

The words were soft but unemotional, and Dempsey wondered if he had perhaps misjudged the submariner as not up to the bloody task of leading a task force such as theirs.

"Kuznetsov is the primary reason Ember's joining this mission. We know Kuznetsov is GRU. And despite not having hard proof, the President, like us, is convinced that Zeta is playing an active role in Petrov's Ukrainian campaign. It didn't work out with Viktor Skorapporsky. So, we take our next shot. Amanda Allen is going to be spending some quality time with Sylvie Bessonov to try to confirm our suspicions and get the names of as many Zeta personnel operating in Ukraine as possible. In the meantime, I look forward to meeting you all in person in the coming weeks, and I'm honored to be part of Ember. I wish I had more time, but Baldwin needs to brief you on hard data points regarding the mission, and I . . . well, I need to pack."

Without ceremony, Casey smiled, turned to shake Jarvis's hand, then stepped out of frame.

"All right, folks," Jarvis said. "That's it for me. Godspeed and good luck."

The feed went black, and Dempsey looked at Grimes, then Munn. "No bullshit, did either of you know about Casey?"

They both shook their heads.

"Seriously, because with the exception of Martin, I'm always the last to know shit around this place . . . What are you guys smiling about? You did fucking know, didn't you?"

"I swear, dude," Munn said, "I didn't know."

Dempsey narrowed his eyes at Munn, then turned to Grimes. "What about you, Freckles?"

She popped out of her chair and went after him. "Oh, you're going to pay for that."

"Uncle, uncle, uncle," he said, ducking his head under his arms as she pummeled his shoulders while Wang and Munn looked on and laughed.

CHAPTER 24

The Oval Office
The White House
Washington, DC
1703 Local Time

"Have a seat, Kelso," the President said as he rose from his chair behind the Resolute Desk and gestured to the seating area.

Jarvis nodded, heels clicking on the wood floor until he stepped onto the huge, oval area rug with the Presidential seal in the middle. He met Warner at the twin gold-colored sofas positioned opposite each other. Warner sat first, crossed his left ankle over his right knee, and pushed up the already rolled sleeves on his white dress shirt. The door behind him opened and he winked at Jarvis.

"I asked for a snifter of brandy for both of us. That okay for you?"

For a moment Jarvis worried he meant because of his medication or his "condition," but he shook the paranoid thought away. "Of course," he said.

The steward poured out two snifters for the men, set the bottle on the coffee table, and left as he had come, without a word. The President took a long pull on his brandy, then set the snifter on the rectangular table between them. He uncrossed his legs, leaned forward, and steepled his fingers.

"Kelso, as you know, the loss of the Vice President is catastrophic to our nation, but it is also catastrophic for me personally and for the smooth running of my administration. I've met with my closest advisors—a small, select group of which I consider you an important member—and with White House Counsel. Even though there is precedent for me to ride out the rest of my term without appointing a Vice President, I've decided that it is something I feel very strongly needs to be done."

If I'm really one of your closest advisors, then why talk to me now after your mind's made up? he thought, keeping his expression as neutral as possible. *No matter; the inner workings of the White House are not only outside my expertise, but also outside my concern.*

"How can I help, Mr. President?" he said.

"Well, Kelso, since you asked . . ." The President was smiling at him in a way that made Jarvis suddenly feel very uneasy, and then it all clicked into place, just before Warner verbalized the worst idea in the history of American government. "I would like you to serve as Vice President of the United States for the remainder of my term."

Jarvis coughed involuntarily as he struggled to keep the absolute repugnance of the idea from showing on his face. He was no bureaucrat and couldn't imagine anything worse. He was a Navy SEAL and now the leader of the entire American intelligence community. To become Vice President was, well, in his mind a demotion.

"Sir, I'm flattered, but . . ."

"Don't be," Warner said, waving his hand. "There's nothing flattering about it. Frankly, it's a shit job, well beneath the talents of a man with your pedigree. But that being said, it's the job I need you for."

"Sir, with all due respect, this is the worst possible time for me to change billets. We are on the brink of war with Russia, I'm managing ongoing intelligence collection and counterterrorism operations in thirty-three countries, and at the same time trying to prosecute your objectives and avoid World War Three. How on earth could I step away to take on what is, frankly, a bureaucratic position in this time of crisis?"

"The crisis is what demands it, Kelso," Warner said, undeterred.

"How is that, sir? My understanding is there is no constitutional mandate requiring that the Vice President be replaced, much less in the middle of an international crisis rivaling the Nazi invasion of Poland. The timing is terrible."

Warner picked up his brandy and stood.

"I have never encountered your equal in tactical and strategic thinking. It's why you're in the position you are, why I have given you free reign with an asset like Ember, and why even as Vice President, I would need you to keep your fingers on IC operations through this crisis and beyond. And yet despite your strengths and capabilities, you still refuse to embrace the crucial role that gamesmanship plays in the global chess match we call geopolitics. Maybe you haven't noticed, but civilization is binary—there's either peace and politics, or war and politics. In either case, the common denominator is *politics*. Now, whether this shortcoming of yours is a conscious choice or a skill set you lack, I cannot say—I would presume the latter; otherwise you would have attempted to master the skill like everything else in your career."

Warner's voice was calm but commanding as he paced beside the table, leaving Jarvis awkwardly in his seat to be lectured by the President of the United States. "You've spent a lifetime evaluating risks and prosecuting threats with direct action. That's all fine and good for a military man, but as the leader of the most powerful nation on Earth, it's only half the picture. Let me ask you this . . . if something were to happen to me, the Speaker of the House would become President. Do you really trust that gutless, showboating politico to rebuff Russian aggression in Ukraine, to protect our forces and allies, and to bring our brave men and women home victorious?"

Apparently, it was not a rhetorical question, because Warner—one hand on his hip and the other clasping his brandy snifter—stared at him for an answer.

"No, sir," Jarvis said. "Given the circumstances, he would not be at the top of my list."

"Bullshit," Warner said. "He shouldn't be on any fucking list under any fucking circumstances! As President, I swore an oath to defend and protect the Constitution. That responsibility extends beyond my tenure of service. Choosing and endorsing the best possible successor is not a luxury, it's an obligation. What kind of leader would I be if I dropped dead from a heart attack and left the Speaker in charge?"

Jarvis nodded but held his tongue.

"But here's the real deal, Kelso. Tenet was poised to continue my policies toward Russia. He was leading in early polling and I believe was a shoo-in to win the next election. That's why Petrov wanted him out of the way. And let's not forget, his Zeta minions have already taken a shot at me once. What's to stop him from trying again? So, while I don't *have* to replace the Vice President, what message do you think it communicates to the Kremlin if I tap you—a decorated Navy SEAL, the Director of National Intelligence, and my man going toe to toe with Arkady Zhukov—to fill the role?"

"The exact message I would want Russia to receive, sir."

"With you next in line, my safety and America's safety have never been more assured," the President said, his eyes alight with fire and confidence.

"If I agree to this, I want to continue to oversee and coordinate Ember operations against Zeta," Jarvis said, failing to see any viable exit strategy.

Warner dropped into his seat, crossed his legs, and with the brandy still in his hand said, "Your statement makes it sound like you think this is a negotiation. What you don't seem to understand is that I'm not asking, I'm telling. You're going to be the next Vice President of the United States, whether you want to or not. You've answered every call of duty your nation has asked of you for over thirty years. This is your next billet. The Vice Presidency is where I need you now. I plan to swear you in tomorrow at fourteen hundred hours, and I will make an announcement to that effect tomorrow morning. Decide what personnel changes need to be made to keep things moving as smoothly as possible and notify the necessary personnel on your staff."

With nothing else left to say, Jarvis acquiesced. "Yes, Mr. President."

"Now that that's settled," Warner said, smiling and leaning into the backrest, "who do you have in mind to take over as DNI?"

Jarvis knew who *should* be his successor . . . the woman who had spent her entire career in Intelligence, from her time at JSOC and the Office of Naval Intelligence, to her tenure as his Chief of Staff at ODNI; the woman who had saved his life by taking a bullet for him; the woman who was his most trusted advisor and had her fingers on the pulse of literally everything in the Intelligence Community. But he knew better than to offer her name up for such a monumental, life-changing opportunity without consulting her first.

"Sir, I'll put together a short list for you, but I need to give my candidates a heads-up first."

Warner chuckled at this. "You're not going to do to them what I just did to you, huh? Is that what I'm hearing?"

"Just telling you straight, sir," Jarvis said, with a chuckle of his own.

"And that's why I need you." The President stood and extended his hand.

Jarvis gripped it firmly. Thank God the medicine was working, or the rigorous exercise regime, or maybe both in tandem. Either way, it didn't matter; he was just grateful that his hand didn't shake, tainting the memory of this moment for the rest of his life.

Warner released his grip, flashed Jarvis a wry smile, then said, "Now go tell Petra the bad news about your promotion and get back to me. I imagine the two of you have a lot to talk about."

That's the understatement of the year . . .

"Yes, sir," he said, practically punch-drunk, and walked out of the most powerful office on earth to find Petra.

He didn't have to go far; she was waiting for him in the President's Outer Office, sitting in the chair opposite Warner's secretary's desk. She stood upon seeing him, a knowing look on her face.

"You heard?" he said.

"Just had a meeting with the President's Chief of Staff," she said. "Let's, um, find someplace private we can talk."

He nodded, and she led him out into the corridor and down

the hall to the Vice President's Office. Vice President Tenet's secretary greeted them, nodded at Petra, and let them into the well-appointed and eerily vacant office, with its iconic blue carpet and blue-painted walls.

"So," she said, turning to him once the door had closed behind them.

"That about sums it up," he grumbled.

"What are you going to do?"

"I don't know," he said. "He's already asked me who I recommend as my successor as DNI."

"Who did you tell him?" she asked, her expression rife with curiosity.

"I didn't," he said. "I wanted to talk to you first."

"I appreciate that," she said with a smile. "I think the choice is obvious; it should be Reggie."

He met her gaze but didn't say anything.

"What?" she said, shifting her weight.

"It *should* be you," he said.

For a moment she didn't react, then she burst into laughter. "Me? Have you lost your mind?"

"My mind's as sharp as ever," he said. "You're the perfect candidate, Petra. You're brilliant, prudent, and you're already read into everything going on. There's no one I'd trust more to take the reins at ODNI."

She walked over to him and took both his hands in hers. "I'm flattered, Kelso, I really am. But even if I could make it through the confirmation hearings—which I wouldn't because I don't have the CV to warrant—"

"I already thought about that," he said, cutting her off, "Warner will name you Acting DNI, and then with my endorsement and Warner exerting pressure behind the scenes, I know we could push your confirmation through after the crisis in Ukraine settles down."

She squeezed his hands, stopping him. "You didn't let me finish . . . What I was trying to say is, even if I could make it through the hearings, I wouldn't want the job."

"What?" he said, screwing up his face at her. "What are you talking about?"

This made her chuckle. "Kelso, I don't want to be DNI. In fact, in my mind, taking over as DNI would be a demotion."

"A demotion?" he echoed, confused.

"Yeah, because given the choice between being Chief of Staff to the Vice President of the United States or being Acting DNI, I'll take the former any day of the week. Besides, I don't want to be DNI without you. We're a team. Where you go, I go . . . Assuming, that is, that you want me?"

"Want you?" he managed to choke out. "I'm terrified of becoming Vice President. I don't want the job if it means doing it without you. But the last thing in the world I ever want is to be selfish and force you to hop, skip, and jump around wherever the winds blow me. I don't want to hold you back, Petra. You'd be an amazing DNI."

"Thank you, for believing in me," she said and pulled him in for an embrace, squeezing him tight around the chest. "But if it's all the same to you, I have my heart set on being the Vice President's Chief of Staff."

CHAPTER 25

USS Donald Cook (DDG-75)
Ten Nautical Miles South of the 45th Parallel
The Black Sea
October 1
1045 Local Time

Commander Dustin Townsend adjusted his ball cap and walked over to the nav plot on the bridge to check the ship's position. *Almost time*, he thought, looking at the rapidly closing distance between the *Cook* and the forty-fifth parallel. He checked his watch and was about to ask the OOD for a status report on the ready helo when she beat him to the punch.

"Captain, Growler is in the air," the Officer of the Deck, Lieutenant Levy, said. Dusty had ordered the MH-60R Seahawk in the air twenty minutes ago and was beginning to think the flyboys had gotten lost trying to find their way from the wardroom to the stern.

Evasive maneuvers were impossible to conduct with the Seahawk sitting on the helo deck, and he needed her antisubmarine warfare capabilities to locate the Russian Kilos he knew were lurking out there.

"It's about damn time," he said, and then, with all eyes on him, he gave the order everyone had been waiting for. "Officer of the Deck, man battle stations."

"Man battle stations, aye, sir," the OOD said and turned to the Boatswain's Mate of the Watch. "Boats, sound general quarters."

"Aye, aye," responded Boatswain's Mate Second Class Smith, reaching for his pipe and the long whistle that informed the crew to immediately prepare for action.

The ship sprang to life. What would have looked like total chaos to an outsider was actually a well-rehearsed sequence of events. The clanging of the alarm, the sounds of doors and hatches closing, the thrum of hundreds of boots on the decks as sailors ran to their battle stations.

Over the 1MC loudspeaker circuit the order rang out: "General quarters, general quarters, all hands man your battle stations, down and aft to port, up and forward to starboard. Now set material condition Zebra throughout the ship. Now general quarters!"

A flurry of activity ensued, actions drilled into the crew until they'd become like muscle memory: watertight doors dogged shut to mitigate the impact of flooding, the ship's propulsion system and engineering spaces shifted to the most optimal and reliable configuration, damage control teams assembled and dressed out in PPE, and all personnel assuming the watch stations where they were most capable and effective. Reports flowed to the bridge as subordinate stations rigged their spaces and reported compliance.

Three minutes and forty-five seconds later, *Donald Cook* was ready for battle in all respects and the OOD reported to Dusty.

"Captain, the ship is rigged for battle stations. DC Central is manned and condition Zebra is set throughout the ship."

"Very well, Lieutenant."

"Captain," the ship's Navigator said. "Crossing the forty-fifth parallel, entering contested Russian waters."

"Very well, Nav," Dusty said and turned to the OOD. "Inform the crew we are crossing into contested waters."

Keying the 1MC, Levy said, "Good morning, *Donald Cook*, the ship is crossing into contested Russian waters and will remain at general quarters until the threat condition changes."

She unkeyed the mike and looked at him, ready for the next order she knew was coming.

"Officer of the Deck, deploy the Nixie," he said. "Spool two thousand feet of tow cable. But I want personnel standing by to cut the cable on my order. God only knows what type of maneuvers we might be required to conduct."

The AN/SLQ-25B Nixie's torpedo-shaped TB-14 vehicle was dragged behind the ship on a tow cable. Its primary purpose was to act as a torpedo countermeasure by emitting simulated broadband noise, propeller signatures, and engineering frequencies to provide a false signature to lure an incoming enemy torpedo away from the ship. It was a fantastic countermeasure, but it also came with a serious tactical constraint. Ordering a backing bell while the Nixie was deployed risked entangling the tow cable around the ship's propellers. It was for this reason that he'd specifically ordered that personnel be standing by at the winch station to cut the cable in an emergency.

The OOD acknowledged the order to deploy the Nixie, then informed the appropriate crew. Moments later, a report came in from the ship's Combat Information Center over the dedicated Net-15 comms circuit between the bridge and CIC.

"Bridge, Combat—radar holds a surface contact, designated Romeo-24, bearing three-zero-two, range twelve nautical miles," Lieutenant Commander Brewster reported. Brewster, the ship's Combat Systems Officer, was standing watch as the Tactical Action Officer. Just like the OOD was the CO's representative on the bridge, the TAO fulfilled an analogous role in Combat, managing the tactical employment of the ship's combat systems and communications. "Sonar has identified the vessel as having two screws," he continued. "Acoustic profile is similar to a previous recording of the guided-missile frigate *Admiral Grigorovich*. Romeo-24 is making twenty-eight knots and is on an intercept course."

"Combat, Bridge, aye. Any ES?" Levy replied.

"Bridge, Combat—negative ES." The new contact wasn't emitting any electronic signature, perhaps trying to hide or delay detection.

"Well, that's not a good sign," Dusty said, with a sideways glance at Levy. "Why announce a blockade and then run quiet . . . unless you're setting a trap?"

"It is odd, sir," she said through an exhale.

"Nervous?" he asked, his voice quiet enough that only she could hear him.

"I'd be lying if I claimed otherwise," she said, then added a belated, "sir."

"And I'd be worried if you weren't. The key, Lieutenant, is to swallow the fear but harness the adrenaline. They're going to try to intimidate us. We cannot let them."

"Yes, sir," she said, and he watched her stand up a little straighter.

"I'm going to take a look outside," he said and grabbed a pair of binoculars.

He walked behind the helmsman steering the ship and passed

through the hatch and onto the port bridge wing. He inhaled as he stepped into the sea breeze and the mélange of odors it carried. Today, the Black Sea was serving up a stale, salty tang with a sulfurous undertone. He looked skyward. The October sun was already high in a faded blue-jean sky with barely a cloud in sight. He scanned for aircraft and didn't see any.

But that didn't mean they weren't up there.

The ship's Aegis Combat System was presently monitoring dozens of aircraft, both civilian and military. The heart of the ACS was the AN/SPY-1 radar and MK 99 Fire Control System, capable of tracking well over one thousand targets with radar cross-sections as small as a bumblebee at ranges over a hundred nautical miles. Nothing above the surface of the water could sneak up on an *Arleigh Burke*, not even Russia's stealthy fifth generation Su-57 fighter. He took comfort in that thought while his gaze drifted to the bluegreen water all around him, where half a dozen silent, invisible killers lurked only God knew where. On its best day, the *Donald Cook* was no match for a Russian Kilo submarine lying in ambush operating on battery. A single Kilo could launch six torpedoes without reloading. Even with the Nixie and all other countermeasures deployed, escape was virtually impossible when faced with a salvo of sixty-five-knot, active-homing Fizik torpedoes.

He set his jaw and pushed the thought out of his head.

His more immediate concern was what to do with Aegis, his ship's most formidable asset. The Black Sea wasn't that big, and the Russians knew exactly where he was. If they weren't tracking the massive electronic signature generated by the SPY-1, which they were, then they certainly had him on satellite. The time for stealth had long since passed. The conundrum now was whether to operate ACS in manual or full automatic. In full auto, the system could detect an enemy missile launch, track it, generate a fire control solution, and shoot down the incoming ordnance without any human interaction or input. This capability was critical because at the current range of the Russian frigate, no human could think and react quickly enough to perform these functions and protect the ship. From a belt-and-suspenders perspective, going full auto was a no brainer. But shooting down a legitimate incoming threat wasn't the only thing an *Arleigh Burke* CO had to worry about.

Donald Cook had a history of being harassed by Russian fighter jets making high-speed passes at dangerously close ranges. If past was prologue, then Russian Sukhoi 27s or 30s would be on him within the hour. Having ACS in full auto when that happened could be an unmitigated disaster. In full auto, odds were over ninety percent that Aegis would miscategorize the Russian fighters as incoming missiles and shoot them down.

Dilemmas, dilemmas, dilemmas, he thought with a heavy exhale. *Address one problem, create another . . . I refuse to be the guy remembered for accidently starting World War III.*

"Combat, Captain," he said over Net-15 via handset. "Confirm ACS is in manual."

"Captain, Combat—confirmed, ACS is in manual," came the reply over speaker.

"Captain, I got something on the horizon, ten o'clock position off the bow," the lookout said. "Good viz today, sir."

Dusty nodded and lifted the high-powered binoculars to his eyes to scan the port forward quadrant. The effective visual range from the bridge elevation on an *Arleigh Burke* was about ten nautical miles, which meant that any minute the Russian frigate should break over the horizon. Just as the lookout had reported, he could make out the main mast of the converging Russian frigate at the ten o'clock position.

He lowered his binos and turned to the lookout. "It's Rogers, right?"

"Yes, sir," the young Seaman Apprentice said.

"Well, Rogers, things are about to get real here in a few minutes. The pucker factor is probably gonna hit eleven, if you know what I mean," he said, meeting the young man's eyes.

"Yes, sir, I hear you."

"This bridge wing is your post, but that doesn't mean you can't take cover if taking cover is warranted."

"Yes, sir. Thank you, sir," the lookout said.

Dusty nodded and lifted his binoculars again. He could now see all of the Russian frigate and the frothy white bow wave it was pushing. He watched it for thirty seconds, and when he lowered his binoculars again, the OOD was standing at his right side.

"You think he's going to try to cut us off?" she asked.

"I think he's playing a game of chicken," Dusty said. "He's gonna stay on this zero-bearing rate vector, force us to slow or turn, and then harass us until we reverse course and hightail it south of the forty-fifth . . . but that's not gonna happen."

"We're the stand-on vessel," she said. "Rules of the road dictate he has to give way."

"Yeah, well, I suspect he doesn't give a shit about the COLREGS, Lieutenant."

The OOD nodded. After an uncomfortable pause, she said, "And if he doesn't alter course?"

"Then I'm afraid we're both going to have a very bad day," he said with fatalistic finality. Turning on a heel, he said, "C'mon, time to get my headset on."

He walked back to the bridge with the OOD in trail, and donned a headset so he could talk freely with Combat. "Combat, Captain—cover Romeo-24 with birds and prepare for a three-round salvo of warning shots fifteen hundred yards off our bow with guns. No mount movement without my approval."

"Birds" was Surface Warfare Officer speak for missiles; *Cook* could fire either the antiship or antiballistic variety. "Guns," of course, referred to the ship's five-inch, 54-caliber deck-mounted cannon.

"Captain, Combat—I just want to make sure I understand. Prep a three-round salvo fifteen hundred yards off Romeo-24's bow, or off our bow?"

"Off our bow—bearing zero-zero-zero relative," Dusty said. "I don't want any confusion. We turn the mount toward him and he's going to assume we're aiming at him. We shoot straight ahead, then hopefully the message is clear—we're going straight, so don't get in our way."

"Aye, sir. Covering Romeo-24 with birds and prepping guns for a three-round salvo fifteen hundred yards off our bow."

"Be ready to fire rounds sequentially on my mark. We're going to show this guy we're plowing straight ahead and what will happen to him if he gets in the way."

"Officer of the Deck, Nav—Romeo-24 is now at eight nautical miles still bearing three-zero-two."

"Very well," the OOD acknowledged.

Tension on the bridge was so thick, the air felt heavy, with all eyes fixated on the Russian frigate on a collision course. Minutes ticked by and the sleek-looking Russian warship loomed larger and larger off the port bow.

"Captain," Levy said, turning up the speaker on the bridge-to-bridge radio. "We're being hailed."

"US Navy warship, US Navy warship," a voice said in Russian-accented English. "This is Russian frigate *Admiral Grigorovich*. You entered Russian territorial water. Turn around. Proceed south of forty-five degrees latitude, immediately."

"Officer of the Deck, respond in accordance with international law," Dusty said.

"Yes, sir," Levy said and issued the following response:

"*Admiral Grigorovich*, this is United States Warship Seven-Five, conducting transit passage on the high seas in accordance with international law. As the stand-on vessel, I intend to maintain course and speed in accordance with international law. Request you alter your course immediately and maintain a safe distance from my ship."

A few seconds passed. "Bridge, Combat—no change to Romeo-24's speed or heading," the TAO reported.

"United States Warship Seven-Five," came the Russian reply, "you have entered Russian territorial water. Turn around. Turn around . . . Proceed south of forty-five degrees latitude, immediately."

"Captain, range to Russian warship is twelve thousand yards. Time to collision: ten minutes six seconds," the Navigator announced.

Levy looked at Dusty, her eyes asking the question.

"Stick to the script," he said.

She nodded and keyed her mike. "*Admiral Grigorovich*, this is United States Warship Seven-Five, conducting transit passage on the high seas in accordance with international law. As the stand-on vessel, I intend to maintain course and speed. Request you alter your course immediately and maintain a safe distance from my ship."

Another minute passed with the Russian frigate still not altering course, then the bridge-to-bridge squawked with a new voice.

"US warship, this is Captain Ruskin of the *Admiral Grigorovich*. You enter Russian territorial water. You must turn around. I repeat, you turn around immediately. Proceed south of forty-five degrees latitude."

Dusty felt his temper building. The Russians were violating international law on multiple counts. *He's baiting me,* he told himself. *Don't take the bait...* Jaw set, he stuck out his hand to the OOD and she passed him the mike.

"Captain Ruskin, this is Warship Seven-Five Charlie-Oscar, I am in international water operating in accordance with international law. I do not understand your intentions. You are the give-way vessel and appear to be heading for an intentional collision. Request you alter your course and maintain a safe distance from my ship. If you do not alter course immediately, I am prepared to take defensive action."

Dusty handed the bridge-to-bridge mike back to Levy. "Any change in the target's course or speed?" he asked the nearby radar console operator.

"No sir," the sailor said.

"Eight minutes, thirty-eight seconds until collision," the Nav chimed in.

"TAO, Captain—what is the status of the gun?" he asked Brewster on the tactical channel.

"Captain, TAO—gun is up, online, ready in all respects for surface action bearing zero-zero-zero relative."

"Officer of the Deck, sound five short blasts and verify the fo'c'sle is clear. Stand by for surface action."

The OOD repeated back the order and carried out his instructions. Then, over the deafening cry of the ship's whistle, she said, "Captain, fo'c'sle is clear. Range visually clear ahead. Russian warship remains off our port bow."

"Very well," he said and issued the order. "Combat, Captain— fire warning shots. Fifteen-hundred-yard offset, bearing zero-zero-zero relative, salvo size one."

A moment later, the ship shook as the .54-caliber deck gun fired a five-inch round straight ahead.

"Let's see what they do now," Dusty said and glanced at the OOD.

"No change to Romeo-24's course or speed," the Nav reported. "Five minutes fifteen seconds until impact."

Dusty felt the nervous tension on the bridge tick up another notch. "Combat, Captain. Fire another warning shot, salvo size one," he ordered.

A moment later, a muffled boom shook the ship as the big gun lobbed another warning shot dead ahead, sending an unmistakable message: *Stay the fuck out of our way or suffer the consequences.*

"Still no change, Captain," the Nav reported, his voice taking on a grim, fatalistic tone. "Four minutes until collision."

With gritted teeth, Dusty threw off his headset and quick-stepped out onto the port bridge wing. The sleek, ghost-grey Russian frigate now loomed large off the port side—the angle of its bow unchanged, still on a collision course.

"Russian frigate thirty-five hundred yards and closing fast," the Nav shouted. "Three minutes until collision."

Dusty grabbed a handset and said, "Combat, Captain—fire another warning shot off our bow, salvo size one."

The MK45 cannon boomed, this time a deafening punch to his ears from his station on the bridge wing. He watched the guided-missile frigate for any response—a change in aspect or bow wake—but the Russian frigate just kept coming.

"Damn it," he snapped and keyed his mike. "Combat, Captain—turn the gun. Target Romeo-24."

Maybe this will get that Russian bastard's attention.

The TAO acknowledged the order, and in Dusty's peripheral vision he saw the barrel of the five-inch gun swivel to port as the *Cook* took aim at the *Admiral Grigorovich*.

"Officer of the Deck, I have the conn," he shouted over his

shoulder to Levy, who was standing just inside the threshold of the open hatch door that separated the pilothouse from the bridge wing.

"Attention in the pilot house, Captain has the conn," she announced, informing everyone on the bridge that the Captain now had control of the ship's helm.

"Officer of the Deck, prepare for collision. Do *not* sound the collision alarm," he shouted. The ship was already in condition Zebra and at a battle stations; it and the crew were in the optimal configuration for any casualty. He needed to alert them to the danger, but could not afford to have the collision alarm drown out his commands in the critical seconds to come.

"All hands brace for impact," she announced over the ship's 1MC. "Collision imminent."

"One minute until impact, Captain!" yelled Nav through the hatch leading to the bridge wing.

Dusty watched in disbelief as every ship captain's nightmare scenario unfolded in real life. A wave of fresh adrenaline electrified his body, while at the same time nausea roiled his guts. His mind flooded with a half-dozen thoughts simultaneously, some productive, some not: *That stupid Russian asshole is actually going to ram us. Fuck it, I should blow him out of the water right now. You can't do that, Dusty. Why not? Because hello, World War III. In five seconds, order a flank bell, then try to pivot around his bow. It could work, or it could sink us.*

He charged into the bridge, nearly knocking the OOD onto her ass as he barreled past her through the open door. "Helm, all engines ahead flank," he shouted.

"All engines ahead flank, aye," the helmsman acknowledged from the ship's control panel. The engine order telegraph chimed and the nine-thousand-ton destroyer began to accelerate.

"Thirty seconds to impact," the Nav reported.

"They're turning, Captain!" the portside lookout screamed.

"Which way?" he hollered, looking left, but in a glance, he answered his own question—as the Russian frigate began to heel over.

"Hard starboard," the lookout yelled.

"Everybody grab onto something," Dusty shouted, readying the next order in his mind. If he didn't time it perfectly, if the Russians countered his maneuver, they would collide. These were big ships, barreling through the water with millions of foot-pounds of energy. They did not turn on a dime. They did not stop on a dime. They did not do *anything* on a dime.

Clutching the side of the control panel and staring at the bow of the Russian frigate, which was now pointing directly at the bridge and less than a hundred yards away, he made the call.

"Helm, hard left rudder!" he shouted, then keying the 1MC, he gave an order to the ship's Chief Engineer. "CHENG, set emergency ahead flank. Give me every turn you can make!"

In preparation for command, prospective COs were given a peek behind the curtain to learn the true mechanical and operational limits of the vessels they were about to command. In the case of the *Arleigh Burke*-class guided-missile destroyer, one of these potentially lifesaving tidbits was that the ship's main turbine engines could boost power above the regular limit for a short duration. Since he'd assumed command, he'd not ordered a flank emergency bell. Most of the crew probably didn't even know the option existed . . . but they did now.

As the rudders swept to port, and the twin propellers churned at 110 percent of their rated speed, the *Donald Cook* heeled over hard to starboard. In the bridge, all potential flying gear had been stowed, but the same could not be said for the rest of the ship. The violent roll to the right dumped foodstuffs from racks, books from shelves, coffee mugs from desks and tables, and everything else not lashed down, bolted to a bulkhead, or welded to the deck. Out the portside bridge windows, Dusty watched the *Admiral Grigorovich*'s bow angle change from starboard to port as the *Cook* turned left—toward the Russian frigate—in an attempt to pivot around the nose of the ship about to ram them. Time slowed, and the two massive warships danced in a terrible, awkward dance.

"Oh shit," someone shouted.

The port bridge wing lookout hit the deck and covered his head.

Commander Dusty Townsend—captain of the USS *Donald Cook* and custodian of 381 American lives—watched with equal parts horror and wonder as the Russian ship and his ship curled past one another with less than thirty feet separation hull to hull. At such close range, hydrodynamic forces could suck them together for a broadside collision any second.

"Helm—rudder amidships, steady as she goes," Dusty ordered as their beams crossed. Then, knowing that the *Admiral Grigorovich* was moments from crossing their wake, he keyed the 1MC and said, "Combat, Bridge, cut the Nixie tow cable."

Better to sacrifice the TB-14 willingly than have the winch ripped out of its mounts when the Russian destroyer ran over the tow cable and it became entangled in its props.

"Cut the Nixie tow cable, aye," the TAO replied.

With the rudder eased, the *Cook* righted herself—the list coming off just as the two warships' sterns cleared each other by less than ten feet.

"Holy fucking shit," the CMC said, wiping sweat from his brow. "Nice driving, Captain."

"Thanks, Master Chief, but stay frosty, people, because that was just a warm-up. God only knows what those crazy Russians will do next."

"Understood," the CMC said with a grave nod.

"Bridge, Sonar—the Nixie tow cable is cut," came the report to the bridge.

"Helm, right full rudder, steady course three-five-nine," he said, then keying the 1MC, he said, "XO to the bridge."

The helm acknowledged the order and spun the pilot wheel right to get the *Cook* back on course. Thirty seconds later, the XO was on the bridge, pale-faced and visibly shaking.

"What the hell were they thinking?" she said. "That stunt almost sank us both."

"I know," he said. He lowered his voice and walked her out onto the bridge wing, where they both saw that the *Admiral Grigorovich* was already coming about. "Listen, I think the odds of us getting out of this operation casualty-free are shrinking. We officially just busted their blockade, and I don't think the Kremlin is going to like that. I'm not going to shoot first, but I will shoot back."

"Yes, sir," she said. "We're on the same page, but technically, you did shoot first."

Her words were like a bucket of cold water to the face. Yes, technically they were warning shots, but the record would show that *Donald Cook*, not the *Admiral Grigorovich*, had fired its gun first. And while the rules of the road were on his side, an argument could be made that the United States had been the aggressor in that encounter.

"Yeah," he murmured. "I suppose I did."

She flashed him a tight grin but didn't offer a follow-up comment.

"Is our air support on station?" he said, his brain already thinking two steps ahead. "Because after this dustup, I imagine the Russians will scramble jets to intercept us any minute."

She nodded. "You can't see 'em, but two Raptors, call signs Shaker One and Shaker Two, are up there. And we've got an EC-8 turning donuts in Romanian airspace coordinating."

"All right, good."

"You're worried about the Kilos, aren't you?" she said, reading his mind.

"Yeah, I had to ditch the Nixie," he grumbled.

"I know, but there's no way you could have anticipated what just happened. Cutting the cable was the smart play. We've still got plenty of cable on the reel and a spare TB-14. Want me to have the techs get to work mating it up?"

"Yeah," he said.

"Captain," the OOD called from the doorway. "CHENG just reported exhaust high-temperature alarm on 1A GTM, as well as high temps in the reduction gear lube oil and starboard shaft main bearing. How long do you want to stay at emergency flank speed?"

"Shit, I forgot." He turned toward the open port bridge hatch and hollered, "Helm, make turns for thirty knots."

"Make turns for thirty knots, aye, sir," the helm replied.

"Captain, Combat—we have indications and warnings that two Russian aircraft just took off from Sevastopol," Brewster reported from the old school "squawk box" on the bridge wing. Dusty always found it reassuring that despite the ship's immense technological complexity, some of the most trustworthy and reliable equipment hadn't changed in more than seventy years.

If it ain't broke, don't fix it . . .

Keying a handset, he said, "Copy." Then, turning to his XO: "You need to get back to Combat. I want verbal confirmation from each station that all defensive weapons and countermeasures are ready to go."

"Yes, sir."

"And I want Tactical Tomahawk missions built for the Sevastopol airfield—runways and parked aircraft only. Do not target hangars, the tower, or barracks."

"It's already in the works," she said with a wry grin.

He smiled back, then said, "Get moving, XO. I'm going to stay here."

"Yes, sir," she said and left.

He glanced aft. The Russian frigate had already come about and was now in pursuit. He watched, noting that the range looked to be holding steady. According to *Jane's Fighting Ships*, the *Admiral Grigorovich* was good for thirty knots. He'd know soon enough if the reference book was accurate. When the high temps cleared, he could probably eke out thirty-two knots without alarms, but at this speed he was burning fuel like mad. They couldn't keep this up forever, and he needed to have gas for evasive maneuvers and to flank if necessary on the return trip with the *Oak Hill* . . .

Assuming we make the return trip.

He glanced at the lookout, who was scanning the horizon with his binoculars.

"See anything?" Dusty asked.

"Other than that Russian frigate on our ass, no, sir," came the young man's reply.

"That was a close one, wasn't it?"

"Any closer, sir, and I would have shit my pants," the lookout said.

"Yeah, me too, shipmate," he said with a chuckle.

Me too . . .

"Captain, CCS reports all propulsion high-temperature alarms clear," the OOD said, joining them on the bridge wing.

"Very well."

"Bridge, Combat—two Russian fighters are inbound at eight hundred knots, bearing zero-four-two. Radar signature is consistent with the Su-30 platform. ETA sixty seconds," the TAO reported.

"Combat, Captain—roger. Cover inbound Russian fighters

with birds and issue an emergency warning Military Air Distress," he replied, then turned to the OOD and lookout. "We've got Russian fighters inbound from the northeast. Things are about to get dicey."

"Bridge, Combat—already in progress, Captain. Negative response to queries or warning on MAD and IAD. Inbound fighters, designated Romeo-25 and Romeo-26, are illuminating ownship. Request permission to place SeaRAM in AAW auto mode?"

He didn't answer and gestured with his head for the OOD to follow him to the other bridge wing.

The inbound Su-30s were Russia's equivalent to America's F-15 Strike Eagle. Like the F-15, they could carry a substantial payload of air-to-air, air-to-ground, and antiship missiles. It was the latter he was concerned about—specifically the Kh-31A, a supersonic, sea-skimming missile that could close the distance between them in virtually no time at all. Placing the ship's eleven-cell SeaRAM defensive missile system in antiair warfare auto would buy potentially lifesaving time in the event the fighters launched missiles at the ship, but Dusty also knew the system could engage the fighters themselves if the Russian pilots' flight paths too closely resembled inbound missiles.

"I've got two inbound aircraft," the starboard bridge wing lookout said. "Just above the horizon."

"I know," he shouted and grabbed a handset. "Combat, Captain—no to SeaRAM in auto. Confirm you are covering aircraft with birds?"

"Affirm, Captain, two engagements on standby in the queue. Salvo size two," the TAO came back.

"Roger, standby," he said.

He felt his heart rate pick up, and his pulse was a bass drum in his ears.

The game of chicken he'd just played with the *Admiral Grigo-rovich* had unfolded over fifteen minutes. This round could be decided in the next fifteen seconds. He was betting this was a show of force by the Russians, not an attack. If he was right, nothing would happen. If he was wrong, the ship and 300 of his shipmates could be lost . . . He gripped the metal doorframe and watched the twin black dots converging on his ship grow bigger. They were coming in low and hot. He estimated they couldn't be more than two hundred feet off the deck. The irony of the situation was not lost on him, as *Donald Cook* had been antagonized by Russian aircraft at danger-close range twice before.

Hopefully, third time's not a charm, he thought, then felt the surprising and overwhelming urge to order Combat to blow the inbound fighters out of the sky. ACS had radar lock and a firing solution. With the press of a button, a pair of SM-2 surface-to-air missiles would blast out of the forward VLS missile battery, streak through the sky, and the threat would be vaporized. But as much as a part of him desperately wanted to just make the problem go away, he knew he couldn't do that.

I have to stay the course. Keep a steady hand on the wheel and my eye on the objective.

No sooner had he finished the thought than the Su-30s were upon them. The lead jet was flying even lower than he'd thought.

"Get low," he heard himself shout at the starboard lookout as the Russian fighters screamed toward them at ludicrous speed.

The first Su-30 streaked across the bow, leading the bridge by less than thirty feet and clearing the deck by less than ten, afterburners blazing. The other Russian jet broke the sound barrier fifty yards off the port bow. The deafening sonic boom and accompanying shockwave hit the ship a split second later, shaking the superstructure with enough force to be mistaken for an actual projectile impact.

Time seemed to shift into low gear as he took in everything: the Conning Officer covering his ears; the starboard lookout on hands and knees out on the bridge wing, eyes wide with fear and confusion; the helmsman clutching the ship's wheel so tight his knuckles looked like eight tiny snow-covered peaks . . .

"Jesus fucking Christ," the CMC shouted, spittle flying from his lips. "That asshole almost hit us."

"They're coming around for another pass!" the port lookout yelled.

Fists clenched, Dusty charged across the bridge to the port bridge wing. "Where is our goddamn air support?" he shouted as he watched the two Russian fighters banking for their next run. Grabbing a mike, he yelled, "XO, get the CAP on the horn and tell them to step in anytime. Because if they don't, someone's gonna die!"

CHAPTER 26

Lead F-22 Raptor
Call Sign Shaker One
One Hundred Miles South of Odessa
28,000 Feet Over the Black Sea

Major Meg "Lady Goose" Gregory eased back the twin throttles of the miracle air-superiority stealth fighter her country had entrusted her to fly for the past eleven years. The Raptor responded smoothly, the altimeter marking a rapid descent and her ears popping as she and her wingman, Shaker Two, descended toward the Black Sea. Her maneuver was in response to the order from aerial command transmitted via an EC-8 control aircraft circling over Romania. The entire battle space was a managed operation—with data links from satellites, all friendly aircraft in theater, and a special U2 configured as eyes and an aerial relay station from eighty thousand feet over the Black Sea.

As the two F-22s descended, she applied gentle left pressure to the control stick in her right hand and eased up a touch on the throttle in her left. The jet responded like the Lamborghini of fighter jets that it was, snapping into a hard left bank and pressing her into her seat at four Gs. She felt the familiar squeeze of the G-suit against her torso and legs as it inflated to prevent blood from pooling in her lower extremities. She led the rollout as the directional indicator approached her heading, wings snapping level just as she hit two hundred and ten degrees on the heading tape at the top of the heads-up display. The altimeter read twelve thousand feet, and she made her way down to eight. A moment later the controller spoke again in her helmet, the voice now more urgent.

"Shaker, your bogey is now twelve o'clock, fifteen miles, descending rapidly toward Delta Charlie. Cleared to engage."

Cleared to engage? Are they fucking serious? We're supposed to engage a pair of Russian Su-30s in international airspace?

"Shaker flight," she said, acknowledging. "Shaker Zero-Two, let's get down there and see what they're up to."

Their F-22s would be all but invisible, thanks to the Raptors' stealth technology being a generation ahead of the Russian aircraft. The Russian Su-30s were more on par with the Navy's workhorse F/A-18 Super Hornets, the same platform that only six months ago she and her wingman had dispatched in a training exercise without the Navy pilots ever even making contact. But she wanted to see for herself what the hell these Russians were up to before she engaged and started World War III.

She leveled off at fifteen hundred feet, the two enemy aircraft now designated on her heads-up display as red triangles just outside the green ten-mile ring. Inside that ring, at six miles, was a yellow box indicating the position of "Delta Charlie"—the USS *Donald Cook*. She didn't paint the Russian jets with her own radar just yet—

that would give away her position and ruin her advantage—but
Donald Cook's Aegis system was tracking them perfectly, and that
data streamed to her via data links with the EC-8. To her right, she
was aware of her wingman, "Paris," sliding out to the south, increasing their separation at combat spread. At over six hundred
knots, the distance to target closed rapidly and she picked up the
two Russian fighters visually twenty seconds later.

The lead fighter was low—incredibly low, less than one hundred feet off the deck and offset seventy degrees—crossing right to
left and heading directly at the *Cook*. The Russian's wingman was
only a bit higher, perhaps five hundred feet, and a half-mile north
and in trail. Gregory pulled gently back on the stick, gaining altitude
to twenty-five hundred feet in a few seconds and leveling off. The
Russians, intent, apparently, on harassing the *Cook*, still seemed
oblivious to her presence. She watched as the Russian jet screamed
across the destroyer's bow at danger-close range—the distance between its left wingtip and the conning tower mere feet. She could
see the ant-sized sailors diving for the deck as the jet streaked past.

Holy shit!

The Su-30 pulled up and made a hard left, condensation
streaming from its wingtips in the tight, high-G turn. Gregory
watched the Russian jet accelerate out of the turn, head north, then
make a tight, high-G, two-hundred-and-seventy-degree turn to loop
around behind the destroyer. She'd lost visual on the maniac's
wingman, but her heads-up display said the other Russian was in a
wider circle, also turning counterclockwise and at her three o'clock.

"He's gonna make another run," Paris said in her ears.

Gregory passed over the *Donald Cook* at three thousand feet and
started her own right turn, eyes fixed on the target on her display.

"I'm on him," she said. "High cover—clear my six of his
wingman."

"Shaker Two," Paris acknowledged.

The Russian fighter lined up again with the destroyer, three miles out and below her. Gregory rolled smartly until her jet was inverted, pulled the stick back sharply, and dove the Raptor through a split-S, then rolled level at five hundred feet, directly on the Russian jet's tail, one mile in tow. She pushed up the throttle with her left hand and felt the jet accelerate, closing the distance to less than half a mile almost instantly. She lined the velocity vector over the Su-30 on her display, then, using her thumb, activated the weapons radar. Immediately, a red box appeared around the enemy fighter and a steady warble sounded in her headset just as the targeting computer's soft female voice said, "Shoot . . . shoot . . ."

A tone must have sounded in the Su-30 indicating that the jet had been locked on by an enemy missile, because things instantly went to shit. The surprise apparently distracted the pilot at the worst possible time—just as the Russian was crossing the bow of the *Donald Cook*.

She watched the twin-engine fighter bobble and the left wingtip droop. Had he been anywhere other than over a Navy ship, the subtle bobble would have been meaningless, but here it was enough that the left wingtip dragged across the ship's superstructure, sparks flying and the jet's nose yawing impossibly left. Its altitude dropped, and she watched the pilot struggle for control. For a moment, just as she streaked past overhead in a gentle nose-up climb, she thought the Russian pilot might recover, but then the jet overcorrected right and its other wingtip dipped into the ocean. There was an explosion as the ejection system spit off the canopy, and the jet then began to tumble.

Oh fuck.

She pulled back on the stick and her Raptor snapped up and over, its variable-direction exhaust nozzles shifting automatically to achieve an impossibly tight loop. The hard maneuver activated her G-suit, and she gritted her teeth while it squeezed her legs and abdomen. A heartbeat later, she came out of the turn and pressed the stick forward to level off. Now inverted, she strained her neck to scan the ocean below. She quickly spotted the debris field—what remained of the Su-30 was spread over a quarter mile across the surface of the Black Sea. She didn't see an orange parachute anywhere but only had limited time to scan.

No way the pilot survived that if he didn't eject in time.

She rolled her jet back over and pulled up to gain eyes on the second jet. Her heads-up showed the other red box west and circling, rapidly gaining altitude and speed.

"Shaker One, be advised we have lost radar contact with your bogey. The second bogey is now at your ten o'clock and . . . stand by . . ." Then the controller's voiced tightened. "Shaker, Delta Charlie reports she is being painted by enemy aircraft. Radar lock. Be advised this aircraft is known to carry the Kalibr antiship missile—with a strike range in excess of two hundred miles."

Her HUD showed Paris maneuvering around behind the second Su-30. "Striker One—Two—I have a shot," he said.

"Engage, Two. I'm on my way." She pulled her Raptor left and up toward the approaching threat, trailing her wingman.

"That Russian's not gonna fire, right?" Paris choked into the radio. "I mean for God's sake—there are three hundred sailors on that ship."

Gregory was asking the same question in her mind, but she knew it all depended on whether the second Su-30 pilot had seen the accident or thought *Donald Cook* had shot down his wingman. She watched on her HUD as Paris's Raptor maneuvered for a firing solution on the Russian jet, but if he closed range any more, he'd be too close for a safe missile kill with his AIM-9L Sidewinder.

What the hell is he doing? Shoot, Paris. Shoot, damn it.

She locked her own medium-range missile on the target just as she acquired a visual on the Su-30 and spotted Paris directly on the Russian's tail, ridiculously tight. Then she saw the burst of his Raptor's M61A2 20 mm cannon. She watched the tracers streak from her wingman's fighter over the enemy jet cockpit like laser blasts in a sci-fi movie.

A warble in her ear told her that her own AIM-9Lima was locked on the Su-30. The combination of missile-lock tone and 20 mm cannon tracers streaking by seemed more than the Russian pilot could take. He pulled straight up, afterburners glowing, and then broke north. She never saw a missile leave his rails—if he even had an antiship missile aboard. As the Russian pilot streaked away, she wondered if the pilot had any idea that Captain Steve "Paris" Hilton, United States Air Force, had just saved his life.

She'd been set to pull the trigger.

"Second bogey is bugging out," Paris reported.

"Roger, Two," she said. "Good thinking, brother," she added, then let out a long, slow breath. "Sentry Two-Five, be advised, the first bandit crashed after inadvertent contact with Delta Charlie and bandit number two is departing the area. Shaker flight climbing and resuming CAP."

If anything happened to them on the remainder of this Combat Air Patrol, someone needed to know that the Russian died from his own fuckup, not from American fire.

It might matter—a lot.

"Roger, Shaker One. Good work guys. Delta Charlie reports no other immediate threats. Diverting their helo for recovery of the pilot."

Her heart slowed a touch. Maybe the Russian pilot had gotten out after all. The *Donald Cook* must have seen a chute, right? She glanced over to her right shoulder as Paris's beautiful grey F-22 Raptor pulled in tight beside her. Through the tinted canopy bubble, she watched him shake his head slowly, then make a show of dropping his head and shoulders in relief. She shot him a thumbs-up, which he returned, and then he slid out to the right and dropped below her as they resumed their patrol.

"Sentry Two-Five, this is Shaker flight—we're gonna need a drink pretty soon."

"Roger, Shaker. Your relief is inbound and we have Texaco four-one setting up an orbit to top you off."

Gregory shook her own head now and allowed herself a long sigh. The Black Sea was a pressure cooker—too many ships and aircraft packed into a captive theater.

Someone's going to fuck up and then the real shooting is going to start.

She tossed the thought off for later and scanned the battle space map on the center screen between her knees, looking for the next target. All the while hoping that there was someone above her pay grade out there working to deescalate this nightmare before it got completely out of control.

CHAPTER 27

USS Donald Cook (DDG-75)
Nine Nautical Miles North of the 45th Parallel
The Black Sea

Dusty gripped the railing on the port bridge wing with both hands. He watched as the Russian fighter pilot's parachute hit the water and collapsed into a flat orange wrinkled disc on the surface three hundred yards off the port beam. He contemplated slowing, the man-overboard rescue instinct strong in him from two decades of conditioning.

No, he thought, shaking his head. *The helo can get him.*

He grabbed a headset from the bridge wing station and slipped it on his head. "Growler One, this is *Donald Cook* actual," he said, hailing the MH-60 that he'd ordered airborne before crossing the forty-fifth parallel.

"Go for Growler One," the helo pilot, Lieutenant Harts, came back.

"Did you see what just happened?"

"Watched the whole fucking thing, Captain," Harts said. "You guys okay?"

"No casualties here, but I doubt the pilot survived. Looked like he did try to eject, however. I saw a parachute splash down off our port side."

"We saw it. I'm repositioning into a hover over the splash zone now. Want us to conduct search and rescue or leave him for the Russians to pick up? That frigate back there is closing fast."

"Scoop him out if you can and bring him back to the *Cook*. Anything we can do to look like the good guys in this scenario only works in our favor," Dusty said.

And it would be nice to have a bargaining chip in my pocket, too.

"Roger that, Captain," Harts said, and after a brief pause added, "Well, he's not dead, 'cause there's movement under the chute . . . Looks like he's trying to clear it."

"Captain, TAO—the other Russian fighter is bugging out," Brewster reported from Combat.

"Copy," Dusty said. "Do we have new bogies inbound?"

"Not yet."

"Roger that. You let me know the second that changes."

"Yes, sir."

"Growler One, SITREP?" he asked, leaning over the railing to look aft. They were steaming at flank speed, and the splashed pilot was well in their wake now.

"He's clear of the chute and waving at us. We're dropping the rescue sling. We'll see if he takes it . . ."

"Captain, XO—we're getting an alarm on the SLQ-32 operator console. We think the Su-30 must have clipped the starboard ESM antenna assembly when it hit us."

"Shit," he said. *Of course he did. Why clip the railing, or the deck mount, or the hull when you can hit an antenna* . . . "All right, secure power to the starboard ESM until we can look at it. The last thing we need is an electrical fire."

"Secure power to the starboard ESM, aye," she said.

"Captain, Growler One—the Russian pilot's in the sling," the helo pilot reported. "We're winching him up."

"Nice work, Growler One. Return to ship once he's secure and give us a heads-up on his injuries so I can have medical standing by."

"Copy all," Harts came back.

"Bridge, Combat—we are tracking two new surface contacts inbound," Brewster reported. "Romeo-27, bearing zero-seven-nine, has a sonar signature matching the *Admiral Grigorovich*-class guided-missile frigate. Romeo-28, bearing three-five-five, has a different signature. We believe it is a Project 22160 patrol ship, but that is unconfirmed. Both vessels are on intercept courses."

"Wonderful," Dusty murmured. He hung up his headset and made his way back inside the bridge.

"Captain, do you want me to slow for helo recovery?" the Conning Officer asked, catching his eye. "We've got a helluva squat at this speed."

Dusty blew air through his teeth. His OOD was right; helo recovery at this speed was a risky maneuver. "Slow to twenty knots for the recovery, but keep the speed on until Growler is ready for his approach."

"Aye, sir."

He walked to the captain's chair, slid his right ass cheek up onto the cushion, and grabbed a headset. Just taking a little weight off his feet—which were barking mad—felt damn good. He was about to tell the CMC to take a look at the starboard ESM antenna assembly and see what he could see when the XO hailed him from Combat.

"Captain, XO—I've got the CO of the *Oak Hill* on chat," she said. "You wanna swap?"

"Copy," he said, then quickly added, "Hey, XO, make sure we get a quick turnaround on SAR ops. It should practically be a touch-and-go—offload the Russian pilot, then back in the air."

"Understood, Captain," she said.

He removed his headset, departed the bridge, and walked aft to Combat. Upon entering, he was hit by a blast of dry, chilled air and the sterile odor of electronics and vinyl.

"Captain in Combat," the closest sailor announced the moment he crossed the threshold.

He paused to let his eyes adjust to the low-level light in the overcrowded information hub. The space he'd just come from compared to the one he'd just entered was, literally and figuratively, night and day. For Dusty, entering CIC felt like stepping out of the real world and into a video game. If not for the rocking motion from the waves, he could easily forget he was on a ship. Most of the sailors within sat at workstations in front of flat-panel monitors lit with graphic representations of data streams from the *Cook*'s myriad sensors. Others manned various weapons control panels, navigation displays, or communication equipment.

"I'm heading to the bridge," the XO said, scooting past him on the right. Swapping command locations was their default protocol. Even in peacetime, they rarely occupied the same space at the same time. Physical separation accomplished two important objectives: first, it prevented a single incident from incapacitating or killing the ship's #1 and #2 in command at the same time; and second, it distributed the command presence.

He nodded at her and she was gone.

"Over here, Captain," Brewster said, gesturing to a laptop set up on the TAO's desk.

Dusty sat down at the keyboard to message with the CO of the *Oak Hill*, Commander Needham. Thankfully, this was not the first time the two men had worked together. *Hey, Josh, you still on the line?* he typed.

Several long seconds later, the reply came. *Hey Dusty, FYI—we are underway and steaming south.*

Dusty nodded to himself but knew that wasn't the whole story. Both ships' positions were being tracked, communicated, and updated in real-time to each other's CIC computers, as well as to the Task Group Commander on the *Ford*. This statement was simply prelude; Needham was touching base about something else.

All good. How is that rust bucket you call a ship? he fired back.

Seaworthy . . . you guys okay?

Dusty laughed and then typed, *We're one itchy trigger finger away from somebody, or a whole lotta of somebodies, getting blown up.*

We've been watching. Looks like our friends in Sevastopol are not making life easy.

Shit no. The sooner we rendezvous, turn around, and start steaming south together, the better.

About that, Needham typed. *As a courtesy, I wanted to let you know that I really appreciate you walking into the lion's den to escort us out.*

This comment piqued Dusty's interest. *"As a courtesy"? Huh?* Sure, when everything was said and done he'd fully expected a thank-you call from Needham, but to take time to message about it now . . . No, the *Oak Hill's* CO was trying to tell him something else.

As a courtesy? he typed, prompting.

Yes, all 402 souls aboard the Oak Hill *are in your debt.*

His mind instantly did the math. *Four hundred and two souls? That's ship's complement. What about the 400+ embarked Marines they were carrying? Holy shit, they left the Marines behind in Odessa! Those sneaky grunt bastards . . . Talk about big brass balls.*

Thanks for the heads-up, Dusty typed. *And I want you to know it wouldn't matter whether you had 400 or 800 souls aboard*—Donald Cook *has your back. See you soon, Captain.*

You too, Captain, the CO of the *Oak Hill* wrote, then logged out.

"Everything all right?" Brewster asked.

"Not sure," he said, his gaze going to the middle distance. "The *Oak Hill* departed without her Marines aboard."

"On purpose?" Brewster asked, his eyes going wide.

Dusty nodded.

"Well, that can't be good."

"Yeah, we'll see," he said, then added, "I'm heading back to the bridge. Keep a close eye on those incoming Russian ships."

"Yes sir," Brewster said. "Always."

Dusty moved with purpose out of CIC. The moment he exited, he was hit by a wave of warm, humid air and was instantly light blind. Squinting hard, he quickstepped to the bridge, where he found the XO and the OOD both wearing headsets and talking together.

"You have something for me?" he said, noting their serious expressions.

"Yes, sir. Sonar just reported an active ping from bearing one-seven-zero," the XO said.

A lump the size of a golf ball materialized in his throat. "The *Admiral Grigorovich?*"

"No sir, Romeo-24 bears one-eight-two," the OOD said.

"Is the helo in the air?"

"Not yet, sir."

"Why the fuck not?"

"Um, as I understand it, the pilot needed to, uh . . . you know," Levy said.

"No, Lieutenant, I don't know."

"He needed to take a shit, sir," she said with a tight-lipped grin.

"So, we have a Russian Kilo ranging our stern and our helo pilot is in the head?" He turned from Levy to the XO. "XO, what part of touch-and-go was I not clear about? If that Kilo launches a torpedo and I turn this boat, we'll dump that Seahawk overboard."

"I understand and I apologize, Captain. I was just whipping that horse when we got the report from sonar," the XO said, her gaze downcast.

Hot with anger, he grabbed the 1MC. "Lieutenant Harts, this is the Captain. You have ninety seconds to get your ass back in your Seahawk or it is taking off without you. And if that happens, then report to the bridge immediately for lookout duty."

"Oh snap," the helmsman said under his breath, and chuckled. "Cap'n's pissed."

Dusty turned to Lieutenant Levy and said, "OOD—Green Deck!" Giving the order to launch the helo immediately.

"Yes sir," she said, but before she could utter the order, the XO piped up.

"Hang on—deck crew says the pilot's running onto the flight deck now . . . All right, he's in the cockpit."

Dusty shook his head. "Fucking aviators. Next time, I bet we'll find him in crew's mess getting autodog," he said, and then imitating the pilot's laid-back Kentucky drawl: "Relax, bro—I was just getting some *fro-yo*."

Everyone on the bridge laughed at that, including the CMC, which was saying something. A little comic relief to break the tension before they got blown up was probably a good thing.

"Growler's in the air," the XO said and handed him her headset, preparing to return to Combat. "The pilot's asking for you, Captain."

"Before you go, there's something else," he said, dropping his

248

voice to a whisper. "The *Oak Hill* departed port *without* the 26th MEU. They must have offloaded all the Marines last night before the ship got underway."

She blew air through pursed lips. "So what does that mean for us? Are we going to have to go back and pick the Marines up if things get worse?"

Dusty thought for a second and said, "Probably the opposite. Unless this thing winds down in a hurry, I have a feeling they'll be in Ukraine for quite some time."

She nodded. "Any strategic adjustments you want to make?"

"Depends on what happens when the other frigate and patrol boat show up," he said. "And if their submarines keep pinging us."

"Roger that," she said, and departed for Combat.

He slipped the headset on over his ball cap. "Captain on the line."

"Captain, Growler One," the helo pilot said. "I figured I had a minute while EMS was offloading that Russian pilot. Looks like I figured wrong."

"While *you* were taking a crap, Harts, we got pinged by a Kilo. If that sub-boat captain had decided to launch a torpedo at us during that window, I would not have been able to execute torpedo-evasion protocols. The ship can't maneuver with your bird on her back."

"Understood, sir. Won't happen again . . . So, uh, you want me to go find that Kilo for ya'll? Drop a couple sonobuoys on his ass?"

"I think that's a great idea," Dusty said. "Just watch out for that frigate behind us. I suspect he's not so pleased with us at the moment. Happy hunting, Growler."

"Roger that, sir. SITREP to follow when we have something, Growler out."

"Combat, Bridge—any more pings from the Russian submarine?" he asked, looking out the starboard door at the water.

"No, sir," Brewster said. "Too bad, too, otherwise we'd be able to pinpoint his location. As it is, one ping only gives us a line of bearing."

"You scanning for periscopes with the SPY-1?" he asked.

"Yes, sir. I have a radar operator dedicated to it and sonar is doing their best, but with us hauling ass in a straight line, sonar is pretty much useless. So long as the towed array is stowed, it's gonna be impossible to hear, let alone locate, a diesel submarine operating on batteries."

Dusty pressed his lips together. Brewster was telling it straight. Hunting submarines required patience, frequent maneuvering, and a speed and configuration that did not diminish sonar performance. The helo was dropping sonobuoys, but his gut told him there were multiple Kilos tracking him right now and there was no way Growler could find all of them.

A lone thought occurred to him that suddenly made him feel a little bit better, if only momentarily. "Well, TAO, so long as we're surrounded by the Russian Black Sea surface fleet, I don't suspect the Kilos will be firing any torpedoes in our direction. But if our Russian escorts suddenly bug out and we find ourselves alone in open water . . . well, that's when we need to start worrying."

"I tell you what, Cap'n—it ain't easy being an *Arleigh Burke* alone in a Russian swimming pool. They can kill us from the air, from the sea, and from below. I don't even want to know how many cruise missiles and torpedoes are pointed at this ship right now. Hell, never in a million years did I think I'd say this, but if I had the choice between driving on the surface or being on a sub where I can submerge and disappear, I'd pick the sub."

"Yeah, but then all your sperm would be irradiated and you'd be shooting blanks for the rest of your life. Trust me, SWO is the only way to go."

Brewster laughed at this, and so did a few others listening on the line—the first levity on NET-15 in hours.

"Nav, how long until we rendezvous with the *Oak Hill?*" Dusty asked.

"We're making thirty-one knots and she's making twenty-four. At this rate, we'll intercept her track in forty-two minutes."

"Good," he said. "Any new airborne threats?"

"Not yet, Captain," Brewster said.

"What's the status of our Russian pilot?" he said, realizing he'd not received a status report from the Corpsman on their "guest" and probably should have by now.

"Captain, we're being hailed by the *Admiral Grigorovich,*" the OOD said. "Captain Ruskin is on the bridge-to-bridge. You want to talk to him?"

"Damn," he grumbled. "Somebody tell the Corpsman to get his ass to the bridge with an update on the pilot."

"Yes, sir," Levy said, then nodded to a subordinate watch stander to make the call.

Dusty exhaled loudly and took the bridge-to-bridge call. "This is Warship Seven-Five, over."

"Captain Townsend," the Russian skipper said, his voice equal parts irritation and self-righteous superiority. "You are making many very bad decisions. If you are not being careful, you might find your ship on the bottom of the Black Sea."

The fact that his Russian counterpart had called him by name pissed Dusty off. Yes, that sort of information was open source, but making things personal just escalated the tension. If this asshole started mentioning his wife and kids by name, shit was gonna get real serious, real fast.

Using the most condescending and sarcastic tone he could muster, he said, "Russian frigate, this is United States Warship Seven-Five operating in international waters with due regard for international law. Request you state your intentions and maintain safe distance, over."

The Russian didn't respond for a long moment, before finally saying, "You have taken prisoner a Russian pilot and officer. We want him back."

Dusty rolled his eyes. "Warship Seven-Five has conducted search and rescue operations in international waters while proceeding on duties assigned. The status of any persons located adrift is a matter for the international courts. I recommend you contact the United States government through official channels if you'd like to know more. I am not at liberty to discuss the status of any persons under my protection."

In his peripheral vision, Dusty could see that the ship's Corpsman, Chief Donovan, had arrived on the bridge and was making his way over.

"Unacceptable," Ruskin said, dispensing with call signs and radio protocols. "We will be sending our helicopter to retrieve our comrade."

"Russian frigate, this is Warship Seven-Five. My flight deck is not certified for Russian aircraft and I cannot ensure the airworthiness of your helicopter. I have already observed the quality of your airmanship during the previous engagement, which risked serious damage to my vessel and harm to personnel. Warship Seven-Five, out."

Dusty removed his headset and turned his attention to the Corpsman. "What's up, Doc? How is our Russian pilot?"

"You want it in layman's terms or doctor speak?" Chief Donovan asked.

"English, please."

The doc nodded. "Well, Cap'n, he's pretty fucked up. I don't know how fast he was going when he hit the water, but he hit hard. To be honest with you, I don't know how he got himself into the rescue sling. Bunch of broken ribs, broken right arm, broken right leg . . . he's got feeling in his toes, but I think his spine is broken."

"Geez, that doesn't sound good," Dusty said.

"No, and that's not even the worst of it. He's bleeding internally. His BP is dropping and his belly's getting bigger, and as you know, I am not properly equipped to operate on him. If we don't get him to a hospital soon, he's not going to make it."

"Hmmm," Dusty said, rubbing his jaw. "Can he make it four hours? Because that's about how long it's gonna take us to meet up with the *Oak Hill*, turn around, and clear this Russian blockade."

The doc blew air through his teeth, then shook his head. "I don't think so, Cap'n."

"Shit," he said and crossed his arms against his chest.

"Maybe we need to give him back to the Russians," the CMC suggested.

Dusty shook his head. "Then we lose our leverage."

"But if he dies on our watch they'll blame us."

"I know," he said, oozing with frustration. "I'm gonna talk to the XO; she's good at coming up with solutions to impossible problems like this." He grabbed a headset and walked her through everything he and the Corpsman had just discussed. "So, what do you think?"

"What if we split the baby?" she said.

"What do you mean?"

"We could fly him to Mihail Kogălniceanu Air Base in Romania. Didn't the Marines send an FRSS team there in addition to staging the F-35s? They could operate on him there and, technically, he's still in American custody."

"Not a bad idea . . . but then Growler would be out of pocket for the remainder of our transit. I don't like the idea of giving up our only ASW asset."

"Good point, but doesn't the *Oak Hill* have a helo? We could keep Growler engaged and use their bird for the CASEVAC."

"Nice," he said but hesitated.

"What's wrong?" she asked.

"Well, it's just that if we send him to MK, in effect we're transferring our leverage. As long as he's aboard, the Russians are gonna think twice before engaging us."

"Okay . . . what if we dress him up in one of our uniforms and put a helmet on him so even if the Russians are watching they don't know what we're doing? We squawk about some other reason why the *Oak Hill*'s helo is jumping around. Personnel swap or something like that."

"So sneaky. I love it," he said, his mood suddenly supercharged as she clicked the last puzzle piece into place. "You're a genius, XO, thanks."

"Anytime, Captain," she said, clearly pleased.

With a crooked smile, he turned to the CMC, the Corpsman, and the OOD, who were clustered around him with expectant eyes. "All right, people, here's what we're going to do . . ."

CHAPTER 28

Dnipropetrovsk International Airport
Dnipro, Ukraine
140 Miles Northwest of Mariupol
1845 Local Time

Dempsey stepped out of Ember's Boeing 787 and onto the landing at the top of the airstair.

This place smells like shit, he thought, expecting fresh air but getting a waft of sewage truck instead.

"Well, isn't this another lovely fucking place you've found for us, John?" Munn gave a tight grin over his shoulder as they descended the rusty rolling airstair that had been pushed up against the Boeing by an ancient-looking pickup truck with one flat tire. Dempsey, a large duffle over one shoulder and a hard Pelican case in the other hand, followed his teammate to the bottom of the creaky stairs and out onto the cracked cement.

"Any place that has an actual runway—much less an airstair—is an improvement over most of the places we've fought in over the years, Dan."

"That's fair," Munn said with a chuckle, but Dempsey saw the SEAL-turned-surgeon-turned-spook wink at Grimes, who smiled back, her own gear weighing her down.

Dempsey scanned the area around him while turning in a full circle to get his bearings. Across the runway was a line of corporate jets, a mix of sleek western and boxier Russian designs that, he supposed, embodied the schizophrenic nation of Ukraine—a former Eastern bloc, Soviet Union state trying desperately to transform into a Western capitalist nation. To the north of the runway in the western corner of the airfield was a series of old-school alert hangars with a handful of Su-25 attack jets in front of them, but no vehicles or personnel in sight.

In the center of the field, he noticed the frame of a large uncompleted building—a future terminal they'd learned was being built by the Ukrainian airline Dniproavia, until funds had dried up. Just beyond the trees to his left, he identified the long noses of five MiG-29 fighter jets, each with a generator unit beside it and a modern-looking fuel truck off to the left. There, a jeep sat with its lights on and three heavily armed soldiers paced casually around the line of jets. Beside the main terminal, two Mi-8 armed transport helicopters sat on either side of a row of Mi-24 helicopter gunships. And last but not least, he saw the sewer truck he'd smelled on arrival, rolling in their direction, in preparation to empty their sanitary tanks.

"Not much civilian activity for a supposed international airport," Martin chuckled as he dropped his gear on the ground. "I didn't know this was, like, an active fighter base."

"Ukrainian Air Command East is co-located with the civilian

airport," Grimes said. "And they have helicopters here most of the time—or at least that's what Casey said in the brief. There's an antiaircraft missile brigade command out of here, with S-300s and a bunch of support stuff. There aren't usually fighters at this location, so this must be where the Ukrainian Air Force intends to counter the Russians from."

A black car—flags fluttering from posts above each headlight—appeared on the tarmac, heading their direction.

"Oh look, here comes the welcome wagon," Dempsey said.

The car pulled up and a young man in a Ukrainian military uniform—which to Dempsey looked very Russian in style—climbed out of the front passenger seat. He hustled to the rear door, opened it, then snapped to attention and saluted. A tall, solidly built man emerged, dressed in a smartly appointed uniform. The VIP approached them, hand out in greeting. As Dempsey shook it, the senior officer flashed him a broad, infectious smile.

"I am General Valeriy Antonets, commander of Air Command Centre," the General said in accented English. He shook Dempsey's hand hard enough to signal he was a fellow warrior. "We are very grateful to have our American allies here with us." Antonets released his hand and clapped him firmly on the shoulders with both hands. For a moment, Dempsey worried the man might lean in and kiss both of his cheeks, but instead the General let go and gestured in an arc around them. "It is not usually this quiet here, I assure you. This airfield moves nearly a quarter million passengers for Dnipropetrovsk Airline. That is no London or New York, but busy for a city the size of Dnipro. Given recent events, however, we have closed the airport for commercial travel. Russians are not above shooting down civilian airliners, as you are no doubt aware, and even more so if they can make it look like someone else's fault."

Dempsey instantly caught the not-so-subtle reference to Malaysia Airlines Flight 17. "I hear you," he said, watching the General tug at his thick mustache.

Eyes twinkling with a fire Dempsey recognized all too well, Antonets gestured toward the row of MiG-29s. "Soon the skies will be filled with the sound of our fighters flying sorties, and together with our American allies, we will keep our people safe from Petrov's pigs. I know it might not look like much to you, but what we lack in money and spare parts, we make up for in spirit. Our pilots have hearts of lions. We fight for our homes . . . for our freedom. You understand?"

"We understand," Munn said, smiling. "Better than most."

"And how can I support you while you are here? How can I help make your mission a success?"

"We were told you have supporting documentation that might smooth our travel en route to Mariupol?" Dempsey said, hoping that was still the case.

"Of course," the General said. "When the rest of your team arrives, my plans and operations unit is waiting for you in the office inside the hangar. We will provide photo IDs as well as a letter from the Defense Minister. This will clear the way for you on your travels in Ukrainian-controlled areas but will have little value with any Russians you encounter in Mariupol. Perhaps, it may get you shot."

The General laughed at this, and Dempsey found the laugh contagious, though the message unsettling.

"Our government believes your fate and ours are linked, General," Munn said. "And we completely agree. It is an honor to serve with you against a fellow enemy."

Dempsey turned at the sound of four turboprop engines beating the skies into submission to the southwest. The incoming Super Hercules landed on the main runway and taxied over to the wide ramp beside the administration building.

"It appears the rest of our team is here, General," Dempsey said, and this time, he clapped the General's shoulders, making sure to convey his own strength. "We appreciate the safety our aircraft and crew will enjoy with your jets and missiles protecting the skies and this airfield."

As soon as the C-130J parked, the rear ramp dropped. A moment later, up-armored SUVs drove out and parked in an arc behind the tactical airlifter.

"Whatever your mission is, I hope it is a success," the General said, perhaps believing if he hinted enough, they might read him into their op.

"I hope so, too, General. If it is, perhaps we can help keep this conflict short. If not, I look forward to fighting beside you and your men."

The General let out a big belly laugh and turned to walk beside Dempsey toward the eight-man SEAL team climbing out to greet them.

"Then I hope you have wings, my friend," the General said, clapping him on the back one last time before peeling off and heading to his car. "I only rain down death from the sky! You call me if you need me . . ."

"We'll do that, General," Dempsey said, smiling as he watched the man slip back into his long black car.

"That ain't their whole Air Force, I hope," Martin quipped once Antonets had departed. He looked back over his shoulder at the short row of jets behind them on the alert ramp. The former MARSOC Marine tightened the sling on the suppressed MCX on his chest and unconsciously ran his hands over his ammo pouches. "'Cause we may actually need some close-in air support on this one."

Dempsey nodded, but his attention was on the SEALs as he

squinted to make out the man he was looking for. When a stout, powerfully built operator came strolling down the ramp, fully kitted up for battle, a grin spread across Dempsey's face. He raised his hand, but instead of waving back, Lieutenant Commander Keith "Chunk" Redman stopped on the ramp, put his hands on his hips, and shook his head. The SEAL waited like that until Dempsey was standing toe to toe in front of him.

"You . . . son . . . of . . . a . . . bitch . . ." Redman said. Behind the officer, three of the gathered SEALs were smiling, while the others exchanged worried looks. "I thought this would be just another easy-day rescue op—eight Americans caught in the crossfire between indistinguishable Slavic forces, in the middle of a Russian invasion backed up by advanced fire power, cruise missiles, and nukes. But now that you're here, I know with absolute certainty that the shit will really hit the fan."

"It's good to see you too, Chunk," Dempsey said, extending his hand to the SEAL officer who was close to ten years his junior.

Chunk broke, bursting into a laugh as he ignored the hand and instead wrapped Dempsey up in a bear hug—practically lifting him off the ground. As he crushed Dempsey in the embrace, he quietly said, "Bro, I'm so sorry about how everything went down. I haven't been able to get Newport News out of my head."

Dempsey returned the hug, then gave Chunk's back a slap. "We're still putting the pieces back together, but thank you."

With the somber business concluded, Chunk's trademark tobacco-stained grin reappeared. "Damn. it's good to see you."

"You too, bro." Dempsey looked past him at the other SEALs, some of whom he recognized from their last op together. "What's up, Saw? Riker . . . Trip . . ." He nodded to the three men he'd fought and very nearly died beside the last time they took on Russian special forces.

"Mr. Dempsey," Saw said, with a nod.

"What's up, dude?" Riker asked with a smile.

Trip grinned and gave a mocking two-finger salute.

"It's great to see you guys," Dempsey said. "For real, man."

"Lady Grimes," Chunk said with a ridiculous bow. Grimes swatted him on the top of the head in response.

"Chunk," she said and smiled. "Guys."

"Doc, how are you?" Chunk said, turning to Munn. "Still regretting your decision to work with this death-cheating, terrorist-hunting, spooky-ass son of a bitch?"

"Every damn day," Munn said, and shook Chunk's hand.

"Well," Chunk said, taking a step back as if to survey the lot of them. "I assume that since *you* guys are the 'special task force' that we were to meet up with—and I secretly hoped it was you, I promise—there must certainly be something else going on in Mariupol besides what the Head Shed briefed us on. I'm guessing that the rescue we came to execute is only the tip of some shit-covered iceberg, right?"

Dempsey shrugged but couldn't suppress a wry chuckle.

"Then why don't you step into my office and give me the skinny on whatever James-Bond-save-the-world bullshit you're piling onto our OPORD?"

"I'd be delighted," Dempsey said, leading the way up the ramp into the Super Hercules.

"Make sure we have all the ammo we can possibly carry, guys," Chunk called over his shoulder. "John Dempsey and his team are coming along, so we're definitely gonna need it."

Then he joined Dempsey in the helicopter, leaving his boys to get to know Grimes, Munn, and Martin—all that was left of the Ember SAD.

CHAPTER 29

Lead SUV of a Four-Vehicle Convoy

H-08 Highway

Fifty-Five Kilometers Northwest of Mariupol, Ukraine

October 2

0055 Local Time

"So . . . we're certain that Ukrainian forces are controlling this highway in and out of Mariupol, correct?" Dempsey asked, changing hands on the steering wheel.

"That's the intel," Chunk said from the passenger seat. He opened a laptop and shoved a satellite antenna up onto the dash and went to work. As the SEAL officer tapped away on the secure computer, Dempsey assumed he was asking whoever he had running intel for them—probably all the way back aboard the USS *Gerald R. Ford*—for confirmation on the checkpoint. "Hold on . . ."

Dempsey flipped his NVGs up on his helmet and strained to

see what was going on ahead of them. Whoever was clustered in both lanes of the highway wasn't trying to be covert, as headlights were blazing from at least two large vehicles. He eased off the accelerator and let the SUV drift slowly to a stop without signaling as much with brake lights.

"Home Plate, you got ears on?" Dempsey asked, talking over the Ember microtransmitter in his left ear. He definitely wanted to hear what Chunk's N2 intel guys had to say, but Wang was Ember. And he had Baldwin and the rest of the team in Tampa backing them up.

"Yeah, I got ya, Yankee One. I show you three miles west of Rozivka. I just hacked the radio comms at the checkpoint—God, these guys love shoving consonants together. Can I buy a vowel already?" Dempsey smiled, relieved to hear the old Wang in his ear. "I got a cluster of vehicles on the H-08, just ahead of you and west of town. We have satellite, but no drone this far out. Let me zoom in and see what's going on . . ."

"Check."

"JD, my guys confirm that Ukrainian forces are controlling movement in and out of Mariupol on the west side; for now, they still own the M14 between Odessa and Mariupol," Chunk said, relaying the intel streaming onto his tablet, "but farther east is a crapshoot. The Russians are already across the border and in the city. They seem to control the H-20 from Mariupol north for a good distance. They're moving armor south on that highway, though I have no fucking clue how they got armor in place that fast. Must have had it pre-staged in the DPR. More importantly, my guys are equally clueless who the hell these guys are up ahead."

"I'm afraid I'm not much help, either," Wang added. "These assholes all look alike and I'm not sure how to tell Ukrainians from Russians, let alone good guy Ukrainians from pro-Russian separatists. And the Ukrainian military doesn't have the best command and control going on. So here's what I see—you have a group of nine armed soldiers with a technical, plus two drivers," Wang reported, referring to the heavy machine gun mounted in the bed of one of the vehicles. "No markings on the truck, but they are those big-ass KrAZ-6322 trucks, the newer ones that the Ukrainian Army uses. I'm trying to find out from our friends in Dnipro if Ukrainian forces set up another checkpoint this far out, but as I said . . ."

"No way to know," Dempsey said.

"No way to be sure," Wang confirmed.

The four-vehicle convoy of up-armored Chevy Suburbans that Dempsey and Team Four were cruising in were running blacked out—with no headlights—and all of them on NVGs. So far, there was no indication that anyone at the checkpoint had seen them.

"Russians would be running satellite and probably drone over-flight surveillance, right?" Chunk asked, flipping up his NVGs and looking over at Dempsey in the dim red glow from the low-level dashboard lights. "Maybe these guys are militia? We know the Ukrainians conscript local help when needed."

It made sense, but Dempsey still didn't like it. Something felt off.

"Let's roll up, lights on, and see what we get," he said, fishing out the identification cards General Antonets's people had provided, along with a letter from the Ukrainian Minister of Defense stating that they were operating in an official capacity in support of the Ukrainian Army. If this *was* a Ukrainian military checkpoint, or even local militia, then they were sure to be anti-Russia and their paperwork would suffice.

But if this is Russian military or the fake pro-Russian separatists staffed by undercover Spetsnaz operators, then we're gonna be in some hot shit . . .

"You sure?" Chunk said.

"Maybe we hold back two, just in case."

"Yeah," the SEAL said and keyed his mike. "Vehicles Three and Four, drift wide left and right, hold back and give us some sniper overwatch. Lead and Two are going to roll up and see what's going on."

Dempsey switched on his headlights and accelerated into the left lane as vehicle two, carrying Munn and two of Chunk's SEALs, pulled in behind them. The other two SUVs stayed back, stationary with their lights off, to support sniper coverage.

"They see you now," Wang said in Dempsey's ear. "They're spreading out in cover behind their trucks, and they got someone up on the technical."

Dempsey looked at his tablet, sitting on the center console. It was streaming Wang's satellite feed, which zoomed in on the soldiers beside the trucks.

"I hope they're Ukrainians," he said, looking over at Chunk.

The SEAL officer grimaced. "Me too."

They were still two hundred meters away. If these guys didn't have drones and satellites like Dempsey and his team—and didn't have sentries watching from the shadows farther up the road—then there was a good chance they didn't know about the rear two SUVs. Grimes and Saw, their two snipers, wouldn't have any height advantage, but they could at least take out the heavy gunner if things went to shit.

"Zeus One, in position," Saw reported.

"Zeus Two is set," Grimes called in a heartbeat later.

Dempsey took off his helmet and handed it to Trip, who was sitting in the seat behind him. "I'm gonna need that back," he said with a grin, as Chunk did the same with his helmet.

"Since when did I become the luggage bitch?" Trip said, but tucked the two helmets with NVGs out of view.

Dempsey looked over at Chunk. "All right, here we go. If this is nothing, we'll just let them know we have two more in trail, and then we cover them as they pass the checkpoint. If this is something evil, we're offset and have snipers on the heavy gunner at least."

"Solid." Chunk nodded. "I like it."

Dempsey eased his way into the checkpoint, keeping the speed down nice and low. As they closed the last fifty meters, all the checkpoint shooters—along with the DShK 12.7 mm heavy gunner, turned their muzzles on Dempsey's vehicle. His heart rate ticking up a notch, Dempsey drifted slowly to a stop, turning the Suburban slightly at the last second to open up a line of fire for the SEAL Team Four operator in the middle seat. He rolled down his window, showing his hands. To his right, Chunk did the same.

"Zeus One has the heavy gunner," Saw's quiet voice said in his ear.

"Zeus Two is on the two guys approaching Vehicle One," Grimes said in the calm, singsong manner that meant she was in her sniper zone.

The soldier apparently in charge approached, his rifle slung on his shoulder. A younger man beside him aimed at Dempsey through the windshield over his iron sight.

"AKS assault rifles," Chunk murmured. "That's a Ukrainian military weapon. And those look like for-real Ukrainian uniforms . . . I think."

Dempsey glanced over and gave him a tight grin, keeping his hands out the window.

"The separatists wore them, too, in the war in Donbas," he said, remembering the confusing mix of good and bad guys they'd been briefed on. "And uniforms are easy to get." It was estimated that more than half the combatants in Donbas were covert Russian paramilitary posing as Ukrainian separatists. Casey had warned them that this was almost certainly how the Russians would try to confuse the narrative in this conflict as well.

So, who are these guys—Ukrainians, or Russians pretending to be Ukrainians?

The lead soldier shouted a command at Dempsey.

"I believe he's ordering you to step out of the vehicle," Baldwin said in Dempsey's ear, speaking for the first time. "One moment . . . Voice analysis suggests this is native Ukrainian; however, the Ukrainian and Russian vocabularies overlap by sixty percent, so I'll need to hear more to be certain."

Awesome. Very helpful, Ian.

"No," Dempsey said loudly out the window, then used one of the few Ukrainian phrases he had memorized to explain they were Americans with official paperwork.

The lead officer seemed to relax—but only a little. The young soldier beside him didn't flinch and kept his rifle trained on Dempsey's face, his finger inside the trigger guard.

"Do you speak English?" Munn asked from the passenger window of Vehicle Two beside them. Dempsey realized that was smart—getting straight to the point and speaking in English. The next ten seconds would answer a lot of questions.

The lead officer didn't reply. Instead, he pulled a small tablet—or perhaps a large mobile phone—from his pocket and appeared to snap pictures of them. Next, he cautiously approached the window, where Dempsey slowly and deliberately handed over their ID cards and letter from the Ukrainian Minister of Defense. Beside him, Chunk was squinting to see through the dirty windshield as the man inspected their documents, but Dempsey also noted·the SEAL checking his SOPMOD M4 without looking down.

"You set, Bart?" Chunk said over his shoulder to the SEAL behind him.

Dempsey saw it now—the mussed, spikey hair and the round nose. Damn if the young SEAL didn't look a bit like Bart Simpson . . .

"Set, boss," the SEAL said. "I got the two guys hanging back on the right."

"I'll take the officer at my door," Dempsey whispered, and brought his own hands in, draping his left hand casually over the steering wheel, and the right gripping the rifle slung on his chest.

"Zeus Two has the ready shooter with the lead," Grimes said in his ear, not missing a beat.

The ready shooter still had his rifle raised at the windshield but was aiming a bit more vaguely now, his cheek having come off the stock. Dempsey scanned the other shooters—all of whom had weapons raised but seemed more relaxed now. His eyes flicked up to the gunner on the technical in the back of the truck. The man's right hand was still on one of the twin trigger handles, but his left now held a cigarette to his lips for a long drag.

Dempsey tapped his index finger against the trigger guard as he watched the officer inspect the letter carefully, using the light from the SUV's headlights. Then he made a cursory inspection of the three ID cards for Dempsey, Chunk, and Bart. The officer said something to his cover man, who nodded and lowered his rifle to a relaxed carry. Then he called back to the men beside the trucks. The right-side truck—the one with the heavy machine gun—backed up ten feet or so, the gunner now pointing the deadly weapon down toward the deck. The officer then waved them through.

Dempsey pulled forward and let their SUV drift to a stop near the officer.

"Dyakuyu," he said, thanking him and taking back their documents. "There will be others coming behind us, okay? Understand? *Rozumlyete?"*

The officer nodded and saluted them. Dempsey maneuvered the Suburban between the two trucks, Riker and Munn on his tail.

"Three and Four, give us a half mile or so and then pull up and do as we did."

A double-click in his ear told him his message had been received.

"Hold overwatch a minute until we're clear," he added as an afterthought.

Can't be too careful . . .

The second SUV, with Riker at the wheel, pulled up beside them, Riker grinning and Munn giving him a thumbs-up. Trip handed Dempsey and Chunk their NVGs back and everything was perfect, until it all changed in an instant.

"Yankee One, it's Mother. The lead officer is taking an incoming phone call. Something's wrong—"

"The heavy gunner is back up," Saw reported, his voice tight. "He's spinning around and looks like he's gonna engage . . ."

"They're all repositioning. Get out of there!" Wang cried.

"Take him, Zeus," Dempsey barked as he swerved left and accelerated hard. Riker broke right, just as a short burst of heavy machine gun fire exploded aft and flooded the gap between them. Tracers screamed past Dempsey on his right, but before the gunner could correct and drag the deadly fire across their SUV, the fire abruptly stopped.

"Gunner down on the technical," Saw said.

"Lead officer is down," Grimes called immediately after.

Dempsey jerked the SUV sideways on the road, donned his helmet, and crawled out the passenger door after Chunk just as bullets began to ping off the Suburban's body panels and stars appeared on the bulletproof glass. Unlike the 12.7 mm technical, the regular rifle fire posed little risk of penetrating the up-armored vehicle's cabin. Dempsey pulled down his NVGs, placed his green IR designator on a fighter firing from the back of one of the trucks, and squeezed the trigger, dropping the man. He shifted his aim left, found a second target, and squeezed again.

"North truck driver down," Grimes said, in her zone, confirming another kill.

"South driver down," Saw added.

It was over before Dempsey's heart rate even had a chance to climb. With Saw and Grimes on the roofs of the SUVs behind the blockade, augmented by three more of Chunk's SEALs plus Martin, the deadly crossfire had finished the enemy in mere seconds.

"Clear," Dempsey said, rising from behind the bullet-pocked truck. "On me," he said.

He led the other five men, including Munn, Riker, Chunk, Bart, and another SEAL, up the road, fanning out and scanning over their weapons at the carnage they'd left in their wake.

"Hold until we clear you through, Zeus Two," he called to Grimes.

"Check," she replied.

"Roads are clear, Yankee. I hold no inbound trouble. Repeat, no inbound," Wang said in his ear. "That includes thermal, by the way. But be aware, someone at the checkpoint sent a message off before the incoming phone call and the firefight."

"A message to who?"

"No idea—but it was heavily encrypted."

"More than we would expect from regular Ukrainian Army—which I think we all agree these men were not," Baldwin added. "And they're too sophisticated for local militia or separatists. This event would seem to have a Russian signature on it."

Dempsey thought about the pictures the officer in charge had snapped with his phone.

Fuck . . .

"Well, that means someone knows we're here."

"Agreed, Yankee One. Recommend you clear out quickly," Baldwin said.

They fanned out in a loose perimeter, scanning the checkpoint for survivors. The heavy machine gunner was draped over the truck's railing like someone's dirty laundry, the top of his head missing from the eyebrows up, courtesy of Saw's sharp sniping. The officer in charge was crumpled on his side with a round hole over his left eye and much of the back of his skull missing. *God, I love ya, Grimes.* The rest of the soldiers were sprawled out dead in various positions where they'd fallen.

"Man, I hope we didn't just kill a whole bunch of Ukrainians," Chunk said, shaking his head at the carnage. "Gonna be hard to explain this to General Antonets if we did."

"Yeah," Dempsey said absently, while thinking of their secondary mandate—to find and capture the suspected Zeta and GRU troublemaker Maksim Kuznetsov. Was that who the lead officer had sent their photos to? Was it Kuznetsov who'd called and ordered the attack? He used a boot to roll the dead officer onto his back, then fished the large cell phone from the man's oversized BDU-style breast pocket. He dropped the device into his own thigh cargo pocket. Moments later, SUVs Three and Four arrived at the checkpoint, lights out. Through the windshield, Dempsey saw Grimes riding shotgun, her face lit from below on night vision by the dashboard lights. She gave Dempsey a thumbs-up as they passed, and he nodded in reply.

"Man, that girl is badass," Chunk said with more than admiration in his voice. "Where do I get me one of those?"

"Not at Hot Tuna or any of the places you hang out, boss," the SEAL called Bart said with a grin.

"That's fair," Chunk said as they hustled back to their Suburbans.

"We need to roll," Dempsey said, feeling the urgency as he climbed into the driver's seat.

"Yeah, but the problem is—they know where we're going," Munn added. "There's nothing on the other end of this road other than Mariupol."

"But they don't know about the rescue op," he said.

"And what about the other objective?" Chunk asked as he slid into the passenger seat. "The super-secret squirrel shit you and your team's got going on?"

Dempsey sighed. Any SEAL team could rescue the CIA officers stranded in Mariupol. Ember's tasking was to capture Kuznetsov to prove that this entire conflict was a Russian operation to annex southern Ukraine. In his heart, Dempsey was certain that Kuznetsov, if not an active Zeta, at least reported to the Zeta spymaster—because when it came to Russian false flag operations, all roads led to Zhukov.

"Yeah, well." Dempsey straightened the truck out on the road and continued heading toward Mariupol, lights out. "If this dude is connected with who we think he is, the benefit is worth the extra risk." He glanced at Chunk, who nodded. Chunk got it. He'd been there at the Ember hangar in the aftermath of the Zeta attack.

"Amen, brother," the SEAL said and started packing a dip. "You know I always got your back."

"Hey, Home Plate?" Dempsey said, pinging Wang.

"Go, Yankee One," Wang answered after a second's delay.

"It's probably a good time to let our friends at Mariupol Maritime Logistics know we're coming. Now that someone knows we're here, we're not gonna have time to fuck around."

"Copy that, Yankee," Wang said.

"And keep running your voodoo magic, Home Plate. Find me my target in Mariupol."

"I'm on it."

"We're gonna have to be quick about this whole thing," Chunk said, a polite way of saying what they were both thinking. As usual, Murphy's Law was intervening to make their already overly ambitious tasking virtually impossible.

The Russian Army was already in Mariupol.

And now, it appeared, that Army knew they were coming.

CHAPTER 30

Embraer Phenom 300

33,000 Feet Over Lublin, Poland

0145 Local Time

Arkady crossed his legs at the knees and accepted the cup of steaming black coffee from the attractive flight attendant in the short black skirt and starched white blouse. In regular times, he'd never drink coffee at this hour, but these weren't regular times, were they? Tonight, he doubted his head would find the pillow, and if it did it wouldn't matter—his mind was a cyclone of thoughts and emotions, too raucous and irritated for sleep.

"Thank you, my dear," he said in flawless German, setting the coffee on the polished wood table beside his oversized leather seat.

She nodded and returned to the galley at the front of the executive jet.

His NOC for this trip was Herr Dieter Hemmler, founder and

CEO of an industrial farming equipment manufacturing company that had opened a plant paying rock-bottom wages in Mykolaiv, sixty-five miles east of Odessa. Herr Hemmler was a hands-on guy, and with all that was going on in Ukraine had insisted on meeting with the principals in the operation. While the wealthy businessman did not see any reason to head east of Odessa—each mile of which took one closer to the conflict, and thus, danger—he had received permission from Ukrainian authorities to meet his local partners at Odessa International Airport's VIP terminal, which a large sum of money had reserved for the meeting.

The beauty of the NOC was that Herr Hemmler and his company actually existed. Following a "failed" attempt on his life—carried out by Arkady's Zetas operating undercover—the real Herr Hemmler had decided to manage his business from the privacy of a chalet in Austria. The international security expert Hemmler had contracted to provide body double services had been none other than Arkady Zhukov himself. In this role, Arkady freely travelled under Hemmler's identity with zero chance of crossing paths with the man. The tail number, and even the paint scheme, of this Embraer Phenom matched Hemmler's real jet, which operated out of Dortmund.

Arkady had taught his Zetas for years the importance of building covers and NOCs based on reality. That was how they stood up to scrutiny. The Hemmler NOC was the ultimate demonstration of this methodology. He scowled and indulged in a long sigh, thinking back to Zeta's golden days . . .

Give the Americans another month, and I'll have no one left alive in my ranks to teach such tradecraft to.

None of his operators knew the truth—that Spetsgruppa Zeta was much smaller than anyone realized. The list of operators in the field and their NOCs were small enough that he kept the complete dossier only in his head. Task Force Ember had inflicted tremen-

dous damage on the operation, thinning his ranks by over fifty percent since the assault on the training compound in Vyborg last
June. He had a small team operating in Mariupol, a handful of operators scattered around the world still embedded in their NOCs,
one loose cannon he'd nearly pulled the plug on in Buenos Aires a
year ago, and, of course, Gavriil and his team in Odessa. Thank
God for Gavriil . . .

As if on cue, the satellite phone beside him chirped, snapping
him from his brooding. He looked at the incoming number and
took the call.

"Hemmler," he said.

"I have an update for you," Gavriil said, all business.

"Tell me," Arkady said, sipping his coffee.

"We have a positive identification on a team of Americans
heading into Mariupol. The Americans evaded capture—in fact,
they killed an entire checkpoint contingent—but not before one of
the soldiers sent photos to GRU. GRU notified Kuznetsov and he
notified me. One of them is the American operator we believe to
be in charge of Task Force Ember."

"That is excellent news, but not surprising. How long ago was
this?"

"Within the hour," Gavriil said. "Do you wish me to go to Mariupol and intervene?"

Arkady took a long sip of coffee.

Whereas the previous Prime, Valerian Kobak, had been driven
by passion and, should one call them . . . hungers, Gavriil was driv-
en by the purest of motivators—the desire to win. His competitive
nature was off the charts. But he still didn't quite see the forest for
the trees. Eliminating the Ember threat was important, but the operation in Odessa was *more* important. During his last meeting with
Petrov in the Kremlin, the Russian President had ordered Arkady

to do the unthinkable—target Russian forces in Mariupol with a short-range ballistic missile launched from Odessa. To all the world, the strike would look like Ukraine had attacked the Russian Army, giving Moscow the justification it needed to escalate the conflict and bring the full might of the Russian military down on its recalcitrant neighbor to the east.

But what Petrov did not know was that Arkady had other plans. Yes, Zeta would launch the missile, but he would leave behind evidence pointing to Russia. The attack would bring things to a head in Ukraine, but not in the way Petrov imagined. Petrov's malice and mental instability would reverberate on the world stage, setting cogs of regime change in motion—thereby saving Mother Russia from Petrov and paving the way for another, more capable leader to return her to her former greatness.

"No," he said at last. "You have your mission. Kuznetsov has his."

"Yes, but I don't think he understands who hunts him. I tried to explain what is coming for him, but he is so arrogant. He didn't want to hear it."

"So, you're convinced Kuznetsov is the target?"

"Of course. Ember has been hunting our people for months," Gavriil said, growing exasperated. "And this time they have a full team—a dozen operators."

Arkady rubbed his chin. "In that case, I'm not so sure Kuznetsov is the target. They may be tasked to evacuate the American CIA ISR group in Mariupol."

"Mariupol Maritime Logistics?" Gavriil asked.

"Precisely," Arkady said. "Coordinate with your brother Zeta in Mariupol. If he isn't already making plans, tell him I want Task Force Ember to receive a proper welcome. After that, I want you to focus exclusively on the mission in Odessa."

"Understood."

"How are things progressing?"

"The pieces are falling into place. The asset is en route from Crimea," Gavriil said, "and I'm finalizing the warehouse contract tonight."

"Excellent. I look forward to a full update in a few hours when I arrive."

An uncomfortably long pause hung on the line, one that Arkady enjoyed very much.

"Arrive . . . here? You are coming to Odessa?"

"*Da,*" he said. "Our ranks are very thin. You have Zeus and Ruben, but I fear it's not enough. I once operated like you. I still have some skills."

"Certainly, of course." Gavriil's voice confirmed he didn't know what to think of this twist. "Will you come to me or . . ."

"Meet me at the Odessa airport when you've finished your work," Arkady said. "You can brief me en route to the storage facility."

"And we stay together until the plan is executed?"

"Yes," Arkady said, catching the eye of the flight attendant and raising his cooling cup. "God willing, we execute the mission and exfil together. We can discuss the next steps I alluded to during our last conversation on our journey back to Moscow."

"I understand," Gavriil said, no angst or regret in his voice. Valerian had been a terrifying weapon as Prime, but Gavriil's measured, outcome-driven style would serve him well in the future—in the new Russia.

"I know you do," Arkady said.

Then, as was his habit, he disconnected the call without waiting for a reply.

The flight attendant bent over to pour fresh coffee in his cup, making no effort at modesty as her blouse fell open. She smiled at him.

"Thank you, my dear," he said.

If I were a younger man . . .

Of course, if he were a younger man, he would already be on the ground in Odessa, personally executing his plan to restore Russia to greatness himself. No matter. At least he would be alive to see it. That alone was more than he might have reasonably expected.

CHAPTER 31

Unregistered Domestic Detention Center

Tampa, Florida

October 1

1907 Local Time

The buzzer sounded, the lock clicked, and the door opened.

"Hey, Doug," Amanda said, greeting the big man with a smile.

"Hey, you," the security guard said, closing the door behind her.

"How are the kids?"

He shrugged. "Been better. Dorothy is upset 'cause she lost her ruby slippers, and Toto ran away. I was out all night, pounding the yellow brick road and questioning every munchkin I could find, looking for that stupid dog."

"Did you get him back?"

"Yeah, a winged monkey dropped him off at like two a.m.," he said with a theatrical headshake.

"*Wizard of Oz* on the brain tonight, huh?" she said with a chuckle.

"Yeah," he said, "just watched it with my real kids for the first time."

"Nice," she said, a little surprised. This was the first time he'd ever pulled back the curtain on his real family life. "It's definitely a classic. Did they like it?"

"Oh yeah, right up to the point when the flying monkeys started ripping the scarecrow apart. That freaked them out and we had to take a break. I'm telling you, those friggin' flying monkeys are the stuff of nightmares."

"Hmmm, funny. They never really bothered me. It was the angry, floating wizard head that creeped me out as a kid," she said, and then, getting down to business, "How's Bessonov doing?"

"Same old, same old," he said with disinterest. "Lounging on the sofa, watching TV all day."

Amanda nodded, not surprised at his report, and pulled her Sig P365 SAS subcompact from her ankle holster. She set the weapon, along with her purse, inside the plastic crate beside the "apartment" door.

"All right, we'll see how belligerent she is today."

Doug unlocked and opened the door for her.

The second Amanda stepped across the threshold, she sensed something wasn't right. For starters, the television was much louder than normal. The air inside felt different, as if charged with static electricity. Gooseflesh stood up on the back of her neck as the door closed and locked behind her.

"Sylvie?" she called, scanning the room for her charge.

Essentially a studio apartment, the space was simplistic and small. The windowless living room had a twin bed against the right wall, a kitchenette on the left, and a sofa in the middle that faced a sixty-inch TV mounted on the opposite wall. Her gaze flicked to the screen, where *Starship Troopers* was streaming. Gunfire raged as human soldiers fought giant arachnids in a severed-limb-flying, blood-and guts-splattering gorefest of epic proportions.

Fear blossomed in her chest as her mind pre-imaged a crazed and wild-eyed Russian girl leaping over the sofa and attacking her. She pushed the thought from her head and took a tentative step toward the back of the sofa. "Sylvie?" she called again, debating if she should get Doug.

Don't be ridiculous, she thought, silently chastising herself.

Then, steeling her mind, she strode with purpose around the sofa, hoping to find Bessonov sprawled out on the cushions, fast asleep. But as she gave the sofa a wide berth, she found it vacant. That left only one possible place the Russian could be—in the bathroom. Amanda picked up the television remote control off the armrest and pressed the mute button, silencing the auditory chaos that made it impossible to think.

Better.

She exhaled and shifted her gaze to the crack at the bottom of the closed bathroom door, where a strip of yellow light glowed between the tile reveal and the slab.

"Sylvie, it's Amanda. Are you in the bathroom?" she called and knocked twice on the door.

When still no answer came, she looked up at one of the black-domed security cameras that hung down from the ceiling. Undoubtedly, Doug was watching. She gave the camera a *WTF* shrug, then returned her attention to the bathroom door.

Screw it.

"Sylvie, I'm coming in," she said, turning the knob and cautiously pushing the door inward.

Her stomach dropped at the sight inside.

The Russian girl, barefoot and wearing only a t-shirt and underwear, was standing on the toilet seat with a corded noose around her neck tied off to a fire sprinkler nozzle in the ceiling. Amanda glanced at the girl's sweatpants and hoodie, both of which were lying discarded on the floor. Immediately, she understood—the drawstrings from the waistband of the pants and the hood of the pullover were both missing.

"Sylvie," she said, cautiously raising both hands palms up and out. "What are you doing?"

The Russian Zeta smiled at her—eyes manic, lips curled in a disturbed grin. "Dieter Hemmler—that's the last and most important name I will give you."

"Sylvie, no. You don't have to do this," Amanda said, taking a cautious step forward.

"I don't know if he will use the alias again, because he rarely leaves Russia. But if he does, this is how you will find him. It is the *only* way you will find him."

"Who are we talking about, Sylvie ... who is Dieter Hemmler?"

Bessonov's smile softened—transforming from unhinged to forlorn. "You are a good person, Amanda. In different circumstances, I think we could have been friends."

"No!" Amanda screamed as the Russian stepped off the toilet. She charged forward and caught Bessonov around the waist, trying desperately to hoist the other woman up. "Douuuuug! Help meeeeee!"

Bessonov thrashed and twisted in her arms, raining blows down on the crown of her head.

"Douuuuuug!" Amanda screamed. She heard a door slam, and a moment later all the weight in her arms evaporated as Doug hoisted the Russian spy into the air as if she were a toddler.

"Cut the cord," he shouted. "I got her."

"*Nyet!*" Bessonov screamed, thrashing and coughing, coughing and thrashing.

Amanda frantically scanned the bathroom for something she could use to cut the cord, but detainees weren't allowed any implements of the sort—no razors, no scissors, not even plastic knives.

"In my right pocket," Doug said. "There's a folding knife."

Amanda shoved her hand into his pants pocket and her fingers found the knife. Retrieving it, she deftly opened the blade and then climbed up onto the toilet seat. Bessonov shrieked like a wild animal, twisting and flailing in midair.

"Hurry," Doug said, "She's slipping."

Amanda grabbed the cord and swiped the blade across it, severing the drawstring noose in a single cut.

"*Nyet, nyet, nyet!*" Bessonov screamed, pounding her fists on Doug's powerful shoulders and the back of his bowed head. Unfazed, he carried her out of the bathroom and dropped her on the sofa cushions, where she immediately scrambled away from him. She pulled her knees to her chest, hugging herself, then rocked back and forth, all the while screaming at both of them in Russian. Amanda walked up and stood beside him, absorbing the bombardment of the girl's indecipherable curses.

"Thanks," she said, glancing at him sideways.

"I'm sorry," he said. "I had no idea she was going to try *that* . . . no idea."

"It's my fault," she said, trying to swallow down the lump in her throat. "I'm an idiot for not thinking of the drawstrings."

"Why did you stop me?" Bessonov interrupted them, her rage suddenly transformed to racking sobs. "Why did you rob me of this dignity?"

A half-dozen competing emotions flooded Amanda's mind.

Despite her best efforts not to, she'd become attached to the Russian over the past several months. She felt a kinship, a strange sisterhood of spies. A part of her wanted to wrap her arms around Bessonov, comfort her and tell her everything would be okay. At the same time, another part of her was angry and wanted to chastise the stupid girl.

"Someday, I hope you will feel differently," she said, meeting the Russian's vitriolic gaze. "You have so much left to live for."

Bessonov fired something back in Russian, then dropped her head between her knees and resumed sobbing and rocking.

Amanda looked up at Doug. "I'll cut down the cord in the bathroom and you get that slip noose off her neck."

He nodded and said, "And then what?"

"I'm going to give the new name to my boss. After that . . ." She blew air through pursed lips. "I guess we just take it one day at a time."

CHAPTER 32

USS Donald Cook (DDG-75)
The 45th Parallel
The Black Sea
October 2
0215 Local Time

"Crossing the forty-fifth parallel south," the Navigator announced.

An impromptu cheer erupted on the bridge. Instead of squelching it, Dusty smiled and let his crew enjoy the moment. They'd defied Russian intimidation, executed their mission, and successfully escorted the USS *Oak Hill* out of contested waters with zero casualties and minimal damage to their ship.

He glanced at his Command Master Chief, who'd been uncharacteristically quiet since they'd transferred the Russian fighter pilot to the base in Romania using the *Oak Hill*'s helo. The plan had gone off without a hitch . . . at least so far.

The CMC met his gaze and held it.

Somebody's got something to say, Dusty thought and motioned for the CMC to join him on the starboard bridge wing.

Once they were standing outside, he told the lookout they needed a little space and dismissed him for a quick trip to the head, which the young sailor gratefully accepted. The ship had been at battle stations for hours. Now that they'd crossed back over the forty-fifth, fatigue would set in like a wet blanket. The letdown was human nature, but it would be a mistake to secure general quarters and condition Zebra prematurely. In truth, the *Donald Cook* wasn't out of the proverbial woods yet. Three Russian warships still trailed them and God only knew how many Kilos were tracking them from below. Only after he put some distance between his ship and his antagonizers would he relax the readiness condition.

"What's on your mind, Master Chief?" Dusty asked, looking out at the *Oak Hill* steaming a hundred yards off their starboard beam on a parallel course.

"I got a bad feeling about this, Captain," the CMC said, clutching the rail with both hands. "Russian troops are pushing into Mariupol, and US Marines are in Odessa. It don't take a genius to predict what happens when they meet in the middle."

"Yeah, it could get ugly."

"The *Admiral Grigorovich* backed off after we stood our ground," the CMC said, "and those F-22s up there certainly made a statement, but if this turns into a hot war, we are the big, easy target. If they decide to sink us, we're getting sunk, no matter what we do."

Dusty nodded. "We're a rubber ducky in a bathtub, surrounded by sharks with no place to go. But if it comes to that, I can assure you of one thing."

"What's that, Captain?"

"If we go down, then we're taking a bunch of them with us. We have seventy-five Tomahawks on this tub—missiles that, unlike her Captain, will not go down with the ship."

The CMC grinned at him. "That's what I'm talkin' about, sir."

Dusty inhaled a lungful of salty ocean air and let his gaze drift to the middle distance.

"When's the last time you talked to that Russian CO?" the CMC asked.

"Right after the *Oak Hill*'s helo took off from our stern with the Russian fighter pilot on board."

"What did he say?"

"He asked what we were doing."

"What did you say?"

Dusty smiled. "I decided to tell him the truth."

"After all that, dressing their pilot up in one of our uniforms and sneaking him off, you told him the truth? Why?"

"Because," Dusty said through a sigh, "he called my bluff."

"I don't get it," the CMC said.

"Well, here's the thing, Master Chief. The way I see it, my credibility is the most important tactical asset in my arsenal. During that game of chicken with the *Admiral Grigorovich*, I told him I wouldn't alter course and I didn't. We almost lost our ship in the process, but I showed him that I had resolve and was a man of my word. By telling him the truth about the Russian pilot, I reinforced that I'm a straight shooter even when it might be strategically disadvantageous to me."

"I see where you're going with this," the CMC said, nodding. "So next time you make a threat or a promise, you want him to take you at your word and believe you're going to follow through on whatever that might be."

"Exactly."

A wry smile spread across the Master Chief's face. "Reminds me of my dad growing up."

"How so?"

"He had this thing he used to say—'Son, if you test me, then this belt is coming off. And when that happens, I promise you that your ass will regret it.'"

"And did your ass regret it?" Dusty asked, chuckling.

"Oh, hell yeah," the CMC said, looking out at the water. "If there was one thing I could say about my dad, he was a man of his word. It only took one good thrashing—I fell in line after that."

Dusty clapped his CMC on the shoulder. "Well, by deploying Marines to Ukraine, it looks to me like President Warner just unbuckled his belt. Hopefully, the Russians learn the same lesson you did and fall in line . . . because if they don't, God help us all."

CHAPTER 33

Kovtun Storage (Number 3)
Akademika Vorobiova Street
Odessa, Ukraine
0241 Local Time

Gavriil stood in the center of the empty storage facility—a rectangular, metal-framed building with a smooth poured-cement floor, stretching north all the way to the corner of the street. He stood with his hands clasped behind his back, turning slowly as if inspecting the space carefully. The man beside him—a heavy man with a thick gut grown from a combination of wealth and an utter lack of self-discipline, and the ruddy cheeks and nose of a functional alcoholic—waited patiently, clearly resisting the urge to check his watch again.

The building was sufficient for Gavriil's short-term needs, with the high roof and fifteen-meter-wide rolling doors on both sides that rose to the top of the frame. It would be easy enough to drive the missile transporter in and out of the building. But what was it they said about real estate? Location, location, location . . .

"What will you be using the space for, if I may ask?" the fat Ukrainian warehouse mogul asked.

"Of course you may," Gavriil said, his Ukrainian deliberately speckled with a Western European accent. "As I said, our production line in Mykolaiv is running, but with restrictions on commercial flight operations, we are having trouble with the shipping end for our commercial tractors. We produce one of these behemoths about every fifteen days, and with all that is going on, we prefer to continue production until forced to stop. With the violence to the east and now the transportation problems—well, it is best if we build as many as possible and store them until they can be sold. At least until we know how long the Russians will continue their little temper tantrum."

"*Pfft,*" the obese man said, pulling at his shirt. "Hard to blame this on the Russians, I am afraid. It's time to make peace with our Russian brothers, and then there would be much money to be made for everyone. It's the politicians who ruin everything for everyone."

"Agreed," Gavriil said, smiling at the man. "Anyway, the space is perfect for my needs. Herr Hemmler thanks you for agreeing to meet me so late. I will tell him how accommodating you were and recommend we increase our business with you."

"Yes, please tell Mr. Hemmler we have much more space available to rent."

Gavriil nodded. "The rate for this facility is one hundred and twenty thousand hryvnia per month, is that correct?"

"Yes, well." The man now looked more awake and excited. "That is on a six-month lease, with a month's deposit and the first month up front."

"I see," Gavriil said. "And for a shorter-term lease? Perhaps one hundred and fifty thousand per month, with one month deposit up front."

"Two months deposit up front," the Ukrainian countered.

Gavriil sighed with feigned aggravation. "Very well, two months deposit."

The other man set his briefcase down and retrieved a clipboard. "Give me a moment to write some of these numbers in, and we can sign now if you like. I would like to get on the road as soon as possible. Have you brought a check with you?"

"Of course," Gavriil said. "Will you be able to confirm funds at this hour?"

The man waved his hand and continued writing. "It is fine. We already confirmed your credentials, so if there is a problem with your check, we can sort it out easily. We know where to find you, yes?" The man gave a laugh that shook his sweaty jowls.

Gavriil nodded. "As we discussed, we prefer that our lease be completely confidential. Obviously, if there are rumors of transportation or production issues, it will impact our stock price on the Deutsche Börse."

"Yes, yes," the man said, again waving a chubby hand. "Everything with us is completely confidential. Here, please have a look and sign, if it is as we agreed."

Gavriil made a show of looking over the paperwork. "What of you, my friend?" he asked. "Are you staying in country and riding this out? I heard American Marines are already here in Odessa. Odessa, for God's sake! Leave it to the Americans to overreact and make things worse."

"I am leaving as soon as we are done here," the man said. "I'll head north to Znamianka tonight for a closing I have in the morning, and then I will drive west to Moldova. I have a flight tomorrow night to Madrid, where my wife is already settled in with my children and no doubt spending my money like a mad woman."

Gavriil looked up and smiled, then began to sign the lease, flipping through and initialing where the yellow highlight marks could be found.

"She must be worried about you."

"No, no. She is excellent at turning a crisis into an expensive vacation. And in any case, she is terrified of all that is going on, so I let her believe that I am in Moldova already. All of my staff in Odessa have already left, so I needed to close this out myself."

Now, a real smile curled Gavriil's lips. "So, no one knows you are here with me? Not even your family?"

"No," the man said, but the timbre of his voice changed, as if he had just realized he'd made a terrible mistake.

"How wonderful," Gavriil said, this time in Russian, and the fat man's eyes went wide.

Gavriil dropped the clipboard and smoothly drew the GSh-18 9 mm pistol from under his coat and squeezed the trigger. A single red-black hole appeared in the center of the fat man's forehead, and for a moment he just stood there, mouth open in a curious O, hands flapping. Then he fell straight backward, the back of his head smacking the concrete floor, splattering grey matter about, eyes wide but lifeless and mouth still locked in the same silly O.

Gavriil stepped over the dead man and slipped the clipboard into the brown leather briefcase. Then he stared down at the dead body and made a *tsk* sound. It would be a bitch to get the rotund man's corpse into the back of his hired SUV, but it had to be done.

He jogged over to his vehicle beside the open warehouse door and stared out at the park across the street to the north. Yes, he had found the perfect spot to store the disguised MZKT Astrolog missile transport vehicle and its payload of two Iskander short-range ballistic missiles. Thanks to the warehouse's high ceiling and roll-up garage doors, when the time came to launch, all he would have to do is drive it across the street into the park, raise the missiles, and press the button.

At least, in theory that was the plan, but plenty could go wrong between now and then.

He started his SUV's engine, drove through the open garage door and across the cement floor, positioning the rear bumper beside the corpse. He killed the engine, opened the tailgate, and hopped out. Looking down at the bloated body that had to weigh well over a hundred kilos, he sighed.

I should probably check in with the driver first, he decided and pulled his encrypted mobile phone from his inside jacket pocket.

He dialed a number from memory. It rang only once.

"Da?" a gruff male voice answered.

"What is your position?"

"Just outside of Sychavka," the Russian driver answered. "I pulled off the road to wait."

"Good," Gavriil said, imagining a mental map of Odessa. "You're fifty kilometers away."

"Are you ready to receive me?" the driver said in Russian. "The disguise is good, but this is a very dangerous game. I don't want to drive into Odessa during daylight hours. If I am stopped by Ukrainian police and they search the trailer section . . . it's game over."

"I know," he said. "So, make haste. I'm waiting."

"Da."

The line went dead.

Gavriil looked down at the corpse again, then at his watch. He had one hour to dispose of the body before the transport arrived. After that, he'd pick up Arkady from the airport and they'd return to the warehouse together. Maybe it would be good to have the old man with him. Gavriil had never launched, let alone programmed, an Iskander SRBM before. Not having to rush the launch would be a luxury, and it would give them time to talk—really talk, not just trade riddles over an encrypted phone line.

He understood now that the old spymaster had designs on a coup. He even agreed that Petrov's recent actions made such a radical move necessary. And yet knowing and accepting the reason didn't change the gravity of the task at hand. What they were contemplating was treason. But if the old man believed that Petrov had taken Russia as far as he could, and that new leadership was needed to raise the country from its second-tier standing to the reemergent superpower status it deserved, then Gavriil trusted him. Arkady was a genius the likes of which he'd never encountered before, and he would follow the man to hell and back.

Even if that meant doing the unthinkable . . .

CHAPTER 34

Metro Cash and Carry Parking Lot
Outskirts of Mariupol, Ukraine
0315 Local Time

Dempsey studied the grainy photograph from the document packet General Antonets's people had given him at the airport in Dnipro. Then, he looked at the dude crossing the parking lot to greet him. Unconvinced, he held the picture up, glancing back and forth until the asset was close enough that the resemblance satisfied his inner skeptic.

He hasn't tried to shoot me yet, so I guess it's him, he thought, shoving the photo back in his pocket.

"Greetings," the Ukrainian said. He was tall, dressed in tactical BDUs and boots, but wore a long leather coat instead of a military blouse and kit. He sported a thick black beard and young eyes that—even in the middle of the night—shone with both fire and humor.

"You're late," Dempsey growled. "What the hell took you so long?"

"Apologies, my friend," the man said in heavily accented English. "I regret that we had a few Russians to kill on our way here." He gestured with a hand toward the south, where gunfire now rang almost constantly. "As you can see, this has become quite a bit more than the protests and looting they talk about on CNN." As if in agreement, a loud explosion sounded in the distance. "This is war, yes?"

"You've seen Russian soldiers here in Mariupol?" Munn asked, stepping up beside Dempsey.

The barrel-chested Ukrainian looked Munn up and down. "You have never fought Russians before, I am assuming."

Munn grinned and shook his head. "I wish that were true, my friend."

The man raised an eyebrow and then his arms, grabbing Munn and surprising him with a kiss on the cheek.

"A killer of Russians, yes? So, you are my friend. And you also know that Russians in Ukraine do not wear uniforms. In Donbas, we fought the Russians, only they dressed like civilians and raised a reserve army of idiots from our own country. You can tell the Spetsnaz forces by how they fight. Unfortunately, they are here now."

Chunk looked over at Dempsey and pursed his lips.

Dempsey nodded.

"Do not look so serious," the Ukrainian fighter said to Dempsey. "You are the leader, yes? You have leader eyes. Is like a party, and you are all invited. I will tell you what I know and we will lead you to pick up your people. It is relatively quiet there, I think. Much of the fighting now is along the water, but mostly west of the river and south of the M14 highway. There is heavy fighting also around the government complexes, and a battle rages for control of Extreme Park, for some reason. Where we go to find your people is north of the industrial area along Vynohradna Street and east of the river."

"We're worried that the Russians may know we're coming. They may be planning an ambush for us," Dempsey warned.

"Well, we will see, yes?" the man said with a grin. "If yes, then we will kill more Russians. They will not take us easily like they did Crimea. If they want Mariupol, they will have to stand on our bodies on television and explain why."

Dempsey nodded. "How many are you?"

"Only three, but we have a Range Rover," the Ukrainian said, as if that fact somehow compensated for the other. "It's very nice, leather seats, GPS, top of the line."

"How long to get to the target?" Chunk asked, growing exasperated with the man's antics.

"Perhaps an hour or maybe more. We will need to circle to the north around the heavy fighting to get there. We will see."

Chunk looked over at Dempsey, true concern replacing his usually grinning face. "Gonna be running the hell out of nighttime on the exfil, dude," the SEAL officer said.

"I know," Dempsey agreed. They'd waited in this parking lot nearly an hour for this man and his Ukrainian fighters tasked to take them to the X. They should have just pushed on, but they might need them in a pinch, especially to help distinguish between the good and bad guys. "It is what it is."

They wouldn't have air exfil once they rescued the CIA team, or if anything went wrong—not in this hot area. No one wanted another Mogadishu, to be sure. They could *maybe* get CASEVAC if they got shot up once they were well west of town, but even that was an *if*. Close air support might be available, but probably not in time if they needed it. Russian fighters and attack aircraft were staged in nearby Crimea, while the US Air Force's Raptors and the Marine's F-35Bs were operating out of MK in Romania.

No, they were on their own—well, except for their *guide*, his two friends, and their souped-up Range Rover. Dempsey chuckled. The Ukrainian was starting to remind him of an Eastern European version of Munn, with a leather trench coat standing in for Munn's red-checked lumberjack coat.

"Well," he said. "Best we get going, then."

The bearded man nodded. "You are Navy SEALs, yes? Badass, like *Call of Duty*."

Riker laughed at that. "Something like that," the SEAL said. "But way more badass than *Call of Duty*."

There was some general chuckling all around, but then the bearded Ukrainian's face got deadly serious. "We will see," he said softly. Then he turned and headed for his truck, the shiny silver Range Rover, which Dempsey now saw was pocked with bullet holes.

"Hey!" Dempsey called after him. "What's your name?"

"You may call me Boris," the asset said, then laughed as if he were his own favorite stand-up comedian. "And what shall I call you?"

"Yankee One," Dempsey said, then jerked a thumb at Chunk and said, "And he's Yankee Two."

"Yankee One, Yankee Two ... I love it," Boris chortled. "Death and comedy. This is our life, yes?"

"We'll follow you," Dempsey said, in no mood for joking. "Let's get moving."

Dempsey, the rest of the Ember team, and Chunk's Team Four SEALs loaded up into their SUVs.

"Dude, no way we have time to go after Kuznetsov. We're

barely going to have time to exfil our primaries," Chunk said from the passenger seat as Dempsey pulled the gear lever into drive and accelerated after the Range Rover.

Dempsey shook his head. "Time won't be an issue."

"How's that?"

"Because if I'm right," he said, looking at his friend and one of the finest SEALs he had fought beside, "Kuznetsov will find us."

"Awesome," Chunk said, shaking his head. "Fucking awesome."

The drive to the industrial complex and rail yard where Mariupol Maritime Logistics was located took less time than expected. Even with the stops for Grimes and Saw, who were set up in a twin sniper overwatch configuration, the team was in position across the yard from the target building in an hour. But that didn't change the fact that when dawn came, the sun would illuminate all things depending on the dark—including Dempsey and his night hunters.

"I don't see anything going on," Munn said, handing the night vision binoculars to Chunk, who was standing between him and Dempsey on the running board of the Suburban as they peered over the roof. "Sure we got the right place?"

"This is the only Mariupol Maritime Logistics building in the city," Boris said from where he paced by the hood of the vehicle, seemingly oblivious to the easy target he would make for an enemy sniper. Or maybe the war-torn Ukrainian was a resigned fatalist, like Dempsey and most of the Team guys he knew.

"I didn't mean you, Boris," Munn said, his comment meant for those far away and in his ear. "You did great. It's just that I don't see any activity at all—not even any lights on."

"They're just using good light discipline," Dempsey said, wanting to believe it. "Home Plate, do you have contact with the target? Any comms at all?"

"Negative, Yankee One," Wang said, his voice a bit defensive. "You told me to wait on contact until you were in position."

"And that was the right call," Baldwin chimed in. "We simply have no idea how robust the Russian signals intelligence apparatus in the area might be. Best to avoid contact until you are ready to exfil."

Baldwin was correct about the danger, he thought. Jonah Knight and his people better be ready, because he didn't have time for handholding. Dempsey took the glasses and scanned the area around the target building in both directions and saw nothing of concern. No personnel. No suspicious vehicles. But he knew better than to trust the calm before the storm. Safety is an illusion.

Bad guys could be everywhere.

"Zeus One and Two—SITREP," he called.

"Zeus One in position," Saw said. "All quiet. I have a line on the north side and most of Hazova Street. I got nothing. No movement at the target either, but I can't see inside. Looks like the windows are boarded up from the inside, and I have no light streams."

"Zeus Two," Grimes called in. "East of the target building with lines on the south side of the building. No tangoes. No movement. Quiet. Multiple vehicles in the rear lot, but no one inside I can see."

"Check," Dempsey said.

Time to go. We'll know if it was a mistake in a minute.

"Home Plate, Yankee One—contact Liberty," he said, using the call sign for the CIA team. "And loop us in."

"Roger that, Yankee," Wang said.

Dempsey waited, watching the target building through the night vision binoculars. Moments later, Wang came back in his ear, the transmission less crystal clear than usual. "Okay, MML chief," he said to someone. "You're designated Liberty. Go for Yankee."

"Okay—so I'm putting my security chief on with you," said an unfamiliar voice that Dempsey assumed belonged to Jonah Knight.

After a short pause and a mumble of other voices in the background, a new voice—this one confident and comms savvy—said, "Yankee, go for Liberty."

Dempsey grinned. They were talking to the GRS lead now—a former operator, undoubtedly.

You can just tell . . .

"Liberty, Yankee—SITREP," Dempsey said.

"Yankee, we have eight souls and all are five by. Two pros, one midlevel shooter, and five pieces of luggage, though three went through the short course, like, years ago. You?"

"All pros," he said, and left it at that.

"Roger that," the GRS lead replied. "Anyone wearing a bone frog?"

"Yes, most," Dempsey said, glancing at Chunk and the other SEALs. The question told as much as it asked. Apparently, Liberty One was a former frogman. "How 'bout you guys?"

"Both of the pros."

"Roger that," Dempsey said with a smile.

"Yankee, we have wheels at the rear if needed," Liberty said.

"Yankee—Zeus Two," Grimes chimed in. "They have a panel van backed up tight at the back door, ass end toward the building with the rear cargo doors open. Looks like they have it staged for a quick-load getaway. Probably could pile everyone in the cargo hold in seconds and drive away. But be advised, it doesn't look heavy," she said, implying the van wasn't up-armored.

Dempsey sighed. Pre-positioning the van was a good idea, but if Liberty got caught in a firefight trying to exfil the rail yard, rifle rounds would slice through the van's thin sheet metal skin like a hot knife through butter. They could load up and then swap vehicles at the standoff location, but then the cat was out of the bag for anyone watching. On the other hand, the cat would be instantly out of the bag if Dempsey's convoy suddenly rolled up to the front of the building for a rapid loadout. And he couldn't fit eight people in a single SUV; it would take two. And sequential loading would eat up a lot of time . . . and it would be hard for his shooters to engage the enemy with CIA evacuees sprawled across their laps.

And, and, and . . .

Then an idea popped into his head.

"Liberty, does your panel van have slider doors on both sides or just the passenger side?" Dempsey asked.

"Both sides, Yankee," Liberty came back.

"Okay, Liberty. I think I got a plan. Stand by."

"Roger," the GRS shooter said, his voice calm and measured.

Dempsey looked over at Munn and Chunk.

"I know what you're thinking. Feint a pick-up at the front door, while we run 'em through the van and out both sides into two Suburbans at the back," Munn said.

Dempsey nodded.

"Thing is, we gotta hold one truck back to pick up Zeus One and Two," Munn said. "And if we park one out front as a decoy, we have fewer guns to provide covering fire if the bad guys are dug in and waiting to hit us."

"All true," Dempsey said. "If you have a better idea, I'm all ears."

Munn shook his head. They both looked at Chunk.

The SEAL officer blew air through his teeth. "Having them come to us in that van would be a mistake. We brought these up-armored bad boys for a reason. We need to use them . . . I've just got a funny feeling we're missing something."

"Yeah, me too," Dempsey said. "Home Plate, Yankee—area threat update?"

"Well," Wang began. "You have Russian armor just north of the city at Novosibirska, where they seem to be staging for a push in. You are only about three and half miles as the crow flies—or in this case, the tank shell flies—so well within range, especially if they have spotters nearby who can light targets for them. They have Su-30s and the new Su-25SMs patrolling along the border, so that's some serious shit there. In other words, they've got close air support in the region. Best to make this sneaky."

"What about local thermal signatures?"

"We do see personnel working the rail yard, but we've been watching all the signatures and they seem to be legitimate night shift workers. None appear to be carrying rifles. And we don't hold any stationary signatures in qualifying sniper locations—other than Zeus One and Two."

Dempsey nodded. "Okay, that's good . . . if Russian heavy guns roll in on us, do we have any fire support we can call on?"

"As providence would have it, after what happened at the checkpoint, Director Casey made some calls. We now have two Marine F-35Bs conducting touch-and-gos at Dnipro Airport, if you know what I mean."

"No shit?" Dempsey said, smiling.

"No shit, indeed," Baldwin interjected.

Well, maybe Director Bubblehead knows a little more about Spec Ops than I thought.

Dempsey suddenly wished he had a JTAC—a professional air controller embedded in the team to coordinate air strikes—like he had in the old days. To drop weapons in this urban environment without risking collateral, they would need precision.

"Time to get the F-35Bs on target?" he asked.

"Minutes from when they get the heads-up," Baldwin said. "Also of note, there's an F-22 Raptor CAP turning donuts over the

Black Sea supporting two Navy warships. In an emergency, they could divert to assist."

Dempsey scratched at his beard. "Alert the F-35s, Mother. We're making our move in five mikes."

"Roger," Baldwin said.

"Liberty, Yankee One," Dempsey said, his mind scrambling for a way to make his fellow frogman understand the plan without spelling it out on the comms. Despite the advanced encryption Ember was using, it was prudent to assume the Russians were listening.

"Go for Liberty," came the reply.

"Stand by for relocation. We're coming in hot to the front, but remember *Talladega Nights*. If you ain't first—you're last. And brother, you ain't no Ricky Bobby."

A long pause hung on the line.

"Seriously?" Munn quipped, rolling his eyes at Dempsey.

"Dude, there's no frogman on earth who hasn't seen *Talladega Nights* like twenty times," Dempsey said.

"Yeah, but that doesn't mean he's gonna understand your dumbass secret code," Munn fired back.

"Dude, I got the reference," Chunk said.

"Yeah, but you heard the plan," Munn fired back.

"Yankee, Liberty One—we gotcha. Liberty is standing by at the *front* door—shake and bake, baby."

Dempsey briefed the plan to the rest of the team and gave each driver his assignment, with Vehicles One, Two, and Three working the exfil, while Vehicle Four kept a standoff to pick up Zeus One and Two after the evacuees were safely loaded. When he finished, he looked at Chunk.

"All right," Chunk said, scraping a wad of stale tobacco from his lower lip with a finger and flinging it to the ground with a splat. "Let's mount up and do this bitch."

PART III

The only thing I am ever certain of is uncertainty.

But that has never stopped me from trying,

and it will not stop me now.

—Arkady Zhukov

CHAPTER 35

Rail Car Loading Tower
300 Yards South of Mariupol Maritime Logistics
0422 Local Time

Grimes shifted her right leg where the metal diamond-deck flooring pressed uncomfortably into her knee as she scanned through the TANGO6 sight, her right cheek hard into the butt stock of her Sig Sauer 716G2 DMR. If things went to hell, she would need both speed and accuracy, and the Sig—with its twenty-round magazine, precision-milled barrel, and composite design—was the perfect instrument for tonight's mission.

From her perch, she enjoyed an almost panoramic view of the rear of the target building, as well as the approach road to the west. Her heart rate ticked up a notch as she watched the decoy black Suburban—piloted by Munn, Yankee Three—cross the rail yard on an overt approach to the main entrance of Mariupol Maritime Logistics. Meanwhile, the other two SUVs—with Dempsey and the

SEAL called Bart in one, and Chunk and Riker in the other—were sneaking around the back of MML for the real extraction. The fourth SUV was standing by to pick up her and Saw. If the decoy SUV drew enemy fire, then they would know the MML building was being covered by ground forces and they would adjust in real time. But if the Russians were surveilling them from above—with drones, satellites, or other spooky watch-tech Ember didn't know about—then they were already blown and Dempsey's elaborate shell game was a pointless exercise.

She shuddered at the thought.

After her near-death experience in Jerusalem, she'd managed her fear and feelings of tactical inadequacy by becoming the team sniper. No, not by simply becoming overwatch . . . by embracing the role. Since then, she'd survived a half-dozen deadly moments by channeling her inner calm—that paradoxical conviction in her capacity to protect her boys because Ember truly owned the night. The enemy was blind to Ember's presence and true capabilities, and in this blind spot was where she thrived. Ember's tactics, methods, and technological superiority kept her lethal out to a thousand yards; she was a night hunter, and her enemy, the hunted. But now she could practically *feel* the Russian thermal image cameras probing her, studying her from somewhere up above. The itch between her shoulder blades, that was the crosshairs from the smart bomb on the Russian drone overhead, ready to atomize her at a moment's notice. With all the willpower at her disposal, she resisted the urge to scratch that itch and look skyward for the invisible death she was certain was circling above . . .

Home Plate has my back, she told herself, trying to chase away her anxiety over things she could not control.

She exhaled and resumed her survey of the buildings across the street, looking for shooters and spotters in windows. Her scan led

her to one particular building, about one hundred and fifty yards
northwest of the target, that would be an ideal spot for an enemy
sniper roost. She had line of sight to the roof, but not enough
height to see down onto it.

"Zeus One—Two—you have height on the building bearing
three-forty-five from the X? I can't see the roof."

After a pause, Saw came back, his soft whisper amplified in her
earpiece. "Two, One—all clear."

Saw was set up atop a four-story building thirty degrees to her
right and nearly even with the target building. From his vantage
point, she expected he had angles on the front of the MML building and the approach to the north. Equally important, he had a line
to cover her six if a threat emerged behind her.

Munn's decoy SUV braked to a stop at the front entrance.
Grimes pulled away from her rifle, lifting her head to look through
a separate spotter scope she had set up with a wider field of view.
The feint was on, and Munn and Martin were the live bait. If the
Russians were going to make a move, now was the time. On this
thought she turned left and began scanning the dozens and dozens
of dark rail cars scattered throughout the yard, wondering why she
hadn't checked them before.

*Hiding in ambush inside the vacant boxcars is the kind of thing JD and
Munn would come up with,* she thought, but didn't see anything moving in the shadows.

She swiveled back to check on Munn and Martin. She thought
about the Hellfire missile strikes Ember had ordered on the Russian
SUVs in Kiev the other night and imagined a fire streak from the
sky vaporizing the Suburban where it sat idling.

And then SAD would be just JD and me . . .

"Stop it," she murmured, trying desperately to get out of her
own head.

We're all good. No Spetsnaz troops have burst from the rail cars. No convoy of military vehicles loaded with little green men are rolling in . . . It's quiet.

We're alone.

She pressed her cheek back into the butt of her weapon to resume scanning through the TANGO6. With a twist of the dial, she increased the magnification from 30x to 56x. Then she exhaled long and slow to bring her heart rate beneath her already low baseline of fifty-five beats a minute.

And she waited.

And waited . . .

"Clear," Saw said.

"Clear," she echoed.

Seconds ticked by, and the decoy SUV loitered—engine running, with Munn and Martin inside, waiting to be assaulted. And when she couldn't stand it anymore, Dempsey finally called the approach.

"Liberty, Yankee One—thirty seconds."

"Roger, Yankee," came the CIA security lead's reply.

"Thermals, Mother?" she whispered, still feeling paranoid.

"Same as before," came Baldwin's reply. "We have thermals throughout the surrounding neighborhoods, as we reported, but none clustered like a large, organized force. The warehouse complex northeast has multiple thermals in the largest building, nearly a dozen, but they appear to be working, moving back and forth within the building. The rail yard to the west would be a delightful place to hide a large force, but we see no thermals in the rail cars and only two thermals walking the yard—night watchmen, we presume. The building Yankee is circling now shows no thermals, but the entire building is blue, suggesting it may be a refrigerated storage facility. Refrigerated warehouses are not unusual at a major rail hub for short-term storage of produce and the like."

"Man, he's a talker," Saw whispered in her earpiece.

"Talks when he's nervous," she whispered back.

"I most certainly do not. I'm just . . . never mind," Baldwin said, taking the hint.

She watched Dempsey's SUV circle behind the cold storage facility now and emerge on the other side, Chunk's vehicle in trail. On that cue, she pressed back into her long gun.

Come on, Dempsey. Be the luckiest son of a bitch on earth just one more time . . .

Dempsey's SUV accelerated on the approach, cruised past the van backed up to the rear of the building, and braked hard. He executed a precision backing maneuver, pulling beside the cargo van's driver's side and leaving just enough room to open the Suburban's rear door. She watched as the second SUV made the same maneuver in mirror image on the passenger side of the van.

With slow, four-count tactical breathing, she kept her pulse rate from rising as she scanned for threats. Time slowed while the two SUVs idled like bookends on either side of the van.

Nothing else moved.

A cool breeze across the rail loading tower kissed at the sweat on her neck and sent a shiver down her back. A plastic tarp in the loading area beneath her rustled, and she looked down, then back up.

It's nothing.

"Liberty, Yankee is in position," Dempsey reported.

"Copy, Yankee—stand by for the Ricky Bobby exfil."

"Home Plate—SITREP?" Dempsey called for a final check.

"Good eyes in the sky," Wang reported. "And no concerning chatter, encrypted or otherwise."

"I concur," Baldwin said, unable to remain quiet after his short pout.

"Zeus One—all clear," Saw said.

"Zeus Two, I concur," Grimes said, smiling at her mimicry, which would likely be lost on Baldwin. Perhaps only Munn noticed, if anyone.

"Liberty, you're a go for exfil. Use both side doors and into the trucks. One pro on each side, please, and divvy up half and half."

"Liberty, check."

A sliver of light appeared behind the van and grew into a door-shaped glow on the pavement behind the van, whose back doors were already hanging wide open. She watched through her rifle scope as the first evacuee shot the gap and jumped into the cargo van. He quickly opened the van's slider doors, first the left, then the right.

Grimes scanned again—the rail cars, the building across the street, and finally the cold storage building. All quiet. She returned her gaze to the cargo van, and watched the second CIA evacuee, a woman, shoot the gap from the building. A split second later, the same woman moved from the van into Dempsey's SUV.

But as she crossed the gap, a halo exploded around her head and she pitched sideways, crumpling in a heap on the ground between the vehicles. Grimes gasped, the kill looking so much like a shot from her own weapon that she checked that her trigger finger was, indeed, *outside* the trigger guard.

"Contact . . . contact!" one of the SEALs hollered.

"Taking sniper fire from the south," Dempsey said, his voice cold steel.

"I see nothing," Wang said in a panic. "Where the hell is it coming from? I have no thermals anywhere except Zeus One and Two."

A starburst appeared on the windshield in line with Dempsey's angry, contorted face. The SEAL called Bart, who was sitting next to Dempsey, opened the front passenger door, sighting through the gap between the door and window frame to provide covering fire. Grimes, for her part, repositioned on a knee looking south.

"Zeus One—anything?" she hollered, searching where the sniper fire seemed to have originated.

"Negative," Saw said, his voice still ice.

She scanned through the spotter scope, surveying every window in green-grey night vision.

Nothing . . . nothing . . . nothing. What the hell?

More sniper rounds echoed, coming faster now.

"He's shooting through the roof of the van—move, people, move!" The last call was not meant for radio, but instead came from Chunk screaming into his hot mike for the CIA evacuees to get their asses into the SUVs, where they would be protected by the up-armored walls and roofs.

Grimes continued her search for the shooter, forcing herself to be slow and deliberate, just as she'd learned.

But how the fuck are there no thermals?

"Man down," Dempsey hollered in her ear. "Got a Yankee down."

It's Bart, she thought, but continued her slow scan.

She came to another building, and beside it stood two structures—radio-style towers, but with what looked like smokestacks in the center. And there, atop a scaffolding platform on the farthest tower, she sighted a shiny blob. When she zoomed in, she could just make out the barrel of a rifle sticking out from underneath what looked like a Mylar thermal-reflective blanket.

"I have the shooter," she said, forcing calm into her voice.

She was going to tell Wang not to look for a heat signature—but instead, she shifted to the scope on her sniper rifle, her gloved hand expertly clicking in adjustments for the one-hundred-and-sixty-yard shot. The breeze was now coming from her left since she'd turned, and she accounted for that in the adjustments with a rough mental calculation. She put the red crosshairs of the sight on the head-shaped bump in the silver blob.

Exhale.

Trigger squeeze.

Her bullet tore through where she'd guessed the sniper's head to be, and the shooter's rifle barrel abruptly dropped. A heartbeat later, a body tumbled out from under the silver tarp, bounced off the scaffolding twice, and then silently slammed into the ground.

"Sniper down," she called.

"Nice shot, Two," Saw said. "Where there's one, there's more. Haul ass, Yankees."

Grimes spun back around, elbow laced through the sling of her rifle, and put the spotter scope back to her right eye in time to see Dempsey hoisting a slumped and motionless Bart into the front passenger seat.

"We've got eight packages secure," Dempsey called, pulling the passenger door closed from the inside. "But we have casualties. Lots. Recover Zeus and let's get the hell out of here."

"Hold, One," Saw said. "We got a new problem, bro. Check the building just east of you . . ."

"Where?" Wang cried. "I see nothing. I have no thermals."

Grimes looked toward the building Baldwin had called a refrigerated warehouse, and saw a twenty-foot-wide, garage-style door rolling up, revealing three old military-style Ural-375 trucks.

Oh shit . . .

The trucks rolled out en masse, each carrying a complement of armed soldiers in the open back trailer beds.

"Other way, Yankee," she hollered into her mike.

"There is no other way!" Dempsey reminded her.

She watched in horror as the three trucks spread out across the only road out of the rear approach to the target building and the shooters took up firing positions, all aiming at the two SUVs.

"We're coming around to help," Munn called out, and she saw his SUV on the move.

"Negative," Dempsey said. "Head north, Three."

Grimes watched Dempsey's SUV executing evasive maneuvers, but she didn't know where he could go. With some luck, they might be able to breach the fence and then make it across the railroad tracks. But even if he managed that, she doubted he could clear the ditches beyond. And if he got stuck, they were dead for sure.

"Home Plate, we need close air support right fucking now. You see our issue, right?" Dempsey hollered.

"Calling in the fast movers to clear a path, Yankee," Wang said, his voice more in control now than before.

"Zeus One, Two," she said. "It's up to us now."

"Roger that," Saw came back, as she threw herself prone.

With steady fingers, she made two small adjustments on her scope, sighted in on the lead enemy truck, and went to work.

Hang in there, guys . . . I got your back.

Exhale . . .

Trigger squeeze.

Sight . . .

Exhale . . .

Trigger squeeze.

Sight . . .

CHAPTER 36

With nowhere to run, Dempsey cut the wheel hard, kicking up a cloud of dust and gravel as he angled the SUV in a defensive nose-to-nose position with Chunk's SUV.

"Stay in the vehicles," Dempsey commanded. He had no idea if there could be more snipers, and in fact assumed there were. This was pretty clearly a well-planned and well-organized trap.

It's not the CIA personnel they're after. They could have raided MML anytime. It's Ember they want . . . retaliation for our Zeta hunting spree.

He was about to make another desperate call to Wang for air support, when a kneeling Russian shooter who was spraying Dempsey's door with rifle fire suddenly collapsed, grey-green gore painting the ground from his wrecked head.

Grimes . . . Go, girl!

A split second later, Saw announced his presence as one of the shooters from the middle truck suddenly pitched over the rail of the truck toward them, dead before he hit the ground. As the Russian shooters scrambled out of the trucks to launch their assault,

Grimes and Saw worked the problem. The two snipers had set up a wicked kill box, catching the Russians in a perfect crossfire. In six or seven seconds, a dozen enemy shooters lay dead beside the trucks, but the seasoned fighters quickly compensated and repositioned—some finding a safe angle, some taking cover beneath the trucks, and others retreating back inside the cold storage warehouse. After a brief respite, the Russians resumed pouring fire on the Suburbans.

Dempsey gritted his teeth. The tactical picture was terrible. Against rifle fire, sheltering inside their armored SUVs was the best option. But this oasis of safety was an illusion. Their big black boxes on wheels were easy targets. A single RPG fired from the ground, or single laser-guided bomb dropped from the sky, would end them. And even if the Russians didn't bring the heavy ordnance, they had a numbers advantage with reinforcements in the area. Eventually, the Suburbans would be surrounded with Spetsnaz shooters. Which left Dempsey and his squad in a damned-if-you-do, damned-if-you-don't situation. Necessity was forcing his hand . . . If they didn't get out of the SUVs now and return fire, they'd never get another chance to do so. In a few minutes, the Russians would swarm their position.

Grimes and Saw were in an equally precarious situation. The element of surprise had given them the upper hand momentarily, but now the Russians knew they were out there. Unlike the Russian shooters, who'd taken steps to conceal their thermal signatures, Grimes and Saw were vulnerable as hell. With Russian satellites looking down, they were easy targets.

"Zeus, Yankee—reposition or exfil," Dempsey commanded. "Bad guys have your lines; you need to move ASAP!"

As if a punctuation mark to his order, the sound of an approaching enemy aircraft from the south joined the chaotic noise of gunfire. He could hear Grimes panting in her hot mike as she evacuated her hide. A few seconds later, a burst of light erupted to his right and he turned in time to see an enormous fireball belch skyward. The shockwave hit him a heartbeat later, followed by the scream of the Russian jet's engines as it streaked across the sky overhead.

His throat tightened and so did his chest as he waited for Grimes to check in.

She didn't, but the sound of her rhythmic panting in his ear was the survival confirmation he needed.

"Two, One," he said, calling Chunk. "If we don't exit the vehicles and give ourselves covering fire, we're screwed."

"Agreed. What about our luggage?" Chunk came back, referring to their CIA evacuees. "In or out?"

I don't fucking know, Dempsey thought, wracked with indecision.

"In or out, One?" Chunk pressed.

"Luggage stays in," Dempsey barked, concluding that their only way out was in these vehicles. But before that could happen, they needed to rebuff the assault and cull the Russians' numbers. Jaw clenched, he climbed over Bart's lifeless body, which was slumped in a puddle of blood in the passenger seat. As he opened the passenger door, he turned to his CIA evacuees in the back. "Heads down. Stay low, people."

"It's not going well," Chunk said in his ear, the SEAL's voice barely discernible over the sound of all the rifle fire.

He dropped to the pavement and took a knee, firing immediately at the Russian shooters clustered in cover around the closest troop truck. "Home Plate, if you don't get those F-35s on station in the next two minutes, we're dead. Do you copy?" he called.

"Inbound already, boss," Wang reported. "Lightning flight is using call sign Leather."

"Zeus Two is clear and, damn, that was close," Grimes said, breathing hard in her mike.

"One is clear," Saw said, and moments later a second explosion rose from the roof of the building he'd been on.

Thank God.

Dempsey felt a double tap on his shoulder and looked up.

"Whadaya think, Yankee One?" An unfamiliar bearded face greeted him with a hard grimace beneath a dirty ball cap.

"Liberty, I presume?" Dempsey said, returning his attention to his optics and dropping another Russian shooter.

"Yeah, I'm Brock," the operator and former SEAL said, dropping prone beside Dempsey to sight below the Suburban's undercarriage.

"We can't stay here," Chunk called in his ear. "They're dropping ordnance."

"I know," Dempsey growled, his frustration mounting. "Home Plate, where's Leather?"

Instead of Wang, a gravelly voice said, "Yankee, Leather One—flight of two Fox-three-fives. Full stores. ETA ninety seconds. SITREP."

"Leather, Yankee One—we are two SUVs in the rear parking lot of the target coordinates. We are in heavy contact with several dozen tangoes in three troop trucks blocking access to our only exfil route. We also have shooters in a cold warehouse just north of the trucks. Need ordnance danger close to clear a path. Say again, we need ordnance danger close to clear a path."

"Rog . . ." the fighter pilot replied, drawing out the word with a Texas twang. "Understand danger close. Coming across now to assess."

"Be advised, there are Russian fighter attack aircraft in the area dropping ordnance."

"I wouldn't worry about them," the pilot replied with sublime confidence, as two F-35s now streaked above them at low altitude. "We got your six now, Yankee."

Dempsey watched as the enemy shooters near the trucks, gaining confidence from believing the Ember sniper threat had been eliminated, moved to better firing positions.

"RPG in the lead truck," Riker called, and then Dempsey heard two three-round bursts of American assault rifles. "Got him."

"Yankee, Leather—incoming on this pass. Danger close, so stay low," the F-35 pilot reported. "We're flying south to north."

Dempsey climbed over the dead SEAL in the passenger seat, struggling to get low on the floor of the driver's side and ready to haul ass after the bombing run. He heard the rear door slam shut as Brock climbed in. Dempsey glanced back, met the GRS shooter's steely-eyed gaze. The woman on the seat beside Brock wasn't moving, and only then did he notice her lifeless eyes staring off into space.

"Zeus Two, back in position," Grimes said in his ear.

We got two angels in my truck alone. Fuck me. I ain't losing Grimes or Saw.

"Negative, Zeus, negative!" he hollered. "We're Mike Charlie after this pass. Get to Vehicle Four and haul ass. Meet us on Hazova Road for exfil. Do it now."

"Zeus," Grimes acknowledged, grudgingly.

Leather flight screamed over the top of the target area—one F-35 low and the other offset and higher. Through the windshield, Dempsey saw them pull up nearly vertical, and a second later, four explosions hit—one on top of the other—turning the world bright, hot, and loud. Dempsey squeezed his eyes shut, trying to preserve his night eyes, as he blindly felt for the gearshift lever. Once his vehicle stopped shaking, he put the transmission in drive, opened his eyes, and slammed his boot down on the accelerator. The Suburban's engine roared as the world came back into focus, and he fishtailed momentarily as the big Chevy took off.

Ahead, the Russian troop trucks billowed with flames, and several man-shaped balls of fire ran from the destruction, only to collapse in writhing, fiery blobs a few yards away. One of the flailing figures—a man completely engulfed in flames—ran directly in front of them. Dempsey's SUV hit him, sending the burning fighter flipping up over the hood and then sliding up the windshield in a horror show—chunks of burning flesh exploding outward in all directions, leaving a smoldering smear across the windshield.

"Good fire, Leather, good fire," he barked into his transceiver.

"Leather, standing by," the Marine aviator replied.

Dempsey spun the steering wheel hard left, then hard right, barely navigating around the rearmost truck, which was somehow rolling to try to close the gap. After clearing the fiery mayhem, he accelerated and checked his side-view mirror, relieved to see Chunk's SUV tight on his tail. Bullets ricocheted off passenger-side doors and windows, and then the tailgate and rear window, as they streaked away from what had only seconds before been the refrigerated warehouse—now a pyre of flame and smoke. His expression granite, Dempsey pulled the wiper control lever, activating the wipers and spraying the windshield with fluid to extinguish the smoldering globs of body grease and clear the cloudy smear that made it difficult to see.

"Yankee, you have another enemy fast mover approaching from the north," Wang hollered in his ear, his voice a tight cord.

"Leather has him," the Marine said, a certain joyful undertone in the cool, grumbling voice. "Fox One . . ." the pilot announced a moment later.

In his rearview mirror, he noted Chunk's SUV falling back and increasing the spacing between them.

For when that Russian fighter drops a bomb on me . . .

He looked up and saw a flash as the incoming Russian jet was hit and consumed in a ball of fire. It streaked right to left across the sky like a meteor and crashed in the rail yard, sending chunks of burning debris arcing in every direction.

"Splash one," the F-35 lead pilot announced. "Ivan's wingman just bugged out—heading east into Russian airspace."

"Nice work, Leather," Dempsey called.

"Yankee One, Zeus is in Vehicle Four headed west on Hazova ahead of you," Grimes reported.

"Roger, Zeus," Dempsey replied, relieved at the news.

"Yankee, I show nothing between you and the river crossing," Wang added with crisp professionalism. "But you're still in range of that Russian armor north of the city."

"Copy," Dempsey said. "Keep eyes on."

"Check," Wang acknowledged.

"Yankee, Leather is staying with you as well. We'll clear any other obstacles."

Dempsey caught Brock's gaze in the mirror. The man gave him a nod. With two F-35s running block for them, they'd get out, barring any unforeseen events. Unfortunately, in Ember, just as in the Tier One SEALs, their work could best be described as a neverending stream of unforeseen events.

"Home Plate, you need to coordinate a CASEVAC site for us, and it needs to be pretty damn close. We have multiple casualties. Stand by for a count."

"Working on it," Wang said.

"I have a location," Brock said from the back seat. "It's a farmhouse in Nikolske I rented for contingencies just like this."

"How far?" Dempsey asked.

"Fifteen clicks northwest," Brock said and gave him the coordinates.

"Home Plate, see if that works."

"Roger," Wang said.

"Leather has plenty of gas to stick with you guys until dust-off," the Marine pilot—who would definitely be receiving a case of hooch for this—added.

"Yankee Three, SITREP," Dempsey called. Munn had not been in his ear at all since this thing began—keeping the channel clear, but now he felt his pulse quicken with worry.

"Vehicle Three is five by," Munn said. "Four souls, all good."

"Zeus?" he queried.

"Vehicle Four is four souls and good," Grimes came back, but her voice sounded pained.

"No casualties?" he pressed, wondering if she'd taken damage trying to exfil her sniper hide.

The pause was long enough to put doubt in his mind, but she said, "Four souls, all good, all in the fight."

"Yankee Two?" he asked Chunk as he accelerated west on Hazova Street, screaming across the rail bridge toward the river before the Russians could coordinate something to stop them. Once in the chaos of the city, they might actually be safer. Like them, the Zetas had probably *not* read others in on their operation—and they'd wiped out the team at the X, thanks to United States Marine Corps aviation.

"Vehicle Two has three casualties, all urgent surgical. We're getting them stable best we can."

"And One has two angels and . . ." He looked at Brock in the rearview; the man held up two fingers. "Two urgent surgicals. You got all that, Home Plate?"

"Copy all," Wang replied.

The rail bridge thumped underneath them, and then they shot forward as the road bent right.

"Can your surgicals make it safely to the FRSS in Romania?" Baldwin asked.

Dempsey repeated the question for Brock, who did not have a headset. The GRS man shook his head in the mirror.

"Negative. Time critical for us," Chunk chimed in, beating Dempsey to the punch.

"Understood," Baldwin said. "CASEVAC is already in the air. We're clearing a rendezvous for you. We'll be taking them to contingency Bravo."

"Roger. Copy all," Dempsey said. Bravo meant they would be airlifting the wounded to a civilian hospital in Ukrainian-controlled Dnipro, where they'd launched this op from. Dnipro was three times closer than MK Air Base in Romania—which was over four hundred fifty miles away—and would not require flying around the Russian-controlled Crimean peninsula.

What a friggin' mess . . .

"Hey, bro," Brock said from the back seat.

Dempsey looked in the rearview mirror and met the man's gaze.

"We now have three angels," the operator said, grim-faced.

Dempsey gave a curt nod.

What a disaster this op had been. Ember's suspicion that Maksim Kuznetsov was Zeta and that Zeta would find them had all but been confirmed. Why else would the Russians have been waiting in ambush and taken measures to hide their thermal signatures? There was no way to know if Kuznetsov had died in this fight, but Dempsey's guess was no . . . odds were, the man was supervising from a safe location.

But it didn't matter.

Dempsey would go on hunting Zetas until every last one of them was dead and Arkady Zhukov himself knelt in his gunsights.

But when that day finally comes, Dempsey thought, clutching the steering wheel tight with both hands, *I think I'll holster my weapon . . . and kill the bastard with my bare hands.*

CHAPTER 37

From his hotel room balcony, Gavriil watched a ribbon of purple in the east turn slowly deep red as the sun clawed its way above the hazy horizon. Wrinkling his nose, he sipped at the mediocre coffee he'd made from the coffee maker in the room's dinette. He'd had to run it through twice to make it strong enough to be palatable. It tasted like plastic, but the caffeine was already sharpening his mind.

It had been a long and exhausting night. After disposing of the fat Ukrainian's body, he'd taken delivery of the Astrolog missile transporter and secured it in the warehouse. Next, he'd picked up Arkady at the airport and driven him back to the facility to see the Iskander missiles and talk with the missile technician, who would guard the unit until they returned. After that, he dropped Arkady off at his hotel so the old man could get a few hours of much needed sleep. By the time Gavriil got back to his own room, his circadian rhythms were telling his body it was time to wake up, despite the fact he'd never gone to bed.

His mobile phone chirped in his pocket.

He retrieved it, expecting the caller to be Arkady, but instead it was another number—one that raised his eyebrows in both surprise and concern.

"Yes?" he said, taking the call.

"The operation against Ember failed," Kuznetsov said, unable to conceal his anger.

"And why are you calling me?"

"I've lost control of the situation. Otet is not responding," Kuznetsov said, calling Arkady by his Zeta code name. "You are Prime. What should I do?"

"Is Ember out of the city with the CIA personnel?"

"Nearly."

"And you are in pursuit?"

"Negative. We are but three men now and with no vehicles. Everyone else is dead. The Americans called in an air strike against us."

Gavriil's heart rate picked up. "What?" he said, incredulous.

"We had a Su-27 assigned to our operation and they shot it out of the sky."

"You initiated close air support against the Americans?"

"Yes, they had snipers in position. I had no choice."

"*Nyet.* Choice is the one thing we *always* have." When Kuznetsov didn't respond, Gavriil said, "Where are the Americans now?"

"Uncertain. Fleeing to the west. I might have been able to stop them if Russian armor and troops had moved in, but the order has not come. Our forces are waiting outside the city."

"And they will continue to do so until you execute your other mission."

"I told you, Otet is not responding. I need authorization to—"

"Stop," Gavriil snapped, cutting him off. These were not Syrian Kurds they were fighting. The Americans could be listening right now. Despite Zeta's advanced encryption, they most certainly should not be discussing battle plans.

"Apologies," Kuznetsov said.

"Is the other operation set to go?"

"Yes. I have a separate team for that."

He almost said, *Detonate now*, but caught himself. "Conduct the operation," he instructed, assuming control as Prime.

"Now?"

"Yes, immediately."

"The area in question is full of our peacekeeping forces," Kuznetsov said. "The collateral will be—"

"Now," he repeated.

"It will be done," the Zeta said, and the line went dead.

Gavriil pocketed his phone and went back out onto the balcony. The news of Ember's escape did not surprise him, but it made him angry regardless. *No matter what we do, Ember always wins,* he thought, *but I have other problems to worry about.*

He watched as a convoy of four American Humvees exited the soccer stadium and headed to the northern checkpoint. The arrival of the American Marines in Odessa was a new development. They'd not been here yesterday, and now this morning here they were. It was all unfolding just as Arkady said it would, which meant his operation would probably achieve its stomach-churning desired result. But for Gavriil's mission to succeed, Kuznetsov needed to succeed first. They still needed a catalyst to draw Russian armor into the streets of Mariupol. The war for Novorossiya was a step-wise process: Create chaos. Send in peacekeepers. Kill the peace-keepers. Send in the tanks. Blow up the tanks. Then mobilize the entire Russian military for invasion.

And then what?

Would his mentor's crazy plan really save Russia?

Or would it lead to World War III instead?

He looked at his watch and resisted the urge to refill his coffee. He had a few hours until it was time to go to the warehouse to complete the final launch preparations. Instead of drinking coffee, he really should be trying to sleep. Sleep was a weapon.

Perhaps in his dreams, Ember would come to him.

Perhaps in his dreams, next time he would win.

CHAPTER 38

Dnipropetrovsk International Airport
Dnipro, Ukraine
0955 Local Time

Dempsey had never seen Chunk's face so serious before, but then he had never been with the officer after the loss of one of his SEALs. The handful of times when Chunk and his boys had augmented Ember on crazy, save-the-world missions, they had always pulled everyone out of the fire intact.

Not this time.

"I'm sorry, brother," Dempsey said as they stood together on the tarmac.

Chunk clenched his jaw and nodded. "That's the job, bro," the SEAL said flatly.

A CASEVAC helo had picked up their badly wounded CIA evacuees at Brock's farmhouse in Nikolske and flown them to a civilian hospital in Dnipro. The rest of the team had made the three-hour drive back to the airport in their battle-damaged SUVs, carrying their fallen brothers and sisters with them.

In a few minutes, the Super Hercules would arrive to take the rest of Chunk's SEALs to MK Air Base for their hop back to the *Ford*. Saw, who had a piece of shrapnel embedded in the fleshy part of his thigh, probably should have gone on the CASEVAC—but the SEAL sniper insisted he could wait until he got to MK for the FRSS docs to look at it. The latest report from the hospital was that all critically wounded evacuees would survive—including Jonah Knight, the CIA annex lead. Brock and the other GRS shooter, along with their dead, would be going to MK with Chunk's team. From there, it would be a long ride home . . . or to wherever it was that God and country meant to send them next.

What a goat rope, Dempsey thought with a heavy sigh.

He looked at Chunk, wishing he had something, anything, profound to say. He wanted to ask about Bart—to *know* the SEAL, because that would make it personal for him. He wanted it to be personal. He wanted to amplify the pain so that he could harness it later and turn it into combat fury. That's how John Dempsey handled loss . . .

But now is not the time for such things, he decided.

Chunk finally pulled his eyes from the western horizon and turned. "Not a stellar success as a rescue mission, huh?" he said, real pain in his voice. "Won't be teaching this one in SQT anytime soon."

Dempsey clenched his jaw. "It was a trap, bro. Our evacuees were the bait . . . and Ember was the target."

Chunk nodded.

"It could have been worse. We're probably lucky we got out at all," Dempsey said. "Reports are coming in of a massive explosion in Mariupol's city center, with dozens of civilian casualties and a company of Russian peacekeepers dead. Details are scant, but whatever happened, it was enough to finally mobilize Russian armor and troops. They've already taken complete control of the city."

"Damn," Chunk said, shaking his head. "What about our little party? Has that been leaked to the press?"

"Not yet, and now that Mariupol is an all-out war zone, what happened with us will disappear . . . like bubbles in a wake behind a fast boat. If nobody's talking about two Marine F-35s bombing Russian forces and shooting down Russian jets already, then they're not going to."

"Well, we got 'em out, I guess," Chunk said, gazing west again. "Most of 'em, anyway . . . That's what matters most, right? No man left behind."

"No man left behind," Dempsey echoed, but couldn't help but wonder if it had occurred to the SEAL officer that, had Ember's SAD *not* augmented Team Four's mission, perhaps there would have been no ambush waiting for them. Heck, they might have faced no resistance at all . . .

And three wounded CIA officers would not be having surgery right now.

And there wouldn't be three more stars on the wall at Langley.

And Chunk and his teammates would not be pounding tridents into the top of Bart's casket in CONUS.

Then again, if Ember hadn't been there, maybe the Russians would have hit Mariupol Maritime Logistics early and killed everyone before the cavalry arrived.

The drone of a twin-engine UC-12W Huron approaching from the southwest shook Dempsey from his rumination. "Here comes your ride," he said.

"Yep," Chunk said, pulling out a can of Kodiak snuff and packing it with a few practiced snaps of his wrist. "So, what's next?"

Dempsey looked at Chunk. "Whadaya mean?"

Chunk raised an eyebrow. "Dude, I know you're not done here in Ukraine. And I know you guys well enough to predict your Head Shed is already making plans to decapitate the outfit that ambushed us, tore up our CIA agents, and killed Bart. I've been down this road with you before . . . or do your spooky bosses erase your memory after every mission with one of those flashy pens?"

"Sometimes, I wish they could." Dempsey chuckled and clapped Chunk on the shoulder. "But you're right . . . we're not done here."

"So promise me."

"Promise you what?"

Chunk didn't answer, just balled up his fist and pounded it twice against his heart.

Dempsey understood. "When we find the head of this snake, we'll lop it off . . . for Bart and everyone we've lost since we started dancing with these Russian bastards." He glanced back at where Chunk's SEALs and the GRS guys were organizing gear beside a row of body bags set to make the long trip back to CONUS. "There's no one—and I mean no one, brother—we'd rather fight beside than you guys."

"You know where to find me." Chunk stuck out his hand.

Dempsey shook it, then pulled the SEAL officer in for a hug. "Godspeed, Chunk."

"Hooyah, frogman," the stout warrior said and left to join his guys. Minutes later, everyone and everything was loaded into the plane.

"Don't fuck up our trucks," Riker shouted with a grin from the airstair. "I'm guessing whoever gave 'em to us is gonna want 'em back in one piece."

Dempsey looked over at the SUVs, two of which were riddled with bullet pockmarks on the bodies and stars on all the windows. "Then they're already going to be pissed," he hollered back. "But don't worry, we'll make sure to tell them which ones Team Four drove."

Riker laughed and disappeared inside the cabin.

Chunk gave a two-finger salute and followed suit.

And then the Beechcraft was taxiing away.

Moments later, all that was left was the ghost vibration in his ears.

"Now what?" Munn said, stepping up beside him.

"Back to the Boeing, I guess," Dempsey said. "Call me crazy, but I have a feeling our work's not done here."

CHAPTER 39

Filvarok Hotel

Odessa, Ukraine

1030 Local Time

Arkady stared into the middle distance, tapping his index finger on the modern wooden desk in the decadent hotel room that he—or, rather, Herr Hemmler—had rented. He'd gotten a few hours' sleep, but not enough. Espionage and sleep were incompatible bedfellows. He sighed.

He felt vulnerable.

Tap, tap, tap . . .

And weak.

Tap, tap, tap . . .

No, not weak . . .

Tap, tap, tap . . .

Depleted. That was a better word . . . like a body after a prolonged period of exertion.

It was fascinating to contemplate. Take the world's fastest man, set him in a race against his closest competition, and nine times out of ten he will prevail. But force this man to run the same race over and over again on a single day, each time pitting him against new runners, and eventually he will lose. When a champion has expended all of himself in the pursuit of victory, that is when he's most vulnerable.

Is that the game Kelso Jarvis has been playing with me? he wondered. *And Petrov, too?*

Over the past year, his two greatest adversaries—one abroad and one at home—had been fatiguing his intellect and draining his will. *Even the mightiest lion can be driven to exhaustion by a relentless pack of hounds . . .*

He stopped tapping and his mind went to Catherine Morgan. He'd lost many Zetas in recent months to Ember—twenty-seven, if he included those slain in Vyborg—but her loss was the most devastating. He was not the type of man who took either his resources or good fortune for granted, but he had grown too comfortable and reliant on both her counsel and the intelligence she'd harvested. With her murder, he'd lost his only insight into DNI Jarvis's mind and the movements and activities of Ember. Compounding the loss, they'd captured Bessonov—so while he'd lost his view inside Ember, Ember had gained insight into Zeta they'd not had before. He'd kept most of this from Petrov, projecting confidence and lying through omission to obscure the terrible truth—that Zeta was in its death throes.

I've been deluding myself, he thought, shaking his head. *Like an old, desperate man in a casino, feeding one coin after another into the machine, hoping for a jackpot and not stopping until all the money is gone.*

His satellite phone rang. He glanced at the caller ID, which appeared as all zeroes, and his stomach sank.

"Da," he said, taking the call.

"Where the fuck are you?" Petrov shouted in his ear.

He hesitated a moment, debating whether to answer truthfully, before saying, "In Odessa."

"Who told you you could go to Odessa, Arkady? Hmmm? I certainly did not. Do you not remember the last thing I instructed you to do?"

"Yes, I remember your words very distinctly, Mr. President. You said, 'Get out of my sight,' and then threatened to have me imprisoned in Lubyanka."

"Before that, you insolent son of a bitch," Petrov seethed.

"You tasked me to initiate an attack that would justify Russian military intervention, which is exactly what I'm attempting to do."

"I did not tell you to go to Ukraine personally."

"That is true, but at the same time, you did not prohibit it. To do this job properly, I need to be in Ukraine."

"You better hurry; the Americans are deploying forces. And are you aware that Kelso Jarvis—a fucking Navy SEAL—is now the Vice President of the United States?"

"I am," he said, letting out a long breath to calm his growing irritation. "This operation will not be affected by who sits second chair in the White House. But we must be careful and calculated with this attack. It's not so easy. It has to look real, and it must never be traced to Russia. But I do have an update for you: The asset is in Odessa. We will be able to proceed on schedule."

"Get it done and come back to Moscow. I need you here. I want to talk about deploying your operatives in a coordinated blitzkrieg-style covert offensive. I want to target top US and NATO commanders and deal a swift, simultaneous blow that creates massive chaos in the ranks while we escalate our efforts to reclaim Novorossiya."

"Okay, I'll be on the next flight out tonight," he said.

"See that you are," Petrov said and ended the call.

Arkady set the phone down on the desk.

The bastard finally called my bluff, he thought and began running scenarios in his head. Like a chessboard in his mind, he took turns playing both sides—white and black, his pieces and Petrov's—and every time the outcome ended with him losing.

"Shit, I think he knows," he murmured. "Which means I can't win . . . not without help."

He resumed tapping his index finger.

Tap, tap, tap . . .

Tap, tap, tap . . .

"Okay, fuck it," he said, shaking his head in disbelief at what he was about to do. He picked up the encrypted sat phone and called his lone surviving Zeta in Washington, DC, with an intact NOC. Samantha Bryant was his newest and least experienced Zeta inside the Beltway and was already proving to be a disappointment. In two years, she'd failed to accomplish anything other than becoming a staffer on the Hill who'd bounced between two different Congressmen.

She answered her mobile phone on the seventh ring. "Hello," she said.

Wherever Samantha was, it was noisy—a bar or crowded restaurant, he surmised. "Yes, hello," he said, with a neutral American Midwestern accent. "I'm calling from Capital One on a secure line. May I speak with Ms. Samantha Bryant?"

"Speaking," she said.

"Ms. Bryant, I'm calling to inform you that we have detected suspicious activity on your card and we are freezing your account. Can you please call our fraud department back at the number listed on the back of your card?"

"Yes, of course," she said, her voice taking on a fresh and urgent tone.

"Thank you for using Capital One. Goodbye," he said and severed the call.

Three minutes later, his other phone rang. "Authenticate," he said, answering it.

"Morning glories bloom at night," she said, calling him from a much quieter place now.

"And sunflowers follow the sun across the sky," he said, completing the challenge protocol.

"I'm secure," she said, unable to hide her nerves.

"Are you sure?"

"Yes. I mean, I think so . . . I'm in an alley behind the restaurant we're at."

"Why don't you go for a walk, Samantha? Walk and talk, that's the way we do it."

"Okay, I'm moving. I'm walking . . ."

"Listen to me, Samantha, I need you to do something for me. Something that, depending on how you execute the tasking, will draw unwanted attention to you. Something that may result in you being taken into custody and questioned. But that is okay, because what I need you to do is more important than the work you're doing in Congress."

"You want me to burn my NOC, is that what you're saying?"

"No," he said, rolling his eyes. "I want you to execute the tasking as quickly and covertly as possible. Use whatever contacts or methods you deem fit. No one knows your network better than you. This is not an either-or scenario, Samantha. Complete the mission *and* attempt to preserve your NOC. Do you understand?"

"Yes sir," she said. "What are my orders?"

He let the question hang on the air for a moment, testing his resolve more than hers. Finally, he said, "I need you to get a message to someone for me."

"Who?" she said, her curiosity piqued.

He let out a heavy, depleted exhale. "The Vice President of the United States."

CHAPTER 40

Office of the Vice President
West Wing of the White House
Washington, DC
0815 Local Time

Jarvis tugged at his shirt collar and grumbled his displeasure.

"What was that?" Petra said, looking up from the notebook computer propped on her lap.

"I said this shirt collar is too damn tight."

"I'm sorry, that must be aggravating," she said with what almost felt like spousal empathy.

"I'm serious, Petra. It's driving me crazy. I don't know if I can wear a tie every damn day for the rest of my life." He got to his feet and began to pace.

She tilted her head a few degrees to the right and fixed him with a knowing stare.

"What?" he snapped.

"Nothing," she said, but the corners of her lips tipped up just so.

"It's not nothing. You're giving me that look again."

"What look?"

"That one you give me whenever you think you've figured something out about me that I failed to recognize," he said, stopping long enough to mimic her head tilt and expression.

Instead of pushing her buttons, it had the opposite effect. "You're going to make a great Vice President," she said, her lips finishing their curl into the most endearing smile he'd ever seen.

Marry me, he thought. *Marry me right now. I don't want to do this alone.* The compulsion to say the words seemed so loud and overpowering in his head, he worried for a split second he might break down and do it. *No. Not like this. It needs to be . . . perfect.*

Instead, he said, "The thing is, I never actually said yes. It just happened . . . It feels like this was forced on me."

At this, her expression changed from fangirl to dubious juror. "You're not the kind of person who lets life happen to him. The President sounded the call of duty and you answered it. We talked about this. Remember?"

"But I never actually said yes." He resumed pacing.

"Mmm-hmm," was all she said.

"In fact, I told the bastard no."

"Must not have been a very convincing 'no,' *Mr. Vice President*," she said, then seemed to work very hard not to chuckle at his expense.

"It's not funny," he growled, despite failing to suppress a smile of his own.

"No, no, not funny at all. Being forced against your will into being second in command of the most powerful nation on Earth is no laughing matter," she said with just enough sarcasm to break down what was left of his petulant wall of self-pity.

"I see what you're doing and it won't work," he said, already feeling his shoulders relax a little.

"Listen, Kelso, I know this is not what you wanted." She put her computer aside to give him her full attention. "And I know Warner bulldozed you into this. But *he* sees the same thing *I* see in you."

"Now *you're* making me uncomfortable," he said, raising his eyebrows.

"Ha ha, very funny." She got to her feet and went to him. "We don't get to choose our fate. On the contrary, fate chooses for us. And in this moment in time, when faced with these circumstances, fate picked you to be Vice President."

"What if I don't believe in fate?"

"Fate doesn't care," she said. "It's agnostic to our whims and moods, or haven't you noticed?"

Jarvis inhaled deeply, exhaled through his nose, and stared at her.

She placed her right palm on his chest.

"But I have Parkinson's," he said.

"Yeah, well, I have acid reflux and my right knee is catching," she replied, not missing a beat. "Our bodies are fallible and imperfect—whatcha gonna do?"

"Wait a minute," he said, narrowing his eyes at her. "What's going on with your knee?"

"I think I might have torn the meniscus," she said with clipped irritation, then shaking her head added, "That's not the point of this conversation. The point I'm trying to make is the same one I made when we got the diagnosis a few months ago. Whether you're DNI or Vice President is irrelevant. In either case, you are serving your country at the highest level, and you're doing it with the mind, body, and soul fate has given you." She reached up, and with deft fingers loosened and removed his necktie, then undid the top button on his collar. "That being said . . . no reason to be miserable while you're at it."

"Thank you," he said, standing up straight with Vice Presidential bearing.

"You're welcome," she replied and handed him his now neatly folded necktie.

A knock came at the door.

"Come," he barked in his command voice.

The door cracked open and Warner's Chief of Staff stuck his head in. "The President wants to see you in the Oval Office."

"Tell him I'll be right there," Jarvis said with a perfunctory nod.

The other man nodded back and disappeared without shutting the door.

"You ready?" he asked, turning to Petra.

"Yeah, just let me grab my laptop," she said, fetching her computer. "All right, let's go."

They stepped out of his office, walked down the hall, past the Roosevelt Room, and entered the Presidential Secretary's office. Warner's secretary waved them both into the Oval Office and shut the door behind them. President Warner looked up from his chair behind the Resolute Desk, where he was on the phone, and gestured for them to take a seat. Together, they sat on the open sofa across from where Warner's Chief of Staff was sitting, furiously typing text messages.

"Yes, you have the green light, General," Warner said into the handset as he stood. "That's correct . . . yes . . . the Vice President is going to do it . . . all right, keep me updated, thank you, that will be all." With a dour look on his face, he placed the telephone handset in its cradle and walked over to join them. "I'm going to keep this brief," he said and sat down beside his Chief of Staff. "I just gave approval to the Joint Chiefs to deploy the Marines to Mariupol."

Jarvis glanced at Petra, then back at Warner. "But sir, that is going to be interpreted as an escalation."

"Which is why you're going to go on television and tell the world the opposite"—the President made a show of checking his watch—"approximately ninety minutes from now."

"I don't understand, sir," Jarvis said, screwing up his face.

"I know, because this is not the world you come from, but it is the world you live in now—a world where reality is defined by words, not actions. By outcome, not intent. So, when you're standing behind that podium in the Press Briefing Room and the reporters ask you if this move should be construed as an act of war against Russia, you are going to look at them like they are all crazy and tell them the opposite is true. You're going to point out how badly things are spiraling out of control in Mariupol, and then tell them it leaves us no choice but to send US Marines to *assist* the Russians with peacekeeping efforts. And when they push back at you, you're going to take it up a notch and say that it is our intention to work hand in glove with Russian forces because we and the Russian share a common goal . . . to quell the violence in the streets and make Mariupol safe for everyone, Ukrainians and Russians alike."

"With all due respect, sir, that's ridiculous. The veneer on that message is so thin, it's transparent. They're going to eat me alive and then they're going to run to the Russian Ambassador for comment and he'll claim there has been no dialogue concerning cooperation and that Russia sees this move as provocation."

"No," Warner said and smiled. "He's not going to say that."

"How can you be so sure?"

"Because you're going to preempt that scenario by insinuating that cooperation was his idea. You're going to make him sound like the voice of reason and thank him for being the type of ambassador we need in these desperate times. A concerned partner who reached out and asked for our help, because after all, the Russian troops in Mariupol are there to keep the peace, not to wage war."

Jarvis laughed, but when Warner didn't react in kind, he said, "You're serious? You want me to lie?"

"Oh, I'm dead serious, Kelso. This is the way the game is played. Welcome to politics, Mr. Vice President."

Jarvis didn't say anything; his mind was already churning through the probable question-and-answer scenarios he would face in this melee with the press.

"I can see you're already putting together your battle plan," Warner said, grinning wide. "Good. Stick with military metaphors; it's appropriate for a man with your pedigree. I want you to treat this press briefer like any other engagement, except instead of firing bullets, words are your ammunition."

"Yes, sir," he said. "I won't let you down."

"I know you won't," Warner said. "That's why I made you VP in the first place."

Jarvis nodded and turned to Petra.

She took the nonverbal cue and said, "We don't have much time. We need to get to work drafting your remarks and get updated on everything that's happened in theater over the past six hours so we don't get blindsided, so . . . unless there's something else, Mr. President?"

"No, no, by all means, you are excused," Warner said, then shot his own Chief of Staff a sly, knowing look.

Jarvis pressed to his feet, nodded at the President and his Chief of Staff and excused himself.

When he got to the door, Warner called after him. "Oh, one more thing, Kelso . . ."

"Sir?" he said, turning.

"Make sure you wear a tie."

"Yes, sir," Jarvis said, cursing in his mind. "Of course."

Officially chided, he and Petra exited and headed back to his office. Once they were out of earshot, he turned to her and said, "Are you fucking kidding me—did that really just happen?"

"I'm afraid so," she said.

Great, he thought. *I've let the President turn me into what I've always despised most. The one thing I promised myself I would never become—a politician.*

"What's that expression you used to use at the Tier One all the time?" Petra asked, her heels clicking on the floor as they walked in step.

"Embrace the suck," he said, shooting her a sideways glance.

"That's the one," she said and gave his arm a quick squeeze. "I think it's time we embrace the suck."

CHAPTER 41

Ember Tactical Operations Trailer (TOT)
SOCOM Compound
MacDill Air Force Base
Tampa, Florida
0816 Local Time

Mike Casey strode down the hallway of what the team had cynically dubbed the Ember TOT—substituting a T, for Trailer, for the C in the ubiquitous Tactical Operations Center acronym. During his turnover and indoc with Baldwin, the Signals Chief told him that TOT was actually the second acronym they'd adopted. Apparently, Dan Munn had originally dubbed their nascent headquarters at MacDill the *Tactical Information Trailer* and insisted on using its acronym at every opportunity, but Baldwin had shut that down. It wasn't the first time an off-color acronym had found its way into the DoD lexicon. When Casey was a junior officer in the submarine training pipeline, a subset of instructors at Naval Nuclear Power

School were tagged as *Direct Input Limited Duty Officers*. When he'd shared that story with Baldwin, the man's cheeks had actually gone pink.

"That's horrifying," Baldwin had said, quickly deciphering the acronym. "You're kidding me?"

"I wish I were," Casey had said, shaking his head. "And it stuck for years, too, before finally being purged from the books. Thankfully, all the DILDOs were good sports about it. As a submariner, I'm something of an expert at being on the receiving end of offensive humor. I'm telling you, having a sense of humor about military service—and life in general, for that matter—is definitely a tactical attribute."

This had earned a chuckle from Baldwin, and they were off to the races afterward with a smooth, amiable handover of control of America's preeminent counterterrorism black ops task force. Unfortunately, having a good sense of humor wasn't enough to deflect the shit storm presently raining down on their heads. The President had set Defense Condition 2 and the world was on the brink of war. Both the American and Russian propaganda machines were running at redline, churning out disinformation in every conceivable media channel to camouflage the reality that a hot war had already started in Mariupol . . . a hot war in which Ember's SAD and their "cousins" from SEAL Team Four had already been bloodied.

"Director Casey," said the analyst everybody called Chip, sticking the upper half of his torso into the hall past a doorframe. "I think we have something you're gonna want to see."

Casey nodded and walked into the trailer's only conference room, which had been transformed into an ops center. In submariner speak, this room was equivalent to the conn, the nerve center and communications hub for all tactical activities. What he found most interesting was that everybody just seemed to hang out in the room all the time, leaving their respective offices sitting vacant. As a former CO, he took this as a very positive sign.

A crew that's tight together, fights together.

"Whatcha got for me?" he said.

"It all started when Buz made an offhand comment about how the Russians have a bad habit of inadvertently telegraphing strategy in their propaganda," Chip said.

"How so?" he asked, glancing at Buz, who was sitting beside Baldwin in a chair pulled back from the table, legs crossed ankle over knee. The "retired" Cold War expert gave him a nod, smiling under his eighties-style mustache.

"They do it all the time," Ember's spook in residence explained. "A state-sponsored media outlet will post an article about how some enemy of the Kremlin is suspected of this or that misdeed, and then weeks later that same person is arrested, ousted from power, or turns up dead."

"Why would they do that?" Casey said. "To desensitize the public in advance?"

Buz nodded. "Exactly. The Kremlin loves to disparage its targets prior to taking action. Russia is pathologically image conscious, like a middle school girl at the dance trying to make sure everyone sees them as one of the cool kids. And just like an insecure teenage girl spreading mean rumors about the pretty girl, they often construct a negative aura around a particular adversary, so that when the hammer strike comes later, they've already built a case against their target in the court of public opinion and established themselves as the good guys."

"Interesting," Casey said. "And you've seen enough instances that you believe it's predictive?"

"It doesn't always pan out," Buz said with a spymaster's twinkle in his eye, "but there are certain bylines I never ignore."

"And you think you found one I need to know about?"

"Three days ago, *Russian Times* posted this article." Buz motioned for Chip to show Casey his tablet. The headline read, "Kiev Readies Weapons of Mass Destruction for Use on Citizens in Mariupol." A photograph beneath the headline showed a mobile ballistic missile launcher with ordnance raised and ready for launch. "The author tries to make the case that the Kiev government blames pro-Russian separatists for the civil unrest in Mariupol and that it will take proactive steps to avoid another war of secession like in Donbas."

Casey screwed up his face. "They're claiming Ukraine is going to bomb its own people?"

Buz nodded. "Yep. The author says they did it in Donetsk and they'll do it again."

"Are those Iskander missiles?" he asked, focusing on the picture.

"Very good, sir," Chip said, jumping in. "A pair of Iskanders shown on an MZKT-7930 transport erector launch vehicle."

"Petrov is putting those damn Iskanders everywhere—Kaliningrad, along the Belarusian and Ukrainian borders, and more recently on the Crimean peninsula."

"A true statement," Baldwin said. "The Iskander is the successor to the Soviet-era Tochka SRBMs that came into service in the mid-nineteen seventies. The Russian military is systematically phasing out its inventory of Tochka missiles and replacing them with Iskanders."

"Okay," Casey said, rubbing his clean-shaven chin. "So you guys think this article indicates Petrov is somehow planning to provoke Ukraine into firing Iskander missiles on Mariupol, thereby giving Russia an excuse to escalate?"

"Well, here's the thing: the Ukrainians don't have Iskanders.

The missile was developed by Russia after Ukrainian independence. Ukraine *does* have an inventory of Tochka missiles, carried over from back in the days when it was an extension of the Red Army," Buzz said, "but no Iskanders."

"Hold on . . . show me that picture again," Casey said, turning to Chip. The young analyst passed him the tablet. "But there's a Ukrainian flag painted on the side of that transporter."

Buz grinned at him like a kid who'd just snuck a cookie from the jar. "And the photo caption is mislabeled, identifying the missiles as Grom-2s."

Casey cocked an eyebrow. "I'm not familiar with the Grom-2."

"Grom-2 is the homegrown Ukrainian SRBM," Chip said. "The Ukrainian Tochkas only have a range of one hundred fifty kilometers, and Russia won't sell Ukraine the Iskander because that platform would be capable of hitting Moscow. So, Kiev tasked the Ukrainian defense contractor YMZ with getting to work on an SRBM that could potentially do the job."

"Are the Grom-2s even in service yet?" Casey asked.

"Kiev officially says no, but we suspect otherwise," Baldwin said.

"Guys, I think I see where you're going with this," he said, loving the strategic thought process they were using, "but I gotta tell you, it's a stretch. There's a lot of speculation here. If you can get me something resembling proof, I'll run it up the flagpole, but without hard evidence . . ."

"Oh, we've got proof," Buz said, smiling under his mustache. "Collectively we've just spent the past six hours putting all the puzzle pieces together, and we're ready to brief you."

"Then I'm all ears," Casey said, pulling out a chair.

For the next twenty minutes, Baldwin and the others made their case—showing him signals intercepts, security camera grabs, and satellite imagery. With a ninety-five percent confidence interval, they'd placed Arkady Zhukov in Odessa traveling under the German Hemmler NOC that Amanda had harvested from Bessonov yesterday. They also had a facial rec hit at a hotel in Odessa on the Zeta they believed was behind the assassination of the Vice President in Kiev. They had encrypted comms between a phone being used on Zhukov's biz jet and the Zeta in the hotel. And the coup de grâce, they had satellite imagery of an 8x8 heavy haul truck, resembling the Iskander transporter, driven into covered storage at a warehouse near the Odessa airport—the same warehouse where they had a signal hit from the Zeta operator's phone—only five hours earlier.

Casey shook his head in disbelief. "Guys, it's amazing work, but two things I don't understand. One, how did you put this all together so quickly; and two, why am I just hearing about this now?"

The Ember gang collectively looked at one another, as if silently negotiating whose turn it was to be the sacrificial lamb. After a pause, Baldwin said, "Sir, the thing about Ember, and maybe any team engaged in intelligence collection and assessment in today's world, is that without a spark the fire rarely catches. In this case, we had two sparks. First, Amanda providing us with Arkady Zhukov's German legend from Bessonov. Without that, we wouldn't have had any SIGINT to prosecute. We pulled satellite imagery for every SIGINT ping, and it just so happened that Buz was sitting next to Chip when he was looking over the satellite imagery for the warehouse near the Odessa airport. We weren't working a missile theory. That epiphany was all Buz."

Casey looked at the old spook.

"You can put a dress and lipstick on a pig," Buz said, knitting his fingers together behind his head, "but it's still a pig . . . and the

MZKT Astrolog transporter is one pig I can recognize anywhere: blocky design, step-up cab with a forward-sloping windshield, and the eight-by-eight chassis. I knew immediately what I was looking at. As soon as I saw it, I remembered the *RT* article about Ukraine planning to launch WMDs at Mariupol. So, we worked backward. Using imagery sourced from multiple partner satellites, Chip reconstructed the vehicle's track. We traced it all the way back to Crimea."

"What type of potential damage are we looking at here?"

"The MZKT Astrolog carries two Iskander-M variant missiles," Chip said, jumping in with nervous enthusiasm. "Iskanders were designed to be used in theater-level conflicts to hit either soft targets, like troop concentrations, or hard targets, like communication bunkers. They can be equipped with a wide variety of warheads: conventional, fuel-air explosive, EMP, high-yield frag payloads, or a hundred-kiloton tactical nuke. Each missile can be independently targeted, guided, and launched. They are supersonic, cruising at Mach six, and programmed to conduct antiballistic maneuvers."

"Wonderful," Casey said through a sigh. "What's the range?"

"The published range is five hundred kilometers, but some sources indicate that's a conservative number."

"How far is Mariupol from Odessa?"

"Five hundred kilometers."

"Of course it is." Casey inhaled deeply as a hypothetical scenario began to unfold in his mind. "Ukraine forfeited all their nukes in the nineties ... the Russians wouldn't fire tactical nukes because they'd lose the element of plausible deniability ... The Marines from the 13th MEU are moving east toward Mariupol as we speak. Instead of targeting the population zone, why not make the Marines a target? It's what I'd do if I were Arkady. And in the propaganda campaign that follows, you call the event a tragic case of friendly fire—collateral damage from a desperate act of retaliation by a desperate nation." He looked at Baldwin. "Tell me more about the fragmentation warhead."

"It has a high-explosive yield and is quite deadly—capable of spraying fifteen thousand pieces of frag per warhead over a five-hectare area," Baldwin said. "It is worth noting that this is the same warhead installed on the Ukrainian Tochka missiles, so again, this would only bolster the Russian propaganda narrative we are hypothesizing."

Casey looked from Baldwin around the room, with his gaze finally settling on Buz. "Anything else I need to know?"

"This type of stealth repositioning of assets and hardware, along with advance propaganda, has all the hallmarks of a Russian false flag operation. In the past, I'd try to convince you that this op was Arkady Zhukov's brainchild. Today, thanks to this team, for the first time in twenty years, I finally have his fingerprints on the crime before it happens."

Casey extended his hand to Buz.

For a moment, the old spy didn't react, as if Buz were questioning his sincerity. But then he leaned forward and clasped the submariner's, and his newest boss's, hand.

"I understand from DNI Jar . . . I mean Vice President Jarvis, that this day has been a long time coming for you, Buz," Casey said.

"Yes, sir.

"And that pursuing this man took a helluva toll on your career and reputation . . ."

"That, it did."

"Then I think congratulations are in order," he said, giving Buz's hand a final pump before releasing it. "Looks like Ember SAD is going to Odessa."

"Yes, sir."

"Do you want to give them the good news, or should I?"

"Prevent the missile launch at all costs?" Buz asked.

Casey nodded. "Plus bonus tasking."

Buz smiled wide at this. "Capture/kill?"

Casey grinned back. "If it's all the same with you, I was leaning more toward the kill side of that equation. I don't think Zhukov gets to walk away this time."

"Did you clear that with the big boss?" Buz asked, unable to hide his anticipation.

"Not yet, although I have a pretty good feeling what his answer is going to be," Casey said. But his submarine skipper's mind was already beginning to contemplate contingency scenarios. "In the meantime, we need a backup plan in case Ember can't get there in time."

"I'll have Chip prepare a list of all the assets in the region with the capability to shoot down a ballistic missile for you," Baldwin said.

"Perfect," he replied, but his mind immediately went to the *Donald Cook* and her Aegis Combat System and SM-3 antiballistic missile cache. "You know what, Mr. Baldwin, scratch that. No point reinventing the wheel. Just get me the Ballistic Missile Defense Officer Europe on the phone."

Thirty minutes passed—two of which were spent talking with the O-5 Ballistic Missile Defense Officer and twenty-two of which were spent arguing with the Vice Admiral in NSA Naples in charge of Sixth Fleet. After that conversation, Casey was patched through to Commander Dustin Townsend on the USS *Donald Cook*.

"*Donald Cook* Actual," came the voice on the other end of the line, as clear as if he were in the next room. The CO sounded weary as hell, Casey thought, and after the ordeal the *Cook* had gone through over the past forty-eight hours, he could relate. As a submarine skipper, he'd known a little something about long hours.

"Captain Townsend, this is Commander Mike Casey," he began, hoping the Navy rank might help smooth things along. "I assume you saw the flash message traffic with your new national-level tasking?"

A pause lingered on the line, and Casey could well imagine what was going through the Naval officer's head.

"I don't know who you are, or who you work for, Commander, but when a three-star sends me a message, I read it pretty quick. So, tell me, what can the *Donald Cook* do for your little sideshow?"

"I'm afraid this is much bigger than a sideshow," Casey said. "We have intelligence indicating that Iskander short range ballistic missiles could be launched from Odessa targeting US forces in eastern Ukraine. We have a covert direct-action operation spinning up to stop it, but if that fails . . ."

"Let me guess, you want us set to intercept the missiles if they launch?"

"That's correct. *Donald Cook*'s Aegis Combat System and SM-3s are the only viable antiballistic platform in theater."

"Well, you see, Commander, there are several major problems with your plan. Number one, I'm not in a position to oblige your request. To intercept those missiles, we'd need to be parked off the coast of Ukraine, but we are steaming south below the forty-fifth parallel. Number two, the Iskander is a fast fucking missile. If your operation fails and they launch, I will literally have seconds to respond, and there is no guarantee the SM-3 will successfully intercept the Iskanders. And number three, if I launch missiles north of the forty-fifth parallel, there is a better than fifty percent chance the Russian Black Sea fleet will assume I'm launching at them and sink my ship. So, um, as much as the *Donald Cook* would like to help you, I think you'd best look at another option."

"I hear you, Captain," Casey said, "and as someone with experience commanding a fast attack nuclear submarine in similar ass-puckering situations, I understand your reservations. But unfortunately, I'm going to have to pull rank."

Casey looked at Baldwin. "Mr. Baldwin, if you could send that follow-on 'eyes only' message to Commander Townsend . . . the one from the President."

Baldwin nodded and looked at Chip, who sent the message with Presidential authorization for the operation. In the background, Casey could hear Townsend being informed of the incoming flash traffic.

After a long pause, Townsend said, "You're really going to send us back into the lion's den?"

"I'm afraid so, Commander," Casey said, bowing his head. "And I pray for all our sakes, I don't have to use you."

CHAPTER 42

Ember Executive Boeing 787
35,000 Feet
En Route to Odessa, Ukraine
1551 Local Time

Dempsey tuned out the droning voices of the talking heads on the flat-screen TV, tapping away nervous energy with his right thumb on the armrest of the recliner while his left booted foot kept cadence. Munn sat beside him in an oversized recliner of his own, legs up and ankles crossed. While Munn flipped through the channels on the TV, switching news feeds every thirty seconds or so, Dempsey fidgeted in his seat.

"Why the hell do you do that?" Dempsey said, unable to stand it anymore.

"Do what?" Munn grumbled over his shoulder.

"Flip around between all the cable news channels like that. Do you really think CNN is gonna report something that you don't already know? We're the recipients of the best, most carefully crafted real-time intelligence assessments on the planet—these bozos don't know anything."

"Yeah, well, I want to know what everyone else is thinking about everything that's going on, okay?" Munn said without looking back at him. "Besides, what else should I be doing? Until someone tells us why we're going to Odessa, I'm gonna watch the news."

"New Director, same bullshit," Dempsey said through a sigh. "Hurry up and wait . . . Nothing ever changes."

Across from them, on the leather sofa, Martin let out a long snore.

Dempsey and Munn both looked at the kid and busted up laughing.

"Must be nice," Munn said. "I'd wake up so stiff that I—"

The lounge door burst open, cutting Munn off. Grimes leaned halfway in, her face bright with anticipation, and said, "The Director's on the line. The brief is now . . ."

Munn beat Dempsey to his feet and gave Martin a gentle kick with his boot as he passed.

"'Bout time," Munn said, new fire in his voice. "Martin's getting bed sores."

Dempsey followed Grimes into the mobile TOC, noticing the fresh, quarter-sized stain of blood on the white Kerlix dressing wrapped around her left arm and shoulder. She seemed to move without much pain, so he decided to keep the concern to himself, though he would ask Munn about the wound later. Despite his eagerness to get back in the fight, the sight of the submarine commander staring at them from the briefing monitor instantly refreshed his grumpiness. He wondered again how in the hell a dolphin-wearing sub geek could possibly be in charge of the most secret and lethal direct-action covert operations team in the world.

"I hope everyone got some rest," Casey said as Ember's SAD members all dropped into their chairs.

Dempsey ignored the new director's question, folded his arms across his chest, and spoke for the group, "What've you got for us, boss?"

A picture of a Russian missile transport vehicle filled the left half of the screen, with what looked to be real-time satellite imagery on the right.

"We believe that the Russians intend to conduct an attack on Mariupol using Iskander short-range ballistic missiles," Casey said.

"That doesn't make any sense," Dempsey said. "In our last brief, you told us that Russian armor and troops moved into the city after that massive IED detonation in the city center killed all those civilians and their peacekeeping contingent."

"All true," Casey said, his expression neutral. "But we believe this is just the next phase of a premeditated series of strategic escalations. The transporter has been disguised, repainted with Ukrainian markings. We believe Petrov will pin the attack on Ukraine and use it as a justification for a full-scale invasion."

"Well, then that's insane," Martin chimed in, fully awake now. "They'll be killing their own troops."

"Yes," Casey said, "But not just their own troops. Marines from the 13th MEU in Odessa have been sent to Mariupol. They will be on station by midafternoon, deploying beside the Russians as a peacekeeping force."

"What?" Dempsey exclaimed, incredulous. "Whose bright fucking idea was that?" He pictured the same Russians who only hours ago had tried to obliterate his team engaging the Marines in bloody combat.

"This move was authorized by the President and will be announced by Vice President Jarvis within the hour," Casey said. "And while I have not been read in on the details or logic of this plan, knowing the architects, I trust the rationale is sound. That being said, the decision was made *before* our team here in Tampa pieced together the false flag Iskander missile plot. Which means it is our job to stop this launch before it happens. Not only is the potential loss of American lives tremendous, but I fear the cascade of events that would follow could lead to a global conflict with hundreds of thousands dead."

"This has Zhukov's signature all over it," Dempsey growled, hands balled into fists. "Do you have a location?"

"We do," Casey said. "The missile transporter is in Odessa. And your instincts about this being a Zeta operation are correct, Mr. Dempsey. We have imagery and facial recognition demonstrating that the Zeta operator who led the attack on your convoy after the Ultra op in Kiev is present, and we believe the launch is imminent."

"We're due to touch down in thirty minutes. We need to put a mission package together ASAFP," Munn said, now in full operator mode.

"Yes, and we've been working on that, but first there's one more thing . . ."

Dempsey tapped his boot against the leg of his chair, impatient for what he could tell was the Ember Director's big reveal.

"We believe Arkady Zhukov himself is on the ground in Odessa, coordinating this mission in person . . . I've already briefed the President. Your kill order is authorized." Casey paused to let all four operators and the cybergenius Wang let out a whooping cheer before adding, "Our first priority, of course, is to stop the launch . . . but I think this group has demonstrated the ability to walk and chew gum. I'll leave the mechanics of achieving both objectives to you."

"In that case, I say drop a fucking smart bomb on the missile transport and let SAD go get Arkady," Dempsey said, practically punch-drunk with euphoria over the news. The day he'd thought would never come was finally here—Arkady fucking Zhukov in the flesh.

"I'm afraid it's not quite that simple, John," Baldwin said, taking this as his cue to begin his brief. The screen filled with a satellite view of what Dempsey assumed to be Odessa. The image zoomed in slowly on an area north of the large international airport. "As you can see, the warehouse with the missile truck is located here . . ." A yellow arrow appeared on the screen beside a long, rectangular building, and Dempsey immediately saw the problem. Not only was the facility in the middle of a busy, crowded business district, but it was only a block away from a residential neighborhood and directly across from a large two-story building, and just down the street from a much larger multistory building with an attached parking deck.

"Let me guess," Dempsey said. "Hospital?"

"Here," Baldwin said, and a red arrow appeared on the large building down the street from the target.

"And that," Munn grumbled, pointing at a different building, "must be an elementary school, because, well, of course it's a fucking school."

"Actually, here," Baldwin agreed, lighting up a blue arrow on a bright green-roofed building a block away. Then he designated the building directly across from the target. "The building you are referring to, Dan, is a retirement center with thirty-five full-time residents. Obviously, an air strike is out of the question due to the unacceptable risk of collateral damage and high civilian casualties. A direct-action mission has the lowest risk and greatest chance of success. This is further enhanced by the fact that we have so far seen only two individuals coming and going from the warehouse—both are present now, by the way—and we detect no obvious QRF presence in the immediate vicinity."

"That's what you said about Mariupol," Grimes chimed in, unconsciously rubbing her bandaged shoulder. "And we all know how that turned out."

"Not exactly the same scenario, but true nonetheless," Baldwin said. "I think it is prudent to assume a covert presence of Zeta support and fighters have been tasked to backup an operation as critical as this. Consideration was given to using an element of the 26th Special Operations–capable Marines in the area—"

"No, it has to be us," Wang barked.

"—but the sensitive nature of the mission," Baldwin continued, unfazed, "and the need to prosecute Arkady Zhukov, gave the mission entirely to us. That being said, let it be a comfort to you that we have a QRF of Marines only minutes away if you need help."

"Right," Dempsey said, drawing out the word, sure that Baldwin did not intend the comment to be as mocking as it sounded. He checked his watch, then turned to his four teammates, who all looked like they'd just been given intravenous caffeine. "All right, people, we have the mission of our lives to prep, and we have twenty-two minutes to do it. Time to kit up!"

CHAPTER 43

Kovtun Storage (Number 3)

Three Miles North of Odessa International Airport

1640 Local Time

Gavriil watched carefully as the former Russian missile technician—now a midlevel agent in the GRU—inspected the launch panel on the side of the MZKT Astrolog missile transporter. He realized that, for the first time in nearly five years, he wanted desperately to smoke a cigarette, and he chastised himself for the craving and the lack of mental discipline it suggested. Perhaps the proximity to this weapon of war and the nostalgia for his early days as a soldier brought on the craving. More likely it was the combination of the diesel fuel smell and the technician who reeked of tobacco. Smell, he had been told, triggered more powerful memories than almost any other stimulus.

"Are the prelaunch checks complete?" he asked the technician impatiently. He'd already memorized the entire operations manual for the Astrolog truck, the launch system, and everything he could digest about the Iskander-M missiles. He was confident he could operate the system, drive the vehicle into position, and fire the two missiles if it came to it. But it would be better to have a proficient tech present in case an unforeseen electrical or mechanical problem reared its ugly head ... which it always seemed to do at the most inopportune time.

"Yes, we are at the stage where I enter the target coordinates. It is better to have the programming done now and stored in the system memory. That way, at launch time, we only have to confirm the prompts. It saves us much time," the tech said.

"I will program the target coordinates myself," Gavriil said, pacing away from the man and the irresistible aroma of cigarettes.

The man turned, both eyebrows arching. "Then why am I here, comrade?" he said, retrieving his pack of Belomorkanals from his shirt pocket. He shook one free and put it to his lips as he searched his other pocket for a lighter. "I have all the necessary clearances, my mysterious friend. I am GRU, after all. You need not keep the targets from me, and in any case ..." He snapped open a metal lighter and lit his smoke. "I will know soon enough."

"It is our protocol. I myself have not yet been informed of the target coordinates," he lied, "so as to maintain complete operational security."

"Is that so?" the other man said, a flash of something in his eyes.

The billowing smoke was almost intoxicating, and Gavriil had the urge to shoot the man now just to rid himself of the temptation. It was an unfortunate necessity of the operation that this man must die, but they both had their roles to play. Gavriil understood his; this poor fool did not. When the body of a known GRU agent—a part of the GRU task force linked closely to Petrov—was found beside the truck by the authorities, the dominos would begin to fall. With all of the other breadcrumbs they would leave behind, Gavriil imagined it would take only hours for the Americans to link the devastating Mariupol missile attack to Petrov. As expected, Arkady's plan was coming together. Hopefully the spymaster's foresight about what would happen in the days that followed was equally prescient.

"Then what to do now?" the GRU agent asked, smoke streaming from both of his nostrils like some ancient dragon.

"We wait," Gavriil said, his hands behind his back.

"Perhaps we go and get something to eat? And maybe a drink?"

Gavriil sighed. This was the GRU inner circle?

"*Nyet*. We must stay here—and indoors—until after dark when we receive our coordinates and conduct our operation. When it is done, we'll have a steak dinner and a bottle of vodka. My treat. *Da?*"

The man shrugged, but his eyes narrowed. "It is the American Marines we are attacking, I assume?"

Undistracted by the man's left hand bringing the cigarette back to his lips, Gavriil noticed his right hand slipping under the flap of his jacket, undoubtedly going for his weapon. Gavriil was faster, however, retrieving the compact GSh-18 pistol from his waistband, aiming, and firing in one fluid motion. The bullet tore through the missile tech's head just beside the bridge of his nose, and the man instantly collapsed, his own larger Makarov P-96 pistol clattering to the ground. Gavriil shook his head. The pistol the GRU man carried was like wearing a T-shirt saying, *I am Russian military covert operations*. Like the GSh-18 Gavriil had chosen to use for the murder, the Makarov would leave little doubt as to who had been behind the missile attack.

He holstered his weapon and exhaled. It was a relief to have it done. Between the smoking and the questions, he could barely stand it anymore. In any case, he always worked better alone . . .

He *tsk*ed when he saw the rather large spatter of blood and other gore on the side of the truck. That would require cleaning. Behind him, he heard a quiet click. Gavriil whirled, pistol up and ready, as he shifted left to take cover. He scanned left and right until he found his target—a lone and familiar silhouette, backlit from the sunlight streaming through the partially opened door.

"You shouldn't do things like that," Gavriil said, heart pounding as he lowered his weapon. "You're not supposed to be here before dark. Has something gone wrong? You take a great risk . . ."

"Yes, yes," Arkady said. "It is wonderful to see you, too. And nothing is wrong. I'm simply here to help."

Gavriil felt anxiety rise to join his confusion. *Do you not trust my ability to execute this mission? Or am I another loose thread to be snipped?* Gavriil shoved the GSh-18 back into his waistband. If Arkady intended to kill him, there would be no stopping it. Just as Gavriil had been tasked to take the life of the Prime who preceded him. If today was his day to die, then today was his day.

Arkady laughed, and it echoed in the cavernous warehouse as he approached. When he reached Gavriil, he set down the large metal suitcase and the brown paper sack he carried, and opened his arms wide. "You look worried, my son," the spymaster said, embracing him, a large smile creasing his face. "Don't be. I'm not here to micromanage, but I am here to help. This operation cannot fail. It is bigger than you, than me, than Zeta. Today we begin the long and arduous operation of saving Russia from the enemy within. A phoenix will rise from the ashes of the chaos we unleash here, and I will need you in the coming days. Our next operation will be more difficult than anything we've undertaken before, and it is one I will not survive."

Gavriil looked into the eyes, at once both young and old, of the man he had loved and hated while always admiring—and fearing. Now, he finally understood.

"Yes," Arkady said, nodding. "You see the end game now. You will carry on my mantle."

"I . . . I don't know," he stammered. "I will serve Russia—and you—until my last breath, but I don't have your gifts."

"Don't worry; I'm recruiting a potential ally for you," the old fox said cryptically. "But we will talk about that later." Arkady's eyes went to the corpse on the floor. Chuckling, he said, "I see you executed one aspect of the plan a little prematurely."

"Yes, well, he was asking questions . . . and he was going to shoot me."

"We have enemies everywhere," Arkady said, nodding. "Never forget that."

Gavriil stepped over the dead GRU agent, snatching a large green towel from the step beneath the control panel of the truck. He began to clean the mess off the side of the truck. He was about to say, "I leave such things to you; I am just a weapon," but he stopped himself. That was the response Arkady would have wanted to hear from him five minutes ago, but not now, he surmised. So instead, he said, "It is sometimes difficult to tell friend from foe until the last second."

"Believe me, I know," Arkady said and nudged the paper bag with his foot. "I brought food. Let's share a meal and talk about the operation. What support elements do you have in place?"

"I have a single controller, two armed spotters, and one sniper. Other than that, it is just me."

"A small footprint is very wise—" The chirping of a satellite phone interrupted him, and he fished the device from his pocket. He held up a bony finger to Gavriil and put the phone to his ear. "Yes?"

Gavriil studied the old spy's expression, searching for a clue as to the nature of the interruption, but as always, Arkady's face gave up nothing. He disconnected the call and dropped the phone back into his pocket.

"It's the Americans," he said, his face still a mask, but his voice grave.

"What of the Americans? I have seen the Marines at the stadium and out conducting patrols. It is impossible that they will stumble on us here."

"Not *those* Americans," Arkady said. "The Ember Boeing just arrived at the airport. They are taxiing over to the government ramp as we speak."

"Shit."

"Yes," Arkady said, pulling at his chin. "An unfortunate development."

"They can't possibly know about this operation, nor about our presence here. How could they?"

"How, indeed? But they are here nonetheless," Arkady said, his mind working the problem. His cheeks suddenly blanched. "It's my fault."

"They don't know you. It must be me. Somehow, they tracked me from Kiev."

"No, I don't think so," Arkady said, shaking his head. "The Hemmler NOC is blown. Bessonov must have broken."

Gavriil paced away from the truck, then turned back to his Director. "Let me program the weapon to target their jet. This is our chance to take them out—completely and finally."

Arkady seemed to consider this for a moment, but Gavriil already knew the answer—whether from some subtle body cue or facial tic, or because he understood Arkady's long-term goal for Mother Russia. "No," the spymaster said. "It would ruin everything. We have to launch now."

"In broad daylight?"

"It is the hand we are dealt, my son," Arkady said. "How long to program the missile, plant the clues, and execute the plan?"

"Most of it is done," Gavriil said, his mind ticking off the few tasks remaining. "I need thirty minutes."

Arkady squeezed his arm and smiled. "Good." He knelt and opened the metal suitcase, which reminded Gavriil of a luggage bomb from an old American spy movie. Gavriil watched as the old man pulled out a tripod device—like a miniature replica of a cell phone tower. He extended it to its maximum height and connected it to the metal box with a thick cable.

"What is that?" Gavriil asked.

"A portable EM jammer. It will interfere with all communications signals for a one-mile radius." Arkady stood. "It is very powerful, but as such has a limited amount of battery. Once activated it will work for up to ninety minutes. You'll have to tell your team in advance. They will lose comms, too."

"That's a problem," Gavriil said.

"I know, but again, the alternative is worse."

"How does it work?"

"Just push this button," Arkady said and pointed to a green button on an electronic control panel.

"And if something changes? What if we need to abort?"

Arkady shook his head. "There is no going back now. There will be no abort. We execute the mission and exfil directly to the airport. While Ember is in the city, we will be escaping right under their noses."

Gavriil nodded, still stunned at the turn of events. He shook his head clear and radioed each member of his team, briefing them on the revised timeline and the electronic jamming that would be implemented. With that done, he lifted the dead missile tech into the cab of the transport vehicle, then walked to the missile launch control panel to enter the target coordinates.

"Gavriil?" Arkady interrupted him, uncharacteristically using his given name.

"Yes?" he said, looking up. The spymaster's eyes held something different, something he had seen only a glimmer of before. Respect? Admiration? Even love, perhaps?

"The plane leaves in one hour, with or without you."

"*Da*, I know."

"And the same holds for me. If I am late, detained, or injured, do not wait for me." Arkady's expression went hard as granite. "Do you understand?"

Gavriil hesitated a moment, then said, "I understand."

"Good," the old fox said, and with a fatalistic smile pressed the green button in the center of the open metal briefcase. "For Russia."

CHAPTER 44

Ember Tactical Operations Trailer (TOT)
Tampa, Florida
0950 Local Time

"What do you mean you've lost *all* comms?" Casey said, rising from his chair to pace—a luxury he never had as the CO of the *Tucson*, where his stateroom was so small he could barely turn around.

"Just that, sir." Over the encrypted communications Wang's voice sounded strained, but also rife with static. To Casey, it sounded like the cyber kid was running his voice through some '80s rock synthesizer. "Everything is down, boss—encrypted radio, encrypted GSM, even LOS using the Predator. I can't raise anyone on the team on any channel."

"Is it your equipment on the Boeing?"

"Negative, sir. We're being jammed, but it's not like anything I'm even remotely familiar with . . ."

Casey waited through the strained silence as Wang worked the problem. He'd learned long ago how to read a room. Good leaders knew when to ask questions, when to give orders, and when to shut the hell up and let people work. This seemed to be one such time.

"Damn it," Wang said, his frustration mounting. "I can't access anything in the target zone—Wi-Fi networks, police scanners, pedestrian mobile phones—anything that transmits or receives over the air is down. It's like a ten-block radius suddenly got shoved under a lead bucket or some shit. We have a Predator overhead," he said, referring to the drone providing their video stream, "but I get nothing but snowy static back from the feed. What the fuck?"

Casey looked over at Baldwin, eyebrows raised.

The Signals genius pursed his lips. "Hmmm, curious. Not like anything we've seen." Baldwin held his fingers to the earpiece in his left ear. "Richard, stream your feed directly to me."

"You're seeing what I'm seeing—or not seeing, I guess."

"Yes, yes, I know. That's not what I'm saying. Share your direct feed with me for analysis." Baldwin shrugged and raised his eyebrows. "Chip and I will figure it out."

Casey rubbed his temples. What was he overlooking? "Where was SAD when we lost contact?"

"Their last position was turning onto Buhaivska Street," Wang answered. "They're less than five minutes from the target."

"Assuming no obstacles and normal low-suspicion speeds inbound, they will be on target in . . . three minutes and fifty-five seconds," Baldwin said.

"Yeah, okay, so four minutes," Wang grumbled.

"And now they're blind and deaf," Casey said. As he had learned to do long ago, he swallowed down his anxiety, and instead of cursing, he said simply, "Very well." In his mind, he started playing out different scenarios for how the SAD team might adapt to this new wrinkle. "Will they continue on mission, or will they pause to sort out the problem?"

"Pause?" Wang laughed out loud. "Uh, no . . . that word does not exist in John Dempsey's vocabulary."

"Yeah," Chip replied. "There's no stopping them now."

"I concur," Baldwin said with less bemusement. "They will use their last, best intelligence and continue to pursue their mission objectives. They will expect us to deconflict the comms problem, while they adapt and overcome. In the two plus years I've known him, I've yet to encounter a scenario in which John believes he cannot execute his mission. Case in point, when Ms. Allen was being held hostage in Syria, we lost comms with John and he single-handedly—"

"I get the point," Casey said, cutting Baldwin off. "So, knowing that, what assets do they have available for ISR that do not require our network to operate?"

"They took the PIXIE case with them," Wang said, his voice still strangely distorted, like something from an old sci-fi film.

Casey looked to Baldwin. "What is the PIXIE case?"

"Microdrones, but it would be difficult to use them in broad daylight. They operate as a swarm and would be rather conspicuous, but they would be able to operate in a disruptive EM environment."

"How's that?" Casey asked. "They don't transmit?"

"Bluetooth is their primary channel, but they use artificial intelligence to navigate and are capable of communicating entirely over line of sight via IR flashers. They were conceived for situations like this."

"Interesting," Casey said. "I'm not familiar with the PIXIE program."

"Well, you wouldn't be." Baldwin chuckled. "It's something we developed internally, with a little help from DARPA."

Why does that not surprise me? Casey thought, and looked to Chip, who clearly had something he wanted to say.

"I bet they'll just go old school," Chip said, his voice as much a question as a statement. "They'll loop around the block a few times, set Grimes up in a window where they can see her, that sort of thing."

"Okay, but that doesn't help us. What do we know from earlier ISR on the target area? I don't want them walking into another trap like they did in that rail yard in Mariupol. We don't have F-35s at our disposal this time to bail them out."

"The Predator saw plenty of thermals, but this warehouse is located in a heavily populated area. I had signatures everywhere, but nothing that overtly appeared to be spotters, snipers, or a QRF . . . Still, Zeta is like us; they know how to hide in plain sight."

"Okay," Casey said, rubbing his chin.

"We could send in the Marines?" Chip asked hopefully.

"No," Casey said. "We need to keep this black." He looked at Chip and Baldwin, then over at Allen, who had just entered, concern on her face at the pulse she had taken of the room. "Dempsey and his team are professionals—the best in the business, I keep being told. They'll improvise. So, let's work the problem, people, and figure out how to get our eyes and ears back."

CHAPTER 45

Ember Up-Armored SUV
Odessa, Ukraine
1651 Local Time

"Dude, why are you driving so slow?" Dempsey said, glancing at the speedometer from the passenger seat. For some reason he'd agreed to let Munn drive, a decision he was now beginning to regret. "My friggin' grandmother drives faster than you."

"First of all, I've met your grandmother, and the only thing that woman does faster than me is down expensive scotch, which is not something to brag about," Munn fired back. "And second, I'm driving slow on purpose—to give Wang time to get his shit together."

Wang, who normally would have come back with a defensive zinger, did not reply—because comms with the Boeing had gone down the moment they closed within ten blocks of the target, a development Dempsey knew to be telling in its own right.

"Do you think they know we're coming and are jamming our comms?" Grimes said from the back seat, her voice uncharacteristically uneasy.

Dempsey considered her question for a moment, then said, "Probably."

He knew the near miss in Mariupol had spooked her. Getting *almost* bombed tended to have that effect on people. From the day he'd joined Ember, their secret sauce had always been tactical and technical superiority. When the enemy was a bunch of Afghani goatherds with AK-47s, their tactical advantage remained comfortably large. Even false flag operations run by Iran's VEVAK had been no match for Ember's superiority. But when the enemy was Russian covert operatives, their advantage became practically nonexistent.

The key to victory is to seek parity with your enemy—said no one ever.

"What are you smiling about?" Munn said with a sideways glance.

"Nothing," Dempsey said, "just thinking about how nice it's gonna be to order a big fat Kansas City strip at Bern's when we get back home, and have Mike Casey pay for it."

"Dude, I told you not to do that shit to me," Munn said, shaking his head. "Now you're gonna have me thinking about steaks the entire op, and my aim is going to suck."

"Your aim always sucks, let's be honest."

"For once, can you guys knock it off and get serious?" Grimes said.

"No reason to get bent outta shape—"

"Jus . . . just stop," she stammered, cutting Dempsey off. "For once, could you please just stop?"

"All right, Freckles, we'll shut up."

"I told you, I don't like that nickname," she said, using her exasperated voice. "I'd rather you go back to Long-Gun Lizzie."

"Okay. Sorry," Dempsey said, and everything got quiet. Martin, who was riding in the back next to Grimes, hadn't said a word since leaving the airport. Dempsey twisted around in his seat and looked at the Marine. "You good, Luka?"

"Oorah, brother," Martin said, but his face was all business.

Dempsey twisted around a little more to make eye contact with Grimes, who shot him her *I'm epically annoyed with you* eyes. In response, he flashed her his best *love ya, kid* big brother smile and held it until she shook her head and looked away.

"Do we pause?" Munn asked.

Dempsey laughed out loud.

"No," he said. "With every ounce of strength we'll accomplish our mission," he added, paraphrasing a line from the SEAL creed.

"Agreed. But if we don't get comms back, what do you want to do?" Munn said.

Dempsey pulled out the tin of Kodiak he'd snagged from Chunk and packed a wad into his bottom lip. "Every time we operate with Chunk, he gets me back on this shit."

"Don't change the subject, bro. You didn't answer my question."

Dempsey gutted the first swallow of tobacco juice. He pulled a tablet PC from his vest pocket and pulled up the imagery of the warehouse where the Astrolog missile transport vehicle was being stored. "They certainly can't launch the missiles from inside. At a minimum, they're gonna have to drive that Astrolog out into the street . . . so, I suppose we could conduct a little ISR and see what we see."

"Do a perimeter drive-by?" Munn said.

"Yeah," he said, hollow and unconvincing.

"Great idea," Grimes said, her voice oozing with sarcasm. "That way if there are pre-positioned Zeta snipers, they can cut us to ribbons right away."

"It's a risk, yes," Munn countered, "but the problem is, we're running out of time. Casey thinks the launch is imminent, so we don't have the luxury of surveilling this thing to death like we normally would."

"We don't even know how many Zetas we're dealing with," Grimes said. "We don't know if they're augmented with local assets or Spetsnaz shooters like we augmented with SEAL Team Four in Mariupol."

Dempsey exhaled with irritation. Why did it always have to be like this? In combat, nothing was ever simple, easy, or obvious. There was always a rub . . . always some unknown variable waiting to bite you in the ass.

"The last thermal pass from before kickoff showed only three people in the warehouse," he said.

"And thermals everywhere else around, any of which could be operators, snipers, a QRF like the one hidden in the cold storage facility—anything," Grimes said. "I think the fact that our comms are down is a strong indicator we are working against an experienced Russian team that has prepared for our intervention. We should expect friction at every point."

"Grimes is right," Martin said, finally speaking up. "Going in blind and deaf would be a big mistake. Even if it's just for ISR."

"All right," Dempsey said, turning around in his seat once again to look at Martin and Grimes. "We'll park two blocks out, get the PIXIEs in the air, and take a look."

"They're going to see the swarm. Hell, everybody on the street is going to see it," Grimes said.

"Then what do you suggest, Elizabeth?" he said, getting short for real now. "This is the mission. We're out of options and out of time. It's either we drive a loop or use the PIXIEs. Those are our two choices."

When she didn't respond, he turned to Munn. "Pull over along the curb."

Munn nodded and eased the SUV into a gap along the curb. Instead of shifting the gear lever into Park, he left the transmission in Drive, engine at idle, and held the brake depressed with his left foot in preparation for a quick getaway. Without Dempsey having to give the order, Martin climbed through the gap between the middle row captain's chairs into the SUV's rear cargo area, where he opened the lid of a large plastic hard case containing forty-eight fist-sized drones. Working quickly, he lifted out the first tray of a dozen drones and set it down inside the lid. Beneath the first tray, a second identical tray was stacked atop two more.

Dempsey opened the PIXIE app on the tablet and initialized the startup sequence, just as Wang had taught him. The software, which relied on no small amount of AI, did the rest. The first flight of triangular-shaped micro-UAVs buzzed to life in their cradles, then lifted off in a tightly spaced, unified hover.

"You can open the cargo hatch," Martin said over the thrum of thirty-six miniature-ducted rotors.

Munn pressed a button on the console, and the powered tailgate drifted open. With a swipe of his thumb, Dempsey guided the first flight of drones out the back of the SUV and into the air. Martin and Dempsey repeated the process with the next three flights until the swarm was fully deployed.

"Dude, what are they doing?" Munn said, craning his neck to look out the driver's side window at the drones. "They're bumping into each other."

"Here," Dempsey said, making no attempt to hide his aggravation as he passed the tablet to Martin. "Wang promised me these things used AI and I wouldn't have to troubleshoot them, but he was apparently full of shit."

Martin accepted the tablet and got to work, opening the application settings menu.

"You do realize you just gave a *Marine* an expensive and complicated piece of computer technology," Munn said, looking at Dempsey. "Words and numbers are like kryptonite for grunts. Hell, there are no crayons involved at all . . ."

Martin paused his tapping, flashed Munn a middle finger salute, and said, "I think the problem with our comms must be local because it's affecting the drones too . . . They must be jamming across the spectrum."

"Shit," Dempsey grumbled. "I was hoping it was just over-the-horizon comms that were down. This changes everything. We're dead in the water until Wang finds the source and shuts it down."

"Not necessarily," Martin said, looking up with a shit-eating grin on his face. "Apparently, the *Marine* was the only guy paying attention during the PIXIE training session, because these little guys have a backup comms option."

"Oh yeah," Dempsey said, nodding. "I do remember Wang saying something about a zero-ES stealth mode—whatever the hell that is—and then he started blabbing, blabbing, blabbing and I tuned him out."

"Look out the windshield now," Martin said, climbing back into his middle-row seat.

Dempsey leaned forward and looked up. Where moments ago he'd seen a chaotic blur of ghost-grey shadows tumbling over each other, he now saw a stable swarm. "What did you do?"

"Changed them over to IR comms. If we were on NVGs, it would look like a swarm of fireflies on crack, with each drone flashing its neighbors multiple times a second."

"Like a remote control and a TV?" Munn said.

"Yeah," Martin said. "Same principle as our helmet strobes. IR signaling, only visible in night vision or by an IR receiver. Except instead of strobing, the drones are communicating by signaling each other with infrared light pulses."

"Nice work, Luka," Dempsey said and extended his hand to get the tablet back. Then, with a crooked grin, he added, "When we get back to Tampa, I'll put in a transfer request with Casey for you from SAD to Signals."

"A guy tries to take initiative, and look what happens," Martin said, shaking his head. He deployed the remaining drone flights and then, grinning, handed the tablet to Dempsey.

On-screen, Dempsey now saw a split image, with the right side displaying a fuzzy cloud on a map of the city, and the left side, an unusual panoramic camera view. Wang had explained that every drone had multiple cameras and that when working together, the swarm functioned like a dragonfly's compound eye, with the AI software knitting together all the camera feeds into a 360-degree viewing experience.

"That's fucking weird," Munn said, looking down at the revolving and ever-changing video feed on the screen.

Dempsey directed the swarm around the corner and down the block by dragging his finger over the map, tracing the path he wanted the drones to take. Unlike with a regular drone, the PIXIEs did not require a pilot. He wasn't even steering them, just communicating the target location. The swarm AI did all the navigating and the flying.

"If you tap that eyeball icon on the upper left, the imagery will change from video to thermal," Martin said, leaning forward in his seat.

Dempsey pressed the icon and the streaming video changed to the high-contrast heat-color scheme utilized in thermal imagery. He remembered from the training that he could manipulate the video "bubble" with standard touchscreen gestures—pinching, swiping, rotating, et cetera. It took him a moment to get the feel for it, but the AI was so intuitive that he quickly mastered the interface and conducted a systematic survey of the approach and the buildings across the street from the target warehouse, while his teammates looked on.

"Whoa, that's pretty fucking cool," Grimes said, leaning forward and looking over his shoulder.

"Don't tell Wang I said it, but he's really outdone himself this time," Dempsey said, and placed the tablet on the center console armrest so everyone could see. "All right—coming up on the warehouse now . . . Hard to tell with all the structural interference, but I think that is the missile transport vehicle . . . The engine's cold, but it looks like someone is working on something on the driver's side."

"He could be programming the missiles for launch," Munn said.

"Maybe . . . probably," Dempsey said as he steered the floating lens around the screen. "There's another heat signature . . . probably a sentry . . . yeah, I think we can consider this target confirmation."

"Can I drive for a sec?" Grimes asked.

"Go for it," Dempsey said and lifted his hand off the tablet.

Grimes repositioned the video bubble and began systematically scanning the upper-level apartments across the street for potential shooters. "Third floor, across the street—one, two, three, four windows in from the north corner—could be a problem, possible shooter and spotter duo . . . I'm gonna try and see if I can see anything through the window without them seeing us. Switching off thermal . . . This guy pacing is definitely a shooter . . . and then this guy, on the fifth floor of the building kitty-corner, in the middle apartment, could be a problem . . . or he could just be watching porn by the window. We won't know for sure until he gets prone."

"Scroll back down to street level," Munn said once she'd finished her scan. "Yeah, good, now slide up the street . . . okay, stop, zoom in on that homeless guy sleeping against the side of the building. Could be coincidence, but his location has sight lines to the warehouse and both the possible snipers. I think he's their eyes. I'm no signals expert, but I imagine they're jamming across the spectrum, and this guy is their watchdog."

"Agreed," Dempsey said. "Let's loop the PIXIEs around the block. Check the back of the warehouse, get a complete tactical picture, and then we can plan the assault."

"What the fuck is that?" Munn said, pointing to a large object positioned tightly against the rear wall of the warehouse as it came into view.

"Looks like a construction dumpster," Martin said. "And it's blocking the door."

"Fuck," Dempsey growled. "There goes that idea."

"Were you thinking a rear breach?" Grimes said.

He nodded while zooming in on the bottom of the metal container to see whether it had rollers or skids.

And it has skids . . . of course it does.

"Think we could move it?" Munn asked.

"No fucking way," Dempsey said, his expression going to a scowl. "But even if we could, it would take too long and make too much noise . . . Shit, we're going to have to go in through the front."

"I don't like the numbers," Munn said, scratching at the five-day scruff on his neck. "I'd feel a helluva a lot better if we'd kept Chunk around and we had another stick."

"I know, but you go to war with the army you have, not the army you want. Right now, this is our army," he said, gesturing in a circle, "and we're just gonna have to find a way to get it done."

"If we don't get comms back?" Grimes said. "Then what?"

Dempsey blew air through his teeth. "Then I guess we better get our psychic connection dialed in, because we're blackholing these assholes, one way or another."

CHAPTER 46

Vice President's Ceremonial Office Complex
Eisenhower Executive Office Building
Next to the West Wing on the White House Premises
Washington, DC

Jarvis paced back and forth alone in the small SCIF that most Vice Presidents rarely, if ever, used. But that changed the moment Warner strong-armed him into assuming the role while retaining sole oversight authority of Ember. He had elected *not* to read the new DNI, Reggie Buckingham, in on the Ember program. With war in Ukraine all but inevitable, and the rest of the IC to manage, Reggie had enough on his plate without the live wire that was America's most secret and deadly task force.

For now, at least.

The hard truth was, Jarvis didn't want to give up control of Ember—not now, not ever. It wasn't hubris, but he doubted anyone, other than perhaps Petra, could deploy the team as they were meant to be deployed. Okay, maybe it was hubris . . . but he didn't care. Ember was his creation. His baby. Perhaps, after this brief stint in politics, he would relieve Casey and step back into the role as Ember Director. He smiled at the thought of a return to simpler days, but then quickly pushed the idea from his mind. It wasn't something he'd likely have control of. His professional fate would be determined like it always had: He would serve where he was needed and at the pleasure of the next Commander in Chief.

He stared in frustration at the snowy static on all three workstation monitors—and then at the static satellite image of Odessa International Airport on the screen on the wall. He resisted the urge to lean over and key the mike on the boom extending from the desktop stand and demand to know what in the hell was going on. He resisted because he had no reservations about the man he had put in charge of Ember. Casey had a brilliant strategic mind, and that was precisely what Ember needed right now.

He let out a long sigh and took a swig of water from his stainless steel tumbler. Then he began to pace.

Whatever the hell is going on, Dempsey will find a way around it, he told himself. *That's why I recruited him. That's why he's the best in the world at what he does.*

A knock on the door made him turn to look over his shoulder. *Who in the holy hell . . .*

A beep sounded and the magnetic lock released. Petra walked in, and her expression immediately concerned him.

"Everything okay?" It was a rhetorical greeting—if everything were okay, she wouldn't be standing in the doorway to the SCIF.

"I know the timing is terrible, Kelso," she said. "But something has come up."

He glanced back at the screens. "Now?"

"Yes, sir, Mr. Vice President," she said, the formal title not a reaction to his expression of doubt, he knew, but meant to convey the gravity of this new development.

He waved her in. "What's going on?"

She let the door click shut behind her, sealing them in the soundproof room.

"A woman showed up at EEOB," she began, "asking for a private audience with you."

Jarvis rolled his eyes. "Another nut job?"

"Well, that's what the staff thought, but her credentials checked out, so they contacted me to see how to best handle it."

"Who is she?"

"Her name's Samantha Bryant. She's a midlevel staffer for Congressman Bacon."

Jarvis shook his head. "Never met Bacon, never heard of her."

"Me neither, but something she said made the hair on my neck stand up. You need to talk to her."

Petra wore the same eldritch look on her face now as the night she'd killed Catherine Morgan.

"Tell me," he said, meeting her gaze.

"She says she has a message for you from Arkady Zhukov that she'll only deliver in person."

A shiver snaked down Jarvis's spine, the words having the same effect they'd had on Petra. "Has she been questioned by anyone?"

"No. I shut that down," Petra said. "She's in cuffs, just in case. Been through the body scanner and two pat downs."

"So, she's not here to kill me?" Jarvis said with a smirk.

Petra smiled. "She'd have to get past me first."

He glanced anxiously at the monitors behind him, which were still streaming static. "Okay, I'll give her three minutes."

Petra nodded, keyed the door open, and disappeared. When

she returned, she had an attractive young woman, perhaps mid- to late twenties, in plasti-cuffs with her.

"Have a seat," Jarvis said, gesturing to the small round table in the center of the room. "I understand you have a message for me?"

"Yes," the woman said, sitting down, her hands in her lap and her knees pulled together. "I was approached a few hours ago by a man—"

"We'll have time for backstory later, young lady," he said, cutting her off. "Right now, all I have time for is the message from . . ." He snapped his fingers, as if trying to remember an unfamiliar word he'd just learned, and looked over at Petra. "What was the name you said?"

"Zhukov, Mr. Vice President," Petra said, playing her role perfectly.

"Arkady Zhukov," the woman echoed, her voice a tight string.

"Right, Zhukov," Jarvis said, then, keeping his expression perfectly neutral, added, "I don't know this man. Who is he?"

The question flustered her for a heartbeat, just long enough for him to see a wave of uncertainty flitter across her face.

Gotcha . . .

"I . . . I don't know who he is," she stammered. "But the man who gave me the message told me to tell you: 'Black and white are in mutual zugzwang. But there is a way out.'"

Jarvis stared at her, waiting for more. When she didn't continue, he said, "That's it? That's the message?"

"Yes," the woman said.

He looked at Petra, his eyes asking the question: *What the hell is a zugzwang?*

Petra pulled out her mobile phone, queried the dictionary, and showed him the screen:

Zugzwang: From the German meaning "compulsion to move." A situa-

tion in chess where a player is compelled to move to his own disadvantage. A common development in the endgame, especially in matches where only kings and pawns remain.

Jarvis laughed—unable to help himself—as both women stared at him.

"Mutual zugzwang indeed," he murmured. "Well, if there's nothing more, Miss Bryant, I think some of my colleagues probably have questions for you."

"Wait," she said, her cheeks blanching. "There's one more thing. He made me memorize it."

"Go on," he said and listened as she rattled off an eleven-digit number beginning with seven. He looked at Petra. "That's a Russian phone number."

She nodded as her pencil finished scribing the last number. She then repeated the number back to the woman, confirming each digit.

"Who else did you tell this to?" Jarvis asked.

"No one," she said, a soft sob now in her voice. "I was told to tell only you. He said they would be watching me and that I would be killed if—"

"Okay, okay," Jarvis said. "Who do you have out there with her?" he asked Petra.

"Two members of your Secret Service detail."

His mind was racing at Mach 2, the options—and their consequences—flashing through his head like mathematical algorithms on a Cray supercomputer. "Have them turn her over to ODNI. She's Reggie's problem now. He can interrogate her, then make a trade with Moscow. Maybe we can get Ben Farris back for her."

Jarvis returned his attention to the workstations. For a hopeful second, the screens began to flicker, but then the snowy static returned.

"Moscow?" the woman said, her voice panicked. "What? Why . . . ? I told you, a man approached me—"

"So you said. I hope you enjoyed your time in the United States, Miss Bryant, because you won't be returning." He glanced at Petra. "Get her out of here."

Once Petra had turned over the Zeta spy to the Secret Service agents and they were alone again with the door shut, she said, "So, you think that was real?"

"'Black and white are in mutual zugzwang,'" he said, shaking his head at the beauty of the message. "Oh yes, it's him."

"How can you be so sure?"

He thrust a finger at the screen. "Kings and pawns . . . he's talking about Ukraine, Petra. Warner and Petrov are playing the world's most dangerous chess match. We're nearing the endgame, and both sides are compelled to move to their mutual disadvantage."

"But there is a way out," she said. "That was the second part of the message."

"Yes, and I think he's talking about Ember and Zeta and what's happening in Odessa right now."

She nodded. "Are you going to call him?"

He turned to face her. In times of crisis, she was so beautiful . . .

"Do I really have a choice?" he said.

"No," she said and turned the scrap of paper with Zhukov's phone number so he could read it. "You don't."

He took a deep breath, picked up the encrypted, untraceable desk phone, and dialed.

CHAPTER 47

Ember Up-Armored SUV
Odessa, Ukraine

"Absolutely not," Dempsey said, shaking his head at Grimes. "I'm not sending you alone into that apartment building without comms. Martin is going with you, period, end of story."

Munn eased the SUV to a stop, double-parking beside a row of cars at the rear of the apartment building across the street from the target warehouse.

Grimes felt her stomach go heavy, like she'd just chugged a cup of liquid lead. "But a two-man frontal assault on that warehouse is crazy. Especially, if Tango Two turns out to be a shooter," she said, referring to the heat signature they'd labeled the secondary, possible sniper. "I won't have a line on him."

"I know," he said, "but I have a plan to make it impossible for him to do his job."

"What's that?"

"I'm going to hover the drone swarm in front of his window. He's not going to be able to see shit."

She bobbed her head side to side, imagining herself trying to shoot through an undulating cloud of four-dozen drones blocking her sight line. "Mmm, that might actually work."

"We only need fifteen seconds," Dempsey said, his hands moving over his kit, checking his loadout as he talked. "Just long enough to round the corner, advance one block, and breach."

"Okay, I can live with that," she said and turned to Martin. "Looks like it's you and me."

The young Marine nodded. "Ready when you are."

Munn put the transmission in Park, turned on the vehicle's hazard flashers, and handed Martin the vehicle's key fob. "Take this. I have a feeling you'll be our exfil."

Martin accepted the fob and stowed it in a Velcro flap pocket on his kit.

"Radios stay on TAC-1, just in case Wang comes through," Dempsey said.

Grimes checked her radio and gave him a thumbs-up. "Good to go."

"Good luck," Dempsey said, then shot Martin a look that she took to mean, *Look after our girl.*

The compulsion to state the obvious—that she wasn't the one who needed looking after—was overpowering, but she held her tongue. "How will you know when I'm set?" she said, reaching for the door latch.

"A little bird, or four dozen, will let me know," he said, tapping the tablet computer with his index finger. "We'll hold until then."

She nodded, pulled the door latch, and jumped out of the vehicle. She hated operating in daylight. Without the night, she felt incredibly vulnerable . . . almost naked. She shoved the thought from her mind, despite being acutely aware of multiple pairs of civilian eyes on her and Martin as they charged into the apartment building, kitted up in full battle rattle. She reached the entrance door first and tried the handle.

Locked.

Martin drove a booted foot into the slab beside the handle. She heard a loud crack, but the door held. He took a step back, then plowed into the door with his shoulder, and this time it gave way. A middle-aged Ukrainian woman checking her mailbox in the little foyer screamed as Grimes quickstepped into the space, sighting over her Rattler. She instantly assessed the woman as a nonthreat and cleared left. Martin drifted in behind, cleared right, then moved toward the stairs. He cleared up the first flight, then swiveled to watch their six as she advanced. Upon reaching the first landing, she dropped into a tactical crouch and cleared the switchback flight.

"Clear," she said, and Martin swept around her while she shifted her aim back down the stairs, her turn to watch their six.

They worked in tandem, methodically and expertly ascending the switchback flights to the third-floor. Unlike a typical fire escape stairwell, this staircase was the primary conveyance for the building's residents. It had wide treads, an open architecture, and lacked doors at each level, which meant that the building probably did not have an elevator. Using hand signals, Martin indicated he would clear right. She nodded and silently counted them down.

Three, two, one . . .

The Marine pivoted around the wall into the hallway, clearing right. She followed him, clearing left.

"Clear," he said.

"Clear," she echoed, swiveling right and chopping a hand toward the target apartment. Like all good operators, she'd created her own mental map of the building, assigning cardinal directions and predicting the number of apartments on this floor based on the number of exterior windows. "This one," she said, her voice a harsh whisper as they approached the target unit.

Martin nodded and drifted past the door, falling in beside the doorframe.

She pulled up short, taking a knee on the other side.

It had been months since she'd breached a room. After taking on the role as overwatch, all the breaching had fallen entirely to the guys. Despite the liquid lightning coursing through her veins, she felt a flutter of butterflies in her stomach. Charging blindly into a room, knowing you faced coin-flip odds of getting cut down by ready fire, was unnerving no matter who you were.

Unless, of course, your name is John Dempsey . . .

She exhaled and looked at Martin. He nodded once and stepped off the wall and into position. Grabbing a flash-bang off her kit, she said, "Three . . . two . . . one . . ."

On "go," she pulled the pin and Martin snapped a front kick, splintering the doorjamb. With perfect synchronicity, she tossed the grenade through the expanding gap as the door arced inward. During the millisecond delay between the release and her squeezing her eyes shut, she registered two male figures in the room—one holding a spotter scope and the other lying prone. The grenade detonated a heartbeat later, with a blinding flash and a thunderclap that rattled her teeth. Training and muscle memory took over and the next thing she knew she was in the room advancing, with Martin on her right, sighting over her weapon.

Trigger squeeze.

Trigger squeeze.

She put two rounds into the Russian sniper and Martin dropped the spotter as the man went for a gun. She walked up to confirm the kill and saw that one of her rounds had hit her target dead center mass between the shoulder blades and the other had punched a hole in the sniper's skull—entering at the base of the neck and exiting through his face. Blood and chunks splattered the carpet, wall, and windowsill. She stepped up to the window and waved once at the drone swarm hovering fifteen feet away at her elevation, then she looked at Martin.

"Help me move this," she said, nudging the dead sniper's body with the toe of her boot. "I want to set up here."

"I got him," Martin said, dragging the corpse clear by the ankles, leaving a smear of crimson in his wake.

"Thanks."

"I'm going to go see about blocking the door."

"Check."

While Martin used a chair to wedge the apartment door shut, she got to work—unslinging her Sig 716G2 and setting the tripod in the exact spot the Russian sniper had selected. For a moment, she considered looking for a towel or sheet to throw over the gore, but the truth was she just didn't fucking care anymore and simply stretched out prone atop the bloody mess. She pressed her cheek against her weapon and sighted through the TANGO6 scope at the street and warehouse below. She heard Martin return a moment later and take station beside her.

Without taking her eye off the optics, she said, "What are you doing?"

"I'm your spotter," he said, in that black-or-white, matter-of-fact manner only Marines could pull off.

"Like hell you are," she said. "You need to get down there and provide covering fire."

"I'm not leaving you alone," he said. "JD was crystal clear on that point."

"Trust me, they need your help more than I do," she said, glancing up at him.

"Look," he said, pointing out the window. "Somebody just walked out of the target building."

With heat in her cheeks, she turned back to her optics. "Shit," she said, seeing the front door to the warehouse swinging closed as a male figure walked away, mobile phone pressed to his ear.

"Did you get a look at his face?"

"No, because I was arguing with you," she snapped. "Damn it."

I know better than to take my eye off the fucking scope, she thought, cursing herself for the lapse in discipline. A chill chased over her entire body as her crosshairs found the back of the target's head. She exhaled and put tension on the trigger as the man turned back, appearing to holler something toward the door.

"Holy shit, it's him," she said.

"Him who?" Martin asked.

"One—this is Zeus, do you copy?" she said into her mike, praying for a miracle as she spoke. "One, Zeus—do you copy?"

"Comms are still down," Martin said, answering the question she didn't ask.

Her mouth went dry. Her pulse thrummed in her ears. The compulsion to take the shot was overpowering. *Fuck authorization*, said the voice in her head. *I'm going to take the shot . . .*

But her index finger refused to move and the man she was ninety-nine percent certain was Arkady Zhukov disappeared around the corner.

Outside, she heard a muffled crack followed by a woman's scream. Dempsey had engaged . . .

"It's on," she said and swung her barrel down and sighted on the Russian spotter dressed as a homeless person. A machine pistol lay on the ground next to the sprawled-out figure bleeding on the sidewalk. As usual, Dempsey had been right. She pulled her cheek off the scope for a full-perspective look at the street below. Two familiar crouching shapes, quickstepping in tandem, crossed the street, sighting over rifles. She pressed her cheek back against her Sig and scanned the front of the warehouse for targets. Dempsey and Munn arrived a split second later, taking breaching positions on opposite sides of the main entry door. She watched Munn quickly and deftly set a breacher charge. But before he could detonate it, the double-wide garage door that dominated the front façade of the warehouse mushroomed outward and went flying into the street. For a split second, her brain thought a bomb had gone off, but instead of flames and smoke blasting out of the hole, she watched the Astrolog missile transporter barrel out through the gap.

"Oh my God," she heard herself say as the massive vehicle careened to the left and then went roaring northwest on the narrow street, smashing and ramming cars left and right.

The rear-deck missile enclosure completely blocked the cab from her angle, not giving her any lines on the driver. So, she did the only thing she could do and took aim at the rear tires of the 8x8 heavy-haul vehicle and fired. She was pretty sure her rounds flew true, but it didn't matter.

It's like shooting a monster truck with a BB gun.

She popped to her feet and slung her Sig. "We're done here," she said to Martin, but the Marine was already a step ahead of her, clearing the apartment door.

"SUV—pick up and pursue?" he said, bringing his rifle up.

"You read my mind," she said and sprinted after him into the hall.

CHAPTER 48

Gavriil shoved the slumping, dead GRU agent off him with his forearm as the heavy truck bounced from wrecked car to wrecked car. The problem with the high-tech jammer Arkady had deployed was that now Gavriil was just as blind and deaf as the Americans. If Arkady had not hollered back at him that the Americans were coming, he would have been caught alone in the warehouse and his mission would have ended in failure.

But how many Americans are assaulting? And where are they?

His sniper team and spotter, if not already dead, would buy him precious little time. Worse, he needed to assume the Americans had positioned their own snipers, so any attempt to launch from the street—technical difficulties of an obstructed launch aside—meant he risked getting cut down by a sniper's bullet before missiles away. Taken together, all of this had driven his decision to flee.

He needed separation from this location and a height advantage and knew exactly where to get it. He crossed the first intersection—a large delivery truck on his left screeching to a halt centimeters before collision—and pressed the accelerator to the floor. The Astrolog's engine growled, and the monster 8X8 transporter shook, bounced, and rolled down the street. He heard gunfire and glanced in his side mirror. Two operators were in the street, firing at the back of the truck, but they quickly shrank from view.

When he reached the hospital, he cut the wheel hard right and vectored toward the parking garage. He glanced at the height-restriction barrier hanging down over the entrance. A second later, a horrible screech sounded as the top of the truck scraped the barrier. Hopefully there was no damage to the launchers in back, but he was not worried about the height—he had planned carefully for this contingency and he had several centimeters of clearance on the ramps leading to the roof of the parking deck—and that was before he'd removed a considerable amount of air from the enormous tires, giving him even more clearance. No, his worry was the *width* of the lanes during the circular ascent to the roof. While the cab did articulate with the bed of the MZKT-7930 truck, in the missile configuration there was precious little play during turns, and the damn truck stretched to nearly ten meters . . .

He turned the wheel left and then right. Sparks flew and metal screeched as he dragged his cab along the side of a high-top van, and then he was in the center of the two narrow lanes leading up and down the ramp. He pressed hard on the accelerator, building the momentum needed to continue the ascent and overcome the friction of repeated contact with the concrete walls. Assuming he made it to the roof, he'd need two minutes to set the stabilizers so he could raise the missiles, and a few more minutes to launch them. He *should* be out of any firing lanes from snipers the Americans might have in play, so if he hurried . . .

More sparks accompanied a horrible squeal as he navigated a

tight turn, the Astrolog's right side dragging across a cement column. Gavriil corrected, easing left, and, with gritted teeth, came out of the turn—leaving a trail of marred concrete in his wake. He laughed, the adrenaline stoking feelings of invincibility as he found the perfect balance of speed and turn radius to navigate the tricky ascent. Now on level two, he spotted a series of low-hanging pipes crossing the gaps between the cement ceiling ribs. Probably part of a fire department standpipe system, he imagined, as he slammed into the first set. He ducked reflexively as the top of the cab sheared the two parallel pipes cleanly in half; metal clattered to the deck and water exploded everywhere. Gavriil activated the windshield wipers to clear the brown water from the dirty windshield—the truck having not been cleaned after the long drive from Crimea.

As he approached the turnoff for the fourth level, he heard a horn blaring. Through the spray of water from the third pipe he had just sheared off, he watched a grey Renault two-door slam on its brakes. With nowhere else to go, Gavriil pressed harder on the accelerator, slamming the front of the Renault with his wide, square cab. The Renault's hood compressed like an accordion. Inside, a wide-eyed man wearing blue scrubs and a white lab coat gripped the steering wheel in horror. Using the Astrolog's front bumper, Gavriil pushed the Renault backward up the ramp. A constant and whining screech of metal over concrete sang in discordant harmony with the squeal of rubber flaying off the sedan's tires, and Gavriil clenched his jaw in aggravation as he felt his time advantage slipping away. He had only minutes until the Americans descended on him—or simply obliterated him and the truck with a Hellfire missile from above.

Feelings of panic and inadequacy flooded his mind.

"Nyet!" he shouted. "I will not fail."

The truck lurched as it shot up the final ramp, the cab grinding across the ceiling before emerging on the roof deck. The Renault spun off to the left. Gavriil brought the truck to a stop, leaned out through the open window, and looked at the wrecked sedan beside him. The doctor emerged not from the driver's side—that side of the vehicle was more badly damaged—but from the passenger side. He stumbled and weaved in shock as he backed away from his car, the front wheels now turned impossibly out and backward. The doctor looked up at him, dazed and frightened, just as Gavriil raised his pistol and fired a single round that went through the man's forehead, just above his left eye. He collapsed dead on the roof beside the destroyed sedan.

Gavriil stepped on the accelerator, and the Astrolog rumbled across the nearly empty roof deck. He maneuvered the truck beside the wall of the hospital—perhaps the Americans would be reluctant to drop ordnance on him if they risked killing civilians. Such concerns seemed to be his enemy's Achilles' heel. Then he engaged the air brake and pulled the lever that deployed the massive outboard stabilizers to convert the truck into a launch pad.

"You can do this. You can do this," he murmured as he climbed out of the cab.

Just a few more minutes and it wouldn't matter what the Americans did . . .

CHAPTER 49

Dempsey stopped shooting at the Russian missile transporter as it disappeared down the street.

"You gotta be kidding me," he muttered and turned to look at Munn. The doc, who had taken a knee beside him, was sighting into the gaping maw where the warehouse's garage door had been just seconds ago.

"Should we clear it?" Munn said.

Dempsey was so pissed off, he wanted to scream, but he checked his anger and got his head back in the game. Thank God Munn had kept his wits, because they hadn't actually breached the warehouse and the Russians could have left shooters behind to ambush them. On the other hand, those sneaky bastards had probably rigged the building to blow instead.

"We ain't going in there," he said, backpedaling and waving Munn to do the same. "Catching that truck before it launches is the only priority."

"Agreed, but I don't want to get shot in the back, either. What if they left shooters behind?"

A high-pitched burst of static pulsed in Dempsey's ear.

"I'm back, bitches!" exclaimed a triumphant Wang over the comms circuit.

"It's about damn time," Dempsey growled. "Please tell me you have eyes?"

"Does Superman have X-ray vision?" Wang quipped. "I've got a Predator in orbit and took control of the PIXIE swarm."

"Are there any warm bodies left in this warehouse?"

"Negative," Wang said. "It's a black hole."

"Zeus, are you up?" Dempsey said, glancing at Munn and chopping a hand in the direction of the fleeing Astrolog. Munn nodded and they both took off running down the street.

"Zeus is secured. Three and Four are coming to you," Grimes said.

"We need wheels, ASAP," Dempsey said, his arms pumping and boots pounding the pavement as he pushed himself to his maximum speed.

As if in reply, he heard the squeal of rubber in the near distance behind him.

"We got you," said Martin. "Coming up on your left."

Dempsey and Munn veered to the right side of the lane as the SUV came screaming up from behind. The vehicle passed them, braked to a hard stop ten meters ahead, and had the rear liftgate rising. Dempsey reached the vehicle first and dove into the rear cargo compartment, followed by Munn a second later.

"Go," he shouted, and Martin hit the gas so hard, the acceleration nearly sent both of them tumbling out onto the street.

"Talk to me, Wang," Dempsey said. "Where's that launch vehicle going?"

"Guys, you aren't going to believe this," Wang said, "but that missile truck went into the hospital parking garage."

"That doesn't make any sense," Munn said, screwing up his face.

"If he can get to the roof deck, it does," Dempsey said. "He'll have an unobstructed launch vector, and he knows we won't take him out with a Hellfire because it's a hospital. The risk of collateral is too high."

Munn nodded. "Then we've got to get to him before he can get set."

"No shit," Dempsey said.

Martin, already driving at a lunatic pace, stomped on the accelerator. Dempsey clutched the headrest of the middle seat in front of him so he wouldn't fall out as the SUV rolled and bounced violently.

"Guys, I think I saw Arkady Zhukov exit the warehouse," Grimes said, turning to look at them, her calm and serious tone out of place given the tornado of chaos they were dealing with.

"What?" Dempsey said, his eyes going wide. "When?"

"Seconds before you guys got set for the assault. I couldn't see his face, but I know it was him."

"Wang . . ."

"On it," came the clipped reply.

"I have confirming evidence," Baldwin said, joining the party line for the first time. "We just registered a transmission from Zhukov's mobile phone in the vicinity."

"Where in the vicinity?" Dempsey barked.

"Triangulating . . ." came Baldwin's cool reply. "We have him in a vehicle, presumably heading for the airport."

This new wrinkle infuriated Dempsey. If they'd had comms during the op, this never would have happened. He would have been able to prosecute Arkady *and* stop the missile transport by . . .

By what? the voice asked in his head. *Splitting the team?*

He'd already done that.

Why did I release Chunk? Stupid, stupid, stupid . . .

"Guys," Wang said with fresh tension in his voice. "The Russian driver is on the roof and extending the stabilizer skids in preparation to launch."

"Are the missiles raised?" Dempsey asked.

"Not yet," Wang said.

"How many levels is the garage?"

"Looks like five."

"We're never going to get to the top in time," he said, looking at Munn.

"We could use ascenders," Munn said.

"How do we get the lines up there?"

"We could use these grappling launchers," Munn said, tapping one of the hard cases between them.

"I'm almost at the garage, guys," Martin said. "Fifteen seconds."

"We don't even know if those fucking things work," Dempsey said, shaking his head.

"They work, gentlemen," came Baldwin's reply.

"Have *you* tried them?" Dempsey said.

"Well, no, but I would not have procured them had the demonstration by the contractor not been convincing," Baldwin said. "I was quite excited for you to try them."

"Split the team," said a new voice on the line, one that took Dempsey a second to register as belonging to Director Casey. "Three and Four, pursue Arkady. One and Two, use ascenders and stop the missile launch."

A surge of hot anger exploded in Dempsey at the intervention, despite the fact that this very order had been poised on the tip of his tongue. Was he angry about the decision, or the fact that Casey had beaten him to it?

"Check," said Munn, acknowledging the order for all of them, while flinging the hard case out onto the sidewalk in front of the parking garage.

The SUV skidded to a stop, with Martin braking and cutting the wheel into a slide. Grimes swung around in her seat and made eye contact with Dempsey, her expression asking the question: *Are you sure?*

"Just make sure you end that sonuvabitch," he said through gritted teeth and jumped out the back of the Suburban.

The second his boots hit pavement, Munn tossed him an ascender, which he clipped to his kit. Then the SEAL surgeon picked up the shotgun-shaped grappling launcher and pointed the business end toward the top of the garage.

"Here goes nothing," Munn said and squeezed the trigger. The launcher made a *whump* sound and fired a projectile with a Kevlar-woven, cut-resistant Novabraid cord seventy-five feet in the air. At apogee, spring-loaded tines popped out of the projectile. Then it arced down and disappeared from view behind the concrete wall on the upper deck of the parking tower.

"He's raising the missiles," Wang said. "Hurry."

Munn ejected the spool-fed line magazine and tossed it to Dempsey. "Haul in the slack and go, dude," he said.

Line in hand, Dempsey jogged to the base of the building and quickly worked the line, pulling in the slack until he felt the four-pronged hook catch. He pulled it tight, then checked the hold with his body weight. Another *whump* reverberated behind him—Munn launching a second line up to the roof deck—while he fed the nylon rope into his ascender's serpentine drive mechanism. Then he clipped the safety traveler to the line below the ascender and squeezed the ascend trigger button. The pulley mechanism grabbed, took up tension, and jerked Dempsey a foot into the air.

"Go," Munn said, working fast to get his line trimmed and ascender set. "I'll be right behind you."

Dempsey nodded, squeezed the trigger, and the ascender's electric motor whirred to life. The compact battery-powered device defied gravity—rapidly hoisting him up the five-story elevation. Large air gaps between concrete levels made it impossible for him to "walk up" the side, so he let himself hang and instead used his feet to keep from spinning like a dangling yo-yo.

When he was six feet from the top, he eased off the ascender trigger and slowed. Here, against the top slab of the vertical concrete wall, the soles of his boots finally found purchase. Below, Munn's ascender motor let out an electric whine and his Ember brother came zooming up to join him as he got into position just below the top of the wall.

"Talk to me, Wang," Dempsey said, thinking that a status report would be nice before he stuck his head over the wall and had his melon split by a ready shooter.

Wang started to answer, but his words were drowned out by the roar of a missile booster igniting. The roof deck trembled. Smoke chased fire into the sky, and there was nothing Dempsey could do but watch as the Russian Iskander short-range ballistic missile streaked toward Mariupol at five times the speed of sound.

CHAPTER 50

USS Donald Cook (DDG-75)
North of the 45th Parallel
The Black Sea

My crew is exhausted, my warship is running low on fuel, I'm surrounded by the Russian Black Sea fleet, and I haven't had time to take a shit in two days . . . why did I choose this job again?

These were the thoughts running through Dusty's head as he stared out the bridge windshield at the Ukrainian shoreline. Ukraine had given the *Donald Cook* permission to enter within twelve nautical miles from land. Ukraine had *not* given that same permission to the Russian Navy, but it didn't matter. They were all here together, one big floating happy family covering each other with missiles, guns, and torpedoes . . .

One must never forget about the torpedoes.

"Captain, are you okay?" said a voice beside him, shaking him out of his fugue.

He turned to his Battle Stations Officer of the Deck, Lieutenant Levy. "Say again?"

"Is everything okay, sir?" she said, meeting his gaze with anxious eyes.

"I don't know," he said earnestly. "I just have this feeling . . ."

When he didn't finish his thought, she said, "Yes, sir, me too."

He thought back to the conversation he'd had with the CMC after crossing the forty-fifth parallel south, during that oh-so-brief moment of respite before the powers that be decided to send his ship back into the lion's den. And as he replayed the words in his head, he knew what he needed to do.

"Lieutenant, I want you to hail the *Admiral Grigorovich* on the bridge-to-bridge. Tell them I want to talk to Captain Ruskin on a secure channel. Give them the ship's satellite phone number. Tell him to . . . no, scratch that, *request* that he call me at his earliest opportunity."

"Sir?" she said with a quizzical expression.

"No, I didn't misspeak, Lieutenant," he said with a tired smile. "You heard me right."

"Yes, sir," she said and did as ordered.

He listened as she dialogued with her male counterpart on the Russian guided-missile frigate, and when she was done, he said, "Good work, OOD. I'm going to Combat. Just keep turning racetracks at this bell."

"Aye, sir," she said.

He walked out of the bridge and straight to Combat.

"Captain in Combat," a sailor announced the second Dusty stepped inside.

He paused a moment for his eyes to adjust to the low-level light, then walked over to where the XO and TAO were talking.

"Captain," the XO greeted him.

"XO," he said with a nod, then, "Anything for me before heading to the bridge?"

She thought for a second, then said, "I'm assuming you've decided to give our Russian escorts a heads-up about our defensive tasking, hence the bridge-to-bridge call to the *Admiral Grigorovich*?"

"That's correct," he said.

"You know, some parties on our side might construe that decision as a flagrant violation of OPSEC."

"Indeed . . . some parties might," he said, meeting her gaze. "What about you?"

"I think in this scenario, communicating our intentions only furthers our ability to execute our mission. If we were tasked to launch an offensive salvo, it would be a different story. But in this case, we're a defensive contingency plan. Probably not a bad idea for the Russians to understand this."

"Good to hear we're of the same mind on this," he said.

"Yes, sir," she said with a nod and headed off for the bridge.

As if on cue, the ship's satellite phone rang. Brewster answered it, and after a brief exchange with the caller, he handed it to Dusty. "Captain Ruskin of the *Admiral Grigorovich* is on the horn for you."

Dusty accepted the sat phone and raised it to his ear. "Captain Ruskin, this is Commander Townsend," he said.

"I must tell you, I am surprised by your request to talk," the Russian captain said in a crisp, even tone. "Are you calling to coordinate the safe return of our pilot?"

"No," Dusty said, "but I do have an update for you on that topic. Your pilot is out of surgery and in critical but stable condition. He suffered multiple fractures and injury to internal organs, but the doctors tell me that he is expected to live. We will make every effort to return him to you when he is in condition to travel."

"Thank you for this information, but if this is not the purpose of calling, tell me what is?"

Dusty inhaled sharply. *Okay, here goes nothing.*

"Captain, I'm going to be honest with you. I'm breaking protocol by having this conversation. In fact, if my superiors hear about this, I will probably be stripped of my command . . . but I believe that's a chance I have to take."

"I understand," the Russian replied.

"Captain, we have intelligence that a rogue entity may have taken possession of a short-range ballistic missile transport vehicle in southeastern Ukraine with the intent of targeting either Russian or American forces in Mariupol. Maybe both. Efforts are in play to prevent this launch from happening, but in the event those efforts fail, the *Donald Cook* has been tasked with shooting down those rogue missiles with our SM-3 antiballistic missiles. I am informing you of this because I do not want any misunderstanding in this scenario."

"Commander Townsend, imagine our roles are reversed and you command the *Admiral Grigorovich.* Imagine your orders are to defend Russia and Russian soldiers. An American warship you are watching has violated Russian sovereign waters. American Marines have invaded Ukraine to attack Russian peacekeeping forces. Then the American warship you are covering launches missiles at an unknown target. How am I to know you are not targeting Sevastopol? Or St. Petersburg? Or Moscow? Remember, Captain, you already fired the first salvo, and I chose not to return fire. I cannot promise to show such restraint a second time."

Dusty felt a surge of anger. This was the sort of spin-doctor bullshit that sent his blood pressure to the stratosphere. *We did not violate Russian waters; Russia blockaded the Black Sea. American Marines did not invade Ukraine; Russian forces did. And for God's sake, you're not*

414

the peacekeepers; we are! These were the things he wanted to say. He wanted to speak truth to power and put the Russian in his place, but to do so would only cause the little trust and common ground they had built to disintegrate. So instead, he decided to speak from a place of humility, rather than ego.

"You're right, I did shoot first, but those were warning shots and we both know it. But I didn't call to debate who was right and who was wrong in the last engagement. I didn't call to argue about the strategic motives of our respective governments in Ukraine. I called to talk to you, captain to captain. You asked me to put myself in your shoes, to imagine what I would do if I were the captain of the *Admiral Grigorovich* . . . well, I have. I imagined myself standing on the bridge of your ship. I imagined myself watching the *Donald Cook* fire missiles without warning, and I imagined me assuming the worst possible intentions and returning fire . . . and *that* is the reason I called. I realized that the only possible chance I had to complete my mission without mutually assured destruction was to communicate my intentions to you—captain to captain."

Several long seconds elapsed before Captain Ruskin replied. "I have not received any intelligence on the situation you describe . . . How do I know if what you are telling me is truth or misinformation to help you complete your real mission objective, which is to attack Russian targets? You are asking me to trust you, but you are my adversary. I am sorry, but you ask too much, Captain."

"I know, but I had to try," Dusty said. Then, after an exhale, he added, "If launched, the SRBMs will have west-to-east trajectories. The launch will happen in Odessa. I will respond with two missiles, Captain, fired on intercept trajectories. Launched only after our radar system detects a missile launch from mainland Ukraine. No more than two. That's my promise to you."

"Launching missiles under any circumstance would be a mistake," the Russian CO said. "That's *my* promise to you. *Dasvidaniya,* Captain."

The line went dead. Dusty clipped the sat phone to his belt, bowed his head, and began rubbing his temples.

"That good, huh?" Brewster said.

"Cover all Russian ships with birds," he said, with a fatalistic grimace. "And put fire control in automatic."

Brewster acknowledged and executed the order while Dusty paced. Hands clasped behind his lower back, he gazed at Combat's three command monitors, each displaying different tactical information and constantly updating.

"Captain," Brewster said urgently. "Intel reports indications of probable ballistic missile launch from northern Odessa. SPY is sectored to that search area."

Dusty's breath caught in his throat and he looked at the screen with the Ballistic Missile Defense System overview.

"Captain, ACS has a new track, designated one-zero-zero-one, probable ballistic missile based on speed and trajectory . . . track one-zero-zero-one first-stage booster cutout, missile is confirmed ballistic. Probable impact point is Mariupol."

"Kill track one-zero-zero-one with Eagles," Dusty ordered, giving the command to fire the SM-3s.

"Aye, sir. Killing track one-zero-zero-one with Eagles."

Lights flashed, an alarm sounded, and the ship shuddered.

"Captain, Eagles away, salvo size one. Time to intercept, two minutes fifty-three seconds," Brewster reported.

In the span of milliseconds, the ship's SPY-1 radar had detected the Iskander SRBM launch in Odessa, the Aegis Combat System had calculated an intercept solution, and the MK41 vertical launch system had fired a single SM-3 Block IIA antiballistic missile. At a speed in excess of Mach 8, the SM-3 was rocketing toward its target while receiving continuous midcourse guidance from the *Donald Cook*'s much more capable radar and targeting system. Only during the final phase of the engagement would the missile's own kinetic warhead take over homing duties and intercept, delivering a 130-megajoule kinetic energy package to explode the target.

Dusty looked at the flat-screen display showing the two missiles' positions and trajectory. An odd feeling washed over him as he watched the converging colored lines stretch out on the monitor. The battle being waged was happening at many, many times the speed of sound. Calculations were being performed by CPUs at close to the speed of light and adjustments were being ordered entirely without human input. Success or failure was entirely out of his hands, which meant all he could do was watch.

"Captain, we're being painted by the *Admiral Grigorovich*," a console operator reported.

"Very well," he said, readying himself for the hell that was coming next. "TAO, confirm only a single launch detected from Odessa."

"That's confirmed, Captain. Only one track detected," Brewster said.

"Combat, Bridge," came the XO's voice over NET-15. "The *Admiral Grigorovich* is repositioning guns—taking aim at ownship."

"Copy, XO," he said, grabbing the nearest mike. "Maintain course and speed."

"Captain, Bridge—aye."

Brewster looked at him, eyes asking the question: *Should we respond in kind and turn the gun?*

He shook his head.

The tension in Combat was so palpable, he could practically

taste it. The same terrible thoughts tumbling in his head were undoubtedly harassing everyone else in the room. *This is not happening . . . Is this really how it's supposed to end? Dear God, I just want it to be over.* He shut them all down and embraced the moment for what it was. He was the ship's captain, and this was the moment he'd prepared for his entire life. He would not fail his crew. He would not lose his focus.

The satellite phone clipped to his belt vibrated and rang, piercing the silence.

He looked down at it in stunned disbelief for an instant, before moving to take the call.

"*Donald Cook* Actual," he said.

"Commander Townsend, this is Captain Ruskin," the Russian CO said, his voice tinged with an emotion—aggravation, arrogance, urgency?—Dusty could not quite place.

"Yes, Captain."

"We detected a missile launch in Odessa on our radar. The missile your ship launched is on an intercept course with that missile? Confirm," Ruskin said.

"That is correct," he said.

"What is your next move?" the Russian CO asked. "Think very carefully before you answer."

"We're going to loiter until I receive confirmation from my people that any additional threat has been neutralized. If a second missile is launched from Odessa, we're going to shoot that missile down, too."

"Captain, Mark India!" Brewster boomed, his report indicating the SM-3 was at the intercept point.

"Battle damage assessment, TAO?" Dusty snapped, nerves on fire.

"Assessed as probable kill based on deceleration," Brewster reported, from where he was leaning over a Fire Control Technician's console. "Wait . . . we have multiple new tracks on ACS at India. Confirming debris fall, Captain. Good kill!"

A cheer erupted in Combat.

"I'm not sure if you could hear that, Captain," Dusty said with a relieved smile. "But that was my crew celebrating a successful intercept. We just saved lives, Captain. It's impossible to say how many—could be dozens, could be hundreds—but what do you say we save some more by keeping this channel of communication open until the rogue threat is neutralized and our respective governments find a way to deescalate this mess?"

"Is a nice plan, but I cannot make any promises as long as your ship remains north of the forty-fifth parallel," the Russian said. "If your ship were to turn south, however, I would take this as—how you say—a show of good faith."

Dusty considered the Russian's request. Commander Casey had told him there were *two* missiles on the launcher, which meant the threat was still active. Casey had also told him that the *Cook* was the contingency plan in case the primary intervention failed. Was the primary asset still engaged? How long until he received word about the fate of the second missile? How long until he received new tasking? He played out a series of probabilities and options in his head before finally answering.

"All right, Captain, give me fifteen minutes," he said, "Just fifteen minutes and you'll get your show of good faith."

"Five minutes," the Russian came back.

"Ten."

"Ten minutes," Ruskin said, that strange, inscrutable tone returning to his voice.

The line went dead. Dusty exhaled, clipped the sat phone to his belt, and looked at Brewster.

"Sounds like you reached an understanding of sorts," the TAO said with a tenuous smile.

He nodded and mirrored Brewster's expression with a tenuous smile of his own. "I bought us a reprieve, but no guarantee."

"Ten minutes?"

"Yeah, ten minutes for some spooky assholes in Odessa to stop World War Three," he said and looked up to heaven. "And I pray to God whoever they are, they do it fast."

CHAPTER 51

Parking Garage

Public Emergency Hospital

Odessa, Ukraine

"Fuck," Dempsey said, drawing out the word, as the Iskander missile streaked away into the blue.

He squeezed the ascender's trigger and hoisted himself the last three feet up to the top of the concrete wall, lifted his Sig MCX rifle over the edge, and blindly hosed down the upper deck of the parking structure, emptying his magazine.

"Dude, what the hell are you doing?" Munn said, snugging up beside him.

"Trying to win," he growled, swapping for a fresh magazine.

"There could be people up there!"

"Then they need to duck," he snapped. "Cover me; I'm going in."

Overhead, the collective buzz of four-dozen PIXIE micro-drones caused him to glance up. The swarm moved fast, faster than he thought it was even capable of flying, toward the target.

"I hold one Russian standing at a launch console on the opposite side of the transport vehicle," Wang said on the comms channel. "He's obviously trying to program another missile to fire. I'm going to dive-bomb his ass."

"Check," Dempsey said, and with a grunt, hoisted himself up and over the wall.

He landed with a thud on the concrete deck, dropping into a kneeling firing stance. He scanned over his weapon for shooters while Munn squeezed off three short bursts of covering fire above his head. Seeing no immediate threats, Dempsey unclipped the ascender from his kit and tossed it aside with a metallic clank. Seventy-five feet ahead, the Astrolog missile transport taunted him, with its second and final missile raised into the launch position. The driver's side was facing the hospital wall. Dempsey sighted, scanning for human legs to shoot in the gaps between the four pairs of oversized tires spaced along the length of the truck.

Must be standing behind a tire . . .

Munn plunked down beside him and let out an old-man grunt, while the PIXIE swarm arced over the top of the missile launcher and disappeared to harass the Russian operator.

"Go now!" Wang said in his ear. "He's still trying to enter the launch instructions."

Dempsey took off at a full sprint, not waiting for Munn. For a split second, he debated whether to round the front or rear of the Astrolog, but instinctively defaulted to his golden rule: *When in doubt, go left.* As he crossed half the distance to the target, he yanked a frag grenade from his kit, pulled the pin, and sidearm pitched it low and hard. The grenade flew true, splitting the gap between the truck's second and third axles, where it skidded across the concrete and disappeared under the truck's chassis. Dempsey arced wide—using the Astrolog as a shield—while dropping into a combat crouch and bringing his weapon up. The grenade detonated a heartbeat later with a loud crack.

"You wounded him," Wang said in his ear as he picked up speed and closed on the rear bumper. "But he's still on his feet. Hurry!"

Dempsey flicked the fire selector switch to full auto and rounded the back of the Astrolog in a deep crouch. A figure stood hunched at the launch control panel in the middle of a cloud of swarming microdrones. The Zeta was typing on a flip-down keyboard with his left hand, while holding a pistol in his right, arm extended and aiming at Dempsey. A single round whizzed over Dempsey's head, but he didn't hear the shot over the roar of his own weapon as he unloaded half his magazine into the Russian.

The Zeta's body spasmed as fifteen rounds of 5.56 pummeled his torso. He crumpled a millisecond later—like a puppet whose strings had just been cut—landing on his back staring upward with his legs folded awkwardly underneath. The hand holding the pistol went limp, and it clattered onto the concrete. Dempsey advanced, his muzzle pointing center mass at the fallen operator, while he scanned for a "last laugh" present the Russian might have rigged to blow—a suicide vest or grenade. Seeing neither threat, Dempsey moved closer until he was looking down at the man.

He immediately recognized the dying operator as the Zeta from Kiev.

The Russian coughed, his breath wet and raspy, as dark blood leaked in twin rivulets from the corners of his grinning mouth.

"I win," Dempsey said, lowering his rifle decisively. "*De oppresso liber*, motherfucker."

"Good job, Yankee," the Russian said through a gurgle, and with the last remaining life in his body, gave Dempsey a wobbly thumbs-up.

Munn appeared around the front end of the Astrolog, sighting over his rifle, just as the Zeta's hand dropped lifelessly to the ground.

"Hooyah," Munn said, looking from the dead Zeta to Dempsey. "Got 'im."

Dempsey nodded at Munn and immediately turned his attention to the launch control panel on the side of the truck. "Wang, the interface is in Russian," Dempsey said, his heart rate picking up as he scanned the LCD panel for something that looked like a countdown timer. "I don't recognize most of the words. What am I looking for? Is there an override I need to activate?"

"Hold . . ." Wang said as the PIXIE swarm coalesced above Dempsey's head.

The next voice Dempsey heard belonged to Buz; the command came hard and punctuated: "Don't touch anything."

"Where's the countdown timer?" Dempsey snapped. "How much time do I have?"

"This ain't an episode of *Looney Tunes* or *Mission: Impossible*," Buz said, and Dempsey could practically hear the old spook chuckling at his expense. "There's no countdown timer. He just didn't get a chance to finish entering the launch commands."

Dempsey exhaled with relief. Then, rolling his eyes, he said, "Fine, then walk me through how to reset the damn thing and lower the missile."

Over the next several minutes, with the combined knowledge and efforts of Buz, Baldwin, and Wang, the team safed the missile and launcher, with the PIXIE swarm serving as their eyes and Dempsey acting as their hands. Just as they secured missile number two, Director Casey reported that an SM-3 antiballistic missile launched from the USS *Donald Cook* had intercepted and destroyed the first Iskander missile before it reached Mariupol.

Munn clapped Dempsey on the shoulder. "We did it, dude! We fucking stopped Zeta."

"No, we stopped this asshole, but we haven't stopped Zeta," Dempsey said, looking up at an F-35 streaking by overhead. "These operators are the weapons. They're interchangeable. Arkady Zhukov is the real threat. Zeta isn't dead until he is. That's up to Grimes and Martin now."

CHAPTER 52

East Perimeter of Odessa International Airport

Grimes watched the fence line stream by in a blur as Martin piloted the SUV along the perimeter of the airport. She closed her eyes and did a series of long, slow four-count tactical breaths. The adrenaline coursing through her veins and her elevated pulse and respiration rates would significantly degrade her precision on the Sig 716. She couldn't permit that to happen.

This would be the shot of a lifetime.

This would be the shot that defined her career.

"Slow down, Yankee," Wang said on the comms circuit, and she felt Martin brake. "There's a gate in the fence line in fifty yards . . . that's your turn. There's a military vehicle at the gate waiting to give you escort. South takes you to the military side of the field, but you want to head north."

She opened her eyes and saw the perimeter security gate already rolling back. A blue compact SUV was waiting for them at idle, with two security personnel in the front seats. She gripped the handle on the A-pillar as Martin took the turn at speed and entered the airport.

"There's a large corporate hangar at the end of the road, just behind the passenger lounge building," Wang said. "It gives you perfect lines on the Embraer that Zhukov will be boarding. He's still inside, but you need to hurry. If you set up on the west side of the roof, you'll have a clear line. There's an exterior ladder you can use for roof access."

Grimes rolled her head to release the tension in her neck, already setting up the shot in her mind. As she took more long, slow breaths to check her rising heart rate, she pondered whether Arkady had spotters positioned to spoil their infiltration.

He probably still has dozens of Zeta agents spread all over the world. So why would he not have personnel positioned here for security?

Is that what Ember would do? Probably not. Any real footprint would compromise the NOC, and the Russian spymaster had cultivated this legend carefully over many years. And yet, she knew better than to make assumptions. The Russians didn't think, or fight, like Ember clones. They had their own tactics and methods.

Martin circled around the back of the large hangar, following their escort vehicle. The little blue SUV screeched to a less than subtle stop, forcing Martin to brake hard behind it. Her mind on the prize, she leapt out the passenger side door, tightening her sniper rifle to her side and gripping the MCX Rattler in a combat carry. She ran to the metal ladder bolted to the side of the corrugated metal building, but Martin beat her there and stopped her before her boot could hit the bottom rung.

"I'll go up first, for security." When she started to object, he cut her off. "I can't make the shot, Elizabeth. Only you can."

She gave him a curt nod, then flashed a crooked smile at the two BDU-clad Ukrainian soldiers who were watching from beside their vehicle, mouths open. She didn't know what they'd been told on the radio, but their instructions clearly hadn't included any mention of an attractive, athletically built female sniper who was kitted up and ready to kick ass.

Pulling herself tight against the rungs to keep her sniper rifle from getting hung up on the metal safety cage, she followed Martin up the ladder. The former Marine climbed swiftly, like a damn spider monkey, and she forced herself *not* to overexert in an effort to keep up with him. She needed her heart rate in the green zone and her arms not burning with lactate to do her job.

Martin rolled over the ledge and moved left, and she followed seconds later, moving right, clearing the roof through the holosight of her Rattler, then surging forward.

"Clear," she said.

"Clear," Martin echoed. "Go! I got your back."

She hustled across the expansive flat roof at a slow jog, still aware of her breathing and heart rate, unslinging the sniper rifle as she did and snapping out the attached tripod. Seconds later, she took a knee at the three-foot raised ledge along the flat roof, set the tripod on the ledge, and pressed her cheek into the side of the stock.

"Yankee Four is Zeus," she said into her hot mike, announcing to everyone listening that she was set.

She started her scan through her scope: The Embraer bizjet sat on the ramp, still attached to a generator box on a trailer behind a parked service vehicle. The plane's two fuselage-mounted engines had their intake fans spinning at speed, creating a strobe effect on the guide vanes behind. She saw no security personnel on the ramp—no shooters scanning rooftops and no bodyguard beside the open clamshell-style airstair door. She watched a ground crewman and the pilot walk around the nose of the jet conversing, and then continue talking as the worker set about disconnecting the generator. She shifted her scan to the cockpit, and through the windscreen sighted the other pilot in his seat, presumably running the preflight checklist.

They're leaving any minute.

She raised her head, looking over her optics for a wide-angle survey of the tarmac. She had no view of the corporate passenger terminal entrance, but from what she could see of the ramp, there was a fifty-meter walk to the jet—a fifty-meter killing zone that Zhukov would have to cross. Plenty of time and space. She decided on a headshot taken at the midway point, equal distance from cover at the terminal and the jet. Doing so would leave time for a second shot if needed. Noting her distance, elevation, and the light breeze, she clicked in her adjustments.

Satisfied, she exhaled and rolled her head one last time.

Come on, asshole . . . come on out and play with me.

Ghost images of Shane Smith, Simon Adamo, June Latif, and Dale played like snapshots in her mind, but the instant she felt the heat rise in her cheeks and her pulse began to quicken, she chased them away. She would visit them later—when the deed was done and the score sheet was balanced. Right now, she needed to be cold. Right now, she needed to be a machine.

She exhaled, slow and controlled.

"Alpha Zulu is on the move," Wang said.

She squeezed her eyes shut for a moment, then opened them and pressed her cheek more tightly into the buttstock of the sniper rifle. A paradoxical calm spread over her like a warm blanket.

Zhukov emerged from the shadow of the building, alone and carrying only a brown leather satchel. He had the slumped shoulders of an old man but walked with a young man's energy and confidence. Despite the fedora-style hat he wore low on his head and the shadows created under the brim by the high afternoon sun, she knew without a doubt it was him.

"I have him," she said, her voice a breathy whisper.

Her adjustments already made, she placed the center of the red crosshairs directly where his temple would be under the hat, then moved it forward slightly, correcting for his forward pace. Ten more yards and she would take him.

A soft, subtle hum suddenly sounded in her earpiece, but she ignored it, her finger slipping inside the trigger guard. Five more yards . . .

The voice in her ear was much harder to ignore. "Zeus, this is Kilo Juliet—hold."

The urge to lift her head from her sight nearly overpowered her, but she kept the crosshairs just ahead of the target's temple, her brain scrambling to make sense of the transmission. Had she really heard it, or was she losing her shit?

"Zeus—acknowledge," the voice commanded, and now her brain processed it as belonging to Kelso Jarvis.

Zhukov was approaching the midpoint . . . She applied gentle pressure to the trigger to ensure a smooth pull.

"Zeus," she barely whispered.

"Elizabeth, listen to me. There's nobody on this frequency but us. It's just you and me talking, and I need you to abort."

"Say again?" she said, not trusting her ears.

"I need Arkady Zhukov to get on that plane alive. Do you understand?"

She blinked hard, then adjusted the crosshairs slightly forward as the target increased his pace toward the jet.

"You want me to let him go? Just let him get away after . . . after everything he's done?"

She pulled more tension into the trigger, just barely feeling the rearward travel. She exhaled fully and watched the crosshairs begin to shudder slightly before stabilizing right where she wanted.

"Zeus, I'm ordering you to stand down. I promise, you'll get your shot, but not today."

How could he ask this of her? After Shane? After Simon and June? After seeing Dale in his bed with a tracheostomy tube snaking out of his throat? After *everything* . . .

But was there anyone on the planet, other than perhaps Dempsey and Munn, whom she trusted more completely than the man in her ear?

She relaxed the trigger tension.

"Acknowledge, damn it . . ."

"Zeus," she whispered, and heard the break in her voice and felt her throat tighten. "Copy all."

"No one can know we had this conversation. Not yet. Play it however you need to, but the party line is we did *not* let him go on purpose. Confirm you understand?"

"Check," she said, the taste of the word traitorous and stomach-turning in her mouth.

The soft hum disappeared and Wang's voice filled her earpiece. "Take the shot, Zeus. Do you read me? Jesus Christ, he's getting away!"

"I don't have it yet," she lied, her body trembling with equal parts ire and disbelief.

She watched the Russian spymaster reach the plane. He stopped and turned, not looking back at her but off to his left. For the first time since the hunt began, she *really* saw him—his face large and clear in her scope. Arkady Zhukov, the head of Spetsgruppa Zeta—murderer of half the Ember task force and God only knew how many other American patriots.

Her finger tightened on the trigger.

What if the call was a ruse? What if it wasn't Jarvis at all, but a Zeta impersonating him?

She pulled more tension into the trigger, now sliding the cross-hairs back onto the Russian's forehead.

Fuck it. I'm going to do it . . . I'm going to take the shot.

But despite her heart's battle cry, her index finger refused to move.

A tear spilled onto her cheek.

"I'm obstructed. I don't have the shot," she choked out through a sob.

"Obstructed? Obstructed by what?" Wang said, shouting now. "For Christ's sake, Zeus, take the shot!"

She picked up her rifle and hustled to her left, placing the tripod back on the ledge and pressing her cheek back into the stock. She lined up on the sight just in time to see the most elusive man in the world disappear through the door of the jet. The airstair pulled up, the door closed, and the ground crewman pulled the chocks.

"Damn it!" she exclaimed, her frustration real, but not for the reasons her teammates would think. "I missed him. I was obstructed and lost the shot. Do you want me to stop the jet?"

"Negative. We've been directed to let the jet go," came Director Casey's reply in her ear, his voice ripe with authority but, like her, frustratingly confused. "Signals will track it and hopefully get us another chance."

"Copy," she said, and wiped the tears from her cheeks with her shirtsleeve. Inhaling deeply, she collected herself. She couldn't face Martin like this . . . so she watched the Russian's private jet taxi across the ramp toward the main runway. Only once she'd regained her composure did she stand, shoulder the Sig 716, and jog back across the roof to where a wide-eyed Martin stood gobsmacked.

Jarvis was going to owe her a helluva lot more than just an explanation for this. He'd not only asked her to stand down from the kill shot on the man who'd assassinated her friends, but he'd also asked her to betray her team and lie about it.

"What happened?" Martin asked.

"I just didn't have the line," she said, and without meeting his gaze, shouldered past him to the ladder on the side of the building.

And so, the charade began.

CHAPTER 53

Ember Executive Boeing 787
Westbound Over the Atlantic Ocean
October 2
2130 Local Time

Dempsey rolled his neck and arched his back, getting a series of satisfying pops, and then slipped into the chair beside Grimes. She didn't look up, just kept staring at her hands, which were resting on the polished dark mahogany conference table. He searched for something to say but came up empty. Zhukov was in the wind, and that was a bitter pill to swallow. He felt it, too, the anger and resentment and unslaked thirst for vengeance.

But maybe not the guilt . . .

He put a hand on her shoulder and gave it a gentle squeeze. She looked up at him, emotional pain visible in her bloodshot eyes, and then back down at her hands.

"I'm sorry, JD . . ."

"For what?" he said, forcing a chuckle. "Dude, we stopped World War Three, we took another deadly Zeta off the planet, we saved the lives of hundreds of American Marines, and maybe four times as many civilians in Mariupol, and we did it without losing anyone. That's a pretty good day, Lizzie."

She gave a soft snort and closed her eyes. When she finally looked up at him, the pain was still there, but so was something else. She opened her mouth to speak, hesitated, then simply sighed.

"What is it?" he said.

She shook her head.

"Listen, Elizabeth, you gotta let it go. If you didn't have the shot, then you didn't have the shot. Signals is tracking Zhukov right now. The entire IC is on this, but more importantly, Ian is on it. We're gonna get tasking any minute, and then we'll reroute this plane, kill box that son of a bitch, and end this." When she didn't respond, he said, "Lizzie, look at me . . . This is not over, okay? I promise you."

"I know," she said, her voice a tense whisper. Then, glancing around to see if anyone might be listening, she leaned in. "John, the thing is—"

The forward door to the TOC slammed open, interrupting them. Munn stomped into the room, tapped a button on the primary workstation, and the center monitor on the opposite wall flickered to life.

"Dude, what the hell?" Dempsey said, looking at Munn.

"The Vice President of the United States wants to say a few words, if it's all right with you," Munn fired back and dropped into the chair beside Grimes.

"Ordinarily I would begin with congratulations," came the booming voice of the greatest SEAL who'd ever lived, and the one man who would always, no matter what, give it to them straight. Hell, Jarvis had *created* Ember, after all. Dempsey gave Grimes's hand a squeeze and shifted his attention to the screen where Jarvis beamed down at them from an unfamiliar SCIF. "But before we discuss Ember business, there's someone I think you guys should meet and thank personally."

The screen split in two, and a Hollywood-handsome naval officer wearing a blue ball cap with *USS Donald Cook DDG-75* on the front and scrambled eggs on the brim appeared in the right panel.

"Commander Townsend, while I'm afraid I can't introduce this team due to OPSEC, I did want to let them thank you personally for your ship's bold and flawless operation. Team, Commander Townsend's *Arleigh Burke* shot down the first Iskander missile that got away. He and his crew risked their lives, operating in contested waters and facing down the entire Russian Black Sea fleet, to get into position for that kill shot. The *Cook* is now safely steaming south of the forty-fifth parallel towards Constanta, but I think we and the world owe them a debt of gratitude."

"Sir," Munn began, taking the lead. "Thank you, and your entire crew, for your courage, competency, and professionalism. Without you, none of us would be heading home right now. We know the risks you and your crew took to execute this mission. Bravo Zulu, Captain. And you're gonna wanna keep an eye out for a crate of something special heading your way in the next few days—enough New York strips so the *Cook* can throw the best damn steel beach picnic in the history of Sixth Fleet."

Thank God for Dan Munn, Dempsey thought, looking at his friend with wonder, having no doubt in his mind that five grand worth of USDA Prime was already en route to the warship. The man wore his heart on his sleeve, and Dempsey wouldn't want it any other way. Without Munn, he wasn't sure he'd even be here.

Without Munn, he wasn't sure how much longer he could do this job.

At least until Arkady Zhukov lies dead in a box, but after that . . . I'm not so sure.

"Well," the young CO said with a humble smile, "whoever the hell you guys are, we're glad you're out there. If we were able to help in some small way, that was our honor. But I would be remiss not to return the gratitude, because we were on standby to shoot down two possible SRBMs, and as it was, we only had to take out one. Now, I'm just a lowly warship captain—not read into the code-word-level stuff it is that you folks do—but I can handle basic arithmetic. So, thank you for getting the other one. And thank you for the steaks. Be safe."

"Fair winds and following seas, Commander," Munn said.

And then Townsend was gone, leaving only the newly minted Vice President of the United States still on the screen. Dempsey felt himself once again consumed by the thrill of the hunt. Baldwin was back as Signals Chief doing what he did best. Dick Wang had his mojo back. Ember's new Director, Mike Casey, had proven himself a capable leader of the Ember team, despite his bubblehead pedigree. And now Jarvis held the second most powerful office in the United States. Ember was better positioned now than it had been in months to execute its charter, and he couldn't wait to hear the update on Zhukov's whereabouts so they could finish what they'd started in Odessa. In some ways, Grimes not having had angles for the shot might prove a blessing . . . the catharsis he would feel squeezing that final trigger and ending the Russian bastard would be unimaginable.

"Here's a quick summary of where we are," Jarvis was saying. "The Marines remain in Mariupol, but they're working now in a multinational peacekeeping role—with UN blue helmets scheduled to arrive later today—in cooperation with the Russian forces. Petrov has pulled most of their ground forces and all of their armor back across the eastern border. They are now respecting the no-fly zone established earlier, though they do maintain combat air patrols over the Black Sea. The Kremlin is still clamoring about our F-22s and F-35s in Russian sovereign airspace, but that's just noise now."

"Right," Martin said with a loud chuckle. "If they keep it up, you can ask them to explain what their heavily armed Su-27 was doing in Mariupol when it crashed."

"Well," Jarvis replied, a good-natured grin on his face, "I say we let the bureaucrats figure that shit out." As he spoke the words, Dempsey noticed something flash across the man's face—a sadness, perhaps—as he remembered that the "bureaucrats" now included him. "In any case," the Vice President continued, "we have pulled our air assets back as well, and in fact, the STP and air element from the 26th MEU are redeploying back to the *Essex*. Russia is still patrolling the Black Sea like they own it, but they have grudgingly agreed to allow the *Essex* and the *Oak Hill* to retrieve their Marines in the coming weeks."

"Bravo Zulu us," Munn said, a big goofy grin on his face. "Looks like we saved the world again, boys . . . and, uh, girl," he added with a wink at Grimes, who gave him a *halfhearted* middle finger, not yet quite over the missed shot in Odessa, Dempsey surmised.

"This is all great, but let's get down to business," Dempsey said, unable to wait a second longer. "Where did Arkady end up and where are we headed to tie up that last loose string?"

He could feel the energy in the room at the question. All of them were waiting for just that order, he knew. Jarvis's face changed, and he seemed to choose his words carefully, making acid churn in Dempsey's stomach.

Dear God, please don't let us lose him again.

"Oh, I thought you all knew," Jarvis said, and the sickening feeling worsened. "Zhukov returned to Moscow."

Dempsey stared at the screen, unable to speak.

"Sir," Munn said, breaking the silence. "We were under the impression he'd flown to Germany under his NOC."

Jarvis shook his head. "No, I'm sorry. He's in Moscow."

"Fine," Dempsey snapped. "Then we take him in Moscow."

Grimes laughed at this.

He turned on her. "What's so funny?"

"You," she said. "We wouldn't last forty-eight hours in Moscow. That's mission impossible, John."

"Maybe for *you*. But I don't care where the bastard is," he snapped. Setting his jaw, he returned his gaze to Jarvis on the monitor. "Send me to Russia, sir, and I'll personally end Zhukov. Hell, I'll take out Petrov while I'm there—consider it a freebie."

"JD, dude," Munn said, using his *let's all calm down* voice, "I want to nail this sonuvabitch, too, but you're not thinking straight."

Dempsey glared at his friend. "If we don't act now, God only knows what that evil psychopath will come up with next. I, for one, am sick of playing Russian roulette. How many more spins of the cylinder can Ember survive? Hell, can the world survive? Damn it, Dan, if not us, who?"

"I understand how you feel, John," Jarvis said, and for the first time since he had known the man, Dempsey thought he heard real conflict, maybe even doubt, in his idol's voice. "But I need you to give me the benefit of the doubt—benefit of the doubt earned by years of service and mutual respect—that I have a plan in the works for Zhukov. He might have slipped away this time, but this is not the end of the story. I need you to trust me on this. Can you do that?"

Dempsey looked at Grimes, who shook her head, and he

watched a tear spill onto her cheek. He got it—hell, he more than got it. If she hadn't failed, then they wouldn't be having this horrible conversation. But she *hadn't* failed, had she? The line hadn't been there . . .

"Yes, sir," Dempsey said, answering for the team. Then he looked away.

He did trust Jarvis—probably more than anyone on the planet—but this time, something felt different.

"You're headed to Tampa, but just long enough to get some well-deserved rest and gear up for the next mission," Jarvis said. "You have my gratitude. You have the President's gratitude. Hell, you have the whole damn country's gratitude. But most importantly, you have my word that when the time is right, Ember, and only Ember, will get the tasking to end Arkady Zhukov."

Dempsey looked back up at the screen. Now, *that* was the voice of the man he would follow to hell and back. Finally, Captain Jarvis the SEAL was talking to them, instead of the Vice President of the United States.

"We appreciate that, sir. We'll be standing by."

Jarvis broke the connection and the screen went black.

The air in the room felt suddenly heavy, almost suffocating. For several long seconds, nobody spoke . . . nobody moved. Then Wang stormed out, mumbling something about "bullshit" under his breath. Dempsey didn't stop him.

Feeling the eyes of his remaining teammates on him, he said, "All right, you heard the Vice President. Let's get some rest on the flight home, and then we can start prepping for whatever Director Casey has for us next. And I want you guys to start thinking about how to best get this team up to full strength and full complement. Recruitment is obviously going to be a priority when we get home. The Ember mission is far from over."

Everyone nodded and pushed their chairs back from the table. Grimes flashed him a tight smile and gave his shoulder a squeeze as she followed him out of the TOC, toward the bunkroom. As Dempsey unlaced his boots and stripped off his clothes, he couldn't help but wonder if his own mission with Ember was perhaps coming to its end.

Yes, there was much work to do . . .

But he just felt so fucking tired.

CHAPTER 54

Moscow, Russia

October 7

1802 Local Time

Tatia Lebedev wrapped the Hermès pashmina around her neck and chin and stepped outside into the cold. The lavender-hued scarf was the only splash of color she wore in today's otherwise black and grey winter ensemble. She'd seen it in a boutique and asked *him* to buy it for her . . . not because she wanted it, but as a test. When she saw the astronomical price tag of 80,000 rubles—equivalent to roughly $1,200—she thought he'd balk, but Petrov didn't even blink. There were rumors in the West that the Russian President was the richest man in the world—richer than Gates or Bezos—rumors that Petrov vigorously and repeatedly pooh-poohed, but she believed it true. Unlike the American entrepreneurs who had earned their fortunes, Petrov had looted his.

He was the world's richest robber baron, and oh, did he wear it well.

She nuzzled the baby-soft cashmere scarf and inhaled the scent to help mask the stink of diesel exhaust lingering from the late-afternoon Moscow traffic. She spritzed the scarf periodically with perfume, Coco Mademoiselle, and was repeatedly amazed at the power of scent to turn heads.

Men were such primal creatures.

She hailed a taxi and told the driver to take her to the Bulgakov Museum—a humble homage to the twentieth-century Soviet dissident-novelist and playwright Mikhail Bulgakov. The driver, a middle-aged Cossack, tried to chat her up about the weather, and when that didn't work, shared his interpretation of *The Master and Margarita*, but she ignored him. She was thoroughly and completely hardened when it came to men. Their advances were like bees at a picnic—unwanted, bumptious, and minatory.

A world without them would be dull but oh so zen . . .

The driver stopped at the curb in front of the museum and she paid him in cash, leaving only a modest tip. She had never been to the museum before. She'd once asked Petrov if he wanted to go, but he'd crinkled his nose at her as if she'd farted in bed.

"Bulgakov was a fool and his prose is garbage," he'd said and ignored her the rest of the day.

"Your typical bullshit comment," she murmured, reliving the memory and talking to his ghost. "You haven't read a word of his work."

Lost in thought, she walked up to the life-sized bronze statue of Koroviev and Behemoth, the two most famous and entertaining characters from *The Master and Margarita*. A smile curled her lips at the sculptor's personification of the devil's henchmen and Moscow mayhem makers. *Just as I imagined*, she thought, and let her fingers glide over the back of Behemoth's left paw where the patina had been rubbed away by the caresses of thousands of tourists and Muscovites.

She didn't really want to go into the museum, but she had no choice.

Tradecraft dictated this little side trip.

Petrov was a paranoid and jealous man. Certainly, she was being watched.

She paid the admission fee and walked through the exhibit, which co-existed inside an occupied residential apartment building. The museum, nothing more than a single flat, wasn't much to see— a glimpse of Soviet-era communal living in 1930s Moscow under Stalin's rule. She stopped to look at Bulgakov's writing desk and his typewriter. Little else of interest was on display. Dishes and silverware, trinkets and trivets. The most interesting part of the self-guided tour was the graffiti-covered stairwell leading to and from the flat. She paused, step-by-step, to read hand-scrawled quotes and excerpts from all of Bulgakov's beloved novels. Contrary to what some might think, she understood that the graffiti here was etched in homage, not defilement, by pilgrims to commemorate and celebrate a place of great spiritual courage and brazen Communist-era defiance by one of Russia's great literary geniuses.

If only I could be so brave.

If only I could be so clever.

As she stepped back outside, a single drifting snowflake landed on the tip of her nose and melted. She glanced up. The clouds looked bloated and pregnant. By midnight, Moscow would be covered in snow. She retrieved a charcoal-colored cashmere beret from her coat pocket and pulled it down over her bleached-blond hair. Then, shoving her hands deep in her pockets, she turned right and walked to Café Tchaikovsky, the coffee house that Arkady Zhukov had suggested she visit on a Thursday afternoon after work when she was ready.

Today was a Thursday afternoon . . .

Upon stepping inside, her first observation was that Café Tchaikovsky was *not* a coffee shop, but rather a posh full-service eatery and patisserie catering to the dinner crowds in Moscow's theater district. The establishment was cavernous inside, with seating on two stories and balcony dining around a central iris that offered views of the restaurant below.

"Do you have a reservation?" the hostess said in greeting.

"No," Tatia said, flashing the woman a warm smile. "I'm just here for a coffee."

"Then you've certainly come to the right place."

"Is Svetlana working today, per chance?" she asked, scanning the bar and barista stations for a candidate matching her imagined semblance of Arkady's point of contact.

"*I'm* Svetlana," the hostess said, her demeanor turning suddenly collegial and warm. "I'm working the front today."

"Oh," she said, pausing to run a quick calculus in her head about what to say next. "I'm a tea drinker, you see, and a friend of mine bragged that of all baristas in Moscow, you were the best, and surely the one who could convert me to coffee."

Svetlana nodded and smiled. "Your friend is too kind. I'll tell you what, if you have the time to sit and relax, I could seat you upstairs and then duck behind the bar to make you something special. How does that sound?"

"Wonderful," Tatia replied, slipping off her beret and stuffing it into her coat pocket.

"Follow me," the hostess said, leading her to a flight of stairs.

But instead of seating her on the second level, Svetlana walked her past all the vacant booths and tables to the back of the restaurant.

Glancing over her shoulder, she led Tatia past a server's station, around a wood-paneled wall, into a short corridor with the men's and women's restrooms. Using a key from her pocket, Svetlana unlocked and opened a third door, located between the bathroom doors with a placard beside it that read HOUSEKEEPING SUPPLIES in Russian.

Tatia glanced at the woman, her eyes asking the question.

"Hurry," was all Svetlana said before ushering her across the threshold. "Proceed until you reach the next door. Then knock five times."

"Okay," she said, but the woman had already shut and locked the door behind her.

Tatia took a deep, calming breath, her nerves finally starting to get the better of her. Also, she was beginning to get warm. She undid her pashmina from her neck, let the ends of the scarf fall limp on each side of her chest, then unbuttoned her winter coat. At the far end of the short hallway, which could not be more than five meters long, she noticed a dome-mounted video camera on the ceiling. She stared at it, digesting the fact that she was being recorded right now, here in this place.

"Shit," she muttered through an exhale. "Now, he has leverage on me."

Steeling herself, she walked down the little hallway, and when she reached the end, knocked five times on the door. When the door opened, she was immediately greeted by the sound of music— a symphony orchestra playing, and playing beautifully.

Of course, she thought, *I'm in Tchaikovsky Concert Hall.*

Café Tchaikovsky abutted the Concert Hall, and she'd just been ushered through a private and managed accessway. She stepped across the threshold and was greeted by a man dressed in an usher's uniform.

"This way, please," he said and bid her to follow him.

Singing joined the symphony, baritones and sopranos in beautiful concert and yet somehow challenging each other for dominance.

"Requiem," she whispered, the music causing gooseflesh to stand up on her arms.

"That's correct," her guide answered without turning.

The music and voices grew louder as he escorted her into the auditorium and around the curving perimeter on the uppermost level. She stared down from the balcony, over the railing and across the sloping concert hall full of empty seats.

"Dress rehearsal?" she asked, watching the musicians and choir perform Mozart's requiem mass in D minor, composed and unfinished in the year of his death, 1791.

He nodded and led her all the way around to the other side of the hall to another locked door, which he opened, ushered her through, then closed and locked behind her. Although she'd never been in such a room, she recognized where and what it was—the chamber behind the concert hall's iconic pipe organ. Standing alone, waiting for her, was Arkady Zhukov.

"Hello, Tatia," he said with a father's smile.

"An unusual choice of venue," she said, her gaze going from him to the towering silver pipes and back again.

"We needed a place to talk where nobody can listen," he said and took a seat on one of two folding plastic chairs, while gesturing for her to do the same. She complied, but not before repositioning the vacant chair at a more comfortable distance. No need to get so cozy so quickly.

When he said nothing, she took the reins. "They're looking for you."

"I know," he said with an inscrutable smile—born not of arrogance or indifference, but something else. "But I'm very good at hiding."

"And right under their noses . . . very bold."

"They know most of my tricks, but not all of them." After a pause, he said, "I wasn't sure you'd come."

She nodded. "I wasn't sure, either, but here I am."

"Why did you come?" he asked plainly.

This question made her very, very happy. No games, no bullshit, just straight and to the point. "Because I hate him."

"Interesting," he said, leaning forward to rest his elbows on his knees. "Is it the man you hate, or what he represents?"

"Both," she said. "There is no joy in him. No love. His greatest passions are chaos and inuring the dependency of others. He's bad for Russia, and he's bad for the world."

Arkady didn't say anything for a long moment, which made her uncomfortable, but she resisted the urge to fill the silence.

"My father was a poet. Unpublished, but not because of lack of talent. In the years since his death, I've committed his entire body of work to memory, and now he lives here," he said, pressing his right hand to his heart.

"Do you have a favorite poem?" she asked, not sure how to best manage his non sequitur but certain he had a point to make.

"Too many favorites, but what you said reminds me of a verse in a particularly poignant poem he wrote about Stalin."

"I would like to hear it."

He nodded, closed his eyes, and said:

> "To burn a man, to burn a book,
> Extinguish hope where all do look.
> Eyes right, eyes right, soldiers all
> Might the Godless King never fall."

"'Soldiers all,'" she echoed with a wan smile. "Yes, I think so."

"Is that why you're here, to enlist in my army?"

"Now that I know the truth of him, how can I stand by and do nothing?" Then, plucking one of the graffiti-scrawled quotes she'd seen in the stairway at the museum, she said, "After all, cowardice is the most terrible of vices."

His face lit up at this, and he met her gaze. "On this, it seems we both agree. So, tell me, Tatia, are you auditioning for Margarita in this dark satire we're writing?"

"No," she said, "I'm already playing the part."

Her answer seemed to please him immensely, because he smiled broadly, sat up, and slapped his knee. "Okay, then."

"Okay, what?"

"We try and see where it goes."

She screwed up her face at him. "That's it? That's all you have to say?"

"What did you expect?"

"Something formal. A promise, detailed instructions, a plan . . . something official."

He laughed at this. "I'm sorry, I shouldn't laugh, but that's not how it works, my dear. I'm still gathering my pieces. The board is not set; the game hasn't started."

"I think you're mistaken, old man," she said with a pitying smile. "Petrov is already playing."

"No," he said, getting to his feet. "That match is already over. We're starting a new game. Someone will contact you when I'm ready to make the first move."

"Trusting you could get me killed," she said, not liking the amorphous nature of the alliance they'd just forged.

"I can say the same in reverse. That's what makes this business so uncomfortable," he said. "And thrilling."

In the background, the choir and symphony stopped playing,

and the sudden silence set her nerves on fire. "What the hell am I supposed to do in the meantime?" she asked, her voice dropping to a whisper.

"The hardest thing imaginable," he said, stepping close to give her a kiss on the right cheek. "Convince Petrov this conversation never happened."

EPILOGUE

St. Pete Beach
St. Petersburg, Florida
October 9
2045 Local Time

Dempsey stood with his hands balled into fists and stuffed in the pockets of his cargo pants while he stared out at the dark ocean. The water lapping against his shins was much cooler than the last time he'd been here—more than two years and a metaphorical life-time ago. But just like that long-ago evening in May, the gentle rhythm of the surging and receding surf calmed his heart. Calmed his soul. He inhaled the salt air and the quiet . . . Kate's eventide, he remembered naming it. And just like that night—when Jarvis had told him not to come here, that it was a place for Jack Kemper, not John Dempsey, and that the memories of this place no longer be-longed to him—he let his mind chase ghosts in all directions on the dark, empty beach. On that fateful night, Jarvis had worried Dempsey might be recognized. He no longer worried about being recognized. As the months had become years, the memories of Jack Kemper had slowly dissolved from this place, and now that concern had been turned on its head—with him fretting instead that there was no one left who cared to remember the SEAL Senior Chief he'd once been.

And anyway, this time, Jarvis had *told* him to come.

He glanced over his shoulder, counted up five floors on the pink stucco condo complex, and found the windows dark. He knew Kate—and her new husband—still owned the condo, because he had seen pictures of them and Jake together on her Facebook page. Dempsey smiled, pleased to find that such thoughts no longer burned with the ache of regret and loss. Instead, they filled him only with peace and contentment at the thought that the woman he'd once loved—would always love—had found the happiness that she deserved. It wasn't that he had finally said goodbye to her in his heart—he would never be able to bring himself to that point—but he accepted the loss and felt gratitude that God, or the universe, had seen fit to give her the life she'd wanted but that he'd never been able to provide.

He let out a long, shaking breath and felt a slight chill. Perhaps it was the cool water licking at his legs, but more likely it was something else that ushered his thoughts to Jake. His only son—still just a boy in his mind's eye and his heart, despite the heroism Jake had shown in stopping the terrorist at the Atlanta Aquarium all those months ago. He imagined Jake in the cold Pacific Ocean, sand in places he'd not known he had places, arms linked to his BUD/S teammates. Chunk had checked on Jake at Dempsey's request, and Dempsey felt no surprise at all to find that Jake had not yet rung the bell, hadn't yet given up his quest to fill his father's boots.

Nor would he.

And that must be such a heavy burden for Kate's heart.

But Jake had the hot warrior blood of his dead SEAL father coursing through his veins, didn't he? And what if he found out that his dad was not really beneath the marble in Arlington, but had instead chosen the illusion of death? That he had chosen to leave forever to continue his fight with evil . . .

Would my son forgive me?

He shook the thought away—too difficult an idea to contemplate—and stared at the distant horizon. He waited, half expecting Shane Smith to step from shadows and wade in to join him, boots and khakis still on, just as he'd done that long-ago May evening. But Shane didn't, of course. And never would.

Dempsey looked up and down the beach and felt a horrible heavy loneliness settle on him like a cold, wet tarp. Kate . . . Jake . . . Shane . . . all gone. As were the brothers he'd come here that evening to mourn, the SEAL brothers he'd lost during Operation Crusader in Yemen. The death of Jack Kemper and the birth of John Dempsey had all occurred here—right fucking here—that night in May.

The men responsible for the deaths of the Tier One SEALs—including that traitor Kittinger—were all dead by his hand. Now the network of Russian Zeta operators responsible for the deaths of Shane and the other Ember team members were also dead by his hand. And, he supposed, Jack Kemper—buried in the empty coffin in Arlington—was also dead, also by his hand.

What was left to be done, now that Arkady Zhukov had escaped and disappeared, likely forever?

"Lots of memories, I'm sure," a voice said behind him.

He turned to look at the Vice President of the United States walking toward him on the dark, quiet beach.

"Didn't mean to startle you," Jarvis said.

"Something only you could manage. I'm surprised you made it here alone," Dempsey said, taken aback by his own casual, informal tone. He noted that his mentor was barefoot and dressed in grey cargo pants and a black T-shirt, a black *Punisher* ball cap, created as a fundraiser by some Team guys honoring other Team guys lost to the endless wars. The VP had his hands in his pockets as he entered the surf.

"Once a SEAL, always a SEAL," Jarvis said, his voice thick with nostalgia. "When I can't slip the leashes of my security detail, I'll know I'm finally old." He smiled, then chuckled and said, "Although, truth is, they're actually up in the vehicles at the street behind us, so . . ."

"Right," Dempsey said with a laugh. "Different world now for you."

"Different world," Jarvis agreed. "For both of us."

Dempsey looked back out at the dark ocean and let the words hang there. That black ocean, hiding creatures and currents, and a myriad of other terrifying things, was still a siren's call to comfort and escape for him. A part of him imagined wading in, without a word or backward glance, then lunging forward, pulling stroke after stroke after stroke farther and farther into the heart of that ocean.

Into the heart of the ocean that had saved him more times than he could count.

Into the heart of the ocean that he loved.

Instead, he turned to the Vice President of the United States. "What's next, sir?" he asked, his right index finger subconsciously finding and tracing the faded serpentine scar wrapping his left forearm.

Jarvis blew air through his lips while his eyes chased the dark water to its invisible horizon. Dempsey wondered if Jarvis was thinking the same thoughts he had been. If anyone would, it would be this man.

"What do you want, John?" he asked, gaze still on the sea.

"Sir?"

"Both of us, I suspect, have been asked—by people we love, by people who care about us—when will we have given enough." Jarvis turned to him now, eyes peering into his soul. "Our answer has always been 'If not me, then who?' But there does come a time, John, when men like us can simply accept the deep, heartfelt thanks of a grateful nation and move on . . . and find another kind of peace."

Dempsey didn't answer the implicit question, and instead boldly asked, "Are you at that point, sir?"

A long silence passed before Jarvis turned to him with the most doleful smile Dempsey had ever seen. "No." he said softly. "Almost . . . but not quite yet."

Dempsey nodded. He wanted to tell Jarvis the truth—confess that he didn't have another life to run to, that for someone like him, *another kind of peace* didn't exist—but those words were too difficult to say.

Jarvis didn't let him off the hook, however. "What about you?"

"If not me, then who?" Dempsey said with a sarcastic grin, deflecting the one question he was afraid to answer.

Jarvis chuckled. "Right."

They stood together and stared out at the sea for a long, but strangely comfortable, silent moment. In the end, Jarvis broke first.

"In that case, Mr. Dempsey," the Vice President said, his eyes once again burning with that old, familiar bright fire, "your nation has another mission for you."

"Anything, sir," he said, and meant it. "Especially if it involves Arkady Zhukov."

"It does . . . but with conditions that I'm afraid you may find difficult."

Dempsey turned and looked at his boss, head swimming with questions, but ready to learn what awaited him behind yet another curtain.

"Walk with me," Jarvis said, turning to lead the way.

Dempsey followed.

"What I'm about to tell you is for your ears only . . ." Jarvis began, and then he patiently and methodically described where the *operator's journey* Dempsey had begun decades ago would take him next.

GLOSSARY

18-Delta—Special Forces medical technician and first responder

ACS—Aegis Combat System

AIP—Air-independent propulsion

AQ—Al-Qaeda

BDU—Battle Dress Uniform

BMD—Ballistic Missile Defense

BND—Germany's Federal Intelligence Service

Bright Falcon—Code name identifier for the Russian Zeta Operation and Training Center in Vyborg, Russia

BUD/S—Basic Underwater Demolition/SEAL training

CASEVAC—Casualty Evacuation

CHENG—Chief Engineer

CIA—Central Intelligence Agency

CIC—Combat Information Center, known as "Combat"

CMC—Command Master Chief

CO—Commanding Officer

COMSUBLANT—Commander, Submarine Force Atlantic

CONUS—Continental United States

CSO—Chief Staff Officer (special warfare)

CSO—Combat Systems Officer (surface warfare)

DC—Damage Control

DCS—Distributed Command System

DDG—Designation for Guided-Missile Destroyer

DILDO—Direct Input Limited Duty Officer

DNI—Director of National Intelligence

DoD—Department of Defense

DPU—Dive Propulsion Unit

DS&T—Directorate of Science and Technology

EAB—Emergency Air Breather

EBE—Emergency Breathing Equipment

EEOB—Eisenhower Executive Office Building

Ember—America's premier black-ops counterterrorism task force

EMP—Electromagnetic pulse

Exfil—Exfiltrate

FOB—Forward Operating Base

FSRU—Floating Storage and Regasification Unit

FRSS— Forward Resuscitative Surgery System

GSW—Gunshot wound

HALO—high-altitude, low opening

HUMINT—Human Intelligence

HVT—High-Value Target

IC—Intelligence Community

Infil—Infiltrate

ISR—Intelligence, surveillance, and reconnaissance

JO—Junior Officer

JSOC—Joint Special Operations Command

JSOTF—Joint Special Operations Task Force

KIA—Killed in Action

LAN—Local Area Network

LNG—Liquefied Natural Gas

MARSOC—Marine Corps Special Operations Command

MEDEVAC—Medical Evacuation

MEU—Marine Expeditionary Unit

MK—Mihail Kogălniceanu Air Base, Romania

NCTC—National Counterterrorism Center

NET-15—Preferred tactical command and control communication channel on an *Arleigh Burke*

NOC—Nonofficial Cover

NSA—National Security Agency

NVGs—Night Vision Goggles

ODNI—Office of the Director of National Intelligence

OGA—Other Government Agency

ONI—Office of Naval Intelligence

OOD—Officer of the Deck

OPSEC—Operational Security

OTC—Officer in Tactical Command

PJ—Parajumper/Air Force Rescue

QRF—Quick Reaction Force

RPG—Rocket-Propelled Grenade

SAD—Special Activities Division

SAPI—Small Arms Protective Insert

SBS—Special Boat Service

SCIF—Sensitive Compartmented Information Facility

SDV—SEAL Delivery Vehicle

SEAL—Sea, Air, and Land Teams, Naval Special Warfare

SecDef—Secretary of Defense

SIGINT—Signals Intelligence

SITREP—Situation Report

SM—Standard Missile

SOAR—Special Operations Aviation Regiment

SOCOM—Special Operations Command

SOG—Special Operations Group

SOPMOD—Special Operations Modification

SQT—SEAL Qualification Training

SSN—Designation for a fast-attack nuclear submarine

STP—Shock Trauma Platoon

TAD—Temporary Additional Duty

TAO—Tactical Action Officer

TOC—Tactical Operations Center

TOT—Tactical Operations Trailer

TMU—Tactical Mobility Unit

UAV—Unmanned Aerial Vehicle

USN—United States Navy

VEVAK—Iranian Ministry of Intelligence, analogue of the CIA

Zeta—Clandestine Russian covert action and espionage activity

ABOUT THE AUTHORS

ndrews is a US Navy veteran, Park Leadership Fellow, and
submarine officer with degrees from Vanderbilt and Cornell
ities. He is the author of three critically acclaimed high-tech
Reset, The Infiltration Game, and The Calypso Directive.

Jeffrey Wilson has worked as an actor, firefighter, paramedic,
jet pilot, and diving instructor, as well as a vascular and trauma surgeon. He served in the US Navy for fourteen years and made multiple deployments as a combat surgeon with an East Coast–based
SEAL Team. The author of the faith-based inspirational war novel
War Torn and three award-winning supernatural thrillers, *The
Traiteur's Ring*, *The Donors*, and *Fade to Black*, he and his wife, Wendy,
live in Southwest Florida with their four children.

To be notified when Brian and Jeff's books are available for
preorder and/or sale, sign up for their newsletter at:

www.andrews-wilson.com

Made in the USA
Las Vegas, NV
18 May 2022